THE ROAD TO DONETSK

a novel by

Diane Chandler

"A touching love story that illuminates the aid business.
Compelling and enjoyable."
Clare Short (former Secretary of State for International Development)

Published by Blackbird Digital Books, London
Second Edition – November 2016
ISBN- 9780995473546
Copyright Diane Chandler 2015
Cover Design by Mark Ecob

For Nick

"I might remind readers why, with all its faults, this is a lucky place to be living in."

Andrew Marr, The Making of Modern Britain

Prologue – April 2014

Donetsk was on the news again today. It's become headline material, even out here; the hostages, the burning buildings, the thugs – and those Russian tanks gathering in ever greater clusters along the border. Afterwards, I managed finally to get through to Svetlana. She says it's tense in the village, that some of the youths have left to join the pro-Russian activists. Her relief that her son is too young was palpable down the phone line, and my concern for her rebounded at me as a long-distance echo, "If you need to get out, then come here."

Those youths from the village, now hurtling through the streets of the city, launching their petrol bombs, they were barely born back then. I can still see their hot little faces, just awakened from their naps, as they ducked around our legs in the wooden hall which served as the kindergarten – along with its many other communal roles. I see them hoisted onto the shoulders of the men returning from the mine, the pinpricks of coal dust emblazoned in their foreheads. It will be those children who are fighting in Donetsk now. But then, of course, most of them followed their fathers down that mine, with its rickety ceiling props and high methane levels, so what do you expect? The country has barely changed since it won its independence over two decades ago. The inertia of Ukraine, I used to call it, and people would nod vigorously – yes that's just the word. Inertia.

Back then though, there was so much hope, so much commotion. We Westerners were crawling over Ukraine, passing on know-how in the ways of democracy and the free market, helping this bold new nation through its transition from communism. But did we ever really know where that transition was to wind up? Not where it is today. Ukraine means 'borderland' in old East Slavic and perhaps Russia was never really going to let go, perhaps it allowed Ukraine to fray at its borders, scrunching it

1

back in when the threat of union with Europe seemed like it might actually happen.

At least the winter is over. The TV pictures show a landscape that is still barren, but I know that it will be strewn with sunflowers before this conflict reaches its zenith. There are blue skies and sunshine, a warmth in the air, and the soldiers at the checkpoints can feel it on their backs, even if the inevitable still awaits them. In the village, come April, spring was always quick to arrive and life would begin again; the chatter at the well, the goats straining on their chains, the whitewashing of the squat houses with their roofs of corrugated iron, the storks taking flight from an old chimney top.

The TV cameras homed in on the airport, on the offices of the regional government – I even caught a glimpse of that hotel. How can there be conflict in a city I know so well? Where all the buildings are so familiar – so benign? I can feel myself there, as if it was all just yesterday. What is going to happen to all those people I knew? I picture their faces, I see them laughing, dancing at a party deep in the forest, or contemplative, stirring sugar into strong black tea, and the memories overwhelm me. The past twenty years fall away, and I remember so vividly that first time I went to Donetsk – with Dan.

1

"You wanna come to Donetsk with me?"

I was sitting at my desk awash with documents when Dan phoned. We'd met the day before at the launch of my programme.

"Donetsk?"

"It's where the coal mines are. Thought you'd know that, Vanessa?"

What if I'd said no? What if I had never gone with him that day? But that provocation in itself was sufficient, plus the fact that this was of course a prize of an invitation. And, I admit, he had been on my mind.

"Of course," I said, "down in the east. When were you thinking of going?"

"Flight's in two hours."

"This morning?"

"Yep. You got your passport?"

"Yes, but we're not leaving the country, are we?"

"No, but Ukraine's still communist in all but name and there'll be checks."

"OK," I said.

"I'll pick you up in thirty." And he hung up.

I flustered about the office, checking my handbag for my passport, which had not left my side since my arrival in Kiev a few weeks before, and stuffing background papers in my briefcase. I have to smile when I look back on those eager days – I even forgot to pack my camera. From behind her computer, Irina threw me sullen glances, while Sasha sent faxes with his back square on to me; they must both have found this impromptu day trip as bizarre as it was.

When he pitched up with his driver, Dan was slouched on the banquette seat, his arm loosely thrown about its back. He wore chinos and a crimson

3

polo shirt, while his cream jacket was bunched up on the back window, its stripy lining spilling like the silk of a hot air balloon. Not without some trepidation, I climbed in beside him, wishing I'd worn a longer dress that day. As we set off for the airport he turned to me with his languid smile.

"Settling in OK?"

"Yes thanks, making good headway with the programme."

"Well, you made an impressive start yesterday."

"Thanks." I felt myself flush.

He contemplated me for a few moments. "You've just got to know that they'll play you, these people, they'll tell you what they think you want to hear. But can you second-guess them? That's the real skill to this game, it can get tricky."

I laughed, only vaguely clear. "Thanks for the tip. I'll have the chance to suss them out when we get down to the detail at our workshop next week." I paused but he said nothing, so I added, "I really want to get it right."

"Sure you do."

As he smiled at me, I took the chance to observe him. He must have been in his late thirties – a good ten years older than me anyway – his cheeks held the crease that comes with age, a baggy line drawn out from the nose down to the corner of the mouth, only in Dan's case it was as marked as Yogi Bear's. His hair was coal black and dishevelled – messy even – and his eyes, the colour of walnuts, were gentle. Presence, that's it, I thought, that's what he has. Even then I could feel it wreathing itself around me like the hot day. He reached behind him for a paper bag and offered me a doughnut.

"Thanks." I held it for a moment as he bit into his.

"You get a place yet?" He sucked sugar from his fingers.

"No, still at the hotel." I took a bite of my own and gulped it back. "Once we've finished the programme design, I'll head back to the UK for a month or so while we put the contract out to tender, then I'll find an apartment in the autumn."

"Ah." He scrutinised the last of his doughnut. "Yours have any jam in it?"

"Little bit." I flipped my hand to show him the red ooze.

"Mine didn't. But then life does that to you, don't you find?"

I watched the tip of his tongue working on the last grains of sugar at his lips, before turning to the view from my window, my thighs peeling like Sellotape as I shifted position on the vinyl seat. Get a grip Vanessa, you're a professional, I chided silently, still callow enough to enjoy the weight of that word when applied to myself. I could see why so many people had told me about Dan, but I was not about to be waylaid by some guy, however high up the ranks he was. I was in Ukraine on a mission – well I was there to change the world, wasn't I? We travelled on in silence, entering the birch forest which surrounded Borispol airport.

"What projects do you run in Donetsk?" I asked eventually.

"IFI mainly." He turned and saw my frown. "Inward foreign investment."

"Oh yes, of course."

"Most of it from the States – plenty of rich pickings down there. We're setting up an IFI department for the Governor, which is the purpose of our meeting today."

"Is there scope for the Levshenko Programme down there?"

He snorted. "There's scope for everything down there, Vanessa."

The plane to Donetsk was a squat propeller affair, which looked like some cartoon character from a kids TV programme as if it should have a face and a cheeky smile. We were last on, having enjoyed the VIP lounge, which consisted of a couple of benches in a side room and a glass of iced water. As we made our way in through the hold, I pulled up short at the scene before me. Beside the heaps of cases, several people were standing around, chatting and smoking. A row of worn canvas loops hung down from the ceiling, and I realised that these passengers were going to be strap-hanging during the flight. Incredulous, I turned back to Dan, who winked at me.

"Different strokes, Vanessa."

He took a window seat at the front of the plane, placing his briefcase in the saggy overhead netting, while I placed my own by my feet, intending to brief myself on Donetsk during the flight.

"So what's the population?" I asked, fastening the tatty seatbelt.

"About a million," he said, lengthening his own; there was a hint of a paunch.

"And how many coal mines?"

"Well over two hundred." He glanced at me. "Does that trump the UK?"

I turned down the corners of my mouth in what I imagined could pass for a sage look and nodded slowly. "Pretty much the same, before the cull."

He raised his eyebrows at that, as I remember, and it did feel thrilling to

5

have filled a gap in his knowledge.

"They're gonna have to close half the mines," he said, "That's a hundred thousand men, in terms you or I care about."

I tutted gravely. "How are we going to find jobs for all of them?"

"Aw, may as well skip a generation, focus on the youth." He yawned as he spoke.

"Surely not?"

I frowned sharply at him, but Dan was reaching across me for a glass of red wine from a tray offered by the stewardess. I declined the drink, my expression overly cross as I grappled with his cynical reaction. My empathy for the unfortunates of this world broiled inside me and I wasn't going to let him off there.

"You can't just give up on them," I said, as he put his nose to the glass and breathed in. "In the UK, we got thousands of miners back into work. Loads of them started their own business too, guys with a passion, a hobby maybe, which they managed to make a living out of when the pit closed."

Dan took a lingering sip of his wine. To anyone else, this message may have been clear – leave the technical stuff till we get to our meeting – but not me, I persisted.

"There was one miner I knew who just lived for his roses, spent all his time in the garden, deadheading and stuff. Now he set himself up in horticulture – and he made good money from it too. Another guy I knew started recycling old conveyor belts from the mines, making new things with them ..." I scrabbled through my mind to remember what things. "Tool bags, for example."

I waited until Dan turned to me. "Roses and tool bags, eh?"

His mockery smarted, and at first his eyes held only amusement, but then they softened, until finally he seemed quite unguarded. A professional giant exposed.

"You have to start somewhere, don't you?" I muttered.

He continued to watch me until finally he said, "I guess you do."

It was me who broke the moment, reaching forward to unclip my briefcase, while Dan closed his eyes and settled back in his seat, the wine glass held balanced at a loose angle on his thigh. He remained silent until take-off, and once we were airborne it was impossible to talk over the din of the propellers anyway, so I spent the flight flicking through my documents, highlighting in yellow as I went. Clearly, I was trying to impress Dan, but he was oblivious to me, making hefty inroads into a John Grisham paperback. As would I these days, of course – I never used to retain the facts in those background papers anyway.

When we came into land after an hour or so, I found myself gripping the armrests. I'd not flown much before and had no particular fear back then, but as we approached the runway the plane seemed to be tilting over. Across the aisle, I could see the tarmac skidding outside, but a glance at the window beside Dan brought only glimpses of sky, and I still swear today that the plane landed on one wheel first, tipping us sideways at a terrifying angle. I braced myself, eyes screwed shut against the squeal of tyres.

"It's OK," I heard Dan say gently, "we're not gonna die today." I felt his hand on my forearm, the warmth and weight of it both calming and rousing, and I opened my eyes with a lingering smile of thanks.

Then I caught a movement in the seat behind. A woman had stood up and was reaching for her carrier bags in the baggage nets.

"Saditsya!" Sit down!

Even I understood the command of the stewardess. The woman snapped back at her and made a great show of smoothing her skirt before sitting down again. But then, once the plane had come to a standstill, I snapped off my own seatbelt and I too jumped up.

"Saditsya!"

This time the passengers joined in with the stewardess and Dan grinned at me. "Got to wait for the pilot to get off."

A good five minutes then passed before finally a stout man, eyes bleary, skin flushed, ducked through the door of the cockpit and walked the short length of the aisle, to thunderous applause, both from cabin and baggage hold.

A black Volga from the regional government swept us into the city of Donetsk. We passed swathes of factories spewing toxic clouds into the cobalt sky, which soon lost its battle to camouflage them and became engulfed by billows of grey. When we crossed the vast river, my eye was drawn to the rows of flower tubs which lined the bridge, each of them packed with roses, the vibrant pinks and oranges of the blousy, old-fashioned heads softening the view across the water to the Soviet monoliths beyond. Finally, we drew up at that colossal building in the main square.

The Governor of Donetsk, Vladimir Zukov, was a short barrel of a creature who bustled out of his office and bore down on Dan. As they shook hands, the man clasped Dan's arm, the way American statesman do on TV, then he pushed him through the door and swung his arm around my waist to propel me in too. I tried to ignore the squeeze he gave me on the way.

Inside his office, a wall of windows had been thrown open to the stunning July day and a breeze rifled the heaps of papers on his desk. On the wall behind it hung an enormous framed photo of Leonid Kuchma, the new President of Ukraine, who had been elected just days before, his eyes gleaming somewhere in the distance, seeking a glorious future – or perhaps a glorious past. Across the whole of another wall was a tapestry of the Donetsk coat of arms, the bottom section a swathe of coal-black, the top half a striking royal blue. A fist, chunky and chiselled, was holding a hammer high up in that sky, beside a luminous gold star, and, as I gazed at the image, I was startled to find myself welling up. I blinked back the tears, staggered by the emotion it had stirred in me.

We took our seats and the Governor boomed at Dan in Russian, while the translator Dan had arranged for my benefit struggled to keep up. "Dan, you are my friend, my buddy, and you are good friend of Donetsk."

"Good to be back here, Vladimir, good to be back." Dan's voice was full of rich warmth. "And this is Vanessa Parker, from the Levshenko Programme."

The Governor threw me a quick nod – I'd say he thought I was Dan's love interest – and with a flash of annoyance I did fleetingly wonder if there'd been other women he'd whizzed down to Donetsk, to ease his negotiations. But then this man was far too professional and I swiftly quashed that thought.

"Ah, such good times we had in Chicago, Dan ..." the Governor cried, adding in English, "... in Vindy City."

More grey suits joined the meeting and greeted Dan effusively, with again the briefest of glances my way. So I sat back, biding my time, and observed Dan in operation; the genial smiles, the locker-room bonding, as he talked about the need for tax breaks for American companies who might invest in Donetsk, as he won them around to his point of view. It didn't occur to me that Dan might also have been trying to impress me – such was the awe I felt for the deputy head of the USA's colossal aid programme for Ukraine. At that point, Dan was the epitome of strength for me, possessed with gravitas, although it would only be a matter of hours before I was to witness his fallibility. Finally, he took the chance to introduce me properly and I sat forward eagerly.

Vladimir Zukov cocked his head at me. "Aha, you are also here for official business?"

The translator captured his undertone perfectly with an intonation which infuriated me, and I launched into a defiant opening gambit about my own aid programme, about how I was in Ukraine to help create new jobs in the wake of communism. But the instant I mentioned the budget – a hefty sum for an aid programme back then – the Governor interrupted me.

"Three million pounds, you say? I hope we will see some of that money in Donetsk, in our city of million roses." He swept his hand towards the open windows. "We are most important city in Ukraine, we have educated people and coal mining, which is biggest industry in my country." He paused. "Sadly many coal mines must now close."

For a brief moment I sensed a connection, a chance to be taken seriously. I felt the power of that tapestry on the wall beside me – the stark simplicity of a miner's fist and the memories it evoked of those I had known. But before I could let him know of my passion to help, the man had slapped a palm on the table and declared that the meeting would continue over lunch. The moment had passed. Then he contemplated me, raising an index finger as a teacher might to a four-year old. "After lunch, we will show you real coal mine."

The other Ukrainian men chortled then, even Dan smiled, I noticed, which felt like a betrayal of our unspoken Western solidarity in that room. I raised my chin to the room.

"That would be great," I cried, a little wildly then. "I've been down lots of coal mines. I used to manage a programme for miners who lost their jobs in the UK."

The 'manage' was stretching it a bit – I'd been an assistant – but the translation was met with a momentary silence, with the surprised glances I'd been courting, and I sensed myself edging from bimbo to someone of potential value. And so I went on, my heart racing, committing myself further to this region far from Kiev, without any go-ahead from my philanthropic boss Bogdan, whose personal wealth was fronting our programme, and who had never once even mentioned Donetsk. How much of it was the tapestry – all those miners to be thrown out of work? How much of it was the way these men had dismissed me in front of Dan? Even today I'm still not sure, but I was a woman possessed.

"I will be launching a massive programme in Kiev, but I could set up a pilot project here. Dan has taken me through the needs."

I shot a glance at Dan. He looked surprised, lips parted with amused interest, which fired me up further.

"I could set up a mini Job Centre at one of the coal mines due to close. This would counsel the men, help them find a new job, retrain them even, if need be."

While speaking ad lib, I was mentally running through the cost of all this; probably no more than a couple of hundred thousand pounds, which we could easily absorb. But I was also aware that the Governor, who had been preparing to stand, had settled again in his seat, that the grey suits had shifted forward in theirs. And so I went further. Much further.

"Job Shops. That's what they're called in the UK. And if our pilot Job Shop is a success, then we could help you roll it out to other mines in the region."

I can still see myself in that office, making policy on the hoof as I sought to prove myself to this man. And to Dan, of course. The way an aid programme takes shape – it was all so willy-nilly.

Over lunch, I was suddenly one of the lads, I was in the tent. The table was heaving with chicken legs, with pig liver pâté, with a baked fish on a platter, and the Governor plied me with vintage wine from Moldova. In those days, I was no wine drinker – I was more used to vodka nights out with Carole, my friend from home – but I found myself knocking back the 1965 Cabernet Sauvignon which the Governor had laid on for Dan, and leading the relentless laughter. After the food, we progressed to the toasts, with cognac, which came at me fast and furious, each drained glass instantly replenished by Vladimir Zukov for the next one. Dan stood, addressing me with a playful smile, and made the traditional Ukrainian third toast to the ladies, while all six men bowed to me and I giggled tipsily, a palm to my chest in modest acceptance. Then I sprang up for the next one.

"A toast to the Governor," I cried, "to your beautiful city of a million roses, to our future collaboration through the Levshenko Aid Programme."

Amidst all the cheers, the thumps on the white linen tablecloth, Vladimir Zukov slammed his shot glass against mine and clicked his fingers for the attention of our interpreter.

"May I call you Vanessa?" He leant towards me.

"Please do." I leant forwards too. "Actually, my close friends call me Ness."

"Ness? Like the monster? In Scotland?"

At that I collapsed into giggles, banging my fist on the table, an action which by then was the universal language at that lunch.

"You'd better have some coffee, kiddo, you've got a coal mine to get through."

I turned to Dan as he spoke. Again his look was open, quite unguarded. And I'd say that was the moment. I'd say the kiddo did it.

2

My arrival in Kiev a few weeks earlier had not been how I'd imagined it. It was May 1994, I was twenty-six years old, and Bogdan had flown me business class, my first time ever, so I stepped off the plane feeling even more benevolent than when I'd boarded in Manchester. At the perimeter fence, a row of trees was blooming with pink and mauve pastels, creating a soft lens effect against the concrete buildings beyond; my new boss had told me I'd be arriving in the lilac season.

"Kiev is renowned for these few weeks of each year, my dear," he'd said, an avuncular hand to the small of my back, "and how my heart yearns to be going with you."

But there was to be no grand welcome in arrivals. The hall was cluttered with pasty men wielding cards with names that were not mine. When I found my own, I smiled gratefully at the face above it, a swarthy one which stood out from the rest. The young man smiled back, jerking his chin in welcome, while I felt his quick assessment of me, cursory but thorough, as if he was storing the data for later. Physically, he would have clocked a skinny body dressed entirely in denim, spice red hair, and feet rubbed red by synthetics (in the days when I still doggedly refused to wear leather). Beyond that, I hoped he would feel the compassion I had brought with me to his country.

"Gaspazha Parker? Welcome in Ukraine. My name is Sasha," he said.

"Hello, please, call me Vanessa."

I spoke slowly and clearly for him, as I'd imagined myself doing, and I thrust my hand into his. His palm was dry against the clamminess of my own and his look betrayed the slightest flash of advantage. Then he took my case and nodded towards the exit. I found myself sticking close, following the white T-shirt hanging from his jeans, a crescent of caramel flesh just visible where it had scrunched up and out.

We joined the dual carriageway into the centre of Kiev, and Sasha put his foot down, dodging the many potholes at high speed. For a while I sat with a fixed smile and clenched the sagging seat, but eventually I relaxed a little and as we entered a dense birch forest I spoke up.

"It's great to be here finally, Sasha, and to meet you. Bogdan tells me you're the office Man-Friday?" I'd forgotten my policy of simplicity, but he'd understood.

"I am office manager," he said.

"Oh. I thought that was Irina?"

"She is programme manager."

That was to be my job title. I felt the sting of a flush to my cheeks. She was supposed to be my assistant, had Bogdan not made things clear? I needed to sort this quickly. "Can we go straight to the office?" I asked, "I'd like to meet Irina too."

"Irina said I must take you to hotel."

"Please? I am really keen to meet her." And tackle this head on, I thought, though the quickening of my heartbeat might have said otherwise. As a girl who wanted so much to please I couldn't bear the thought of conflict.

In response, Sasha merely clicked his tongue, and we drove on in silence for some time. I sat gazing into the trees scudding by and mulled it over. Bogdan did already run some tiny projects in Kiev and it was likely that Sasha meant those rather than the grand new programme I had arrived to manage. Either that, or it must have been a language glitch. Emerging from the forest, we came upon a series of factories poisoning the air with their streams of yellow and brown, which seeped into the car and cloyed at the back of my throat.

I tried again. "Are you from Kiev, Sasha?"

"My father is Georgian"

"Ah." Hence his swarthy complexion. "Have you lived here for a long time?"

"I came to Kiev at age of ten years."

"And you like it here?"

He slid his hands further up the steering wheel. "Our lives are difficult."

"I know," I said. But what did I know? Other than what I'd read? Other than what I'd been told by Bogdan? And I made it worse. "I'm hoping our new programme will help improve your lives."

13

I still cringe, all these years later, when I hear myself. It's one of those moments when I actually whimper out loud, usually in the dead of night. When the gaffes of your life creep all over, stopping in places to slide inside you and wriggle around – I'm still here, I can still shame you. But back then I really was there to change the world – and I thought I could. If he considered me vacuous, however, Sasha simply nodded.

We sped on towards the city and past an abandoned development of tower blocks, some already ten storeys high, with the cranes left hanging in mid air. The unfinished pods caught my eye, the blue sky visible through each one of them, and I could feel my camera sitting in a bag at my feet. They would have made a fascinating photo (economic blip, or hope abandoned?) but even I knew better than to take the camera out and shove Sasha's difficult life in his face. I felt his glance on my cheek.

"Is your first visit to Ukraine?" he asked.

"Yes, I'm very much looking forward to it."

"Your first time with aid programme?"

"Well, I've been working on a similar programme in England, social regeneration in the mining regions." I frowned at my complex words. "I helped coal miners find new jobs when the pits closed."

"I think you will also help us here," he said.

I smiled, and returned his compliment. "Your English is excellent, Sasha."

For that I was granted the makings of his own smile, and I caught sight of a gold eye-tooth. My shoulders softened against the car seat and we fell into a more companionable silence while I smiled idly at the sights from my window. Down below us a river came into view.

"Is that the Dniepro?" I asked. I'd read that for centuries this river had served as a trade route from the northern Baltic down to the Black Sea, that now it was contaminated by the aftermath of Chernobyl.

Sasha nodded and pointed across the expanse of water to a hillside statue, a cloaked figure holding up a cross. "Volodymyr, great founder of Kiev."

"Oh yes, I read about him, back in 837, I think? That's a lot of history."

His head dipped; I appeared to have notched up another peg.

The outskirts of Kiev reminded me of Salford back in the early eighties when I first moved there with Mum; vast stretches of tufted wasteland between random clumps of buildings. The apartment blocks were straight from the high rise estate I used to skirt round on my way home. Here, the pavements thickened with people and I studied their faces, inscrutable to me as they hurried along. We pulled up at a traffic light which was strung up on a line overhead, and I watched the people streaming inside the blocks, followed their invisible progress upwards to one of the tiny windows and tried to imagine their lives.

A sharp rap on my window snapped me from my thoughts and I turned to see an old woman leering at me. Instinctively I jumped back, then began to scrabble in my pocket for cash and made to wind the window down, but Sasha tutted and reached across, shoving my fingers from the handle.

"Eta bizniz, Vannysa!" he said, scowling the woman into submission.

As she backed away, he set off in a screech of tyres, while I grappled with his reaction – how could an old lady begging be any kind of business?

When we reached the city centre, Sasha turned onto a wide boulevard. Here the concrete blocks suddenly gave way to the most remarkable buildings, many of them ornate with sculpture or plastered with colour. The pavements were swathed with lilac trees. Many years later, I was to learn that every flower has a meaning of some kind, and that lilac is the floral symbol of lost youth. It still brings a smile to me now as I recall how those trees swayed shaggily overhead in canopies, their pastel cones reaching out to me, as if greeting my arrival.

"Boulevard Kreschatyk," Sasha said proudly and slowed down for me to absorb the scene.

"This is amazing." I gazed out on the six-lane boulevard, which is Kiev's answer to the Champs Elysées, and actually far more impressive. "OK if I get my camera out? I'm into photography – I mean I enjoy photography."

That earned me another click of his tongue. "I understand, I am into paintings."

"Ah. Which are your favourite artists?" I removed my lens cap.

"I find paintings in old houses in Ukraine and I sell to foreign expats."

"Oh, I see." I grinned to myself.

He smiled back at me. "You want buy, I sell. Good price."

"OK, I'd like to see them sometime."

And I snapped a shot of him, gold eye-tooth and all.

The building which housed the Bogdan Levshenko programme was well situated, in the old Jewish Quarter of Kiev, but our office was sunk below the street. My stomach churned as I followed Sasha down the steps that first afternoon. He opened the door onto a musty room and I saw a young woman in a dress of canary yellow sitting behind a desk directly

15

ahead of me. Having prepared my opening greeting, one of warmth and cheer, I marched in, smile in place, hand outstretched.

"Hello, you must be Irina? I'm Vanessa."

I beamed at her, taking in the pale pixie features, a small beaky nose and a cupid's bow at her lips. Like me, she would have been in her late twenties, and she too wore no make-up, indeed her ice-blue eyes needed none. It took more than a few unsettling moments for her to stand, during which she held my eyes with hers – intelligent eyes, somewhat anxious perhaps. Then, finally, gracefully and soundlessly, she stood and offered a chilled, limp handshake.

"How do you do." There was a slight whine to her English.

"It's so nice to meet you. I've heard from Bogdan that you're doing a wonderful job running the office."

I caught the barely perceptible frown, but she didn't respond, just gestured behind me. "You will sit here."

I swung round to see a desk jammed into the tight corner behind the door. My chest began to thud and I turned back to Irina, making a point of studying her own desk, centre stage in the office. Whether I bottled it, or whether some instinct told me I should not rise to this, the moment was brief, and I placed my briefcase on the desk. Its metal surface was scratched with Cyrillic writing; profanities for all I knew.

But then, instead of squeezing in behind the desk, I swung myself up on top of it, in what I hoped was a boss-like manoeuvre. Legs dangling, I smiled at Irina and surveyed the office. Old metal filing cabinets lined the room. The plaster peeled away from the walls in butter curls and the edges of the stained beige carpet trailed nylon threads, leaving patches of concrete exposed. Beyond the barred windows, I could see only feet clipping by on the pavement outside. Sasha was leaning on the windowsill observing our standoff with an amused smile, until suddenly, Irina let out a string of instructions at him. Ignoring her at first, he then slowly heaved himself up, took a kettle and made for the corridor.

So there I sat, legs swinging with a bluffness I did not feel. Of course, I should have made small talk, should have commented on the office, asked her about her family or something, but what did I know about managing a tricky situation? So I blundered in.

"Once I've settled in, I'd like you to brief me on how you run things here, Irina, OK?"

"Why have you come here?" Her face remained inscrutable and I half thought I must have misheard her.

16

"To manage the new programme," I muttered, adding in my confusion, "to help Ukraine."

"Huh." It was the sound of perfect scorn. "Ukraine needs no help from West."

"Oh!"

Stung, I jumped down from the desk, slid in behind it and switched on the chunky computer. Her continued glare befuddled my mind; I couldn't begin to fathom her apparent instant hatred for me. Eventually she ceased her scrutiny, picked up the phone and spoke in Russian at rattling speed, so I pretended to sift through my briefcase, pulling out papers, shuffling them into piles. Sasha handed me a cup of tea with a wink, and I sensed he'd spotted a chance for alliance against persecution, which calmed me a little. I sipped at the black tea, savouring the warm liquid and its hefty dose of sugar which washed through me, and I did feel a little better. But I needed to get myself out of there. So I announced that I wanted to change some money and asked Sasha for directions.

Emerging, a bit like a kitten on its first time through a cat flap, into the busy streets of Kiev, I then only made it a few doors down before I flattened my back to a building, palms pressed to its cool stone. Her scorn had stung me to tears, which I blinked back roughly. I'd never actually managed people before, but had visualised myself as the benevolent boss, shepherding her staff, who themselves would be eager and willing. But what really hurt was that I'd arrived that day puffed up with the notion of helping, expecting a warm welcome, and had received instead a kick in the face. Helping people was how I got along, I knew that much. What I didn't realise then, of course, was that it was also a need, one which defined me. Looking back now, it's clear that this was at the root of all that was to happen.

I walked along the pavement in a daze. How was I going to do my job without her co-operation? I'd yearned for a chance to run my own overseas aid programme, to really do good in the world, but I wouldn't know how to begin without her. Why had Bogdan employed her? And why had she taken the job if she was so defiant? As I paced through the old Jewish market, oblivious to the beauty of its white colonnades, it did occur to me that I could just sack her and recruit somebody more malleable. But that would have seemed like instant defeat. And I knew too that I felt sorry for her; there was something about the anxiety in her eyes. So I had to find some way to bring her round. Perhaps I had only to imbue on her the depths of my empathy, show her that I understood how harsh her life must be.

By the time I'd found the money changers and sign-languaged my way through the purchase of Ukrainian currency, I'd convinced myself that she was simply fearful of me and the change I represented for her. Which was all very understandable. On the street outside the office, an old lady sat on a camp stool astride a bucket of flowers, so I bought a bunch of lily of the valley and presented it to Irina.

She looked up at me expressionless. "I have flowers in my garden."

"But ... I thought they'd brighten the office." I felt the heat already spreading on my cheeks and glanced at Sasha, but he was engrossed at the photocopier.

Irina made a point of gazing around her as if insulted, then she fixed her eyes on mine. "The soul of the Ukrainian people is not bright."

I knew that I had flushed a mottled crimson and I began gathering my papers together. "Will you take me to the hotel then, Sasha?"

He nodded and left the room, returning with his jacket and a mug of water for the flowers which had been left trailing on Irina's desk, their perfume and delicacy now suddenly frivolous.

The Hotel Kievskaya was a hideous concrete slab, some twelve storeys high. At the foyer window a grubby curtain had come loose, looping down like the eyes of a bloodhound. As I followed Sasha inside that evening, I took in the varnished browns, the dust motes caught in a strand of sunshine, and I steeled myself; this would only be temporary until I found an apartment.

"I come tomorrow nine o'clock." He nodded kindly, his brown eyes soft.

"Thank you Sasha." I felt quite desolate as I watched him walk away.

The lift cranked its way to the top floor and the doors opened onto a woman knitting, her booted legs crossed, her white shirt straining across her stomach. She ignored me while she finished her row, then she let out a morose sigh, took a key and heaved herself to her feet. At the end of a corridor she opened the door of my room and closed me inside it. I stood for a moment, half expecting to hear her key turn in the lock, then I shuffled to the window, looked down onto the sprawl of the city and sighed. On the inside looking out.

Too troubled to venture out into Kiev, I opted instead for the hotel restaurant, where I ordered varenyki, which the menu said was a typical Ukrainian dish of ravioli stuffed with mushrooms and potatoes. Then I splayed open a document, Ukraine in the Wake of Communism, and stared into it while I tried to make sense of my day. I felt utterly miserable. I'll admit it now, I hadn't just expected a warm welcome that day – I'd anticipated gratitude. I find that shameful of me, but ask any man or woman on the street how they view overseas aid and wouldn't they respond as I had? Aid is a generous giving by us, and a grateful taking by them – as if it's sheer altruism on our part? Well if you scratch away at that warm fuzzy feeling you'll find that it's much more complex than that, but I for one was far too callow to begin scraping.

A man I recognised from the plane sauntered in. He had spent the flight chain-smoking in the aisle and again he was holding a cigarette, a fug of smoke clinging visibly to his suit. He smiled over at me as he sat down at a nearby table. His face was kindly, all rubbery and lived-in, and his head sported a comb-over, leaving tufts of grey to fight it out above the ears. Returning his smile, I half wished he had joined me at my table despite the cigarette.

With all the self-consciousness of the single diner, I set about eating and reading, but could sense the constant scrutiny of my waiter standing just a few feet away. When I glanced up at him he stared me out, quite openly, and I looked away in a flurry – what was it with these people? I put down my cutlery and flattened the spine of my book in an emphatic show of concentration, but then he was at my side and reaching for my half-finished meal. He slid the plate away while I grabbed it back from him. For a few moments we actually tussled over it.

"I've not finished," I hissed, clinging onto the plate, until finally he let go and loped back to his post.

Across the largely empty room, the smoker let out a loud chuckle, which ended in a fruity cough.

"Welcome to the Wild East!" he shouted. "And all its crazy people. I'm Jeff, may I join you?"

I nodded at him, warming instantly to his northern accent.

"Do they always do that?" I whispered as he reached my table.

"They call it service!" He laughed, drew on his cigarette and blew the smoke out, reaching for my hand. "To whom do I have the pleasure?"

"Vanessa Parker."

He sat down. "Very pleased to meet you. Would you per chance be here for an aid programme? Kievskaya's the usual stamping ground."

"Levshenko Programme. I'm here to design and manage it, I've just got here."

"Just arrived? Well that calls for shampoo." He clicked his fingers at the waiter, ordered a bottle, then he leant across the table, head cocked. "I'd heard Bogdan was expanding his programme out here, what great things may we expect from him?"

"You know Bogdan?"

"Oh yes, we go back years."

Drawn by Jeff's paternal twinkle, I too folded my arms conspiratorially.

"He wants to start something major for job creation, but we're not sure what yet. It's up to me to come up with something, design it and then contract it out."

"Well, Vanessa, job creation just happens to be my forte. You're going to need good people for that, here's my card."

He pressed his business card onto the white linen, flipping it with his nail as if playing an ace in black jack. Jeff Osbourne, Expert, it read. Though it didn't say in what.

"Are you here on an aid programme too, then?"

"Indeed I am. For my sins."

Our champagne arrived, Crimean I noticed, and Jeff opened it with a flourish, letting the waiter traipse after the flown cork, while he filled the two old-fashioned coupes the man had brought for us.

He raised his glass. "To Vanessa's arrival in Ukraine!"

I chinked glasses and sipped the lukewarm fizz, nodding benignly at him. I was enjoying the sanctuary of his easy company, although he did remind me of some character in a sitcom with his bizarre attempts to sound genteel when he was clearly salt of the earth.

"And how was your first day in this sublime country?"

"Well, I didn't exactly get the warmest of welcomes from my new assistant."

"Bit aloof was she? I assume it was a she?"

"She said Ukraine didn't need help from the West."

Jeff sucked his teeth. "You're about to spend, how much was it?"

"Three million."

"Three million quid in her country. And she's not welcoming you with open arms, Vanessa?"

Even if they echoed my own thoughts, his words made me uneasy.

"Some Ukrainians get like that. It's arrogant, if you ask me, and she should be careful because there's plenty of bright young things out there."

I smiled, suddenly protective towards Irina. "Oh I'll give her a chance, I'm sure she's just unsettled by my arrival."

He sat back and contemplated me, taking a few long drags on his cigarette before dropping it into the crystal flower vase on the table.

"Anyway, if it's job creation you're here for, you'll be wanting to meet with the Minister for Employment. Balavensky, he's called. And I can make the necessary introductions, if you so require?"

"Jeff, that would be fantastic, thank you."

"Can you parlski the Ruski yet?"

"My parrot is sick, please fetch me a doctor."

Jeff let out a throaty chuckle which brought on his cough again. "I do believe I learnt my Russian from the very same textbook. No problemo, he comes with a charming sidekick, Valentyna Tabachuk, who's fluent in English. Any case, you'll have an interpreter."

A trace of self-importance crept over me then – my very own interpreter translating my very own words.

"And you'll need to meet Dan, too," he went on. "Dan Mitchell, the Deputy Head at USAID, and your guru on all things job creation here."

I scrawled the name on the back of Jeff's card. It was one that would come up several times during my first month in Kiev, always with similar accolades, often with a knowing smile. But, of course, during those early weeks in Ukraine, Dan was on leave back home in Chicago.

3

After our boozy lunch with the Governor, Dan and I slid back into the Volga and I fell into a doze. When I stirred, still bright with alcohol, I found us surrounded by fields of sunflowers. The landscape was yellow for as far as the eye could see, their oversized sunshine heads standing to attention.

"Stunning, isn't it?" Dan was smiling at me.

"Gorgeous." I smiled woozily back.

"If you look closely, you might catch them moving with the sun. They ratchet round to trap its rays."

"Really?"

"Really." His smile lingered, so mine did too.

We soon reached the coal mine. Its tower loomed above us, the vast wheel and iron girders stark against the lustrous afternoon sky. I kicked myself for having forgotten my camera, as we picked our way across the gritty coal sediment towards the office building, its brick blackened, its door hanging from a single loose hinge.

The mine manager was a surly man who greeted us without handshake or smile, and led us into separate shower rooms. I removed all of my clothes, knowing that they'd be ruined after we'd been down the pit, and mildly cursed Dan for not having given me the notice which would have allowed for a change of underwear. Then I pulled on a ragged navy blue boiler suit and boots, and stuffed my belongings into a locker.

Outside in the yard, the manager was silent as he handed us each a lamp and a scratched orange helmet. Aware of Dan watching me, I made a show of scooping my hair up and into it. Then we were given a set of cup-shaped pads.

"Two codpieces?" Dan held them out to me, his face full of question and fun.

"They're kneepads." I threw him a mock withering glance. "Give them here."

I dropped to the ground before him and began to tie a pad around his knee, my fingers scrabbling against the solidity of his calf muscles. The physical contact made me even more conscious of my nakedness beneath the baggy boiler suit, and I wondered if Dan was also naked beneath his. As he helped me up, our eyes met briefly and he raised his eyebrows, as if he was conscious of all I was thinking. I raised my own and turned jauntily for the lift shaft. We handed over the tokens we'd been given and followed the manager and our interpreter into the lift.

The cage swung shut and the lift began its descent into the mine. I peered up into the last chunk of sunlight as it became a sliver before being snatched from us, and then I looked down at my boots in the gloom. The wooden platform wobbled as it dropped, sucking my stomach down with it, emptying my legs and stretching my chest with fear. For some people it is snakes or spiders; for me, since the age of eleven, it has been the sensation of falling and I sank down into myself, all trace of our lunchtime cognac feast suddenly gone. Behind my closed eyelids I saw a flash of the image that has stayed with me since that day. Don't jump, I told myself silently, don't jump.

We dropped further down, the heat intensifying to sauna levels, and the manager began to address us. "Our mines are two times as deep as mines in UK," he said, through the interpreter, whose voice had risen a notch, no doubt with his own nerves. "We will descend to level of one kilometre. And I must inform you that we have many accidents in coal mines in Ukraine, because very often we have build-up of methane gas."

I continued to hang my head, studying my boots as he droned on, while it slowly dawned on me that the man was tormenting us for good reason. I looked up at him.

"Is this mine due to close?"

"Yes," he replied without returning my glance. "Slagansk mine will close before end of year."

So not only were we a blight on his afternoon's work (a lunchtime phone call from the Governor) but we had also come to observe his dying days. I glanced at Dan, whose face seemed to have lost some of its tan despite the gloom, and he raised his eyebrows, seemingly also ashamed. I could tell that he too was sober again.

Our descent took a good five minutes, twice as long as with the pits I'd been down back home in Lancashire. When, finally, the lift reached the bottom of the shaft, it landed with a hefty clunk which jostled us all into each other and I felt Dan's steadying hand on my arm. As the cage door was swung back, I looked up into the large, blackened face of a miner, who gazed back at me in equal astonishment. The coal dust smothering his face was broken only by the startled eyes with their piercing blue irises and flashes of white. A flush of humbling emotion swept me and I glanced down, catching the glint of a silver crucifix on a chain at his neck. When I looked back into his eyes, I saw that they were then frowning, the furrows at his brow deepened by coal dust. Clearly, I was an unwelcome tourist – and also an unnecessary risk.

We each stepped from the lift into the surge of heat, our heads jabbing about like exotic birds, in an effort to seek out and make sense of the light cast by our lamps. The mineral air cloyed at my lungs, causing me to take deeper, grasping breaths of it in a bid for the fresh stuff. I could hear the rumble of machinery at work in the distance and, from along the narrow passageway, a line of miners were approaching us, almost silhouetted with coal dust, their lamps and eyes the only points of light. Turning, I attempted a smile at the miner attending the lift, wanting to assure him that I knew about coal mines, that I would be respectful – reverent even. But he refused me this comfort, closing the cage door and standing back from our group into the gloom.

The mine manager ushered us into a narrow roofless train, not unlike those you see puffing merrily round parks, the children waving at their parents, and I sat down close to Dan, our arms and thighs clamped together, while the man sat in front with our interpreter.

I turned to Dan. "OK?"

He nodded briefly, but he looked far from well, his face beaded with a sweat that seemed to be caused by more than the searing heat alone.

The train set off and we were shunted further underground, this time inwards, burrowing into the earth and away from the relative safety of the lift shaft. I sat in silence as the minutes passed and gazed down at my hands, watching the grime claim every part of my exposed skin, feeling the coal dust gritting up my teeth. Dan's hands beside mine seemed to be shaking. I squashed the urge to place my own hand over his and I glanced away and up at the ceiling, expecting to see a steel canopy of the type that secures British mines, but there was only sporadic wooden propping. I felt suddenly sick. This was not right. Further in we passed ventilation equipment which was so antiquated it reminded me of the bellows in some grainy documentary on the industrial revolution. I swallowed hard and focused on the steady progress of a narrow conveyor belt running beside us, smothered in the day's produce; there was some comfort to be had in the glistening mass which was moving in the opposite direction, back to where there was daylight. Back to where life was still happening.

"This how it normally is?" Dan asked me, his voice a rasp.

"I'm sure it's safe," I lied.

It was instinct that moved my hand towards his then, that made me squeeze it to stop it from shaking, and as I did so I heard an anxious sigh fall from his chest.

When, after several minutes, we finished our journey to the centre of the earth, we stepped out of the train and stood huddled together in the confined space, looking up as the weak lamp above our heads momentarily faltered. Aware of the terrifying mass of rock above me, of the terrible distance back to the shaft, I looked at Dan's blackened face and he nodded back at me. But it wasn't over. The manager pointed to a tunnel, no more than half a metre wide, which had been hewn through the rock.

"We must crawl through this tunnel to reach coal seam," he said.

Dan's response was instant. "No way am I going to get myself through there."

The manager retorted and Dan continued to shake his head as we waited for the interpreter.

"Mr Mitchell, our miners are bigger men than you," he translated.

"Yeah, but they're a lot fitter than I am. Look, I'm really sorry, but I just cannot do this."

Dan turned to me, his eyes pleading with me through the soot, and it was clear that our visit, which had put the manager and his miners to gratuitous hassle, would be an even greater imposition unless I were to sink to my knees in front of that tunnel. So that's what I did. I dropped flat to my stomach and I began to push elbow after elbow, shunting my hips, creeping combat-like in pursuit of the mine manager's boots ahead of me. Our interpreter, in a move well above and beyond the course of duty, flopped down and followed me in. As I crawled my way through, the needles of rock face snagged at my back, the coal dust clogged my eyes and nose, and each breath I took sucked drafts of the dense mineral deep down inside me.

We inched forward like that for what seemed an age until the rumble of drills grew louder and, eventually, we emerged into a low cavern. I struggled to my knees and then to a crouch, unable to right myself completely, and I looked around me. The cave was more brightly lit and, as my eyes adjusted, I saw that it was packed with miners, that they too were forced to bend double in places as they laboured, that some of them had shed their boiler suits and worked in underpants. Their machines were nudging and stroking the walls over and over, shearing sheets of coal which glistened like diamonds at their feet. Once I'd been spotted, one by one they each ceased their drilling, let their machines hang loosely and swung round to contemplate me. Some were startled, others regarded me without expression. While I stared back at them in awe.

The compassion I felt at that moment has never left me. How could these men live through this, working themselves to the end, putting body and soul into their labour – and all of that when they were on the brink of losing their livelihoods? Did they even know about that bit? In the UK, miners had literally worked themselves into the ground, believing this would prevent the doom, but it had all been in vain in the end. I knew miners who had been told at clocking off on Friday not to show up on the Monday; there'd been the sweetener of a year's salary, and then the loan sharks had moved in, whole communities left adrift. We might as well skip a generation, Dan had said, but I was not going to let that happen. It physically pained me to see these men; I didn't just empathise with them, I was inside their suffering, and I was going to use my programme to give them a better life. Single-handedly, as it seems to me now. All of this I tried to convey to them, willing them to read my mind, in the few minutes that I stood and watched the miners watching me, before I silently turned, dropped to my knees and crawled back into the tunnel.

On the journey back to the surface, Dan and I stood close, remaining silent and still. But as we stepped from the cage into the strong summer sunlight, the relief seemed to swamp us both and we laughed brightly, finding ourselves sliding apart, careful to maintain our distance. As if the unexpected intimacy of our shared encounter needed redressing. Dan peered into my face, unhooking his helmet, his hands again sure and steady.

"Is that you in there, Vanessa?" He was flirting with me.

"You're no oil painting right now, Mr Mitchell." I narrowed my eyes at him, shaking my hair free.

Beaming like a pair of astronauts safely back from space, we slotted the interpreter between us as a buffer, slapping him on the back as if he'd been our shuttle commander, and we made our way across the blanket of grit. In my changing room, I looked into the jagged piece of mirror on the wall;

my face was black and my eyes loomed up out of it. I rolled them dramatically to flash the whites, inhaled deeply and blew the air out of me. It felt as if I'd been delivered from death, and it was hard to fathom that these men were still down there beneath me. I kicked the filthy boiler suit into a corner and made for the shower.

I lathered up many times over while I took myself through the possibilities. How many men would there be at this mine? A thousand perhaps? Highly skilled, totally reliable, and resilient, just as British miners had been – even more so considering their appalling conditions. A pilot project within my overall programme could capitalise on those qualities and see them through into new employment, into better lives. I could do this, I knew I could.

I emerged from the shower with black in the crevices of my palms, and could still feel the grit between my teeth. We met up again in the manager's office, where we were served a polite tray of tea.

"Your show time, Vanessa." Dan winked at me. His wet hair was slick as if doused with ink and an impressive smattering of coal dust still clung to his own skin.

Buoyed by his presence, but with great deference, I launched myself into an explanation of how we could set up a Job Shop at Slagansk before the mine closed, to help re-employ the men elsewhere. I put my all into my pitch, but the manager watched me idly, with the passive tolerance of a man ordered to do his duty and simply getting through it. He tossed my information leaflet onto his desk without a glance.

"We have many visitors, who come here for fact-finding." He spoke those last words in English to press home his sarcasm, "but we see never concrete actions."

"I promise you will see concrete actions from me." I felt my cheeks burn as I scrabbled and failed to maintain eye contact. "In fact, I will tell you exactly when you can expect to see us here again, with some actual funding too."

A woman in a floral dress entered the room then. She nodded over to me and began a flurried discussion with the man, hushing her words behind her hand. The manager sighed and ran a hand wearily across his face.

"This is my wife, Tanya. She would like you to visit our village."

I considered the woman. The dress was a flouncy one, as if she was out for some special occasion, and I realised that the tom-toms must be onto our visit, drumming out the beat: there's an aid programme in town. She

27

nodded again at me, her eyes willing me on, so I turned to Dan.

"I'd like to go," I said, "have we got time?"

"Sure." The weight of his sidelong glance agreed that we owed them one.

4

"Shall we dance?"

Those had been Dan's very first words to me. Although we were in a conference hall, not a dance hall. I'd been in Kiev some weeks by then, Irina was still icy towards me and I had not even begun to master the situation. Empowerment is the best way to manage people, so Bogdan had advised me in that floppy emphatic way of his, but in those early days Irina was as empowered as a Tsarina.

"Tomorrow, I will go to job at university," she would announce as she left some evenings, with startling certainty that she did not have to request time off.

Her disdain smarted. I was used to being appreciated by colleagues – liked even – and I just could not read her. As for the work, when I asked her for help with contacts and background information, she would dump files on my desk and return to her own work with the small aid projects which Bogdan had been financing for some years – the training schemes for journalists and the emerging Non Governmental Organisations. At that early stage in my new job, I found that I could work round her, skulking in the office of an evening to plunder the filing cabinets. So I'd decided to roll with her punches for the time being, remaining kind and cheerful, demonstrating that I meant her no harm, and believing that this would eventually bring her round. Which is how my youthful judgement had called the situation.

While muddling along at this man-management, I did however trust my instincts on the development of our programme. I gathered data on the figures and profiles of Ukraine's workforce, marshalled my ideas for possible job creation measures – among them modern vocational training, small business support centres, or managed workspace – and drew up budget scenarios for each one. And I set off on a mission to meet the other international aid bodies, known as donors, to discover their own job creation programmes for a country where mass unemployment was about to strike. Kiev was crawling with donors – the World Bank, the UN, the IMF, the EU, plus a whole raft of national governments, and I took tea in their plush offices, the white cocoons which cushioned them from the chaos of this city.

Windows down, Sasha drove me to and from my meetings, the warm breeze buffeting us along the Boulevard Kreschatyk. And together we discovered a shared, somewhat puerile, sense of humour. I learnt that the skid start he'd demonstrated on our drive in from the airport was his default setting and when one morning he pulled off, tyres screeching, I laughed.

"OK Starsky, less go get'em," I said huskily.

"Who is this Starsky?" he asked with a sidelong frown and flash of gold eye-tooth. Then he sourced a bootleg video for himself and was soon calling me Hutch.

Within a few weeks, I was ready to present the outline of the Levshenko Programme – Creating New Jobs in Ukraine – to the Ukrainian Government, and Bogdan flew over for the launch. Our press release was embargoed until 9am on Tuesday 12th July 1994. Still today I find myself gazing into the yellowed copy I've kept, lingering on the date and time; on the before, when the world had not yet shifted.

"Let us be clear," the Minister for Employment, Ivan Balavensky, began. "Ukraine is great nation. Our country has rich and fertile soil, our country has major industries, including huge output of inter-ballistic missiles."

I watched him, a little further along the podium from me, as he went on to give us output figures for Ukraine's collective farms and for the production of pig iron. A man of hefty build, his skin resembled uncooked pastry and his eyes were lifeless, as if honed by the KGB. When we'd finally been introduced that morning, my handshake too eager against his loose grip, I'd noticed also that his fingernails seemed to be packed with soil. Balavensky was a reformer, my boss Bogdan had counselled, and there were so few of these in the Ukrainian Government that it was key to harness him, to run with him. But listening to him drone on, I doubted his credentials as a modern thinker, as a man who wanted to renew his country. What's more, Jeff had secured me the promised introduction and I'd waited in the Minister's antechamber for his return from lunch, but

30

he'd failed to show. Twice.

"The word 'unemployment' did not even exist in our country until after the fall of communism," the Minister continued, the translation from Russian to English coming through our headphones. "Last year there were almost no jobless people in Ukraine."

You're a dinosaur, I thought to myself, frowning and turning to gauge his impact on the room; the Western donors were lolling at the back, the eager Ukrainians were up front, press release in hand. We all knew that unemployment was already astronomical, but that it was still hidden. Under communism, the unemployed were seen as down and outs, a stigma which still lingered, and this was partly why the masses were not signing on. Moreover, factories were still housing their workforce and educating their children in schools they financed, even if they no longer had any work for them, so men were still technically employed if actually idle.

On the first row, Valentyna Tabachuk, the Head of the Job Centre Network whom Jeff had mentioned, caught my eye with a knowing smile. An attractive woman, perhaps in her late forties, with glossy black hair, a silk scarf at her neck and a slash of somewhat garish crimson lipstick, she had spoken fluent English at our introduction that morning. Indeed, with her easy smile and greeting of a kiss to each cheek, she appeared more Western than Ukrainian to me and I had been drawn to her kindred ways. Resolving to corner her at lunch, I smiled back with a daring roll of my eyes at the Minister's monologue, but then I caught a sudden mention of my name.

"Mrs Vanyssa." Balavensky bent forward around Bogdan's trim figure and held an open palm out at me. "We would like to co-operate with you, but you must come to speak with me in my office, you cannot run this programme all alone."

Amusement rippled through the Ukrainian delegates as I felt the flush hit my cheeks and I opened my mouth to retort. But Bogdan pressed a hand to my arm and I fought to calm myself, my knee jiggling beneath the podium. For a moment the Minister appeared to be noting my reaction, then he wound up his speech.

"We are most grateful to Levshenko Programme for coming to our aid, most grateful to you, my good friend Bogdan. And we will give you all assistance necessary to complete your work here in Ukraine."

I found that last bit bizarre, given that we were there for them. Indeed, with all that I know now, I should not have pushed his comment so readily from my mind, but Balavensky threw Bogdan the most comradely of glances, which my boss returned before taking the microphone, and the moment was gone.

Bogdan spoke in his mother tongue, Ukrainian. I had heard mostly Russian spoken by the various officials I'd met in Kiev, and Sasha had told me that some snobbery prevailed among government circles, that Ukrainian was viewed as more of a peasant language, although its revival was underway – and today of course it's back where it belongs. While vaguely aware of the difference between the two languages, I listened intently to the translation as Bogdan told of his Grandfather, who had arrived in Manchester among the first immigrant families from Ukraine, early in the twentieth century. How he, the Grandson, was now a multi-millionaire, having built his manufacturing empire in the same city. How he wanted to put something back. His words made me feel proud to have been recruited by such a philanthropist and I smiled at his face as he spoke. Clearly a Slav face, but with a complexion that was tanned and healthy – like the 'after' photo against Balavensky's 'before'.

Towards the end of his speech, Bogdan placed a palm across his heart. "My friends, I sit before you today, quite humbly, to announce that I would like to help you with my modest personal contribution through the Levshenko Programme and I have chosen this beautiful woman beside me to supervise my work here." He ignored the withering glance I shot him. "As those of us with Ukraine in their blood all know, women have many facets. Beautiful women may also be intelligent, certainly women may be fiery, those with red hair especially."

There were chortles around the room as he finished, but I scowled at Bogdan's paternal smile, intent on having it out with him later. That morning, at breakfast in the hotel, he'd told me he was going to play it 'their way' and I'd nodded bluffly, not wanting to let on that I had no idea what their way was.

In a bid for calm before I took the microphone myself, I scanned my audience, and I saw fervour in the eyes of the Ukrainians, which heartened me. Now, of course, I would take such zeal for dollar signs (there were thousands at stake) but back then I took things almost at complete face value. A smiling Mrs Tabachuk rolled her eyes at me, as I had done earlier – no doubt in a gesture of solidarity after the sexist remarks – so I beamed at her and then at the whole room.

"We are here to support your transition to a free market economy," I began. "That transition will bring unemployment, and we can help you tackle that. In the UK we have a wealth of experience to share with you, from our huge job losses in the coal and steel regions alone."

The Minister now nodded agreeably at me, as if he'd thrown no missile at all and I looked back down to my notes, gathering my thoughts.

It was then that the door to the conference hall opened. I heard the murmured ripple across the room and I felt his presence, all of that in the seconds before I glanced up. When I did so, I saw that the man was looking back at me, still holding the door ajar, a fold of that red and cream lining bursting from one cuff of his jacket. He dipped his head briefly in apology for his tardiness while I nodded back, and I believe – or maybe I've planted the memory – that our eye contact was a touch prolonged, surprising us both into glancing down. I watched him then, my heart beating fast, as he sauntered past the rows of chairs. He loped like a lion, shoulders lifting and rolling, his head high, surveying the plain. Such an overt and steady display of confidence was thrilling to me and I sensed the first frisson patter through me right then in that room. When he came to a halt, I watched Jeff stand and clasp his hand, as if he'd won the prize of skin contact with this man.

I knew it was Dan, of course. I waited, as did everybody else in that hall, until he had sat, flicking the jacket button open, and settled himself down. Then I cleared my throat and went on, hauling my mind back to the task in hand.

"This manual, for example, contains many strategies for re-employment." I held up a glossy hardback book. "British experts could draw on these and show you how best to—"

I stopped short as a man in the front row raised his hand, stretching his arm like a kid in a classroom, and I nodded to him, waiting as the roving microphone was passed over. This was my first encounter with Viktor, the Head of Ukraine's Small Business Federation.

"Please?" the man began, his smile sickly. "When will you give us this money? And how may we apply for it?"

That floored me. Instinctively, I shot a glance first at Dan, whose eyes were gentle, narrowing to spur me on, and then at Bogdan, who was clearly as confused as I was.

"Erm, well, the money isn't going directly to you, it'll go to pay the UK experts who will come here to transfer their experience and know-how to you."

Viktor's smile froze in his face but his hand was still raised. "Please? In Ukraine we do not need handbooks, we need money to pay our entrepreneurs, to buy desks and computers. We can do the job ourselves, if you will just give us the money. Please, you give us the three million pounds?"

I gawped at his ruddy face, at the silver-grey hair clumped together in greasy shards, but before I could respond, Balavensky cut in with a sharp tirade in Russian, covering the microphone to prevent any translation of his words. I clocked the steel in the Minister's eyes as he took Viktor to task, and the smile left the businessman's face, it even crumpled a little.

In a whisper, I asked Bogdan what the Minister had said, and he scribbled it down – Shut your mouth, you know that is not the official line! I was unable to make sense of that – what official line? But when I glanced up at Viktor again he was beaming at me, so I beamed back in reflex and went on.

"To confirm then, the lion's share will be spent on technical assistance – that is on the transfer of knowledge and experience to you. We will provide some equipment too, a few computers, or photocopy machines perhaps. But, as is the norm with these technical assistance programmes, the equipment component will not exceed 10% of the total programme budget."

Those last words caused a bit of a rumpus; all Ukrainian heads shook at the injustice of the offering and, behind them, all Western heads shook at the audacity of the expectation. It was time to wind up.

"Our next step will be a design workshop to thrash out the details. Then, once Bogdan has approved the programme, it can begin in the autumn."

I sat back to the applause, which was quite vigorous, the Ukrainians having collected themselves again, but the Minister raised his palm to quieten them and dipped his mouth to the microphone on his desk.

"Thank you Vanyssa. You are indeed very beautiful, and your red hair tells us you will be passionate in helping us to solve all our problems." He ignored my scowl. "But, please, let us be your partners, not the beneficiaries of Levshenko Programme. And please, my friend Bogdan, may I also have the chance to approve this programme before you start up in the autumn?"

Bogdan nodded crazily. "Absolutely," he cried, slamming the desk, though his annoyance was palpable.

And I admit I shared his indignation – why should the Minister have a say? It was our bloody money and he wasn't going to hijack it!

The launch was followed by a buffet. This was the first time I would witness the spectacle of a free lunch in Kiev – as if the plane had crashed and it was first man to the escape chute. I watched Dan stand and stretch before buttoning his jacket and motioning a short and silent clap of the hands at me, a smile bursting onto his white American teeth. But then he made for the door and, before I could move, Chelsea Savage from the World Bank was standing at the base of our podium.

Just a few years older than me, Chelsea's taut skin pulled her cheeks high, tilting her lips up at the edges and giving her the air of someone always faintly amused, in a supercilious sort of way. I'd not warmed to her when we'd first met and as I watched Dan slip out of the room, she too turned to watch him go, as if she was deliberately preventing me from following him.

"Nice work Vanessa." Her sugary voice grated. "I guess we could use your programme."

"Sorry?" I tugged my eyes away from the door and frowned down at her.

"Sure. The Bank is short on grants to pay for technical assistance, so when we lend our money to these people, we're unable to back it up with know-how to finish the job. What say we dovetail your Levshenko funds with our loans?"

I stared at her, making a mental note never to dovetail anything of mine with anything of hers.

"Did I give you my card?" she asked.

"Two of them, thanks." I swung away and tramped down from the podium.

In keeping with the spirit of things the room had divided itself into two halves: Ukrainians and Westerners, all of them already tucking into loaded plates, and I searched out Mrs Tabachuk, spotting her by the Minister's side. She raised her smile at me, and I returned it, but made first for the far end of the trestle table, needing some moments of solitude to compose myself.

Irina stood behind the buffet table. She had organised pork cutlets, chicken legs, an array of salads, even champagne. I smiled at her in thanks for this startling effort. With a slow blink, my colleague nodded back at me. In later days, I realised that this was to become her gesture of approval towards me, and I came to wonder if she had witnessed my stand-off with Chelsea, if I had risen slightly in her esteem that morning. With my back to the room, I began half-heartedly placing the odd tomato or gherkin onto my plate. My surreal morning had left me miserable. I felt completely out of my depth with this new job, this new life. The Minister, Bogdan, they both seem to have mocked me, and nobody present seemed to understand that we weren't just going to hand the money over to them. What's more, the World Bank clearly viewed me as some little girl they could manipulate with a pat on the head – but then my lack of professionalism in having snubbed this giant of an aid donor did not escape me either. I let out a hefty sigh; I'd even allowed myself to be drawn in by Dan Mitchell. As Deputy Head of USAID, he was an important contact, but he was clearly also a man with an ego, who swept in and out of rooms, and I was not some simpering female who was about to catch pneumonia on a rainy moor. I needed to get a grip.

As host, I also had to face the mass of delegates sooner rather than later. So with another plaintive sigh I swung away from the table – and smacked into Dan, who must have been making pretty smartly for my side.

"Sorry!" I jumped back.

"Shall we dance?" He smiled and held his arms out, lightly embracing my shoulders before reaching past me for a plate. "You must be the new kid in town?"

"Yes, Vanessa Parker, nice to meet you." I held out a hand – I swear I almost curtsied too.

"Dan Mitchell." He gestured to his full hands, already a chicken leg in one, plate in the other.

"Oh, yes, I've heard your name mentioned."

I feigned nonchalance but his eyes dipped briefly to my cheeks, and for an odd moment neither of us spoke. Around us, the buzz of Western conversation also quietened and I knew that heads had turned, I could feel their scrutiny. As if they too could sense something happening.

5

The sun was low but the day still burned as we slipped once more into the black Volga, left the Slagansk mine behind and drove out to Tanya's village. The woman would like us to meet her friends, she said through our interpreter, who was beginning to flag and was probably wondering what else this day still had to throw at him. As was I. Sitting squashed beside Dan, so keenly aware of his thigh against mine, of the chewing gum wafting from his mouth, I was more than a little bothered.

Most of the houses in Tanya's village were single storey, many of them whitewashed with roofs of corrugated iron. More like cottages, I thought, as we trundled along the gravel road and pulled up at a ramshackle green picket fence.

"My home," she said, opening the garden gate and shooing several scraggy hens with soft kicks. "I keep chickens. Very good eggs," she added.

As we followed her across the mossy grass, I stumbled a little and felt Dan's hand on the small of my back, steadying me. We shared a smile which seemed weighted with the unique events of that overly long day. Tanya took us past an old wooden well, its winding frame crooked, its planks rotten, and around to the back garden, where several other young women were sitting in a circle of stripy plastic deckchairs. They reminded me of the ones we used to take camping when I was a kid.

The women all got to their feet and a girl about my own age held out her hand to me. She was very pretty, with long blonde hair and those grey Slav eyes that beguile.

"Hello, I am Svetlana," she said, and offered us beers.

I could tell from the cadence of her words that her English was good, so I nodded at our interpreter that he would probably not be needed. Then, with the kind of smile that lures you in and holds you close, Svetlana explained to us that each of these women was the wife of a miner, that their husbands all worked at Slagansk and that she would introduce each of them in turn.

"But please, first can you tell us who you are?" she asked.

"This is Dan Mitchell from USAID," I began, but she threw a fleeting look his way and then back; it was me they were after. I went on. "My name is Vanessa Parker and I've just arrived in Ukraine to manage the Levshenko Programme. You may have heard of it?"

"Levshenko ..." Svetlana glanced swiftly round the huddle of women, shaking her head. "No, we do not know that programme, Vanessa."

She'd even pronounced my name right. Her focus on me was intense, like that of an animal sizing up danger, and I learnt later that she too was used to timewasters from the West.

"It's a programme of three million pounds to get the jobless back to work." I returned the intensity of her gaze, wanting so much to assure her of my commitment.

Svetlana nodded slowly and I saw that the other women were carefully watching her, waiting for her benediction. Once they caught the nod, they visibly relaxed, settling into their chairs with more genuine smiles for me, so I pulled out my leaflet and explained a little more.

"Do you think I can help here in your village?" I asked finally.

"Yes, we hope so, Vanessa," Svetlana said. And then these wives of miners began their round table.

First to speak was Lesya, a plump young woman whose thick foundation drew attention to the roughened acne scars on her cheeks beneath. She was learning to cut hair, self-taught with the guidance of a friend in the local town, and charged just a couple of hundred karbovantsiv, the equivalent of fifty pence, to cut hair in the homes of her friends.

"I have many real customers in village too!" she said through Svetlana's translation, producing a pair of tarnished scissors from her pocket and snipping them in the air with a wicked gleam at me.

I shielded my hair with my hands and we all laughed – perhaps a little too loudly in that polite manner of new acquaintances. I sensed Dan smiling at my comical expression and I threw him a flirtatious sidelong smirk.

"Maybe Lesya could do men too?" I asked.

Dan's own hair, now dry again after his shower, was thickly tousled against his face. He grinned back at me and the moment lingered, until Svetlana moved on round to the next woman, Olga, who made and mended clothes.

Although slightly younger than the others, Olga's round face and smile lent her a motherly air as she handed me a pile of blouses, their scratchy fabric embroidered in cheerful cross-stitch.

"These seem very well made," I said, holding one up and beaming at her.

I passed the garments onto Dan, observing him for any sign of ridicule and was heartened to see none; he'd clearly also developed a respect for Ukrainian folklore.

"Can you make other stuff as well as clothing Olga?" he asked.

"Oh yes, cushions and curtains too." She beamed from Dan to me.

"I'm sure Vanessa will leave you her card." I nodded at my cue, and handed several around the group.

In the deckchair beside mine was the tiny Yelena, who sat gripping a large jar of honey with both hands and I peered at the wodge of honeycomb encased within it. When she stood to hand the jar over to me, the woman remained on her feet to make a formal speech about its floral provenance – sunflowers – then she encouraged us to scoop out long sticky skeins of the stuff with our fingers.

"Mmm-mmm." Dan made a humorous show of sucking his fingers then pulled the pot to him and wrapped his arms around it. From Yogi Bear to Winnie the Pooh, I thought, as we all laughed at his antics. He laughed back with me, his face open and so radiant.

"How much, Yelena?" I turned back to the woman.

"One hundred karbovantsiv." A mere twenty-five pence, but she blushed at the prospect of our transaction.

"Thank you." I curled a thousand note into my fist and pressed it into her hand. "Sorry I have no change."

"Niet," No, she protested, unfolding the note and holding it up to the other women.

"You keep the rest." I sensed their unease. "And I'll take another pot from you next time."

Steadily, I looked around the group to let them know that there would be a next time; it was so clear to me that I could work in their village, that any aid I brought to them would be well deployed, it would reach the point of need.

The last young woman Dan and I met that evening was Marina. A slight figure, as many cooks seem to be, she offered round the cakes she had baked, while Tanya handed us more beer. The women watched us eat, encouraging us to load our plates with more, and they told us about life in their village, about how they wanted to earn more cash to support the wages of their husbands. I listened almost spellbound – did they even know that the mine was going to close? It seemed not. If I could help with some small contribution from the Levshenko Programme, Svetlana explained, it would be so very much appreciated. They had heard about something called micro-credit, where small loans were given to enterprising women like them. Would I be able to help them with that?

In streaks of pink, the sun finally sank behind the village houses and the stars began to come through. I tipped my head back drowsily and took in the vast coal black of a Ukrainian country sky, unblemished by buildings or electric light; I was able to make out the Pole Star, the Great Bear and the Milky Way quite distinctly. At some point, I did hear Dan murmur in my ear that we were going to miss the last flight back, but there was no way we could leave, we were both bewitched by those women. I found myself looking from one face to the next – Svetlana, Lesya, Olga, Yelena, Marina and Tanya. They're incredible, I thought, and silently I christened them the Divas. My Divas.

As we finally took our leave that evening, Tanya presented me with two freshly laid eggs, wrapped up in straw and still warm, and I slid them into my handbag where they sat incongruously alongside the passport and purse. Then I held my arms out to Svetlana. We rocked from side to side like old friends reunited, the movement soldering our very new friendship, and we thanked each other effusively, without really knowing why.

When I turned to get into the car, I felt my tears brimming, though I knew not to insult the women by letting them fall. Dan too seemed subdued as we left. USAID had a contract with a hotel in the city, he said, and so we asked one last journey of our driver, paying him and the interpreter handsomely for the extra hours, and we arrived just as they were locking up for the night.

I admit I was disappointed with the peck on the cheek Dan gave me as he got out of the lift, at a different floor to mine even. At the outset of this extraordinary day I'd barely known the man, and yet we seemed to have become so strangely close over the course of it, but I was exhausted and thought that perhaps I had misread him. In any case I didn't want him to think me easy, so I let it go.

That night, I showered again. The water was barely lukewarm – ludicrous when you think of the fuel being produced in that city, but the night was hot and I let it wash down over me. I raised my face to its cleansing force, I soaped my body with palms that swept flat and then lingered over my flesh, and I thought of Dan. Twisting myself into it, I let the water pound my body, my breasts, my thighs, and then I held myself still beneath its torrent.

Afterwards I lay in bed, the cotton sheet feathery against my skin, and listened to the scuttle of the trams outside on the boulevard. I was conscious, acutely so, of the mining of coal which was happening deep beneath the streets of Donetsk, perhaps directly beneath my bed. Through the night, men would be hacking coal from the earth, shovelling it onto the moving belts, sweating and hurting with the physical strain. When I closed my eyes, my lids were jittery with the images of the day, refusing me any rest. I saw again the persistent eyes of the miners, the hopeful ones of the village women – all of them bearing down on me, as if I'd been sent from the outside, from a better place, and could magic them away from there. And yet I could see also the flashes in those eyes – of determination, of humour. Of survival.

Tossing around the bed, I found myself musing about Dan; his warmth, his humour, the ease he seemed to have with everybody we'd met that day. I thought endearingly about his fear in the mine; there was a chink then. And I was just drifting off to sleep, when the tap on the door came. My eyes opened, but I lay motionless, my heart thumping; it must have been the pipes.

The tap came again, and then, "Vanessa, it's me."

41

6

When I look back on that first night together, I remember the wonder I felt at this man lying beside me. It was hard to believe that I had only just met him – hardly knew him –and yet there was something about that day that had drawn us together. It felt as if we were suspended in a world somewhere above our heads. In Donetsk, there was gentle humour too, as there often would be to having sex with Dan. I remember that neither of us had any condoms.

"Not even a small one?" he asked, making me laugh at his false modesty. He beamed down at me. "You're so beautiful when you laugh, Vanessa."

I'd say laughter was more of a need when I was with Dan – streaming out of me like bubbles blown by a child. That following morning, we flew back up to Kiev and sat sleepily together on the back seat of his car, while Dan's driver took us straight to the Arizona, a bistro tucked away behind a busy road on the quay of the Dniepro river.

"I always come here when I fly in from the regions," he said, as we made our way into the courtyard and sat at one of the few small round tables outside. "Need to get some home comfort inside me."

The service was American too, the menus appearing instantly, the young Ukrainian waiter slapping Dan on the back and reaching to shake my hand. For a fleeting moment it struck me that he might be congratulating Dan on yet another conquest; did he bring all the new kids in town here? But Dan's smile was so unguarded and he covered my hand proprietarily with his own as he began to point out the best dishes, so I smiled drowsily back at him.

"I'm a veggie," I said, scanning the bacon and sausages.

"Ah, well, soon sort that," Dan muttered.

"No, it's an ethical thing."

"You haven't sampled my cooking yet." He tapped the side of his nose.

I ordered the eggs with smoked salmon, while Dan rattled off his choices from the full breakfast menu. "Can we get some coffee and fresh orange juice, too?"

As the waiter gathered the menus, I remembered the eggs in my handbag. "Hold on a minute, could you use these for my breakfast, please?" I asked him.

Sadly, only one of the eggs was still intact, the other now a yolky goo smothering my passport. Frowning at the mess, I began to mop up the pages with a tissue.

"Don't worry, passports are meant to be weathered, it'll just look well seasoned from here on," Dan said gently.

"It's not the passport, I should have taken better care of them, they were a gift."

"Just an egg, Ness,"

"It's a symbol though, isn't it? Of all those women can achieve down there."

"I guess you're right." He smiled at me. "You are what's known as a good person, aren't you?"

I shrugged. "You too, methinks."

"Ah, that's debatable."

Closing my eyes to hide the smirk, I sank back into my seat and tipped my head up at the sky. I breathed in deeply, enjoying the languid sound of the air passing through my nose, held it for a moment and then let it out contentedly; I wanted to slow the morning down.

"This feels so decadent," I said, "deliciously decadent."

"Playing hooky?"

"Yeah. And being with you. Can't get enough of you."

"Ditto," he said. "Come here, you're too far away."

I shuffled my chair around the table and pressed my cheek against his; he smelt sleepy. "You've still got coal dust in your hair."

"As if we didn't take enough showers this morning."

I smiled. "I wouldn't have called it showering."

Dan had launched me up against the wall of the cubicle, snagging my shoulder against the jagged edge of a broken tile. The graze still smarted.

Our coffee and juice arrived, hailed by a humorous clearing of throat by the waiter. I drank the juice down in one, its vitamins replenishing after the sleepless night, then I tipped my face up to the sunshine, lulled by the unique morning, by the anticipation of this man beside me.

"Yesterday was probably the most incredible day of my life," I murmured.

I could feel Dan's smile.

"How old are you, Vanessa?"

"Twenty-six." I paused. "You?"

"Close enough for it to be respectable."

"Who wants respectable?"

"And you're from Manchester, right?"

"Right."

"You go to Oxford University?"

"No." Mercifully he didn't dig. But then why couldn't I just tell him I'd left school at sixteen?

"How long you say you're here for?"

"Three years."

"Aha. And why Kiev?"

"All these questions." I frowned at him but he raised his eyebrows for an answer. "Well, I was planning to go to Africa, do a VSO or something – you know, voluntary service overseas. But then Bogdan Levshenko poached me, so here I am."

"Like a pheasant?"

"Like a pheasant."

"Well you're certainly making your mark already."

I covered his hand with mine. "On you, I hope?"

"On me, for sure. On those women down there too, they've all fallen under your spell. Miners will drop next no doubt."

Our breakfasts arrived and we began to eat; the egg did taste exceptional. "Feels as if it's me who is under a spell, actually," I said, forking it up. "I'll probably wake up soon and this will all have been a dream."

"I don't think there's any danger of that. Do you?"

I shook my head. "And you're from Chicago, right?"

"Yep."

"And why Kiev?"

"Just one of a long list of cities where I've laid my hat."

"Only your hat?"

"Mainly my hat." He rolled his eyes at me. "Kampala, Jakarta, Singapore, Buenos Aires ..."

"Always in aid?"

44

"Yep. Beginning to get the aid jade, now."

"Surely not? There's so much to do here."

"Yeah. You'll have those miners running the stock exchange within a year."

"Didn't think you Yanks knew about sarcasm."

"This one does."

I smiled. "Miners are special people though, Dan, they're not like most other men. You'd never find a feckless miner. They're proud men, resilient men, there's no self-pity going on. You can see it in their faces, the strength, the principles, the belief in keeping going."

Dan nodded and waited for more.

"In fact, I used to take photos of them, held an exhibition once, in the foyer of Lancashire Regeneration, where I used to work. A perspective in black and white, I even sold a few."

"I'd like to see them sometime."

I enjoyed that seal of approval from him.

After we'd eaten, Dan stretched his arms above his head. "Do you have to get back to the office today Ness?"

For a brief moment I saw the heavy workload mounting up ahead of me; I was keen to set my ideas for Donetsk in motion. But of course I was also already falling in love.

"Not especially."

"Don't know about you, but I'm feeling quite sleepy myself."

"Me too. Exhausted, actually."

"Come on."

His driver, waiting in the car, started the engine as we climbed in.

"My place, please," Dan said.

The following lunchtime, after Dan had made us a breakfast of toast, lavishly spread with Yelena's honey, I left his apartment to change in my hotel room. Then, on my way to the office, in whimsical mood, I took a wander through the old Bessarabsky Market Hall, where I mooched between the stalls, breathing in the earth on the leafy carrots, smiling compliments at the pyramids of melons. I knew to steer clear of the hunks of meat on the marble slabs, with their cloying stench and the trickles of blood tracing the grain in the stone. Often I would give a few dollars to the old women who approached me between the stalls, and that day I wrongly handed out a hundred dollar note, instead of a single, slipping it absent-mindedly from my purse and into a palm. I didn't ask for it back.

In the office, I received raised eyebrows from Sasha and a crisp reception from Irina, who spent a good few unembarrassed seconds looking at her watch. I waited for her to glance up at me and then threw her an ebullient smile, which I was pleased to note caught her off guard. She sniffed and turned away to a filing cabinet, while behind her back, Sasha gave me the thumbs up.

I would describe Irina's behaviour towards me by then as mild. Mild, but in no way meek. I was continuing to cut her major slack, not only because of her harsh life, as I imagined it, but because I was already conscious that her intelligence was far superior to mine. In truth, I was in some awe of my new colleague. Both her parents were professors at the university, while she herself had majored in philosophy, and still tutored there part-time. Unpaid, I understood.

On that hot afternoon, I tugged my mind away from Dan, from the crumpled sheets in his apartment, and tried to focus on the planning of our design workshop, which was scheduled for the following week. Mechanically, I began to run through the various options for our programme in Kiev, but found myself drawn only to Donetsk, musing how I could easily spend my whole budget down there and just forget about the capital, with its stultifying bureaucrats and donors. I smiled to myself at the memory of the scraggy chickens, of the tales of hairdressing and dressmaking, of cakes and honey. And then, as I was scribbling a reminder to fly Svetlana up for our workshop, there was a knock on the door.

It nudged itself open, and a young man entered and shook hands with Irina, who stood up with a smile of clear respect for him. He wore a lank leather jacket, his trousers sagged where his bottom should have been and, when he turned to me, his pale face and polo neck sweater reminded me of an early Beatles album cover. There was no smile, just a vague frown and a searing intelligence behind the eyes as he summed me up.

Irina introduced him. "This is Yaroslav, he is television news journalist."

"Good afternoon," he said, with a small bow.

Yaroslav had benefited from one of the small media training projects which Bogdan had already financed in Kiev and he wished to thank me, he said. So I took him to the small café on the corner.

"I am very grateful to you, and to Bogdan Levshenko, for opportunity you have given me," he said, in near perfect English.

"You're very welcome, Yaroslav," I said with a benign smile – and that delicious shiver of altruism, as I was still calling it. "I hope the training was valuable for you?"

46

"Yes, yes. I learned from BBC journalist, how to conduct interview, how to ask very good questions." He frowned. "But here is not like in your country, here the bastards they grind you down."

He spoke with a total absence of humour, but I smiled to myself at the thought of a British guy teaching him that phrase along with the technicalities of investigative journalism.

He went on. "I would like to film Levshenko programme. Please, may I come to your workshop next week, Vanessa?"

"That's a great idea! And would we be on the TV news?"

"Yes, I hope so."

"That would be brilliant publicity for us, thank you. Why don't I tell you about our plans?"

I then held forth for several minutes about my ideas for the programme, about the needs I'd identified from the reports I'd read and from my meetings with the other donors. Yaroslav listened to me intently. And once I'd exhausted my ideas to tackle unemployment in his country, he told me about his life.

"I live in suburb of Kiev with my parents. My father worked in ammunitions factory, my mother was rocket scientist."

I did suppress a joke about his mother's work, but he paused as if he were used to expecting it.

"Now, they have no jobs. Our factories are ghost places, our workers sit at home all day, even though officially they are employed still. My father is pensioner, but my mother must find new work, and she rides her bicycle to search for jobs."

Norman Tebbit's slogan, On yer bike, flitted through my mind, but I said nothing.

"Last month, my father received household goods for his pension. He was paid in saucepans and gloves, because there is no money for pension. Can you imagine that Vanessa?" I shook my head mutely. He paused and shook his own head before continuing. "My brother is fifteen, he is at school. His friends, they want to be mafia when they have grown up. The girls, they want to be escorts, so that they may earn dollar salary."

He stopped for a moment and sipped his forgotten tea; I had no wish to reach for mine.

"If we are sick, we must bribe our doctors to get appointment, and then we must bribe them again to get medicine. It is wrong, Vanessa, my country it is so wrong."

I came away from my first meeting with Yaroslav ashamed. Not only because I'd been with Dan that morning, instead of working to change Yaroslav's shitty life, which is the only reason I was in Ukraine, but ashamed also that I had not begun my research with him – with the Ukrainian people. I'd been driven by Sasha from Western donor to Western donor, and yet I'd learnt more in just an hour about this nation from this man – a man, whom later I would come to know as exceptional. Our teatime meetings were to become a regular fixture.

7

On the morning of my programme design workshop I woke early, feeling compelled to help Irina and Sasha set up, but as I showered, the curtain on his bath rail was yanked back and there stood Dan, already at half mast.

"Sexy shower cap."

He swung a leg over the bath and climbed in. Succumbing, I pulled off the cap, and ended up astride him on the edge of the bath, with precarious balance; he said it was a bit like hanging off a yacht. Afterwards, I dashed around his apartment with sodden hair, flushed by the thought of letting Irina down, while Dan sat on the arm of the sofa in his socks and boxers watching me.

"Vanessa, you are not the worker bee, YOU are the queen – you are the strategy," he said, sipping his coffee.

But I don't think I ever was. Not really. As the events of that morning were to confirm.

The workshop was held at the Ministry of Employment, in a sun-strewn conference hall which reeked of wood polish. It was filling with people, many of whom I did not recognise, particularly a line of elderly men who sat on the front row. I had been inclusive – too inclusive Dan had warned – in my open invitation to the workshop.

"It's important to have buy-in from all the stakeholders," I'd told him. "That's how we did it in Lancashire. They need to own the project if we're going to get their full commitment to it."

"They'll run rings round you," he'd said.

"Oh, you're just too long in the tooth."

Mrs Tabachuk, Head of the Job Centre Network and now confirmed as the designated beneficiary for our programme, arrived in the hall, glamorous in a fine suit of royal blue and jangling with gold chains.

Bogdan had insisted on calling her a 'beneficiary' despite the Minister's plea that they should be our 'partner' and had pointed out that most of the other donors also used this term. Clearly, he wanted to flag his benevolence, it being his dosh, but the word beneficiary did sit uneasily with me.

"Vanessa, how lovely to see you again." Mrs Tabachuk greeted me with a kiss to each cheek and then stood back. "What a beautiful suit you are wearing."

"Thank you." I glanced down at my new outfit from Dorothy Perkins, purchased in anticipation of the high-level meetings my Kiev appointment would bring, and then at her tailored suit. "Welcome to the workshop. I hope we'll end up with the perfect programme for you today."

As I watched her take her seat on the front row beside that reserved for the Minister, it struck me that once again her Western countenance and lilting accent had boosted me that morning. I was becoming aware of a complex set of feelings when I spent time with Ukrainian people; the alien culture, the childhood I could not begin to visualise, the values I was struggling to understand. While I sympathised with them and their hard lives, I was still at the stage where their presence bore down on me. Added to which, I'd also come to realise that Irina's whiny English was not peculiar to her – this was the way many of these people spoke our language. To me, it sounded intense and penetrating, as if they were angry with me, and often I'd flinch when they spoke. Later, I was told that when we speak their language it sounds soft – not pleasantly so but in a wishy-washy, drippy kind of way.

The Minister was last to arrive, with a tight nod at me that perfectly captured his reluctance to be present, and I gave him what I intended as a cool and controlled smile in return. After his sexism towards me at our launch, I'd scraped the mass of my hair up onto my head in professional defiance.

When all were settled, I nodded at Sasha, who was manning a flip-chart, felt-tip in hand, and then at our interpreter. The man wore the same salmon-coloured shirt each time he worked for me, and its honeyed drift was ripe, as if he simply hung it up between assignments. Having picked up a little Russian by then, I was also somewhat sceptical of his ability.

I beamed around the room. "Welcome to our brainstorming session. Today we will design together the Levshenko Programme – Creating New Jobs in Ukraine."

My interpreter spoke at length, sentence after hefty sentence – perhaps the word brainstorming took some translating – and I used the time to acknowledge my audience. I nodded at Svetlana, my new friend from Donetsk whom I'd flown up for the occasion, then at Yaroslav, at the supercilious Chelsea, and finally at Dan beside her on the back row; I saw this as my chance to impress them all. Jeff was also present that morning. Bogdan had asked him to help facilitate the workshop, advising me with a wink that it would be good to have some grey hairs present, but my pride had Jeff lodged firmly in the audience; I was going to handle this one alone.

"First we have to draw up a Problem Tree." I waited for my interpreter, who appeared to be outlining the wobbly shape of an oak tree with his hands. Ignoring a flurry of unease, I went on. "We get all the problems surrounding employment in your country down on paper, and then we decide which problems are the cause and which ones are the effect."

Pausing for the translation, I gestured at the flipchart and then scanned the room; most Ukrainian faces were blank, nothing but an impressive and universal avoidance of eye contact. I could sense Dan watching me and I felt the heat hit my cheeks.

"Then we turn the problems into objectives and create an Objective Tree."

The same leafy hand gestures from the interpreter, the same blank reception; people were shifting in their seats now and a slight panic drifted through my chest. I had facilitated so many design workshops in the UK and had never known this. In my experience the audience were always engaged when there was huge funding at stake – and I was simplifying things, so they must have been able to understand. My mind was suddenly choked by the mass of vacant faces, and I was just unable to rethink my words, or even elaborate. So I ploughed on.

"Then we will try and place the objectives into a special matrix, which is known as a Logical Framework."

I attempted a nonchalant stroll to the wall behind me, where I had mounted a scroll of paper showing a table split into sixteen boxes. You can actually design a multi-million pound aid programme with this simple device.

"Down the left side we fill in our objectives and actions." I trailed my hand down the words. "And along the top, we list our indicators, which will measure the success of our actions."

As the interpreter reeled out my words seamlessly in Russian, I ignored Sasha's click of the tongue and beamed at the room to will my message home. "All clear?" I asked.

I seemed to be the only one nodding in response, but I went on regardless. "Let's tackle first our Problem Tree then. What problems do we face?"

Nobody spoke. All eyes turned to the Minister for him to go first, but Balavensky was a man who clearly revelled in the pause and for several moments he remained folded in on himself, as if in contemplation. Finally, wearily, he lifted his large head.

"Main problem in our country is unemployment. Employers still give our workers houses and kindergartens for their children. But our factories are silent and our workers at home."

"Great!" I cried, jumping in to prevent an hour's monologue. "We have our biggest problem – high unemployment."

I swung to my flipchart, wrote High Unemployment at the top of the page and stood back delighted, while Sasha stepped forward to jot the translation beneath. The Minister looked startled, as if a thief had flashed past and nicked his wallet from his hands, but I nodded at him to continue.

"Our youth suffer most, they are idling ..." he began again.

"Good. Youth unemployment. This is one cause of the overall high unemployment, which is the effect. So, we write this beneath it with an arrow leading upwards." I see-sawed my hands between the words. "Do you see the cause and effect emerging?"

Only one person nodded, Svetlana, her intelligent grey eyes narrowing as she spoke in English. "Unemployment of women is also very big problem."

"Right. Female unemployment."

I was swept along now by the logic and, while the interpreter rehashed my words in Russian, I added Female Unemployment to my chart and drew an arrow linking it to the top. Then I stepped back and swept my palm across the chart; you'd have thought I'd just made a canary appear in a cage.

"So why are young people and women suffering especially?" I asked.

There was again a hush, all eyes on the Minister, but he had now sat back and crossed his legs, seemingly resigned to let me continue. Perhaps the spell of his diatribe had been broken by Svetlana, a fresh young woman from the provinces, or perhaps he was secretly pleased not to have to perform his usual spiel. For me he was inscrutable, but his silence was welcome.

Yaroslav, sitting at the back with his cameraman, raised his hand. "Our young people have no training courses like you have in your country."

"OK," I said, swivelling on my toes to write Lack of Training Facilities. "We need new skills to meet the new types of jobs created."

An exclamation was spluttered from the front and I turned back to see Viktor, the Head of the Small Business Federation, on his feet.

"New jobs?" he cried in English, his eyes bulbous. "Government kills all new businesses dead."

Viktor drew a slicing motion across his throat with his finger, complete with gory sound effects, and brandished his fist at Balavensky a few seats down. Incredulous, I glanced at Dan, who shook his head at me in empathy, and I had a sudden flash of him sailing that bath earlier, which calmed me a little. When I looked back at Viktor, he beamed at me, then scowled at the Minister, a change of expression so instant it was comical. He sat down again clutching an expensive-looking briefcase to his lap. And yet my eyes were drawn to his shoes, which were incongruously cheap, scuffed white and patterned with tiny pinpricks.

Meanwhile, the Minister seemed to be in some faraway land, ignoring Viktor, calmly cleaning his nails with his index finger, digging out what did indeed appear to be soil and flicking it away. There must have been vibes coming off him, however, as a menacing silence had settled on the room. Even I decided to water down the problem, choosing to write simply – Small Businesses Need Help and the matter was then closed.

"Right …" I said warily, "any more problems?"

"Job Centres are no use. Bus fare costs more than benefit paid." A shabby man a few rows back spoke up, bringing Mrs Tabachuk instantly to her feet. She swished round to the man, who slunk down into his chair.

"Job Centres are efficient!" she cried. "We are always improving our image."

She spoke in Russian, but the word 'image' remained in English, softly and strangely wrapped up within the guttural Slav, and all the more striking for that. It sounded humorous even, and provoked chuckles among the Westerners. For a few moments, I wondered if perhaps there was no word for image in Russian, if this notion had never existed in the old Ukraine, because nobody needed to bother with it under communism. Whereas, in the West, image was innate to all our lives, image permeated us and our whole perspective on life. Now, all these years later, I often wonder how much more effective I might have been, if I had dwelt further on that fleeting insight of mine, if I had gone on to apply this divergence in our two cultures to all the other realms of disparity between us. I might have shifted a level in my comprehension of Ukraine. For there were so many other differences in the way we made sense of our lives, which I should have incorporated into my work, should have assimilated into my aid programme. Had I done so, I might have had more impact during my years there. Perhaps, even, what was to happen between me and Dan would never have materialized. But I delved no deeper that day, partly because, let's face it, I was pretty clueless back then, but also because I was suddenly absorbed by the strange ambiance which had fallen over the room.

Mrs Tabachuk remained on her feet, animated in language and gestures, while people were listening, people were nodding. My interpreter failed to translate her speech, but I observed her from behind, the sleek back, the lustrous hair, the wafts of perfume. It may have also been that blue suit, but her presence reminded me of Mrs Thatcher and it was at that workshop that I christened her Mrs T.

As she finished, she threw a defiant glance at Balavensky and snapped at him. "Also, we need more money!"

That bit was translated. She had spoken out of turn, with potential repercussions from her superior, and I caught an imperceptible twitch of muscle in the Minister's neck, but he remained bowed behind his mask of boredom. As she took her seat I thanked her and simply scribbled again a diplomatic – Job Centres Need Support. It took a throwaway comment by Sasha a few days later to enlighten me on her daring.

When Sasha had finished transcribing everything in Russian, I gave him a smug nod. It seemed to me that the workshop was swinging along with a mass of intelligence, all of it hanging together with arrows, and I stood aside waiting for my audience to absorb the Problem Tree, imagining that their thought processes mirrored my own. It was then that an elderly man sitting beside Balavensky stood up and wagged a finger at me.

"We need computers for our pensions system. You must add that to your tree of puzzles, Mrs Parker."

I gawped at the man, in fact I nearly laughed in his face. What had pensions got to do with anything? Sasha muttered in my ear that he was the Welfare Minister, and I glanced at his fellow elders along the front row; Dan had been right, chances were we had Transport, Health and Farm Ministers in too, all wanting a piece of the pie. And it was Dan who helped me out, standing then to address the man.

"Minister, you need to have a pensions system before you can computerise it," he said.

The jovial dig brought sniggers from Western and Ukrainian participants alike, while the old man turned with good humour and chuckled at Dan, waved a hand dismissively in the air at his irreverence and sat back down. This was Dan for you; a serious message defused by the warmth in his voice, by the buddy-buddy eye-contact. I could have done with some of that ingenuity myself, but I felt compelled to respond more respectfully.

"I am very sorry, this programme is for job creation, not pensions." I paused for the interpreter.

He was glaring at the Minister. "Niet," No, he cried. "Evident!" It's obvious.

I heard a gasp escape me and bridled at the interpreter; how could he have destroyed my careful words?

Beside me, Sasha let out a sudden string of abuse at the man and shoved him aside. "I translate for you Ness," he said.

But the interpreter shoved him back and clung to my side like some loyal terrier. So Sasha grabbed the man's sleeve, propelling him away from me again, and the two of them began to tussle, not unlike a couple of kids fighting over a swing in the park. Nobody from the audience intervened and I too looked on mutely. Finally, Sasha backed into the flip chart, which clattered to the ground, bringing both men instantly to their senses. They glared at each other, stags locking horns, before the interpreter snarled some Russian at Sasha and left the hall.

"What the …?" I said to Sasha, aware of the sudden silence. He looked at me, contrite then, shucked his jacket into place and he too walked out of the hall.

I turned to my audience. "Let's break for coffee, shall we?"

With the gestures of an air stewardess, I signalled to the table laid out at the back of the hall, and people stood and made for it, quite languidly, as if the disturbance had indeed been a spot of turbulence. Dan appeared with a cup of coffee.

"Gosh." I rolled my eyes at him. "Never a dull moment, is there?"

"Your interpreter was an asshole, Ness. He translated Logical Framework as Sensible Windowframe."

I drew breath sharply, but then as the humour in this struck me I began to giggle, spilling coffee into the saucer.

"I knew you'd see the funny side." Dan steadied my hand with a gentle smile; clearly he could sense the nerves behind my laughter.

"Did they understand any of it? I did try to keep it simple."

"You bet! Just look at this thing." Dan ran a hand across the Problem Tree. "Impressive start, Ness."

That was just the reassurance I needed. After coffee, Sasha returned to my side for the next session as if there had been no outburst.

"All right?" I asked him with a grin.

"Evident!" he grinned back.

From then on, Sasha, office boy, driver, tea-maker, and brunt of Irina's wrath, became my personal interpreter for the whole of my time in Ukraine. Evident! was to become our catch phrase.

I announced to the room that we would tackle next the objectives. Tearing off the Problem Tree sheet, I handed it to Sasha who blu-tacked it on the wall, then I headed the fresh page with Objective Tree and waited. And that room, crammed with intelligent, highly educated people, waited too, watching me like cows chewing the cud.

"So, how do we tackle unemployment?" I raised my eyebrows, marker pen poised. "How do we turn each of these problems into objectives for our three million pound programme?"

They looked mildly up at me, as if waiting to be informed of the solutions. It was clear there would be no further storming of brains that morning, and we broke for an early lunch. I sensed a headache coming on, and bustled at the flip chart, rather than face the masses as they filed out, but Dan was soon by my side.

"Pesky characters, aren't they?"

"Yep." I rubbed at some ink on my fingers, unable to meet his eyes.

"Wanna take a walk?"

I nodded. We wandered outside the Ministry into the welcome sunshine. Dan offered me a sausage roll from a paper bag and I took one, out of politeness, holding the pastry gingerly, while he stuck the other in his mouth and scrunched up the bag.

"I can't understand it," I said as we walked along the leafy pavements relishing the fresh breeze. "They have a chance to decide how to spend three million pounds, so why don't they use it?"

"Ah Ness, it's the way it is here. They expect you to come up with the answers. They always come prepared with their set piece, they toss a problem in the air and then they sit back wanting you to fix it for them. You'll get used to it."

"But they are the ones living through the misery of unemployment, surely they know what specific help they need better than we do?"

"Not sure about that, Ness."

"Well we shouldn't be ramming a programme down their throats, it's wrong."

"Look, in the Soviet Union, you didn't speak out, you didn't offer up solutions, you kept your head well below the parapet. That was how they got through."

"That's ridiculous. Surely there's no fear of speaking out now? There's no KGB anymore, is there?"

"No, they call it the National Security Services now, different name, same building. That one over there, actually."

Dan stopped and pointed at an office block across the road. A grey monster, clad with rough stone which seemed to force itself into the path of passers-by, almost catching at their clothing. I looked up at the dark windows and shuddered.

"Come on, let's get back." I handed him my sausage roll. "Here, you have this."

"You don't want it?"

"It's a sausage roll."

"Oh yeah, so it is." Dan bit into the pastry. "Look, I've got to get back to the office, but I'll swing by later. You'll be fine, might just have to nudge them on."

We lingered on the steps while he pressed his forehead to mine, holding us steady for a few moments. Then I watched him walk away, took a deep breath and went back into the fray, the headache still lingering. Jeff was waiting for me on a bench outside the conference hall, holding a document.

"I do apologise if you think me out of order, Ness, but designing job creation programmes is a forte of mine," he said.

"OK, Jeff," I smiled wanly at him, "let's take a look at it."

He showed me a blueprint of a programme he had designed previously for Armenia, another former Soviet country. I scanned it and found myself nodding resignedly.

"OK, but there has to be something in there for Donetsk too, both for the women and for the coal miners."

"No problemo." He smacked his thighs and got to his feet.

After their lunch, the workshop participants were sated and nicely sleepy. The room had emptied out a little, the elderly chancers on the front row having left, along with all the Westerners, but I was surprised to see that all the key Ukrainians had remained in the hall – even the Minister, beside whom Svetlana now sat.

Reluctantly, I introduced Jeff as an expert in programme design, and he jumped up, flipped the chart to a blank sheet and rubbed his hands together.

"May I be so bold as to suggest the following objectives for our programme?" And swiftly he jotted down the following:

Levshenko Programme

Creating New Jobs for Ukraine

£3 million over 3 years

Objective one: Set up a model Job Centre in Kiev and roll out to regions.

Objective two: Set up a Small Business Development Agency

Objective three: Develop an Employment Policy with the Ministry

Objective four: A Pilot Project in Donetsk (to be defined)

I observed the room while Sasha transcribed his ideas in Russian. Surely there would be some reaction? Suggestions, or at least questions? Without exception, however, the Ukrainians were noting it down, like kids copying off a blackboard. Mrs T, the Minister, Viktor, even Yaroslav was craning his head to catch the next line on the flip chart. Svetlana smiled at me as the final objective was revealed – something she and I could develop together.

At the end of the workshop, my temples thudded and my feet throbbed. Yet, while I waited for the room to empty, a neat queue of people formed at my flip chart. Balavenksy shook my hand with polite thanks, Mrs T was effusive in hers and Viktor bounced up like Tigger to kiss my hand. I was touched by their optimism; had they really believed that all had gone to plan? Hadn't they realised that Jeff had steamrolled them into a one-size-fits-all programme? True, his objectives did somehow capture the essence of our morning, but I'd wanted to hear some demands for specific actions from the Ukrainians, some passion, like I'd had from the women in the garden that night. I wanted to feel the need for our programme. Now, of course, it's clear to me that I simply wanted to feel the need for me.

Once the room was empty, Sasha began to clear away the papers and Irina appeared by my chair with a glass of tea.

"It was good day," she said, and she gave me the second of her slow blinks.

Sasha caught this and winked at me as she turned away.

"And I have a new interpreter." I winked back at him.

When they too had left, I stood and surveyed the room, catching sight

58

of my Logical Framework on the far wall, its matrix still blank. I took a pen, shuffled over to it and began to fill in the objectives down the left hand side. Behind me the door opened, and I turned to see Dan enter the room, clunking it shut behind him and clipping over to me with a broad smile.

"Hey, thought I'd walk you home."

"Hi." I turned back to the wall, relieved that he had left after lunch, that he hadn't witnessed the shambles of my afternoon.

"You got your objectives down then?" He let out a low whistle.

"Yeah." I continued to write. "Nudging wasn't quite the word though."

"At least you tried, Ness. Nobody else would have bothered. Anyways, there's something for everyone there, isn't there?"

As he spoke, it dawned on me that there were indeed distinct objectives – one for Balavensky, one for Mrs T and one for Viktor too. Neat packages of aid for each of them. The thought remained undeveloped, however, because Dan moved against me then, enfolding me in his arms and pressing the length of his body into my back. We rocked together and I felt myself relaxing into him as the feeling of being wanted, of being needed, washed through me.

"My special lady, stay just as you are," he said.

I closed my eyes and let myself sink.

8

That night Dan stayed in my single bed at the Kievskaya. The following morning, a Saturday, he was in the bathroom when there was a rap on the door and a voice, my floor woman. I called out to her to come back later please and rolled over in bed. Then her key was in the door and her apoplectic face in the room.

"What the …?"

I scowled at her, sitting up and pulling the sheet around me. But she strode to the centre of the room screeching – as Dan told me after – that this was a single room and not meant for other guests. She actually stooped to check under the desk and even hovered at the heavy brown curtains for signs of twitching. Then Dan emerged from the bathroom, naked, dangling his tackle at her and whooping like a Red Indian. We both stared at his scrotum with its flaccid penis swinging from side to side, then I checked her face, biting my lip with a half-smile ready to burst. She shook her head, and muttered something – the size of the package, Dan claimed later, though I'd guess it was more along the lines of 'silly boy'.

"Get out you old bat," he said, shunting her by the shoulders gently to the door and depositing her in the corridor. Then he dusted off his hands. "Now where were we?"

Later that morning we set off for the Mariensky Park, a lovely green spot on a hillside above the Dniepro river. The day was a beauty, clear and warm with cloud wisps softening the blue high above us as we walked hand in hand down into the crowds on the Boulevard Kreschatyk. Pedestrianised at weekends, you'd never know that it was lined with shops, the windows opaque, the doors heavy and closed. And though they probably sold only the odd painted trinket or piece of amber jewellery, people still flocked inside. I began to snap discreet shots of them, the

60

women heavily made up with glossy hair, the men thin and pale, their own hair cut close to the scalp.

Along the pavement an accordionist sat planted on a camping stool and I took a few shots of him unawares. As we approached, I hummed along to his rendition of If I were a Rich Man, and he smiled a toothy grin at me smoothly changing his tune to Lara's theme from Dr Zhivago.

"For the lovers," he said, bowing his head at our locked hands.

Dan stopped, clicked his heels to attention for the man and looked to the sky with a loud guffaw. He placed a couple of karbovanet notes in the man's cap at his feet, then he gave my hand a squeeze, a proud one, and we walked on.

We turned off the Boulevard and up through a stone archway into Kiev Passage. Inside, Dan pointed out the bas relief sculptures depicting the famous artists and writers who had lived there. I studied them – a forehead etched with lines, a darkened brow, or a mouth puckered with the weight of the world, and I raised my camera. Though, as always, I was more interested in the view through the archways to the courtyards behind each building, in searching for a better understanding of the Ukrainian people in a sagging washing line or a discarded car wheel.

We moved on up the hill to the white Parliament building – the Verkhovna Rada. Back in 1994, the pro-democracy protest camps, which would arrive in later years, had not yet blighted the surrounding grassy area, and the un-mown lawns were still splattered with dandelions, their flat sunshine heads peeking up through the blades of grass. Together, sky and dandelions set a perfect backdrop to the blue and yellow stripe of the Ukrainian flags, which streamed from the pillars of the Parliament.

"Would they allow dandelions outside Congress, Dan? They'd wrench them up outside our Parliament."

He laughed. "You're right, weeds would not be tolerated in the US of A either. That's what's refreshing about this part of the world."

I bent to pick a dandelion clock and began to blow as we walked. "He loves me … he loves me not …" An extra-strong puff dislodged the remaining seed heads like fairies into the air and I stopped in my tracks. "He loves me."

Dan swivelled me round to him and pressed his forehead to mine. "He does."

A soldier with a sub machine gun clicked his tongue at us to move on, and Dan jerked his head at the man with a scowl. "Lighten up," he growled. Though I was jarred by the hostility and the combat fatigues and tugged at Dan's hand.

We wandered into the Mariensky Park and along the pathway to the fountain, decorated by the mouths of lions spouting froth into the pool. Further down the slope we found a soft patch of grass and lay down on our backs, gazing up into the chestnut trees. I thought back to the TV news of the evening before. Yaroslav had run a brief piece on my workshop, the shaky camera panning the room, then a close up on Balavenksy, a longer one of Mrs T and a quick shot of me. Dan had translated Yaroslav's praise for me, my new friend's words thick with the usual gush of official gratitude for a new international aid programme.

Beside me, Dan yawned. "As cities go, Kiev has to be up there with the best of them. Especially now you're in it too."

I smiled. "I really love living here. Be even better when I've got my own pad, it's going to get trickier with matron haranguing me."

"Expensive – for a decent one."

"Yeah, well, so is the hotel." I yawned myself, masking a slight panic that we were about to arrive at somewhere I wasn't ready to be, and I changed the subject. "Did you really think it went well yesterday?"

"I've told you, I thought you were superb. You're good on your feet, aren't you?" He rucked himself up onto an elbow, dipped his head and brushed my lips with his. "And in other positions."

"Yeah, but they didn't really get it, did they?"

"Look, they got that there's going to be a three million pound programme coming their way, that if they're smart there's a chance to grab a piece of it for themselves to ease their daily existence."

He pulled at a long strand of my hair and curled it round his index finger, winding until his finger grazed my temple, then he freed the curl to bounce back into its natural corkscrew.

"What they'll remember Vanessa, is your smile. What they'll remember is the radiance of you."

He flopped back down. "Anyways, who wants to talk shop on a Saturday? I want to talk you, Vanessa Parker from Manchester, England."

I sighed. "OK, what do you want to know?"

"Everything."

"Well … I'm Twenty-six and I worked in regional development."

"That much I know already."

I swallowed, considering what else to tell him.

"I shared a flat with my mate Carole. We worked together at a firm called Lancashire Regeneration, she has a boyfriend who's moved into the flat with her now."

"Hey, who am I interested in here? Your mate as you so charmingly call her, or you?"

"So, what do you want to know?"

"First boy you kissed?"

"Name was Charlie, I was sixteen."

"Sixteen? I would have figured earlier."

"Chaste is my middle name."

He snorted. "Huh, made up for it pretty smart since then."

Dan was spot on. Once I'd left school and moved up to Salford with Mum, I'd started sleeping around a bit; after all, that's what the daughters of negligent fathers did. I'd never yet managed a relationship of any length, which made what was happening to me with Dan all the more spectacular.

"Your turn Mister."

"Aw, we haven't got going on you yet."

"There's time, come on tell me something about you."

"OK, let's see. I'm thirty-seven, raised in Chicago."

"You already told me that. How did you end up in aid?"

"Well … Mom worked for the State University, she ran their business side."

"The university ran a business?"

He nodded. "Setting up courses abroad, and accrediting them – Chicago's name was in big demand. She used to travel all over the world and I would get to go with her in summer recess, go meet a bunch of academics in Indonesia or China, get a hold of what courses they wanted her to develop for them. Guess that's how I got the bug – see the world and help out a bit on the way."

"Are they still alive, your parents?"

"Yep, still live in the city. Divorced though. What about yours?"

"My dad is, though I don't really see him." I paused for a moment. "Mum died."

"Hey I'm sorry, Ness."

He fumbled across the grass for my hand and, swept by a sudden draft of emotion, I needed to tell him more.

"I'd just come in from work. Still lived with her, you see. She was watching Wogan on telly, you've probably never heard of that, have you?" He shook his head. "I was walking across the room to kiss her, she made to stand up from her chair, and then she just slumped to the carpet."

"You saw it happen?"

I nodded. "Blood clot, they said. On the lungs."

"Jesus, Vanessa"

"I used to take care of her. She was never well, really."

He squeezed my hand. "I'm so sorry for you. You must have been a good daughter."

I smiled to myself, a lump in my throat, and thought back to the fights at home, of how hard I tried to make it better for her.

"Never good enough." I felt the intensity of his gaze on the side of my head. "Think I always wanted to run from it, if I'm honest."

He waited, but didn't press me. "I know that feeling," he said finally.

"So. You!" I cried. "Somehow we seem to have got back onto me. Let me see … So how come you never got married?"

"Oh, I was married."

"Are you divorced then?"

"Yep. Got myself two strapping teenagers back home." His voice tightened. "Raised by some other guy, right now."

Instant prickles hit the back of my eyes. Later I was ashamed to realise that self-pity had got in there before sympathy; this could bring complications.

He went on. "Sheryl resented the work I do. Hated being dragged round the world, as she put it. She ran off with another man, so the euphemism goes."

"Dan, that's awful."

"I'm well rid of her. Miss my boys though."

"What are they called?"

"Spencer and Franklin."

"Great names. Very American."

"They're great boys, I'm proud of them. Spencer, he's fifteen and a budding Olympic track athlete, and Franklin's just thirteen but there's a Wall Street office door already got his name on."

I imagined two shiny-skinned, white-teethed youths, and I pictured them smiling at a school prom, or walking down a corridor lined with metal lockers, which was about all I knew of America back then, from films. I glanced at Dan, his eyes shining with pride, lost then in his two sons, and for the first time I felt a distance between us. He was also an American, a stranger. I couldn't picture how his childhood would have played out, or begin to envisage the years of his life I had not been a party to.

Something jangled beside me and I turned to see a Springer Spaniel flouncing over to us. It slopped its tongue across my cheek and I sat up, took its silken head between my hands and ruffled its ears, until it lolloped off again at its owner's whistle.

"Dogs are the same all over the world aren't they?" I laughed, watching it go.

"Folks too, Ness." Dan came back in a beat as if he'd read my thoughts.

"Are they?" I picked a blade of grass and bent then to tickle his forehead, trailing it down over his lips. He pulled me to him and we canoodled – as Mum would have put it – like a couple of teenagers.

When I sat up again, I looked down through the trees onto the Dniepro, at the ribbons of wake streaming behind the pleasure steamers. On the bank opposite an artificial beach had been laid, the golden sand nudging the tufts of trees beyond, and it teemed with people, who had gathered to cool off in the river, the smoke from their barbecues rising in spires, the squeals of children drifting over to us. Dan pulled himself up too and looked down across the river with me.

"Isn't it still polluted?" I asked.

"Chernobyl, you mean?"

I nodded.

"Possibly, probably. Worse things happen at sea. We should do a boat trip down it sometime, it's all the rage here, I'll buy you a rose."

"Plastic one?" I nudged his shoulder with mine.

"Nah, I'll pull out all the stops for you."

We sat shoulder to shoulder watching the people having fun on the beach, while I plucked at stalks of grass, biting down on them and sucking out the sap, something I hadn't done since I was a child.

"You know, I've been having these guilty feelings. I mean about meeting you, having such a good time, when I came to this country with a serious purpose. But it's not all gloom and doom here, is it?"

He snorted. "No, but any case why can't you save the world and screw me?"

We were still laughing when I caught sight of the Minister. He was strolling further down the hillside, with a young girl's arm tucked into his. Balavensky had seen us first, I knew, but pretended otherwise as he made a show of approaching us.

"Dan, Vanessa, Zdraztvuite," Good morning, he said with a small bow.

"Hello." I was pleased he'd used my first name.

Dan got to his feet and shook the man's hand. While he chatted to them in Russian, I furtively gave the girl the once over; she would have been about seventeen, possibly his daughter, but with a rosebud face which bore no resemblance to his own pasty cheeks. We nodded our goodbyes and they ambled off up the slope.

"His daughter, in case you were thinking otherwise," Dan said.

"Hadn't crossed my mind." I smiled and watched them reach the fountain, where they took one of the benches and sank into conversation, his hand stroking her forearm.

"Think I'm getting the measure of him now," I said, as Dan settled back down with me on the grass.

He groaned. "Everybody takes him for a reformer, someone who is committed to real change in this country, and we chuck aid at his Employment Ministry. It's like spoiling the favoured child with too many cookies. But none of us has the measure of Balavensky, Ness. Think Blofeld stroking white cat and work from there."

I frowned at him. "Maybe you should take people at face value a bit more."

"Don't be too drawn in by these people, Vanessa, keep a hold of yourself. You need to examine each individual, analyse them, work out what their specific self-interest is. They've all got one, something that drives their actions."

"I care about them, they need us here."

"Yeah, but do they care about you? Or are they exploiting you? Look, many of the people we're dealing with here are only in Government to make themselves richer, they don't care about reforms. Some of them have only to gain from keeping their minions weak and vulnerable."

"That's cynical. It's a cruel quirk of fate that they were born in this country, they're just trying to get through as best they can."

He sighed. "Folks really are the same all over, you know. These people are just as smart as we are in the West, just as cunning. More so, given what they've been through. You know the Czech President, Vaclav Havel, the one who rides a bicycle around his office? You know what he said?"

"What?"

"That under Communism they'd learnt to 'live in the lie'." Dan paused for me to absorb this. "Think about that. It would have taken a lot of skill, to mount a pretence on the outside, to live only inside your mind. These people are wily, Ness, they can easily outwit us. They're not to be pitied."

"I do pity them, they have crap lives, and I want to play a part in getting this country right."

He shook his head gently at me. "Way I see it, there's no such thing as altruism. Far as I'm concerned, aid professionals are driven either by power, or by the need to appease their own conscience." He paused. "To atone for something, whatever that might be."

Something flipped inside my chest but I squashed it and cocked my head at him. "And which one applies to you, Dan Mitchell?"

He smiled to himself, but he didn't respond and we sat in silence for some time, while his words bounced around my head. I'd always believed myself to be altruistic, and I'd never considered that there could be any motive behind this; it was just innate to me. But I wondered then for the first time ever – was it power of some sort? Was it atonement? If so, then for what? More likely it was just Dan being cynical.

"You are a very special young woman, Vanessa Parker, very special indeed." Dan lifted my hand and began to shake it loosely, as if he were trying to guess its weight. "Maybe neither of those things applies to you. In fact you may even have broken the mould."

I heard myself laughing, far too brightly. "Whatever I am, I'm big enough and ugly enough to look after myself, thank you."

But the morning had brought us closer. And, in truth, as we lay together on that hillside, I knew that the independence was sliding off me. I'd learnt to stand alone against the world; in recent years defiantly so, never needing, only ever letting Carole in. But I could feel that iron smelting now, could feel myself fusing with Dan, the molten warmth of him glowing within me.

Later that evening, at his place, Dan lay on his back, barrel-chested, while I snuggled beside him on my stomach. We'd just woken from a lengthy doze, a breeze rifled through the open window from the courtyard, and drifting in on us were the sounds of TV, of laughter, of Saturday night.

"You talk in your sleep, you know." Dan broke our silence.

"Do I?" I laughed, though I knew what was coming.

"Couple of times now. 'No! Don't jump!' You shout it"

"Oh I've always had vivid dreams."

"Yeah, but you flip around too, Ness." His eyes remained on the ceiling as he spoke. "Want to tell me about it?"

"I've no idea what I was dreaming about." I veered him off, laughing again. "But if it disturbs you, maybe we should sleep in separate beds?"

"Ha, ha, the lady has such a sense of humour." He clamped a hand across my back. "You are going nowhere."

I put my face to his shoulder and breathed him in, the clean earthy scent of him, and was swept by a feeling of total contentment.

"What you said today, Ness? About helping these people."

"Yeah?"

"Well … I'm just the rubber band that's been stretched too far.

"What do you mean?"

"Just that … well, don't change. Stay as you are."

I smiled to myself in the dusky light of his bedroom.

"You're pure, you're good," he said.

"So are you." I kissed his shoulder.

Dan began smoothing his hand along my back, tracing the dips with his palm. After a few strokes he said, "You going to move your gear here tomorrow?"

I felt my heart quicken, felt it strumming against the mattress. We'd known each other for less than a week and this was a totally ridiculous proposition. But then it wouldn't be as if I was leaving my own home for his; I was in a hotel, my gear consisted of two suitcases, and it wouldn't be any great upheaval. If it didn't work out I could just as easily move out again.

As if he'd read my thoughts, he added, "I mean, just for a while if you like?"

It wasn't really even a decision. "That would be nice."

"Nice." He let the sibilant wash over his tongue. "Yeah, I think it would be nice."

I lay there visualising where my stuff might go. And maybe I sensed the momentous change to my life within the space of those few days since Donetsk, maybe I felt so close to him that I needed to back off a fraction. Whatever, I felt the need to be mischievous.

"Dan?" I asked.

"Van-es-sa?" he mocked my tone.

"Were you scared down the coal mine?"

"Me? Nah."

"So why didn't you go through that tunnel?"

He laughed. "Old war wound. Anyways, don't you guys have a name for Parkers who are too curious?"

"I think you were a bit of a wimp." I braced myself for the tickling; he'd already found the weak spot in my ribs.

"What's that mean?"

"Bit of a big girl's blouse."

"Right, young lady," Dan launched himself up off the bed and reached for me, "let me show you who is the girl around here."

9

One day I found a tiny egg in a nest that had tumbled to the pavement and I brought it into the office. Cushioned on an additional bed of paper from the shredder, the pale blue egg, no bigger than a quail's, sat beneath the heat from my anglepoise desk lamp for a matter of days. I don't suppose I genuinely expected it to hatch, but some sense of nostalgia had me in its grip and I mildly wondered what might happen. Sasha would make comical enquiries as to its wellbeing, peering into the nest, baby-talking to the egg and gently teasing me. Irina, however, treated it with overt disdain, switching the lamp off in my absence.

Nonetheless, I decided to involve her in my programme design. Empower her, I thought, and I asked her to draft the economic and political context, against which our programme would be operating. The so-called risks and assumptions, which could derail an aid programme, and which must be considered and noted before it begins. This move on my part was to be an error.

I'd borrowed Jeff's blueprint of the programme Creating Jobs in Armenia in order to finalise my own. On my desk one morning, I found Irina's contribution on the programme context and I began to read. She too had copied much of the economic and political background from Jeff's programme, which was sensible, given that all the other countries of the former Soviet Union were suffering similar problems to Ukraine. She had noted several economic risks, which could hamper the programme. For example, that there might be no cash for re-employment measures, that the current lack of growth would hinder re-employment. Politically, she had raised the fact that a possible change of government could whisk Balavensky off our programme and replace him with a new Minister, who would then take precious time getting up to speed. In all, her research was comprehensive and impressive. And then Irina had listed a raft of additional background issues that could hamstring the programme. You do not understand our history, the ways of our society, our family structures, she wrote. You do not understand our culture.

I sat, head in hands, and absorbed the pages, her own thesis on the context to our programme. How the shock therapy that the West was imposing on Ukraine, forcing reform right across the board in one fell swoop, would ultimately cause the country to implode. How the West was bombarding Ukraine with experts who were not sensitive to the local environment. How Ukraine, with its rich and tragic history, was a more profound nation than any in the West. She ended with a flourishing quote by Ukraine's national poet Taras Shevchenko –

The Cossack lad his fortune seeks, but never fortune knows …

In foreign lands live foreign folks, their ways are not your way.

There will be none to share your woes, or pass the time of day.

Irina always arrived later than me at the office, something I readily condoned given that she travelled for well over an hour by train and then by bus to get there. When she finally arrived that morning, I took her to the café on the corner and wondered how to start.

"Those are strong views, Irina," I began.

"They are views of many people in my country," she said, blowing on her coffee.

I nodded and composed my thoughts. "But these views are much bigger than our tiny programme. We're just here trying to help on a small scale, we're not trying to reform the whole country."

She fixed her ice blue eyes on mine. "You know that both my parents are professors at the university. They are intelligent people. But do you know how they live? You cannot imagine how hard is their life."

I chose simply to shake my head gravely rather than attempt a response to this.

"You think coming from UK, you deserve better life than they do?"

I got her drift then. "No Irina, I'm not as clever as your parents, I think I was very lucky to be born in England, that's all. But I'm here to help people like them have better lives."

"Huh. Bogdan spends three million pounds in our country, but you think my parents will benefit in any way from this?"

"Look, Bogdan is one of you, even if I'm not. He too is only trying to do good here."

"He should introduce new type of programme then. The West, they tell

71

us they have spent billions of dollars in our countries, but you think we see any of those billions? Your money makes Western experts richer and Ukrainian people stay poor."

"Give the programme a chance, Irina. Once we get the model Job Centre up and running, you'll see how valuable it will be. Yaroslav's mother will be able to use it to find new work, rather than have to ride her bike around. And just think of all the small businesses that our new agency could help to set up. Kids like Yaroslav's brother will be able to make something of themselves, not just dream of becoming mafiosi."

"We will see if it will work," she said mildly, infuriatingly.

"There's micro-credit planned for the women in Donetsk too. Those funds will go directly to the locals, not the Westerners."

"Those funds will be small."

"And there will be some computers and photocopiers too, don't forget."

Irina said nothing after that, but the look she gave me was a mix of condescension and pity, with a hint of derision she must have practiced in the mirror.

"The power of positive thinking, Irina," I said, standing and throwing some notes on the table. "You should try it some time."

As I left her in the café and stalked back to the office, her words both riled and perturbed me. Why had I scrabbled at minor components of the programme for my arguments? I should have had faith in the main thrust of it. I did consider firing her that morning, but again my empathy won out; one, she had a hard life, two, she would have no other income – and three, well what? I didn't want to go there. So I rolled again with the punch. However, after a restless night, the following day I did assert some authority and I removed Irina's thesis from the document, instructing her to photocopy the shortened version as the final one. I later found the birds nest had fallen off my desk, the egg splattered on the floor.

Once I had my final programme document, I touted it at my first donor coordination meeting. All the aid donors in Kiev met quarterly to exchange information and – allegedly – to coordinate with each other. Dan opened it with a tour de table to share information about progress on our various programmes. As a small donor, I was one of the last to speak. I first listened attentively to the IMF, the Bank, USAID, the EC, the UN and the raft of national government donors – there must have been at least ten of them. It did occur to me that I was the only one actively listening; most attendees had brought documents and diaries along and, once each of them had spoken, their focus turned to these.

Emboldened by my first ever attendance, where I would not be expected to know anything, I was intrepid in my opening question. The guy from the German government and an Italian from the UN had briefed us on two of their respective aid programmes. They both dealt with pension reform and I was curious that both actions seemed identical.

"If you are both running programmes to reform the pension system, how do you ensure there is no duplication between the advice you give the Ministry?" I asked, quite blithely really.

The German guy looked bemused. "We show them different pension models and they are free to choose." He shook his head, as if to shake me off him.

"But how do they know which ones to choose?"

"We train them in how to analyse different policy choices."

"But you said you were doing that very same training too?" I looked pointedly at the Italian, who nodded at me with a frown. "So do you share the same training materials to ensure it's consistent?"

An uncomfortable silence had fallen on the room. The two men shrugged at each other, then looked around for back-up, with amused smiles which suggested I was out of order – off my rocker even.

"It doesn't work like that," the Italian said finally.

"But what about the overlap? Wouldn't it be more cost effective and less confusing if it did?"

The question went unanswered and my mouth became suddenly dry. Dan had been sitting through this discussion with a quiet smile, and he regarded me calmly.

"Good point," he said. "Let's minute it."

And to my amazement Dan moved the meeting on.

"Final item today, folks, what do we call the Ukrainians? Beneficiaries, counterparts or partners? Zat is the question."

A humorous groan swept the room and people began tapping their papers together to leave.

Dan held up a hand. "OK. Let's just clarify what term we're all using, right now."

"What does it matter?" Chelsea Savage said. "They get the project, don't they?"

The Italian spoke up. "We still say 'beneficiary' though I think we'll shift to 'counterpart' like you guys at USAID, Dan."

I glared at the man; was that obsequious relief at having been let off the hook by Dan? Thank God the Danish woman interjected.

"We have always called them our partners," she said, "that way we enjoy maximum co-operation with them."

I jumped in. "Surely we should all call them partners? They provide the office space and staff." Again I felt eyes spearing me, the heat rising in my cheeks.

"Counterpart is a good step in that direction, isn't it?" Dan shucked his head.

"But 'counterpart' dehumanises the relationship. It sounds more like a plastic marker in a game of Ludo than a human being."

Silence hit the room again, this time hostile rather than embarrassed. Dan and I locked eyes and I wondered if he even knew what Ludo was.

Finally he rolled his eyes. "OK, let's come back to this at our next meeting folks."

And he wound up the session.

I had to wait for the ambush of reverent handshakes that Dan always commanded before everyone left the meeting room. Once it was empty, it was he who spoke first.

"I know what you're going to say, Ness, but I helped you out there, truly I did."

"Let's minute it?" I mimicked him. "That was supposed to be a co-ordination meeting. Do you all just pay lip service then? Spend thousands developing the same training materials when they already exist on someone else's shelf?"

"It's complex."

"Well try me."

I sat down again. Dan sighed and he too sat down, reaching for my hand, but I tugged it away.

He blew his breath out in exasperation. "Look you can't just insist that one donor has to fund one action and another has to opt for a different aid sector. Like the guy said, it doesn't work like that."

"There were thirty donors at this meeting. Are you telling me they should all be left to run loose over Ukraine, without any effort to link up their efforts?"

"Look. Each donor has its own agenda. Different timetables, different political drives, different cultural drives, surely you can see that, Ness?"

"I can see that we must be a laughing stock."

"OK, one example. The EC can take up to two years to get a programme off the ground here. You know why? Because every member state, all fifteen of them, has to agree to every single programme, so it gets translated into all of their languages and discussed at some grand council. Imagine the politicking there. Then, it's translated into Russian and despatched here to the Government for their approval too. Finally, it goes out to competitive tender. Meanwhile, your fellow countrymen, the Brits, they can start up a programme within weeks. How do you expect those two organisations to co-ordinate? Even if they wanted to?"

"But why can't they at least collaborate? If they find themselves working in identical areas with the same Ministry?"

"Maybe, just maybe, the Germans think their pension model is the best. So why would they want to collaborate with some pesky southern Europeans, with the Greeks or the Portuguese, say?"

I folded my arms and dug in. "Well they could at least share their training modules, the technical stuff."

"They get paid for developing that stuff, that's where the aid budget goes. It's called political expediency."

"It's called waste in my book."

Our eyes burned at each other and I wondered if his heart was racing as fast as mine.

"Is it the same for other stuff too? The duplication, I mean?"

Dan stood then and began packing his briefcase, his back to me. "Reports, surveys, studies, all duplicated."

"We're talking a lot of money here, aren't we?"

He clipped the briefcase shut with a twang. "All told, across the whole of the Former Soviet Union, I guess we are."

"How can you let this happen?"

"Jeez, you think I have any control over this machine?"

"Well you could try!"

Dan made for the door and turned to me, holding it open. "You coming?"

I was relieved that we parted on the steps outside, he for his office and I for my regular swim. As I ploughed my lengths, I struggled to make sense of the meeting. Really it had been too enormous for me, but still I resolved that I myself would coordinate our aid programme with others, and that I would use the term 'partner', even if I had to keep it secret from Bogdan.

When we met up at home for dinner that evening, I sulked a little and the atmosphere lingered.

"Plus everyone has different political motivations for being in Ukraine, Ness," Dan said suddenly as he served me his seafood linguine. "And you cannot hope to have any technical coordination of interventions that are fundamentally political."

I glanced up at him. "For example?"

"For example, USAID's stated objective everywhere in the world is to further the foreign policy goals of the US, whereas your own dear government's mission statement is to alleviate poverty. How do you square that one? What's more, you guys in Europe have closer cultural and historical ties to this region than we Yanks do. You're almost family."

"Well it's not all like that!" I snapped, with no idea of what I meant and fiercely concentrating on winding the pasta onto my fork.

I felt Dan smile then and he let me off further debate, changing the subject to some domestic matter. Our discussions would often end thus, and we would revert to the new lovers we were.

The following day, I took the programme document off to the Ministry of Employment. True to form, the Minister had dodged my phone calls, but I'd secured a meeting with Mrs T, which I knew would be far more productive in any case.

The afternoon was a balmy one and Sasha drove with all our windows down. As we passed the monolithic Cabinet of Ministers, I noticed a platform of men suspended half way up the building. They were painting it white, but the lower part of the building was still the original dark grey colour, which lent it an odd perspective.

"Why are they painting it?" I asked Sasha.

"Our politicians try to paint a black dog white," he said.

I laughed. "They try to change the spots of the leopard."

He grinned. "On this occasion, your English expression may be better one."

When we arrived at the Ministry, Sasha drove straight up the kerb and onto the pavement, ignoring the pedestrians who stopped dead in their tracks to avoid being squashed by his tyres, with not a hint of a scowl on their faces. He parked snugly up against the wall of the building but, dissatisfied with his first attempt, he reversed back again. Without checking his rear view mirror.

"Christ, Sasha, you're supposed to keep looking all around you. You could have killed someone." I jumped around in my seat.

He shrugged, "They will move."

"Didn't they teach you to reverse, or something?"

"No. In Ukraine, no lessons in reverse gear. Anyway, I buy licence from man at State Driving Complex."

I grinned at him, incredulous. "You bought your driving licence?"

"Of course." He returned my smile, a flash of gold eye tooth revealing the extent of his pleasure at my shock.

As we were shown into Mrs T's office, she rose from her desk and greeted me with her usual kiss to each cheek. "Vanessa, how lovely to see you."

"And you, Valentyna." I dared to use her first name, which raised Sasha's eyebrows, though not hers, I was pleased to note.

The woman gestured to her meeting table and I found myself sitting up straight, observing how carefully turned out she was, the lustrous black hair, the tailored grey suit, the fuchsia scarf at her neck. Wafts of expensive perfume were coming at me and the sight of her perfect nails had me scrunching my own bitten ones into my palms.

"So," I began. "This is our programme document, Valentyna. We've had it translated into Russian for you, although your English is excellent, I know."

I heard my obsequious voice, but was unable to get a grip, so potent was her presence.

"Thank you Vanessa, you are too kind." Her laughter tinkled.

"As you will be our partner on the project," I paused for effect, to let her know I was a pioneer, "there are contributions we will need from you. Perhaps we could run through them?"

"Yes, of course." She flicked the document open.

"First of all, I hope it will be OK for you to recruit a Training Task Force?"

"How many people will you need for that?"

"Twenty of your staff, please. Good people we can train up to manage Job Centres, who may then go on and train others. It's called a train the trainer exercise. However, it's not me, but we together who need them, isn't it?" I made a kind of shuttle motion with my hands, indicating the give and take. "As I said, I see us very much as partners on the programme, Valentyna."

"Yes, of course." She made a few notes.

"And, as you know, the Ministry has to provide a building, where we can set up the model Job Centre and Small Business Agency."

"That is in motion." Her smile was very much still in place. Had it dropped even for an instant I might have visualised just how much we were expecting of them.

"Anything else?" she asked.

"Your time, your energy." I let out a frivolous laugh. "Your commitment."

With slight embarrassment at my behaviour, I glanced down at Sasha's pad on the table beside me, he was totting up his business takings. I smiled again at Mrs T.

"All our energies will be with your project, Vanessa," she said. "I will read this document and make sure the Minister is fully informed."

She gripped the paper in both hands, shaking it a little, as if bestowing it with gravitas and then stood up from the table. "We will have lunch soon."

On the way out of the Ministry, we passed Jeff on his way in.

"Hello Jeff?" My eyes were full of question.

"Vanessa. Lovely day for it." And he bounded up the steps.

Sasha suggested coffee, by then a typical ploy to avoid the office and Irina. At Independence Square we found a pavement café, where I ordered a Coke. Sasha lit up and ordered his usual Turkish coffee in a miniature cup. "So I can stand my spoon up," he said; I'd once made a joke about its treacle texture. We sat watching the life in the square. Men were sunk like vultures over chess boards dotted around the piazza, girls in mini-skirts sauntered past us, and a man with a monkey and organ grinder was plying for photo trade.

"That was a good meeting, wasn't it?" I found I was preening myself, pulling at my hair, brushing my shirt.

"She is important woman."

"Yes," I agreed, pleased that by association so was I and that my junior colleague had noted it. "I think she's an excellent partner for the programme."

"You know she is mistress of Prime Minister?"

"Mistress?"

"Yes, you know Ness, they make hanky panky together."

I gasped. That explained her aura, and the respect – the fear almost – she'd commanded at my design workshop. But surely it could only be good for the programme? So long as the affair didn't end.

As if he'd read my thoughts, Sasha added, "Is long time they are together."

"Keep me posted will you?"

He nodded. Sunglasses on, I sank back and scanned the tops of the ornate buildings, the pediments, the roofs, the sculptures.

"Such a beautiful city," I murmured.

"It was more beautiful before. Many buildings here on Kreschatyk were destroyed by Red Army in Second World War."

I raised my glasses at him. "By the Russians? Why?"

"To kill German officers. Germans invaded Kiev and moved into best buildings for headquarters. But Red Army had laid explosives there – and poof."

"They destroyed their own heritage to kill the invaders?"

"Kiev citizens were also killed, many people lived here on Kreschatyk."

"Gosh. So was it worth it?"

He shrugged, that resigned shrug I'd seen too many times in too many people since my arrival. "Victory for Ukraine came at end."

I watched him light another cigarette. "Do you think people here see us as invaders?"

He shook the match out. "No. We like you here, you bring hope to our country."

"Do we?" I thought of Irina's thesis, and of the donor meeting. "Or do we just bring chaos?"

Sasha laughed. "You do good things here. I watch you, people like you."

"Irina doesn't."

"Irina is odd person."

I smiled inwardly, but let the moment pass. "Why do you think we're here?"

"Is simple. To open Ukraine for interests of West. We learn to do free market economy then you can sell exports here."

"That's cynical, some of us just want to help you have better lives."

Sasha turned his mouth down sceptically but made no comment.

"What would you do, if you didn't work for the Levshenko programme?" I asked.

"I would join other aid programme, we have lot of donors in Kiev."

I nodded. Too many.

"And I have my business," he added. "By way, you tell Dan I have new consignment, socialist realism paintings, very good choices."

I threw him a sideways smile. "OK, I'll let him know. Was it you who sold him the paintings on our walls?"

"Evident!" Sasha replied, with a laugh.

"Evident." I laughed back, closing my eyes again to the sun, with the grotesque image of a happy worker imprinted inside my eyelids.

"Hey, Vanessa."

I opened them again to see Chelsea standing before me. "Hi, how are you?"

"Buying in supplies for some R&R across the pond." She waggled a plastic bag, through which I could make out the square edges of CDs.

"Which shop sells CDs?" I looked around the square.

She screwed her nose up. "Aw, none of these Ukrainian ones, they just sell garbage."

I smarted at her scorn and took a surreptitious glance at Sasha, who was making a good effort of appearing oblivious to the comment, staring into the distance.

"You wanna go down to the market." Chelsea pointed to a side street off the Square. "It's all pirate but the quality's great."

After she'd gone, Sasha lit yet another cigarette. "She is hypocrite, this woman." He slapped at the ash on his trouser leg. "World Bank write our laws for copyright. They stop all bootleg goods in Ukraine, but they buy pirate CDs here for themselves. At market, you see only World Bank people." He stabbed his cigarette in the direction of the side street Chelsea had indicated. "Is cheap, is good for us too, but she is hypocrite, this woman."

"Yes she is." I felt a cheeky smile coming on. "So can we go there?"

Sasha laughed. "You are very naughty lady, Ness."

He dropped some notes on the table and we left in search of the market.

10

Over the phone, Bogdan and I drew up the shortlist of four companies, who would bid for the three million pound contract to implement our programme. To my surprise, he wanted to include my old firm Lancashire Regeneration. Once the tender was launched, I could only sit back and wait for the bids to come in, though now I had moved in with Dan, I had no desire to go home to Manchester as planned. I'd also been invited by Svetlana to a summer party down in her village in Donetsk, a place I was itching to revisit.

Dan's apartment was on the fifth floor of a block near the Opera House. From the front it was grand, hues of pinkish stone with impressive dusky grey pillars and sculptured stone frames around the windows. Two mermaid-like creatures propped up the doorway, their breasts exposed, hands braced on their head to take the burden of the overhang, and from the waist down they were scrolls of marble, curling up and round at the tips. The back view of the apartment was akin to most other apartment blocks in Kiev, built of basic brick, though still dusted with memories of a pale pink. An enclosed balcony hung like a small shed off the back of his bedroom.

Inside, the apartment was small but luxuriously refurbished, in keeping with his status at USAID; they'd even installed a PC and bespoke email system – the first I'd ever come across. There was a living room which gave onto the sole bedroom, a black and white bathroom with that vast sailing tub, and a tiny kitchen. On the evening I'd moved in, we'd celebrated with Crimean champagne. A little tipsy, I'd stood Dan's grey Persian cat, Pushkin, on the Formica work surface, nose to the wall, and smoothed its tail out to reach the opposite one. It fell short by a foot or so which had me in fits of giggles, while Dan stood in the doorway, arms folded, face perplexed.

That summer, Dan and I would spend our Saturdays exploring Kiev. One morning he took me to see the university, just a brief walk from our apartment. The sun beckoned us as we set off and the ubiquitous trees were in full leaf, hanging heavily across the pavements. We came across an old lady who had set up stall on the pavement. She was selling a single bunch of bananas, gold dust in Kiev back then, and possibly similarly priced given the lack of interest. As we neared her, Dan began his usual running commentary, sotto voce.

"Are we going to make it past her?"

"Shut up," I muttered, squeezing his hand.

"Is it going to happen? Could it possibly be that we might just avoid a purchase here?"

I stopped at the woman and bought all the bananas, squishy and blackened. Dan had walked on and he waited for me with a gentle smile as the woman thanked me, as the habitual fuzzy glow warmed through me.

"What's up?" I said as I reached him. "You like bananas don't you?" I handed him one, peeled mine and slipped the others into my bag.

"You're too good for this world." He peeled it and eyed the bruised fruit. "Mmm, yummy!"

We walked on eating in amiable silence, unable to speak anyway through the leaden mush of the fruit. At the university we found a vacant bench opposite the main building and sat down.

"Shevchenko University," Dan said. "Named after the national poet."

I looked at the deep red façade, vivid against the foliage bursting around it. "That's red paint, not red stone, isn't it?"

He nodded. "Story goes that Tsar Nicholas had it painted red, in anger at the students refusing to fight during the First World War, to make them face the blood spilt by their fellow Ukrainians."

"Ah." I sighed and scanned the pediment for an inscription. "Irina keeps quoting Shevchenko at me, you know."

Dan chuckled. "Any particular lines?"

"Oh, it's always about how great it is to be Ukrainian, how foreign lands are luring and yet disappointing, that kind of thing. She really doesn't like me." I hadn't told Dan about our run-in.

"Come on, it's not you, Ness, it's what you represent. Lot of people feel that way here."

"That we're threatening their culture, or something? That's rubbish, I'm just here to help them find a better life."

"So you keep telling me. But who says they want our kind of life?"

"Well, we don't have old ladies forced to sell a single bunch of bananas on the street, do we?

He drew me to him. "Mmm, you smell good. The lady's wearing perfume."

"See, I do have an indulgence." I laughed and pulled away, awkward then to have referred so primly to my act of charity.

He threw me one of those ironic glances. "You refuse to wear make-up because it's tested on animals, but you wear a perfume that is produced from the musk gland of the civet cat?"

"What?"

"I'd bet they had to slay six kitty cats to produce one bottle of the stuff."

"You're joking?"

"I am. Guess they use chemicals these days."

He'd let me off the hook, but he was right, I found out later – and for me that was to become a symbol of my ignorance, of my general misguided mission.

"How do you know this perfume anyway?" I asked.

Dan sank back and sighed. "Sheryl wore it too."

The mention of his ex-wife unsettled me. "What happened there, Dan? Are you going to tell me?"

"Like I said, Sheryl resented what I do for a living, hated being trailed around the world – which is how she saw it. But when we hit Singapore for a few years she seemed to settle a little, spent the afternoons playing mah-jong. Or so she told me. It was a buddy of mine at the office." He broke off, ran a hand over his face. "Classic really. One afternoon, I nipped home for some document I needed and opened the bedroom door. Her butt in the air, his cock in her mouth."

I heard myself gasp. "Dan, that's dreadful."

"Oh, I was glad to see the back of her."

"I'll stop wearing the perfume."

"Nah, don't Ness. Smells much better on you."

*

The following Saturday I flew back down to Donetsk for the villagers' summer party. As Dan drove me out to Borispol, I half wished I was not leaving him, that instead we would spend the day on the beach, or cycling in the forest. In departures we held each other like lovers parting for months rather than just the one night.

Svetlana met me at Donetsk airport and we took a bus, then a local train, followed by another bus. The whole journey took us two hours. Once off the bus, I dropped my bag to the ground and let the mass of foliage wash over me, the multitude of different greens, untamed and wild. And I had an odd sense of déjà vu. Spangles of sunshine fell through the leaves onto us and, as we set off for Svetlana's home, I felt the makings of a sweet joy inside me. We shuffled along the gravel road, cutting through an alleyway between the houses and across a patch of tangled grass, where the telegraph wires sagged on their splintered posts. One of them was topped by an empty stork's nest the size of a tractor tyre. Arriving at Svetlana's house, I followed her through a gate in a wonky picket fence, the gaps in it wider than the actual slats. A clump of tall bushes with red blooms lined the path to her door.

"Hollyhocks," she said, smiling behind her at me.

"It's lovely Svetlana. It's like an English country cottage." I gazed at her house in awe, at the touch of splendour added, in the form of carved green frames around the windows. Otherwise, it was like all the others, white and squat with a roof of corrugated iron.

Inside, the first thing that struck me were two steps in the corner which seemed to be radiating heat. Svetlana reached for a heavy iron kettle lodged on the top step, and I realised that this was the stove. Coal had been shovelled into a small opening on the lower step, and a larger opening above was clearly for baking and roasting.

"Would you like tea, Vanessa?"

"I'd love some, thanks." I sat down and looked around her kitchen, at the sloping stone floor, at the curtains on a wire above the sink; it reminded me of my grandmother's house. I heard movement in a neighbouring room.

Svetlana nodded at the door. "My husband is just waking, he worked in the mine last night. The party will begin at two o'clock."

"Is the party to celebrate Independence Day?" We were coming up for the 24th August.

"No! Not in Donetsk, Vanessa. Here people do not want the independent Ukraine, they think only of their glorious past, of the Soviet Union." As she spoke, she held a spoof pose for me, gazing into the far away and long ago, like Judy Garland searching over her rainbow. "Many people in our village were happier under communism," she added.

84

I nodded, careful not to say anything clumsy or offensive, and she went on. "Our party is held each year to celebrate the holiday from the mine. Our men will not have to work for the next two weeks."

The door off the kitchen opened and a man ducked through the frame smiling, his hand outstretched. Also in his late twenties, he was thickset, with wrists the size of the table legs, and biceps which seemed to roll out of his black sleeveless T-shirt. His wet blond hair was combed flat and I was drawn to the beads of coal dust embedded in his forehead; they seemed almost to complement his slate blue eyes.

"Vanessa, this is my husband, Oleg."

Svetlana threw her husband a fond look and I caught a definite glint of sexual tension between them, as he kissed her and squeezed her around the waist, which whisked my mind back fleetingly to Dan.

That afternoon, a series of tumbledown buses used to transport the miners to and from their shifts, was waiting at the edge of the village. I sat with Svetlana, while Oleg made for the back with the other men. There must have been four generations of families on that bus, from walnut-skinned grandmothers to silky babes in arms. Lesya waved, and I gestured to my hair then to hers, to indicate how lovely it looked. Behind her was Yelena, neat and stunning in a red frilled dress, a jar of honey on her lap.

As the bus rocked us along the dirt roads out towards the forest, the whoops and laughter coming at me were as raucous as my primary school trips to the zoo, and I half expected these people to launch into song. Soon there was a great commotion. Villagers were gesticulating at gaps between the great birch trees, but the driver swept onwards ignoring them. Then, without warning, in what felt like a handbrake turn, he swerved the bus off and swung us into the foliage. I ducked in my seat; surely we would hit the thicket? But the bus lurched through undergrowth and emerged into a clearing. I joined in the riotous cheering.

We piled off the bus onto the grass, where shafts of light caught the bright clothes, almost in surprise, against the varied greens of foliage. Olga, the seamstress, approached me arms outstretched, with compliments in Russian for my long sundress, so I stood back holding her hands out and returned them in English for her dirndl skirt and embroidered blouse. She led me by the hand over to the makeshift barbecues, where wisps of smoke were already rising, and she introduced me to her husband, who was blowing at the kindle. Dmitry was a striking man, with a large wedge of a nose and hair so black it shone blue. Built the same as Oleg, he too wore a T-shirt vest, and he brushed his charcoaled hands off on it then held one out to me with a broad smile.

"Can I help?" I asked them both.

"Da." Olga nodded, bunching up her shoulders with a smile.

I followed her to the long lines of trestle tables which had been set up on the grass. She shook out a white linen tablecloth, handing me one end, while Lesya and Svetlana shared another cloth. As we laid the tables, I watched the stools and chairs emerging from the boot in the belly of the bus and being passed, as if down a line of ants, to where we stood. Over among the trees, at the edge of our clearing, children played hide and seek, the older ones taking the younger gently in hand to hide with them. One small boy tried to climb a birch tree, but its branches began too high up the bark and he slid back down it like a cartoon dog on a Tom and Jerry lamppost. While I was laughing at this with the other women, a man wearing shorts, whom I half recognised, bustled up to us and thrust a plastic beaker of white wine at me.

"Welcome, Welcome!" he shouted.

I glanced at his bandy legs and his half-unbuttoned crimson shirt, as he foisted a beaker on Svetlana too, giving her a smacker of a kiss on her cheek, and I realised that it was Vladimir Zukov, the Governor of Donetsk. He handed wine to the other girls then moved on to take several of the older women in his arms, and Svetlana put her mouth to my ear.

"He is from our village."

"Ah, I see."

Humming crazily, the Governor swirled the pensioners round, and I watched as their faces lit up with the attention. Oleg, arriving at the man's side with a giant block of a CD player, caught me smiling to myself at his tuneless zeal, and smiled back with a knowing nod.

"Musika!" the Governor cried, swinging the machine onto a table.

He slapped Oleg and Dmitry heartily on the back, as together they fiddled with knobs and sorted through CDs, then he stood back, finger in the air to command the attention of anybody close by, and waited for the song to begin. Ukrainian – or perhaps it was Russian – folk music roared from the set, to the applause of all nearby, and the man sashayed between the tables, arms out to the music, greeting all in his path, tousling the heads of the children as he went.

Heralded by its horn, another bus reeled out of the trees and pulled up. I ambled over to greet it. Marina picked her way carefully down the steps with a wicker basket brimming with her cakes, placed it down and took me in her thin embrace. Slabs of meat stacked in washing up bowls, salads in enamel dishes and loaves of black bread, were then carried by eager arms over to the tables, which were now decorated with woodland foxgloves in jam jars.

"Ness, this is my mother."

I turned to see Svetlana by my side, with an older woman wearing a dress the colour of lapis lazuli, and printed with lollipop-pink roses which dazzled almost three-dimensionally against the blue. The woman beamed at me, her face etching itself into deep lines which curved around her cheeks, her smile revealing the gaps between her yellow teeth. She reached for a platter of bread from a nearby table and began to address me.

"Vanessa, this is how we prepare our bread," Svetlana translated for her.

Olga, Lesya and Yelena gathered round us, while she explained how the bread was traditionally wrapped in embroidered linen, called a rushnik, and laid out on a wooden platter to serve. She pointed out the ears of corn which decorated the bread, and the salt which had been heaped upon its crust.

"The salt symbolizes friendship that will never fail." Svetlana's eyes held mine as she spoke. "Because, you see, salt is never altered by time."

"That's a lovely symbol," I said, feeling the tide of emotion rising.

"Vanessa, we greet you with this bread and this salt, and we hope our friendship with you will never fail."

"That's what I hope for too." I beamed at them all – at my Divas standing before me – how could it be that I'd met these women only once before and yet I was already so much a part of their group? I felt wholly embraced by their warmth at that moment and I reached for a beaker of wine, raised it to them. "To our special friendship," I said, "may it never fail."

The meal lasted for many hours. I did make the odd foray around the table with my camera, hoping to capture the laughter, the camaraderie, and promising to provide photographs for all who wanted them. But for the most part, I sat as if in a dream, smiling at this new world, understanding little of the language around me, but never being excluded. Indeed, many of these villagers spoke as if their tale were intended only for me, shouting or gesturing to bring it home. Flanked by Oleg and Dmitry, I followed their anecdotes through their mimes, and also the occasional assistance from Svetlana opposite me. I sank my teeth into the small pancakes stuffed with potato and herbs, and felt the sweet vitamin goodness from the tomato and onion salads sinking into my body.

Every so often, I lifted myself from the present, let the voices and laughter wash away, distant and bubbling, and I gazed around me at the forest, at the show of wild violets, at the pads of leaves which cushioned us. Never had I experienced this kind of joy. I was a woman in love, and that surely coloured those moments, opened me up to them, but this feeling was different, it was an overwhelming compassion. I had not before known such happiness in unity with other people.

It was dusk when the dancing began. Plates were cleared, rinsed and stacked, with mutterings of anticipation, and the barbecues were stamped out within the confines of their brick walls. Then somebody struck up a note on the fiddle, another squeezed the opening riffs from an accordion, and around me a mass of people clapped madly and made to grab a partner. I watched Svetlana and Oleg swing round together over the grass, squashing flowers beneath their bare feet, her full skirts swirling out, the muscles in his strong shoulders writhing with the effort of leading her. Olga and Dmitry followed them round. On the fringe, the young children, drunk with tiredness, clasped hands and swung together in staccato jumps, giggling and squealing, while the older ones shirked off the teenager in them to dance wildly with the rest.

"Vanyssa!"

I looked up to see the Governor hovering over me.

"Pozhalusta?" Please? he asked, one hand at his heart, the other behind his back.

I stood and staggered to the grass with him. The band struck up a polka and, as I felt the man's grip around my waist, the ballast of his stomach, the warmth of his beery breath, I smiled to myself; I knew this dance. Not that I'd ever danced it before, but I had seen it in films; you just had to shout one, two, three, hopping from foot to foot and you were off. So I danced myself dizzy, overcome by the wine, the music – by the joy of life. I was happy, and I found myself dancing the polka with the most powerful man in East Ukraine, who might one day, it was rumoured, make a bid to be its President.

11

It must have been late September when I returned from a brief visit to the UK. I'd taken part in the evaluation of the four bids to decide which company would win the contract to implement our aid programme. I looked up at the apartment building after our drive from the airport and searched out the fifth floor window, and I remember thinking, yes, this really is our apartment now, this is home.

Dan wheeled my case inside, with his habitual nod and greeting of, "Howdie," at the female load bearers. He crossed the floor to the lift, taking my hand in reassurance as the cage rattled its way down to us. I would have preferred to hoof it up the eighty-five stairs to our front door, but I squeezed Dan's hand and looked down, comforted by the patterns in the coloured chips on the stone floor. As the doors opened, I tugged his arm, alarmed as usual that he was already propelling himself forward inside the decrepit lift.

"Make sure it's here, Dan."

"It's always here, Ness."

He swung my case inside, jolting the platform, and stepped in. I looked through the gaping crack between the lift and the floor – it was at least three inches. I could envision the depths below, could feel myself plummeting, fingernails snatching at walls until I hit the bottom. I shuddered and stepped in, the platform swinging like a grocer's scales beneath me. The door creaked shut and the lift began to shunt itself upwards, swinging from side to side. There was no point trying to speak; its mechanics were deafening – a thud-thud-thud like a washing machine gearing itself up for full spin.

Then, suddenly, the lift came to a halt. Just stopped dead. I let out a shriek and slammed the alarm button behind me, but if it rang somewhere, it wasn't in our building.

"Fuck." Dan yanked his mobile phone out and jammed in his office number.

"It's Saturday, Dan."

"Always somebody there."

He did get through, and he spoke to the Ukrainian duty manager at USAID, gaining assurance that we would be freed as soon as the man had got hold of maintenance.

"Come here." Dan pulled me to him and held me tightly. "You're shaking. I'm sorry about this, Ness." He pressed his forehead to mine and scrunched the mass of my hair through his fingers. "Mmm, like Maine in the fall," he muttered – a favourite of his.

But when he drew back, I saw the beads of perspiration on his own forehead.

"Are you OK?" I asked.

"Yeah, I'm fine, just that I hate being closed in."

His words took me back to the coal mine and his fear of that tunnel.

"Where's yours come from, then?" I asked him. "Come on, we might as well tell each other our ghost stories and get really freaked out here."

"Oh, it goes way back." He pulled out his phone again. "Where's he gotten to?"

Seeing how nervous Dan was made me suddenly raw with emotion myself. "Shall I tell you mine then?"

"Yeah, you do that." He ran his hands over my bare arms as if I needed warming up.

"OK." I took a deep breath and blew it out of me. "I was eleven. I know that because it was the day after my birthday. It was a beautiful spring day, very sunny, very fresh. We were walking back from town past a multi-story car park, Mum, Dad and me." I paused for a moment. "And there was this boy standing at the top of it."

Dan's eyes were locked on mine but he said nothing. I went on.

"And, well he was balanced there, right at the very edge." I closed my eyes and the image was clear – the cobalt sky, the concrete tiers of car park, the scrawny youth perched at the top. He wore jeans and a green plaid shirt, a garment so thick and cosy that it seemed it might break his fall. I could see the abundant blond hair, the fear in his face.

"And?" Dan asked gently.

I opened my eyes and wondered whether to tell him the whole story, but then I caught a flash of my dad's face and I snapped my eyes shut, wincing to push him out.

"And," I said finally. "And, well, he jumped. I watched him do it. He just launched himself off, arms out, and he soared through the air, for what seemed like an age, all in slow motion. And then I saw him hit the ground."

"Oh Ness." Dan pulled me to him.

"There was so much blood, I couldn't believe it."

"I'm so sorry for you."

I sank into Dan, battling to throw the images off me. That's how I'd learnt to manage these episodes, but still they always lingered.

"It's OK. It was years ago now. But I get really bad vertigo, and I have these falling dreams." I was shivering with nerves and tried to laugh them off. "Can't bear heights and hate being suspended anywhere – like in this lift, for example."

Dan drew back and smiled at me. "Once we're out of here I promise you we'll take the stairs forever more, OK?"

Dan never did get to tell me his own story that day. A burly Ukrainian arrived to free us, and once in the apartment the rush to get naked was animal.

When we emerged from our doze later, Dan showered first, while I sat with a glass of wine and contemplated the new painting he had acquired from Sasha in my absence. A socialist realist scene, it depicted metal workers standing large and angular before their forge. There was something powerful, something mechanical about the brutish workers that reminded me of my dad. The coiled kinetic force of the men, primed to strike their hammers on the molten steel. I shuddered; once my dad had wormed himself inside my head he always loitered there.

In the evening, we strolled up to the Golden Gate and our favourite restaurant, the Pantagruel. You would never have known it was an Italian place, with its absence of any signage, the opaque amber windows and those steps down inside that felt as if they led somewhere strictly private. But every Westerner knew the place, and I've heard that it's still there today. Dan and I sat outside on a newly decked area and drank Slavutich beer.

"So you stayed with your matey Carole in Manchester, did you?" Dan asked.

"My mate yes. We had a great night out together." With too many vodka cocktails, I thought to myself. "You'll love her when you meet her, Dan, she's so much fun."

"Look forward to it. So, good to be back?"

"Great." I covered his hand with mine. "Missed you."

"Missed you too." He placed his other hand onto the pile.

"Anything exciting happen while I was gone?"

"Fisticuffs in Parliament. If that counts?"

"What, an actual fight?"

"Well, more hissy-fit kangaroos than Madison Square Gardens, but yes, an actual fight."

"What was that over?"

"Oh, who has first dibs at being PM this week, or some such garbage."

"Hope Mrs T's lurve is still in place?"

"Yeah, don't worry, I guess he had the best swapsies."

We sipped our beers, falling into silence, and watched the people strolling by. I looked them up and down, their clothes, their shoes, their faces, and began to settle my mind back into Kiev. Even on a balmy Saturday evening, there was little frivolity about these people out and about – no jostling lads preening themselves, no giggling girls strutting wonkily in heels. No fizz.

"A heaviness of being," I said to myself with a sigh.

"Suits you, doesn't it?" Dan spoke as if he were waiting for this.

"They just seem so real, so grounded somehow, as if they know what's what. You can't imagine them being swept away by Britain PLC, by all that commercialism, all that materialism, can you?"

He smiled. "The first-visit-home syndrome."

"What?"

"Going home to all that extravagance, kind of shocks you after here, doesn't it?"

"Yes, that could be it," I mumbled. "Only …"

"Only, what?"

"Well, you know I took Mrs T with me?"

"And she spent her whole time at the mall?"

"Yeah, pretty much. It pissed me off, to be honest. I fought tooth and nail with Bogdan to have her there to quiz all the bidders alongside us. So she could be a real partner."

Dan nodded. "Gotta take a leak, but tell me about it." He left me alone with my thoughts.

I wondered how much to divulge to him. In fact, every single one of the bids had been trite, the constant repetition of anodyne phrases –

development of knowledge base … foster links with … tailored inputs … And without exception, the companies had padded out their bids with endless charts and diagrams – even maps of Ukraine. I had no idea what they actually intended to do in Kiev if they won the contract.

As for Mrs T, we had put her up at a swanky hotel in Manchester and I'd treated her to dinner in Chinatown, really bonding with her. Then the following day, she'd turned up three hours into the evaluation meeting, when we were onto our final candidate, Lancashire Regeneration. And, without even meeting the others, she was adamant that they were her preferred bidder.

"They offer to provide more computers than the others," she'd said. "And also a longer study trip to the UK."

It was as if Mrs T and Lancashire were in cahoots with each other, but I'd never known my old employer engage in anything underhand so I was sure that couldn't be. And, in any case, Bogdan too had wanted Lancashire to win his contract, that had been clear, and their bid did propose the best experts for the programme, so it had seemed a win-win situation. But, still, it unsettled me. When Dan returned to the table I told him none of this; somehow I felt lacking in professionalism, a sense of shame even.

"Mrs T certainly shopped till she dropped," I said instead. "Came into the meeting swinging shopping bags. I mean, where does she get all that cash from?"

Dan rolled his eyes at me. "Come on, Ness."

I found myself shaking my head at him. "You don't mean she took a bribe?" It shocked me to hear myself express it in words. "Lancashire would never …"

"Happens." He raised his eyebrows. "Apart from anything else, she's the PM's mistress, and he's a billionaire off the back of all those cuts."

"What cuts? This country's bankrupt."

"From selling off state assets, from rigging privatisation, from extorting bribes for export permits … Need I go on?"

"Well it's obscene," I said crossly. I still didn't understand all that back then.

"And let me guess here, Lancashire Regeneration won the contract?"

"Yes! Mrs T refused to entertain any of the other bids." I paused. "But then Bogdan wanted them to win too, and I used to work for them, so I do know them, and I do rate them myself …"

I heard myself rambling and fell silent, slumped back in my seat and took another sip of beer. Dan followed suit, looking around nonchalantly, waiting for me to catch up, I guess that's clear to me now. Feigning detachment, I too glanced around, while I thought again about their bid – in a couple of places they'd even written Armenia instead of Ukraine. A slip of the pen? Or a cut and paste jobbie?

"The bid was excellent," I said finally. "They were clearly the best ..."

"Sure they were." Dan drummed his fingertips on the table, as if following a tune in his head. "So who's your Resident Expert? The one who'll be based here to manage the whole show?"

"Jeff Osbourne." I waited for any negative reaction, but Dan nodded mildly at me, so I went on. "I think he'll do a good job, he was far more impressive than any of the others. Most just seemed to want a stint abroad before retirement, you know?"

"I do, there's a lot of them about."

"And Jeff knows the programme, knows the territory, knows the people."

"Of course he knows the programme, he designed it himself, didn't he?"

"So?"

"So ... what's saying he didn't design it to suit himself? Didn't you say he'd copied his blueprint from Armenia? Something he'd done before? Something he can then run with his eyes shut?" He leant across the table. "If that was public money, Vanessa, he would have an unfair advantage. It would be deemed a conflict of interest."

"Well it's not public money, it's from Bogdan's own wallet isn't it?" I snapped. "And we were proud of the team we selected, there are oodles of fabulous experts in their bid, not just Jeff. People with years of experience in stuff such as small business development and fronting up Job Centres."

"Oodles?" Dan mimicked me. "Did you check how many weeks input they'll have on the programme?"

I blushed. I hadn't, but I fired back anyway. "You think you know it all sometimes. Anyway, what's it to you, Dan Mitchell?"

Dan bit his lip, turning the surrounding flesh white. "Not sure, Ness, not sure. Look, I'm sorry, come on let's order." He sank the last of his beer and motioned for the waiter.

Later that night, I did pull out the winning bid by Lancashire, and I did check the time inputs of each of the forty experts who were to work on the programme. The average period they would spend in Ukraine was two weeks per year. They would just about have time to unpack and see the sights before leaving for the airport again. Dan was absolutely right.

12

Our programme finally got off the ground in early October, five months after I'd arrived in Kiev, which seemed a sluggish beginning to me, but which Dan said was one of the quickest start-ups he'd ever witnessed. As for the government building to house our model Job Centre and Small Business Development Agency, Mrs T's influence had clearly kicked in. The Ministry had allocated a three-storey block, turfing out an archaic State Committee to make way for our programme HQ, but the building seemed more like a prison to me. Its brick façade was painted the magnolia of an English living room, the door was a slab of steel and the windows heavily barred, the metal rods fanning up and out from the bottom corner.

"Those bars on the windows look like the way children paint sunshine." I felt the need to be positive for Sasha and Irina as we approached it.

Sasha smiled, but Irina ignored me, her eyes widening in scorn, her focus resolutely ahead. A sign on the door held the Levshenko Programme logo – Bogdan's proud design of an open hand holding an oak tree – but the State Committee's plaque was also still in place and I sounded out its Cyrillic title. "Agrikultur Stateesteek Komeetee ..."

"Ness is making good progress in our language, Irina." Sasha swung the door open, while I smiled hopefully at my office manager but received nothing but a jerk of the chin as she stepped inside.

In the foyer, a small porter's lodge stood to one side, vacant until Jeff had organised security to guard the office equipment that would soon arrive. On the wall ahead of us a brass plaque had been engraved with the words Kiev Small Business Development Agency. I heaved the door open and led the way in, overwhelmed by pungent floor polish. The room was vast, taking up the whole of the ground floor, with high, chandeliered ceilings and those sunshine prison bars lining one wall. Viktor, the Head of the Small Business Federation, whom we had recruited to manage our Agency, stood at a window with his back to us, firing instructions into a brick of a mobile phone. Waiting for him, I surveyed the room, visualising the banks of desks with their phones and computers that would soon arrive, and the advisers who would welcome Ukrainians eager to start their own businesses. But Sasha, impatient as ever, cleared his throat, causing Viktor to swing on his heels and lock eyes with me, his frown of concentration flashing into the contagiously jolly smile I remembered from before. He hung up.

"People is not here?" He held his palms up in question and strode across the parquet to shake our hands.

"They must be upstairs in the Job Centre," I said. "Come up with us, Viktor."

The stairwell reminded me of a municipal car park. It stank of fag ends, our feet echoed on the bare concrete steps, and it was so cold I could see my breath before me. *Like dead man walking*, I thought; what a great welcome for a guy who's just lost his job. On the next floor up I heaved my weight against the door, to be greeted by Jeff who strode towards me.

"Aha! VP our VIP!" Exhaling a copious smoke cloud, he shook my hand, then let out a hefty cough which buffed my cheek.

"Whose idea was it to have the Job Centre at the top?" I asked coldly. "We're supposed to be drawing them in, not laying out an assault course."

"Keeps you fit," he quipped.

I considered Jeff for a moment. I was less enamoured by my Resident Expert, as he was to be called, after what Dan had told me about his potentially dodgy role as both designer and implementer of our programme. Slowly, I drew my eyes away from him and scanned the room. Over by the window stood my best friend Carole, a hand covering her mouth in anticipation. I blinked at her in astonishment.

"Carole!"

"Surprise!" She did a little wriggle with her hips.

"What are you doing here?" I hurried over, clocking the expensive suit and the white blonde hair that was more sharply cut than the last time I'd seen her.

"They promoted me." Carole hugged me to her. "You know old Greg had a stroke, don't you?"

I nodded. The programme supervisor in Lancashire's winning bid, my key liaison person with them, had since lost the use of his left arm and leg.

"Well, I've taken over. I'm your new programme supervisor. Isn't it great?"

My heart sank. "Fantastic."

I was surprised by the strength of my dismay. Carole was my closest friend, but professionally she was ditsy, everybody knew that. And, unlike me, she'd never made promotion from her secretarial position at Lancashire – until then. I stood gazing at her; I didn't want a rookie on my programme, even if she would only be handling the invoices and the admin – and I was riled that she'd chosen to keep it a secret from me. More importantly, I was cross that I hadn't been informed by Lancashire, as if they had taken my agreement for granted.

While Carole lit up a cigarette, I looked around at the handful of other people in the room; three matronly Ukrainian women still sitting in coats and hats, and two Western men in their fifties leaning against the wood panelling, also smoking cigarettes.

I turned back to Carole. "How come you didn't tell me you were coming?"

"Wanted to surprise you." She shoved my shoulder. "And clearly I did!"

"But, you could have stayed with us."

"And disrupt the love nest? No, I'm at the National Hotel, they've done some of the rooms up already – very swanky too."

This upset me further. I knew those refurbished rooms cost $300 a night, and that was our programme money. Why wasn't she at the cheaper Kievskaya, as I had been?

"How long are you here for?"

"Just a week this time, but I'll be back every month, I've got twenty man-weeks of input, so we'll see loads of each other. We can paint the town."

I fixed my smile, hiding two thoughts. Firstly, Kiev was not a town you painted and, secondly, what a waste of expensive man-weeks; she would cost the programme thousands.

"Let's have dinner tonight, you can meet Dan," I said.

"Love to, Ness. And we'll be having lunch together too, not much else to be doing round here today. No furniture, no heating, no interpreter. And no Mrs Tabachuk either." Carole shrugged. "Haven't even met her yet."

I glared over at Jeff, but he who was standing with the two men against the far wall with his back to me. So I looked around what was to become our model Job Centre, our demonstration project which we would later replicate across Ukraine. East facing, with its tiny windows high up in the wall – just like a Victorian prison – this chilly hall would clearly never heat up, even in summer. The stench of cigarettes was battling for dominance with the wood polish, and underlying both of them was a trace of carbolic soap, which was omnipresent in Ukrainian public buildings.

Across the other side of the room, the three women sat patiently, chatting quietly to Irina, and I clipped over the parquet blocks to them. They got to their feet and smoothed down their coats as I introduced myself. Through Sasha, they explained that they would be trained by our programme to be the reception staff at this model Job Centre. After that they would help train up a Task Force of twenty women, who would roll out these skills to the regional Job Centres. I smiled from one face to the next, taking the measure of them – the Three Graces, I thought to myself. I warmed immediately to these women, impressed that they had already grasped their role. They were homely too. The unemployed need a touch of therapy with their employment advice.

It was some minutes before finally Jeff and Carole sauntered over to us and introduced the two other men. I shook hands with Bob and Steve from Stoke-on-Trent, a place I remember because of the way it stood out, mediocre in my mind.

"I don't recall your names from the bid," I said, mentally flipping through the forty CVs in Lancashire's proposal.

Carole stepped in. "We've made some changes. The other experts weren't available, but we were fortunate in securing these two gentlemen to train the Job Centre staff."

"Just like that?" An instant fury suffused me.

"Just like what?" Carole's own eyes steeled too.

"You win the £3million contract based on a raft of experts, whose CVs Bogdan and I pored over and analysed for hours, and then you simply change them without consulting me?"

"Don't panic Mr Mannering," Jeff's raspy voice cut in. "I know Bob and Steve from years back."

"Oh well if they're mates of yours, that's alright then," I said sarcastically and turned to the two men. "Have you worked in Eastern Europe before?"

Bobsteve, as I then saw them, looked nervously at each other. "No, this is our first assignment."

"Have you actually ever worked in a Job Centre?"

"We're social analysts at Keele University."

"You're academics? Oh for Christ's sake, Carole." I glowered at my friend.

"Look, will you just calm down a bit?" she muttered.

"I've heard about so-called experts like you." I turned back onto the two men. "I bet you've come here for some research of your own, some sociological project on post-communist Ukraine, haven't you?"

"Ness, you're being totally unreasonable." Carole took my arm, which I shrugged away from her.

"You're supposed to be here to transfer your expertise to these three ladies, but do you actually have any?"

We all turned then to regard the Ukrainian women. They were standing to one side, their expressions oh so enigmatic, and that brought my rant to a halt. These women were so obviously second-class citizens in that room, but their faces remained as inscrutable as ever. *What would they tell their families that evening?* I thought. I caught Irina's eye, and I swear I saw a hint of respect in them. Indeed it merited one of her slow blinks; another small step forward.

"Let's all go and have a nice cup of coffee at the National Hotel." Jeff let out one of his obsequious laughs.

I ignored him, turned again to Bobsteve. "How long are you here for?"

"Just this week."

"Of course." I nodded resignedly. Dan had been so right; what could they possibly achieve in a week?

"Well we will take these ladies with us for coffee and you can start training them there."

"Absolutely, we're keen to get cracking." Bobsteve nodded, hands fluttering, a nervous sheen to each of their foreheads.

"Goodo," Jeff said, patting me on the back. "Hope you're not going to micro-manage though, Ness? This is my baby, remember?"

"It's Vanessa," I hissed. "And you'd better get your act together quick if you want to see it out of nappies."

13

It was clear that my presence at that coffee was making everybody else uptight too. When anybody spoke, I swung my head to spear them, scouring their words for relevance to the task in hand, and when Jeff cracked his jokes I sighed pointedly at what I saw as distraction. So I left them to it and pulled on my coat. Irina made a show of dragging on her own with a scowl, before stomping from the hotel. I suppose she'd assumed I'd given up.

"Ooh, she's a snippy little madam, isn't she?" Carole said, watching her go. "Why do you put up with that?"

"She has it hard here." I followed my friend into the foyer. "Are you going back up to your room then?"

"Actually, I was hoping you might take me shopping for souvenirs." Carole gave me a sheepish smile.

"Do you actually expect to get paid for today?"

"Nope. Let's wipe today from the slate, shall we?" She smacked her hands together as if to dust them off. "Won't be a mo'."

While Carole nipped up to her room I lingered in the foyer, my eye drawn to a panel of stained glass, and I lost myself in the colourful image of Cossacks astride their horses.

"Vanessa!" Mrs T swept into the foyer. "I hope I am not late? Viktor told me you were here at hotel. I am sorry I come from very important meeting."

More important than this? I thought. "Hello, Valentyna. No, not at all late, they're just starting off with coffee in the lounge."

Carole emerged from the lift and I introduced them, watching each woman give the other the once over, a full overt sweep from toe to top, without eyes meeting in the middle.

"So that is the infamous Mrs Tabachuk!" Carole exclaimed as the woman disappeared into the lounge.

"Why infamous?"

"Oh, just impressive, you know."

I frowned; her words bothered me. "I call her Mrs T."

"Ms Dior, more like. Must have poured the whole bottle on her."

"Did Lancashire give her a sweetener to win the contract, Carole?"

"What? Like in some Le Carré novel or something? Don't be daft, you know Lancashire's whiter than white."

She took me by the arm to leave and I pulled it away.

"Aw, are you still mad at me Ness? Look, it is only day one. We have the trainers and we have the women in situ, that's a good start, don't you think?"

Perhaps she was right, but I was loath to shake off my sulky mood as we left the hotel. We headed off to Andriyivskyi Spusk, a steep winding descent of cobbles which led from the British Embassy down to the old Jewish quarter of Podil. Lined with souvenir stalls, the road was actually more of a wide trench, the kerbs stacked like dry-stone walls, which sloped from pavement to road. In the snow, it was treacherous. It was not icy that day, but still, I took some satisfaction in watching Carole negotiate the pavement in her stilettos. Puerile perhaps, but she had riled me.

We stopped first at a series of stalls selling Soviet memorabilia, the stacks of old army hats, ribboned medals and statues of Lenin heaped up like apples and oranges at a market. The men in the grey army surplus coats stood stamping feet, the wisps of their breath clear against the freezing October air.

'Ushanka!' Hats, they called out to us, removing their hands from pockets for a brief sweep across the merchandise.

Carole slid giggling between each stall, fingering the fake fur, breaking the monotony of their day, while they overtly admired her legs beneath the peach cashmere coat. I watched her flirting and smiled to myself, feeling again some fondness for her; perhaps I had expected too much of the very first day.

"This is perfect." She picked up a black padded slab of a hat, with flaps tied up over its crown.

"You try!" A tall thin guy stepped forward, his smile revealing greying teeth. He took the hat from Carole and pushed it down onto her head, while the men from the other stalls milled around her with their compliments. There was no fighting for her trade, just an opportunity for some humorous flirtation. The thin guy gave her a piece of mirror.

"Harasho," he said.

"He says it looks good." I smiled reluctantly at her.

In fact she looked beautiful, her olive skin framed against the black fur, her blonde skeins fanning out below it. Ten years we'd known each other, an odd couple thrown together by chance in a staff canteen on our first day at Lancashire. It was three hours before somebody had come for us and, without that bonding, I doubt that we would have become friends. But some people need a foil for their humour, and I was hers. In fact, Carole had lightened me up. As a child I'd been too watchful to be funny and I owed my own sense of humour to her.

She untied the flaps on the hat and pulled them down over her ears, laughing into the mirror at herself.

"Now you look like Deputy Dawg." My sulk was finally beginning to lift.

"I do a bit, don't I?" She swung her head, bringing the long floppy ears to life.

We both snorted with laughter then. Soon we had the giggles, like kids in a classroom who've been ordered to stop and can't; whenever our eyes met we set each other off again. That was why I loved my friend so much, she was so full of fun.

"You try one." She handed me a hat.

"No, they're for tourists."

"Ooh, gone native have we?"

"I try and live like a local, yes." I spoke with mock primness.

"How much?" She began bargaining with the man in English, fingering the cheap hammer and sickle insignia. "And this is genuine gold?"

"Kaneshno." Of course. The man frowned with feigned indignation.

She bought the hat, put it on, and the party broke up slowly, as if they were old friends. We moved on.

I pointed out St Andrew's Church across the street, a fabulous structure of white icing and turquoise turrets. "Want to have a look inside?"

"Crikey, you've not found religion out here too, have you?"

"No, but Dan says they're restoring it. Dates back to the 1700s."

"Nah, we've never really done churches, have we Ness?" She linked arms with me. "Come on, I'm having fun."

Further on down the hill, we passed the women who were always there, whatever the weather. Encased in men's coats, and headscarves, they sat open-legged and heavy beside their lines of embroidered shawls. One woman heaved herself to her feet and began speaking at us, while she pinched the linen rushniks for the offering of bread, and the white shawls with their identical patterns of childlike cross-stitch. I smiled to myself, remembering the forest party.

"Nice!" Carole said, fingering one of the cloths.

I tutted crossly at her sarcasm. But it was lost on the woman, who nodded with a broad smile, sending her leathery skin into fans of wrinkles, and foisted one into Carole's hands, patting them closed together around the rough fabric.

"So buy one," I said, "for your Gran."

"OK." Carole shrugged and pulled out a wad of karbovanet notes. "I've got no idea what this money's worth."

"I always give a bit more," I said.

Carole grinned at me. "In everything you do."

As we strolled on, I was struck by the way her peach coat blended in with the dusky pastels of the buildings, though I made no comment.

"You've not told me much about this Dan yet," she said. "He's a bit cultured then, is he?"

"Yes I suppose he is." I laughed. "He's just ... well he's very special."

"Still not seen a photo either." She dug me in the ribs. "Have you had them developed now?"

My many rolls of film had been at Boots when I'd last seen her.

"Got one of both of us, actually." I stopped, rummaged in my handbag and pulled out the photo of us at the People's Friendship Arch, a vast titanium rainbow high above the Dniepro river. He had bought me the rose to go with it too. We were standing polite and straight-backed for the shot, while other lovers waited in line off-camera.

Carole took it from me. "Oh, he's older than I thought." I felt my cheeks smart. "Bit porky too, Ness."

I snatched it from her. "He's lost weight since then. Anyway, don't be such a bitch."

"Just joshing. So I'll get to meet him tonight?"

I shrugged. "Not sure, he might be busy."

Carole took my arm and turned me to her. "Sorry Ness, it's just that he's not your usual choice. You've always gone for the lanky band types."

"Well, like I said, he's special."

"Bet he's good in the sack too, isn't he?"

I cocked my head at her and walked on abruptly, so that she had to skitter after me to catch up.

At the bottom of the hill, we turned into Podil and made for a restaurant near my office. Inside, the heat swamped us luxuriously.

"I'm starving." Carole swept a hand over her flat belly. "What I fancy is a huge salad."

"Why don't you try the borsch soup? It'll warm you up."

"No, these salads look enormous, look at the pictures, and so much choice. Original salad, beans salad, house salad, village salad ..." She drew breath dramatically. "What is a girl to have?"

I smiled to myself, knowing that none of those choices would actually be available. In fact, the waiter offered us just one type of salad, plus pork cutlets and borsch, and we both opted for the soup with pampushki, those soft bread rolls steeped in garlic.

Carole lit up a cigarette and rolled her eyes at me. "Do you really like living in this country, Ness?"

"It's got under my skin." I paused. "And so has the programme."

"Ah, the programme, wondered when we'd have to come to that. Look, this morning was just a glitch, tomorrow's another day."

"I really do believe we can make a difference out here, Carole."

"Saint Ness, patron saint of sufferers everywhere."

"If we get the right experts, this programme could be a huge success. We could set up the model Job Centre for Ukraine, and replicate it right across the whole country. We could train entrepreneurs, just like we did in Lancashire, set them up in their own business. Just think about the possibilities."

She drew on her cigarette but said nothing.

"So don't send me the dross nobody else wants, will you? No more academics writing a thesis on social justice in Ukraine, or some such crap. They should come out here with a serious goal, not on an anthropological jolly. Do you get me?"

"Loud and clear, Ness, loud and clear." She reached for my hand across the table. "You've always been the same, you. While the rest of us were tanking back the Chardonnay after work, you were still helping some redundant coal miner with his CV. It never was just another project to you, was it?"

I shook my head. "This one's gotten to me most though."

"Why can't you be shallow like me? Why won't shoes do it for you?"

We laughed together then. That was probably the most profound thing my friend had ever said – but then that was Carole, seemingly an airhead, but actually acutely self-aware. She had won me over again and I smiled at her with real affection.

"Most of all …" I said.

"Yes?"

"Well, there are some amazing people in the coal region, you wouldn't believe the human spirit down there. I want the Job Shop at the mine to be a crucial part of the programme – and the micro-credit finance for the women. I need Niamh Byrne and Kevin Reed on the job, Carole. Both of them are named in the contract, that's partly why I wanted Lancashire to win it. Please don't mess that up for me, will you?"

"OK, I'll make sure you get them." She jotted the names down on a beer mat.

It was then that Dan swung through the doors of the restaurant with a couple of buddies from the office. They were sharing a joke and their arrival was raucous. My tummy flipped to see him, as it always did, and our eyes met in a smile – though I still believe that he saw Carole first, that those noisette eyes of his flickered at her. He slid his arm around me with a kiss and my eyes strayed to his stomach. I was right, it was quite taut these days, though he did seem to be holding it in a bit.

"Hey Ness, thought you were at your start-up today?"

His colleagues stood like lapdogs beside him, clearly hoping to join us, so I introduced everyone to Carole.

"Enchanté." Dan gave a slight bow and did that click of his heels thing, while his smile became a silly grin.

Carole's face was also working itself up into its best radiance, I could see that, and I felt the tingle of jealousy; clearly he was better in the flesh than on celluloid then.

"She's not French," I said tightly.

"I'm a Mancunian actually," Carole said.

Dan let out a boom of a laugh. "We won't hold it against you."

I watched Carole and waited. On one of our nights out, she would have come out with something crass, like, she would love it if he did hold it against her, but she looked down coyly as the men pulled up chairs and sat down.

"So, are you here with the Levshenko Programme?" Dan asked, shunting his chair in close to hers.

"I am indeed." Carole lit another cigarette, her loyalty finally kicking in then. "And I'm also Ness's best friend from home."

"Oh." Dan looked perplexed.

"I've told you about my mate Carole, haven't I, Dan? We used to flat share."

"Ah yes. Well. It's good to meet you finally."

"By coincidence, she's also our new programme supervisor," I added for him.

At that moment, the waiter loped up to the table and slipped Carole's bowl away from her, the borsch slopping over the edge as he whisked it off with the spoon and side plate.

"Hey, I've not finished that," she cried after him.

She looked to me for help. I ignored her, blowing on my own soup, eyes down, while Dan, apparently back in boyfriend role, was contrite enough to effect a sudden focus on the menu. It was left to one of his buddies to snap at the waiter and have it brought back to the table.

The moment Dan arrived home that evening, I screeched at him. "How could you have flirted with her like that? You behaved like a whore!"

"Come on, Ness, I'm flesh and blood, she's a beautiful woman."

"She's my best friend!"

"I didn't know that, did I? Don't tell me that you never flirt with anyone?" He paused. "With Sasha, for example? It's just a bit of harmless fun."

I blushed as I thought of the way Sasha and I behaved together in the car; he did have a point, but still I couldn't contain myself.

"You didn't flirt with me like that when we first met!"

"You were special! You were more important than that."

He slammed the bathroom door. When he emerged seconds later, he made for me, his eyes ablaze, grabbed my wrist and yanked me through to the bedroom, where we flung ourselves at the bed. That little incident was to prove momentous.

14

While the Kiev training sputtered to a start, I made preparations with Svetlana to set the Donetsk micro-credit and Job Shop in motion, flying her up to relish in doses of her zeal. When next I visited her village, however, it was unrecognisable. Sasha drove me out from the airport in a hire car on a bleak late November day. Together with us were Niamh Byrne, an expert in micro-credit, and Paul Hopkins, who was a consultant in social regeneration.

Niamh, I was thrilled to have on board. A lithe and lively Irishwoman in her late thirties, she was newly on the market for overseas aid projects, having left her City investment bank in search of a fresh challenge. Carole, however, hadn't come up with my ideal choice of expert for the Job Shop – Kevin Reed. A compassionate former British Coal manager, he had lived through the Thatcher job losses and had helped many miners into new work. He had deserted to another aid programme, Carole told me on the phone, and Paul Hopkins also had heaps of experience. Moreover, Donetsk was twinned with Sheffield, which happened to be his home town. An absurd argument, but I was prepared to go with it, given that it was not Carole's fault.

Still wary of Paul, however, I'd spent the flight down grilling him, while he sat beside me pulling at his moustache. He talked up the work he'd done in Poland, glossing over the fact that he'd spent only brief periods there – mere days at a time – that it had been mostly workshops and not one-on-one coaching of miners. Admittedly, I did warm to his northern charm and sense of humour. "Don't worry," he cried over the din of the plane, "these propeller jobbies are safe as houses, it's the jets what fall out of sky here."

In Donetsk, everything seemed to be shut down, turned in on itself. The roses on the bridge across the river were bare sticks, the streets were piled with sludge, and every face was bent to the ground, like in some wintry Bruegel painting. We drove out through a pasty landscape. In the village, I was dismayed to see that the overwhelming greens of my memory had faded into a swathe of grey, as if deliberately spoilt with the drab wash of an artist's brush. We pulled up to the bus stop where Svetlana was waiting for the drive on to the coal mine. Svetlana had once told me that she showered in cold water each morning to start the day 'with a fizz,' as she put it. Observing her rosy sheen that day, I shivered to think how hard her life must be. Still now, on a winter's night whenever I'm in England, when I'm sinking under the luxuriant warmth of my duvet, I think of Ukrainians in their cold beds. And I cringe with guilt at the hand they were dealt. Guilt of the Catholic kind – it's not my fault but still I burden myself with their suffering.

We all stood taking in the village. Heaps of slush peppered with dirt were slumped up against fences and walls. The white single-storey houses that had seemed so quaint just three months earlier now stood squat and naked, all soft-lens foliage ripped from them, their corrugated roofs pressing them to the ground.

"Glad you came?" I asked Niamh.

She laughed. "I'm from Ireland, hon, remember? Gets like this in winter too."

"Well it's all very emerald here in the summer, I promise you."

"Could be Poland," Paul said. And the three of us threw him a lingering glance.

At the Slagansk mine, the morning shift had just finished and the men were eating in the canteen. We joined them, creating a hubbub of interest as we took our trays of stew to a table. With its steam and meaty odours, the atmosphere reminded me of a school dining room; the table tops had even been defaced with knifed scrawls and biro doodles, and the water beakers were those scratched tin ones, their metallic reek all-pervading as I drank from mine. I eyed up the stew, picked out the potatoes from the meat and toyed with them.

"It's not good?" the mine manager asked me in Russian.

"Da." I smiled and, although it was coated with gravy, I slipped a potato into my mouth and swallowed it. That's how important it was to me to get it right that morning.

I looked around the canteen. Svetlana's husband Oleg, sitting over by the window, smiled at me, his slate grey eyes studying me with that considered gaze of his. He nudged the other miners at his table and they too turned to scrutinise this odd party; a woman with a mass of dark blonde hair and freckles, a squat man in a woolly sweater, and me in my jeans and fleece. I nodded to the large craggy faces that turned my way, recognising many of them from the forest. There was Olga's husband, Dmitry, and beside him Lesya's and Yelena's too, all of them looking weary from their six hours of graft underground. Now showered and out of their overalls, these men sat elbow to elbow in their sludge coloured sweaters, their arms the size of lamp-posts, muscle-bound in their bulk.

Over lunch, Paul Hopkins was charming, with hearty compliments for the food. He maintained a running chumminess with the mine manager, who, doubtless pleased I had actually delivered this concrete action, seemed to be enthralled by him. Paul's effort with Svetlana fell flat though, and I noticed her dull eyes as he played to the gallery.

"Shall we start?" she said curtly, pushing her tray away.

"Now?" Paul pulled at his moustache. "Here?"

"Where else? These men need to sleep, they will be in the mine again before it is light."

"OK." Paul stood up. "I'll just clear my tray away."

He carried it over to the rack, nodding at the odd burly miner on the way, then he ambled to the front of the canteen, a hanky drooping from the pocket of his cords. Many of the miners were still eating, their backs to us, and the noise was slow to die down, but the manager introduced Paul as an expert from the UK in getting new jobs for miners. With a kindly smile which embraced the whole room, Paul began.

"When the pit closes it doesn't have to be the end of the world."

Dmitry, who was still shovelling food in, let out an exclamation with a dismissive flick of the hand. We all looked to Sasha.

"This pit is not closing," he translated.

Paul glanced at me, and I at the mine manager, who shrugged.

Paul tried again. "I'm here today to reassure you that miners do find new jobs." Silence. He went on. "We have a wealth of experience to share with you."

A guffaw from Dmitry made me jump. This time he stood to shout something at us. We looked again to Sasha for translation.

"You share your wealth of money with us. You pay our wages," he said.

Paul composed his face into that of a maudlin doctor announcing bad news to his patient and assumed a soothing tone. "We can't do that, I'm sorry. But we can help you in other ways. I've just returned from Poland, where the mines are closing, but where the men are finding new work."

"How you help us?" Oleg shouted in heavily accented English.

Around him there was a fug of smoke. Most of the miners had now lit up and were sitting back in their chairs, arms folded, contemplating our spectacle with the mild interest of hecklers waiting for the gag at a comedy club. But others still sat with their backs square on, in a kind of kiss my arse posture.

"Well, the first thing is counselling, to help you come to terms with redundancy," Paul said.

I let out a silent yelp. I would have started with something tangible. I surveyed the room. Nearly two hundred proud and stoic men who had only ever known the mine. How could they ever 'come to terms' with losing their livelihood? British miners had flogged themselves ever harder, sent production soaring in the dying months, all in the belief that their mine would never close. Like bailing the Titanic with a teacup. Thankfully, Sasha must have been thinking the same, because his translation was lengthy, I could sense him skirting round the words – maybe he even made stuff up.

Paul went on. "We can help you foster a positive attitude, analyse your existing skills and develop with you a personal action plan."

It was like telling them they were to become astronauts.

"Can you give them some concrete examples?" I muttered.

He nodded. "Then we can set up a Job Shop, here on site, to help with your re-employment. We would identify local vacancies and their training requirements. British miners retrained in a host of new skills, many of them went on to work offshore in the oilfields."

I glanced sharply at Paul. Offshore? He was losing it, but still he motored on.

"Welding, bricklaying, joinery, all of this training we can arrange for you." He let out a short laugh. "In Yorkshire we even had a training course for ballroom dancing instructors."

I coughed, spearing Sasha for his attention. He glanced at me with an imperceptible nod; he knew not to translate this.

While Paul rambled on, into the realms of loans and equity participation for entrepreneurs, I thought how Kevin Reed would have done this so much better. He would have spent this first session showing real understanding for their lives, he would have tailored his words sensitively, he would already have done his research on the possibilities for re-employment in Donetsk. He would have given them hope.

Gradually, the miners began shunting their chairs back. It was a gentle and quiet operation, and those I'd met in the forest had the good grace to smile wanly at me as they left the room. Even the belligerent Dmitry. The only hint of disrespect was a soft belch or two as the men filed past us.

And it's strange, but I do remember feeling cross with them for walking out – such a callow word cross and it fitted me well back then. Of course, I was mostly cross with Paul for being so useless. I had stuck my neck out to secure this pilot project in Donetsk and it was not being welcomed. I'd battled to convince Bogdan, who had asked me why I was creating more work for myself, why I didn't just focus on the mainstay of the programme in Kiev, which in itself was vast. But, after all that, these men were not even trying to grasp the extent of all that I was doing for them – they were just not being grateful. But then, do you have to be grateful for something you never requested?

Out in the corridor, Paul shoved Svetlana aside. "Let me through!" he barked, and marched out into the yard, smacking the door back as he went.

I stared after him, shocked at such aggression, but Svetlana's expression was mild, as if she'd been expecting this. Paul's veneer of charm had slid off him, had clattered to the floor. I could see then what Svetlana had sussed, that it had all been an act. He had no real empathy for these men. No respect even. This behaviour is common in the world of overseas aid, I would say rampant even. Men and women who jolly the natives, pandering to them, while secretly believing them to be inferior. All of that was exposed in Paul as he was sucked out of his comfort zone. He'd scurried over their lives, teased out their weaknesses, content to offer his largesse, so long as he avoided exposing his own fallibility. But the moment he felt cornered, his true feelings for them were out. I've met many more like him over the years, but Paul was my first experience of this.

With an impressive skid-start to mark his own annoyance, Sasha drove us away from the mine.

"Well that went well." Paul's voice beside him was hollow. In the back, Svetlana, Niamh and I were solidly silent. He persisted. "You could have told me the men didn't know about the closure."

I gritted my teeth, twitching to snap that he should have done his own research over lunch instead of feigning sycophancy with the mine manager. But there were five of us in that small car and I was learning to

112

save it for later.

Svetlana spoke up. "Of course they have been told the mine will close, but Oleg does not believe it will happen. We cannot imagine our lives without it."

In the hush that followed, I sensed her words filtering through each one of us.

"And have the miners really not been paid this month, Svetlana?" I asked her finally.

She shook her head. "Not last month either."

At that we all fell silent for the drive back to the village, lulled by the squeak of the windscreen wipers which were struggling to cope with the sleet now falling outside.

Once we reached the village, Svetlana directed Sasha to the hall where we were to meet the women. I felt small and stupid at having initiated something far too big to handle, and wondered if I should abandon the Job Shop idea. Especially if Paul Hopkins was in charge of developing it. I glanced at the hair on the back of his head, all mousy and lank, and I bristled.

We pulled up at a ramshackle wooden building with smoke drifting from its chimney. We all appeared to be in some trepidation. Niamh was drained of colour and I squeezed her arm for reassurance.

"Don't worry, these women are amazing, this will be much easier."

"This is meeting place for the whole village," Svetlana explained. "Here, we meet for dancing, our children have kindergarten, our youth play sports. And this hall belongs to the mine, so if the mine closes, we do not know what will happen to it."

Inside, there must have been eighty women milling round. It seemed that half the village had turned out. I was relieved to feel the heat being churned out by a coal-fired stove against the wall. Shivering at meetings was becoming embarrassing for me, especially as my hosts always seemed so comfortable with the cold. My Divas – Olga, Lesya, Tanya, Yelena and Marina, came to greet me with a kiss to the cheek, but I held each of them to me, wanting to convey my empathy for the unpaid wages. And they each went with it, rocking me back to my own rhythm.

Svetlana's mother, her blue dress with pink roses now teamed with a heavy dull cardigan and wellington boots, took me in a bear hug and rattled on in Russian. She hushed a finger to her lips and Svetlana whispered that it was kindergarten nap time. Peeking into a darkened side room, I saw a dozen or so small children sprawled on mats on the floor, with blankets thrown loosely over them. In their slumber they looked so at peace, so oblivious to the harsh life their country had dealt them by sheer fluke of birth.

At the other end of the hall, the women were fussing over a gleaming brass samovar and plates laden with Marina's cakes. I winked at her, and remembered then my gifts. With a flourish, I pulled out bags of shampoo and toothpaste, all brought from England to distribute to the villagers, and I held them up to the room. But Svetlana quietly took them from me and pushed them under the table, denying me the chance to show them off – to my dismay, I'll admit that now.

Soon the women were settled in their seats and Svetlana opened the meeting, first in Russian then repeating herself in English.

"Women of our village have hard lives, especially now as wages are not paid. But we are strong women and we fight to survive, to make lives better for our men and for our children."

Many women were nodding, others sat with their chins lifted in proud Soviet rapture to her words; clearly Svetlana commanded respect here.

"Our fight to survive has given us many skills," she continued. "We have good ideas and we create new possibilities for our village. Today we have opportunity to borrow money, so we can earn money. Niamh is an expert from the Levshenko programme and she will tell us about it."

Niamh, who had been standing behind Svetlana, appraising her with clear appreciation as the girl worked the room, stepped forward.

"Zdraztvuite." Hello, she said, and some of the older women threw their hands up in delight, as if she'd proved herself fluent in their language.

"I'm here to tell you about the Levshenko Micro-credit Scheme for your village. Micro-credit schemes for women first began in Bangladesh and India."

Tanya, the mine manager's wife who kept chickens, called out something, and Svetlana translated. "In former Ukraine, we used to give overseas aid to India, just like you give aid to us now."

"I know that." Niamh nodded, her eyes locked with the woman in respectful acknowledgement. "And I am also aware that Ukrainian women are among the most educated in the world."

I glanced around at the emphatic nods among young and old, the young for the most part attractive and svelte, while the older peasant women had become almost tubular with age, their skin gnarled. At what point did this transformation happen? I wondered.

"Micro-credit provides small loans for women with a good business idea." Niamh said, and then she paused for effect. Later she told me she'd read that 'business' was still a dirty word in Ukraine, still one of life's lower pursuits.

"And when I say business," she continued, "I mean finding ways to feed your families, to live a better life. I mean you Olga, with your wonderful talent for making clothes." Olga's ruddy face reddened further. "I mean you Lesya. Everybody feels good after a haircut, I know you could help me out."

Niamh ruffled her untamed pile of hair, to the clear delight of these women.

"And Marina, you have a real gift too. I have my eye on that cake over there, the one with the pink icing."

The women chuckled again, while Svetlana's mother stood to clock the cake in question and link it to Niamh's possession with the arc of a finger. I observed this highly professional Irishwoman in operation, choosing simple but powerful words, speaking slowly, and all the while maintaining eye contact, and I wondered if I'd ever get there myself. She'd won them over in five minutes; mesmerised them. And then she got down to the detail.

"Small sums of money, which could be just £2 but could also be higher. We have set a limit on your Levshenko scheme of £20 per loan, or $30 if you prefer."

There were sharp intakes of breath; that would buy a month's worth of food in Ukraine back then. Niamh raised her palms, pressing the air for calm.

"However, this would be exceptional. You may use the cash to buy new stock or supplies for your small business, for example jars for preserves." She nodded at Yelena. "Or you may choose to invest in new tools – scissors, for example, or a sewing machine." Lesya and Olga hunched shoulders at each other.

"Now, you don't have to provide collateral on these loans. By that I mean that you do not need to risk a sum of money at the start, or even give up something precious, like a ring for example, which we would confiscate if you fail to repay the loan."

Niamh waited for the room to absorb this. She'd already explained the notion at length to Svetlana, who appeared to be translating effectively.

"Your collective responsibility will be the collateral. That means, if one of you does not pay back the loan then the others in the group will have to pay it for you."

She fell silent, waiting for the women's reaction. I observed the cautious glances from woman to woman and I wondered how strictly we would enforce this rule. Several eyes did seem to flash instinctively at Olga, but she sat facing the front, head held high, probably already calculating how much she would borrow for new reams of fabric.

Niamh went on. "Svetlana will be in charge of the scheme and each of you must pay a little interest on the loan every week. We will set this at a simple 10%. So if you borrow £10 from the scheme, you must pay back a total of £11. Is that clear?"

After a lengthy translation it was evident that these women knew their maths, if not their free market economy.

"Finally, I should stress that these schemes work best with a small circle of women, because you need to know and trust each other well. I would suggest that you begin with ten of you women here today. We can chat more about that over tea and cakes."

Niamh wound up just as the children were waking. They joined us for our refreshments, running in and out of legs, while their mothers thronged around Niamh, respectful to each other as they waited to put their own questions. What was the penalty if they did not repay a little of the money each week? That was for them to decide with Svetlana, Niamh replied. Where would the cash be held? With Vanessa in Kiev, and regular amounts would be sent down via Svetlana. Could the loan be used for chickens? Yes, any livestock that could make them money and would benefit the village could be appropriate. Who would choose the women? They would start with those already operating some sort of business, which would include my Divas. And, finally, how much would the scheme have in total?

And that was my cue. The bountiful Vanessa Parker, who was able to stand and smile with munificence at her flock, wait until all eyes were upon her, and announce that the total available to the scheme over the next three years would be a breathtaking £2000. The ensuing gasps and hugs, and even kisses to my hand, swept me in a tsunami of adulation. What had Dan said that day in the park? That you're in this game either to save yourself, or for the power.

15

"Doesn't seem to have gone so badly, looking back on the day," Paul said later, as we settled down into the familiar Western surroundings of the Irish bar back in Kiev. He took a long draft of his Guinness, wiping the froth from his moustache with the back of his hand and letting out a childlike snap of satisfaction.

"Paul, you were crap," I said. Odd, because I'd prepared something biting and pithy, but his arrogance dashed whatever that might have been from my mind.

"Bit harsh Vanessa. Look love, I know my stuff, I've built a damn good reputation in Poland."

"That's just it, isn't it? You came here with Poland in mind, you didn't try and get your head round these people. Ukraine is completely different."

He shrugged. "Don't see how, really. Anyway, first sesh is always tricky, they'll come round."

"Come round?"

Niamh, who was licking a roll-up cigarette she'd put together, went boss-eyed at me in support. Behind her head, I saw Dan enter the bar and I paused, savouring the way he scanned the room in search of me. He slapped high-fives on several of the other Americans as he made his way over.

"Hey." He slid in beside me with a kiss which smacked the air.

In mischievous mode then, I thought, as I introduced him to Paul and Niamh. I'd called him from the airport to brief him on our day.

"Hey guys, you want something more to drink?" He gestured to the waiter. "So how did it go down there, today? I heard you took on the coal miners, Paul?"

Straight in there too. Paul glanced at me, but Dan thrust his chin up and the Yorkshireman rose to the challenge.

"It was a shit-hole. Rats running round yard, the lot."

I clenched my fists beneath the table. Imagine having to live there. Imagine never being able to leave that place the way you and I are free to. Then Dan nudged my knee with his, a silent signal, and my anger uncoiled itself.

"Dan, could you explain to Paul why Ukraine is not Poland? Why he can't just pull out a one-size-fits-all jobbie over here?"

Dan began throwing peanuts into his mouth. "Sure. First off, in Poland they already had notions of commerce, so the Poles are better placed to pick themselves up if they lose their livelihoods. Number two, foreign business was tripping over itself to invest in Poland when it opened up, including in the coal regions. Three, Poland is gearing up for EU accession, which lends it security, stability and a rosy future."

Dan tossed a peanut in the air, caught it in his open jaw and snapped his mouth shut. I caught Niamh smirking, her roll-up tight between two elegantly pointed fingers, while Paul gave Dan a sneer of a smile; an instant hatred for my lover then. But Dan wasn't finished with him.

"This your first visit?"

"Yeah."

"Well, right now, it seems that Ukraine can teach you more than you can teach it, Paul. You need to understand the impoverishment of this country, the misery of daily existence for these people from the moment they wake in their unheated homes to the moment they go to bed, maybe sleeping four to a room. If they're lucky they may board a tram and travel for an hour or two to a factory for some hazardous labour until it gets dark, and then join a line somewhere in the bitter cold to feed themselves. If they're unlucky they'll be wallowing at home on unpaid leave, scratching round for that last karbovanet note, wondering if they may ever see a wage again, hoping the spring greens come up, that the preserves will hold out until they do. If they're lucky they may live past sixty, a little longer even, if they're female. And if they're unlucky they'll end up in a hospital, where there will be no drugs or anaesthetics and risk pot luck on the equipment being sterilised."

Dan took a dramatic breath, sat back and toyed with his Guinness. In the hush that followed, we all gazed at him; I had never heard such an emotional outpouring from him before. I felt the hairs rise on the back of my hands, a claw-like pattering up my spine and, when his hand reached for mine under the table, I grasped it. This extraordinary man, he wasn't

118

jaded at all.

Finally Niamh let out a doleful sigh, seemingly at the enormity of it, which broke our silence. It also triggered Paul off into a High Noon posture.

"So why are you here, Mr Yankee? When you're such a glass half empty kind of guy?"

Dan shrugged. "US business is investing in Donetsk. Big time, as a matter of fact, in the likes of steel, agriculture, consumer goods. And they're going to need good workers, solid and reliable workers, like coal miners, for example. Plus, the Government is about to declare Donetsk a Special Economic Zone, with privileges for all who invest in her. Could have given them some positives down there today, Paul."

Dan seemed out of steam then and sank the rest of his pint. Paul considered me, his mouth bunched up, eyes glittering.

"Doubt I'll be going back down there, anyhow. Enough for me to be doing up here on the Small Business Agency."

"You're working on that too?" My heart sank.

"Yup."

I mulled this news over. To oust him from the Job Shop in Donetsk would be a result of one kind, but then Viktor needed a decent expert to help set up his Business Agency in Kiev too, so we'd just be shifting the problem. Somehow I would have to find a way to get Paul turfed off the programme completely.

That night, Dan and I lay on our backs listening to the Opera House turning out at the front of our apartment. I could visualise the swathes of booted, fur-encased people descending the broad steps that encircled the building, sinking into the fresh snow, which must by then have been ankle deep.

"Thanks for what you did tonight," I said. "Felt like cavalry to the rescue."

"All part of the service." Dan paused. "You know he'll stick it out though, don't you?"

I nodded. "Too lucrative."

"Ukraine is awash with aid, ergo it's awash with gooks like him."

"He should be ashamed of himself, though. He's arrogant, he's a fake."

Dan slid his hand onto mine and squeezed it. "It's a gravy train, Ness. Everything's moving so fast out here, and everyone wants a piece of the action, even though none of us really understand what's going on. How many Westerners even stepped foot in Ukraine when it was still a part of

119

the Soviet Union?"

"Well, I'm definitely going to try and get him thrown off the programme."

"You'd be wasting your time. Just have to make the best of it. Once firms like your Lancashire have won the contract, they behave exactly as they wish. The deal's done. You and I have little control over the quality of these programmes."

"But my programme has concrete goals. It's going to train twenty women to run Job Centres. That's tangible. I won't pay their invoice if they don't deliver."

Dan shrugged. "So you've set yourself some dinky pointers."

"They're not dinky, they—"

"Look, everything these people have ever known is changing around them, every last thing. And we're here to ease them through that change, aren't we? Think about it. It's colossal. It's not simply a case of ticking a box to prove that you've trained up twenty women."

I glared at him. "Why do we bother setting goals at all then? Why even bother being here? I've managed programmes like this in the UK, they can work, they do work!"

"Ah now you're sounding like Paul the Pole aren't you, kiddo? Ukraine is not the UK."

"Don't kiddo me."

If there is a flipping over and flouncing of bedclothes equivalent to slamming a door, then that is what I did that night. I lay with my heart pounding, thinking Dan had to be wrong, knowing he was probably right. Above all, feeling stupid that I hadn't managed to come up with a decent retort. And how could our complicity have transformed so seamlessly into a quarrel?

I could feel his thigh against my back, the solidity of him. He seemed to be pressing it in as an apology. The longer I stayed rigid and unforgiving, the more I could feel the tug of him, the sexual and emotional tug of him. It reached inside me, dragged me back to him. But still, after every silly argument like this I always wondered how to turn back over.

Outside, the laughter at the Opera House was slow to fade, even though it was below minus out there. It might as well have been a summer's evening, the way these people lingered, extracting every last drop of pleasure from their night out. A cry went out in the street, an American voice. "Ah, you got me!" It was followed by shouting in Russian or Ukrainian; clearly a snowball fight had started between complete strangers. As it developed, more people seemed to be joining in, their cries lusty, their laughs from the belly, and I let out a snigger myself to hear them. The human exchanges between East and West.

"That's what it's about," Dan said softly in the darkness.

"Yeah." I had found the reason to flip back over to him. I loved this man too much for my anger to linger.

The following morning I called Jeff and announced that I would join them later at the Small Business Development Agency, my intention being to try and catch Paul out somehow. Then I sat down and phoned Carole.

"Hi Ness," she trilled. "How was it with tut miners at tut pit?"

"Niamh was impressive. But I want Paul off the project, Carole, he was the most extraordinary waste of space, utterly and completely useless."

The phone connection to her office was poor, so that that my words reverberated and my melodrama bounced back at me with a hollow, pathetic echo – extraordinary waste … utterly useless …

"Paul? I can't believe it Ness, he's such a lovely guy." I heard the fun leave Carole's voice.

"Yes, but he's crap, did you not hear me? He thinks he's in Poland."

He thinks he's in Poland. The childish echo sounded nothing like my voice.

"Yes, well he's got heaps of expertise from Poland, that's why we put him in the bid, he's one of the most experienced experts on the programme, Ness."

I took a deep breath. "Don't give me that smooth talk Carole, we used to work together remember? I've seen you schmooze 'em from the other side of the fence."

"You've got your knickers in a right twist over this haven't you?" Her voice was haughty now. "I mean, he's in the contract, to provide a total input of six man months, if my memory serves me rightly. And you did sign off on that contract. You can't insist that we keep chopping and changing, Ness, just like you can't make us force someone to do this job if he doesn't want to. Like your mate Kevin Reed, for example."

The moment she mentioned Kevin, I realised she was hiding something from me – like the killer who glances to the dead body under the floorboards.

"I've just spoken to Kevin actually," I lied.

"Oh have you now?"

"Yes, and he says he hasn't deserted the programme, that you never even approached him about this contract."

My accusation hung in the air between us before Carole let out a sigh. "OK I might have told you a teensy weensy fib there. Look if truth be known, Kevin's more pricey than Paul, way more pricey."

"So you put his CV in the bid just to win the contract? Without ever seeking his agreement? Without ever intending to use him?"

"Look, he costs us £600 a day and we can't charge you more than £700 per man day, so we wouldn't have made our twenty percent on him."

"Sod your twenty percent, what about the programme? Remember? That thing you're being paid three million quid to deliver?"

"But Ness, I'm between a rock and a hard place here, can't you understand that? And I really want to keep this promotion."

"You lied to me."

I was shaking, partly in fury and partly in dismay at a friendship splintering. The stupid echo came at me, you lied to me. In the ensuing silence I thought our connection had been lost, but then she said, "Get real Ness." And she hung up.

Without dwelling on the call, I headed straight over to our programme HQ. The building stood stiff against the frozen day, the sunshine window bars half hidden behind the snow heaped on the sills.

Beside the door a new brass plaque had been fitted:

LEVSHENKO PROGRAMME

Small Business Development Agency

Model Job Centre

An old weasel of a man now sat in the porter's lodge; our security for the raft of PCs and furniture that had just been delivered to the programme. I decided first to put my head in at the Job Centre, holding my breath in bursts against the sickly tobacco stench as I took the stairs.

I slid into the room and stood silently surveying the scene. The hall was still largely empty, no PCs or office equipment, but Bobsteve were taking a training session with the Graces and, as my arrival seemed to have gone unnoticed, I observed them performing a role-play. Clearly they were learning how to receive the unemployed. One of the women sat behind a desk in a woolly polo-neck and I stifled a snigger as Bob or Steve shuffled up to her, looking down-trodden and very much jobless. He suggested she open her folded arms into a more welcome embrace, so she held them out with a warm, biblical greeting.

"Remember your active listening skills," Bobsteve said. "Eye contact, lots of nods. Show me you're engaged, that you really care about me."

Bloody hell, I thought to myself and made to leave, my scuffle with the heavy door causing them all to look over at me then.

"Sorry," I shouted with a wave, "didn't mean to disturb. I thought the PCs and stuff had arrived, by the way?"

"All downstairs," Bobsteve said with a godly smile. "We would like our share though."

"Ah. OK I'll try and sort it." I left the hall.

In the Small Business Agency, Viktor stood with his back to me, gazing out of the far window and snapping into his mobile. Several shards of his silver hair were sticking out at angles to his head, so congealed was it that day. The scuffed white shoes, I noticed, had given way to shiny black leather brogues. He spoke in what sounded like angry, insistent snatches, tones that would sting an English person, but by then I knew that this was simply the Ukrainian way. Lining the length of the room there were now two rows of smart wooden desks – clearly not sourced in Ukraine – each of them topped with a PC, a phone and a printer. By the door stood a fax and a photocopier, both machines much more advanced than anything I'd ever seen in an office back in 1994.

As I crossed the floor, its parquet reeking of polish, Viktor turned to wave with a hunch of his shoulders. I sat down at a PC and turned it on, whistling at the coloured frame with its neat icons. My own screen was black with a flashing green dash for a cursor.

Viktor hung up and strode over to me, clapping his hands. "Ha! I am so happy with equipment Vanessa." He took my hand and kissed it.

"I bet you are Viktor, this is state of the art."

"State of the art." He tried out the words for effect, then he sank into an office chair and clapped his hands on his knees like an excited child. "Today we begin with technical assistance, yes? With transfer of know-how?"

"Yes." I looked at my watch, it was gone noon. "They should be here soon."

The door opened and Jeff pushed his way through, cigarette in hand, cackling at some joke he was sharing with Paul behind him.

"Vanessa, you're here already?"

"Early bird catches the worm, Jeff."

He ignored my loaded reference. "I do apologise. Paul wanted to buy CDs at the market, and I thought he deserved some fun. Because I hear it was extremely full-on yesterday?"

Beside him Viktor had stood to attention.

"Viktor, meet your new guru, Mr Paul Hopkins. What he doesn't know about small business ain't worth knowing."

Huh, I thought, from expert in mine closure to expert in small business with a flick of the wand. But Viktor took Paul's hand with both of his and shook it vigorously.

"All problems will be solved," he shouted, laughing.

"We'll certainly see what we can do, Viktor." Paul's fake charm had been topped back up to full.

"So, how we start?" Viktor led us to the meeting table at the far end of the room.

Paul settled himself in, holding the pause, clearly basking in the authority he commanded here. "Well, Viktor, I think we need to start with a comprehensive study of the constraints to small businesses in your country."

Viktor, who had been eagerly awaiting nuggets from his new guru, visibly crumpled, some broken capillaries springing up red against the grey pallor of his cheeks. But still his voice was conciliatory, sycophantic even.

"But we all know constraints Paul." He began ticking them off with his fingers. "Heavy bureaucracy, high taxes, impossible interest rates at banks …"

"Yes, but Viktor I'd like to have them in writing, lends more weight to things." Paul spread his fingers on the table for added gravitas.

"But we will use up precious time, we have that already." Viktor looked to me for help and attempted a chuckle that came out more like a whimper. "We need concrete actions. How we sell our goods … how we do marketing … how we do business planning."

"He's right," I said, "you don't need to waste half your time on research Paul, USAID have just published the exact study you need."

I pulled the report out of my briefcase and slapped it down. Dan, with his usual prescience, had given it to me that morning.

"Ha!" said Viktor. "Excellent. So we can start on real work. I have business advisers ready to start at every one of desks. I have advert in newspaper, we can welcome all entrepreneurs who want to start own business. You show us how we do it Paul. Please, my friend."

Again the humility, again his head cocked to the side. But then Viktor stood abruptly to take a call at his window, his back turned to us – clearly some of the respect for his guru had already waned. Jeff, always one to avoid conflict, also stood to make a call and wandered off down the room, flicking ash into a pot plant as he went. Paul threw me a cold stare as he

124

took the USAID report and flicked through it.

"This is from last year," he muttered.

"Yeah, and how fast do you think things change out here?" I snapped. "Rather do desk work than get your hands dirty with real people, would you?"

Paul contemplated me for a long moment. "You know, you're much too cynical for your tender age."

And I decided to take that as a compliment.

16

It was a few days later, early in December, that I drove with Dan to Chernobyl, for a meeting on one of his own aid programmes. We set off well before dawn, my head lulling against the heated leather seats of his Jeep, a thermos of coffee and croissants at my feet.

"Wear old boots," Dan had advised, though he hadn't said why.

Incredibly, in 1994, eight years after the accident which had blown the top off the infamous fourth reactor, Chernobyl was still operational, with two of its other reactors continuing to provide power to the national grid. The Ukrainian Government had agreed to shut the plant down by the year 2000 insisting, however, that the countries of the G7 finance the costs of closure. It was alongside this commitment that USAID was running a programme to cushion the social impact of closure – both on Chernobyl's thousands of workers, who would lose their jobs, and also on the new town built to house them after the disaster.

Dan had designed this aid programme himself and, while its daily supervision was well below his pay grade, he maintained a strategic eye, as he explained during our seventy mile drive north.

"For the G7, it's about making sure the closure happens safely," he said. "This workforce is highly qualified, they earn good wages, they're part of the elite. It's going to be crucial to keep up their morale, to offer them something for when Chernobyl is gone."

"Do people think they might sabotage the plant, or something, then?"

Dan turned down the corners of his mouth. "Nah, not really, just that the accident was actually caused by human error. We've gotta keep an eye on the psychological state of these people while the closure's underway."

"Ah." I gazed out of the window at the plumes of grime on the outskirts of Kiev, visible even in the dark. "Is that your sole motivation too? Safe closure?"

He grinned at me and reached across to tweak my knee. "I'm more in the Vanessa Parker camp than you give me credit for. Far as I'm concerned I want to make sure those workers are not hung out to dry after closure. But six thousand souls is a mere sprinkling of humanity in G7 terms."

His response sent a further drift of warmth through my body and I sank back into the seat smiling quietly to myself.

"So what can you do for them?" I asked him.

"Well, for starters, the closure programme will bring hefty contracts for the West. It's you Europeans and we Yanks who will get paid the squillions needed to decommission the plant, but the firms involved are going to need a local workforce too." He turned to me. "For logistics, waste management, that kind of stuff. And I need to ensure that the good folk of Chernobyl get first dibs on those contracts."

"And after that?"

"After that, well, the new town might not survive without Chernobyl either. That's thirty thousand people in total."

"What's it called?"

"Slavutich."

"After the beer?"

"Town came first, I guess, honoured later by the beer – lest we should forget, even in our most abandoned moments."

Dan smiled as he turned off the dual carriageway. Soon we were cutting along country roads through birch forest, the trees lining our path standing erect in the darkness.

He went on. "Anyways, Slavutich could be seen as a microcosm of what's happening across the whole of Ukraine, if you like – collapse of the enterprise, hence potential collapse of the community. Chernobyl has a paternal role, just like any other state enterprise here, it doesn't simply produce nuclear power, it provides for its workers too, foots the bill for everything in the town: housing, schools, the sports arena, even the theatre." He eyed me, waiting for me to absorb this. "Same story as your Donetsk really. Without Chernobyl, Slavutich will have to diversify its economic base."

"Have you got new business development going on there too, then?"

"Yep. Nuclear physics has its many applications, don't you know, semiconductors, medical imaging, or carbon dating to name but a few. But it's a time-consuming and tricky process when you're nurturing individual livelihoods."

"To which you are dedicated, Dan Mitchell, the self-confessed but not so ardent cynic." I rested my hand on his thigh with a smug grin, feeling closer to him than ever.

An hour or so into our journey, we reached the boundary of the twenty mile exclusion zone. I looked into the vast nothing beyond the check point; the road ahead was spookily unlit, though our headlights swept over the deep snow – no ploughs had ever have bothered going in there.

"The dead zone, they call it," Dan said as we passed the barrier. "Contaminated and dangerous. Still, they say there are old biddies who refused to leave after the evacuation back in '86. What was it one old guy said? He'd rather die at home of radiation sickness than die elsewhere of homesickness."

I smiled ruefully at the thought of an old man, standing outside a home that probably resembled Svetlana's cottage, scattering corn to the chickens from an enamel basin. Peering out of the car window into the blackness, I imagined I might see him there in the far distance, that I might make out a speck of yellow light at his window. Then Dan braked sharply, skidding a little and bringing me out of my reverie.

"Look," he said, "wild boar ahead on the road."

In the dipped beam of the headlights, I could make out a line of three or four crossing our path, their steps jittery, their snouts down as they scuttled for the hedgerow.

"You also find elk here, deer and foxes too, of course, even wolves. Undisturbed by man for nearly ten years now."

We fell into a lull. Dan kept up a leisurely speed, with the odd slither of tyre on snow, creating a peculiar but rather comforting sensation inside the Jeep. Gradually, the wan light of dawn began to creep upon our solitary journey and the fields beside us took on dim shapes. When the sky and snow each emerged from the night into the palest of blues, Dan pulled over and switched off the engine. We glanced at each other and climbed out of the Jeep, our wellingtons sinking into the snow, and we met at the bonnet, where we leant back against the warmth of the engine. The sun began to leach then, washing the deep snow at the extremities of the fields with a light pink, its glow nudging above the horizon, sweeping back the pink and turning the fields to gold. Bewitched by the scene, Dan and I shared a secretive glance. The hush was such that I strained to hear it, as if my ear was forced by the absence of sound to produce a muffled silence, and I held my breath against the stillness, feeling the blood pulsing at my neck.

We stood for a long time absorbing the landscape, respectful, not daring to move. In places, the snow must have been waist deep, while closer to us I could make out the cleft prints of deer.

"Look." With barely a whisper, Dan broke our silence. "Don't move a muscle. Three o'clock."

My eyes found the cat easily in the far corner of the field by the clumps of hedgerow, and I drew a startled breath at its size, thinking it at first to be a small leopard. My heart began to thump and I could feel myself hyperventilating.

"What is it?" I flustered.

"Lynx."

At the sound of our voices, the lynx stopped dead and swung its head, the alarm in its eyes spearing us to the spot. Padded with a hefty grey-beige pelt, its stature was that of an Alsatian dog, but the face was distinctly feline, the whiskers long, the ears curled at the tips. It continued to regard us for a few haughty moments before taking a leap towards the bushes, its paws springing from the deep snow, each one the size of a fur boot.

"Jeez." Dan let out a soft whistle as it disappeared from sight. "That's a first."

"Incredible." I found I was shaking.

We stood rooted to the car bonnet for a further hour or so that morning, holding hands in silent companionship, hoping for one more sighting, but we spotted only deer and rabbit. Finally, we returned to the Jeep in tacit conferral that our human coffee and croissants should not mar the pristine scene.

Chernobyl looked to me like any other factory, an innocuous chimney with barbershop stripes standing between a series of production sheds. As we made our way over to the administration block, however, Dan pointed out the sarcophagus which had been constructed over the burnt-out reactor to contain the radiation. We stopped and studied the shell, a black mass of steel and concrete, which they said had been too hastily built and was, in fact, leaking radiation into the air.

"The accident happened during a planned shutdown," Dan said, as I eyed the block, wondering if it was safe to be this close. "Matter of fact, they were conducting an experiment, monitoring the performance of the turbine generators, and the reactor was barely ticking over. But when the reactor was operating at such low power, it was inherently unstable, and it relied on human intervention to keep it steady, to keep it safe. The technicians were simply careless, didn't observe the safety precautions."

"And?"

"And, there was a sudden monumental power surge, which destroyed the core of the reactor and blew the roof off, blasting radioactive debris several hundred yards into the sky and for half a mile around." Dan glanced at me. "They didn't evacuate the neighbouring town, Pripyat, for a whole thirty-six hours. People didn't know, kids at school, mothers in the parks."

"Oh no, surely not?" I couldn't take my eyes from the sarcophagus. "I can remember that day, the helicopters on the telly."

"Yeah, they lived for all of one day. You'll see the pictures inside, come on."

At the entrance to the office block we were invited to step through an archway detector, as if at airport security. The Geiger Counter took no issue with us in the shape of a bleep, but then it may well have been on silent mode and in fact the official behind the desk was aware of a flick of its needle – we must surely have picked up some radioactive dust on our stroll from car to building. We were greeted warmly by a tall thin man with a beard, Dan's counterpart on the programme, who led us into a meeting room. A Director of the power plant, his voice was weak – scratchy is how I would put it – and he cleared his throat often. I suspected from what I'd read that it might be thyroid cancer. Other men entered the room dressed in a uniform of white overalls and round baker's hats.

While Dan discussed progress on the project with the men in Russian, I studied the display of photographs on the walls, whose captions were in English. There were the helicopters flying overhead, dropping lead, sand and clay, it said, into the gaping maw. Beside them, photos of the dead heroes who flew the mission, all of them in their thirties, I noted, barely older than me. An image of the so-called 'golden corridor' caught my eye, with the four nuclear reactors lining one side and the operations rooms for each of them on the other. I bristled; the walls and floor of the golden corridor were the same yellow pine as the room where I now stood, which meant we were only footsteps away from the stricken fourth reactor. Its brooding presence sent a chill up my back and I hurried on to the next photo.

Some way along the wall was a shot of the operations room for the third reactor, which was still producing nuclear power. With its sweeping bank of knobs and lights, it resembled the Starship Enterprise. Alongside it was a shot of an identical operations room, but that one was burnt out, the counters melted and twisted. I gazed into the blackened mess and for a moment I could imagine the lights frantically red, the claxons bawling at the men as they desperately grabbed at the knobs and switches. The explanatory caption said that the technicians on duty that night had been immediately sent to prison – where they had died some days later.

By the time I had circled the meeting room, I was thoroughly shaken, and almost relieved to come across the pictures of the neighbouring town, Pripyat, on the final wall. Shots of dolls and books scattered on the floor of a schoolroom bore witness to the speed of its tardy evacuation, when finally the alarm had been raised. An armchair stood by a doorway, the plaster peeling off the blue walls captivating me, luring me to reach in and stroke the fabulous duck-egg texture, to pick off the curled sheets of paint. Then my guilt at the thought of indulging in the scene kicked in and I glanced away. But it was the final image that for me was the most arresting. So much so, that I didn't feel Dan come up behind me and study it over my shoulder. It was a photograph of a giant Ferris wheel, its seats like pastel cupcakes, each of them still suspended neatly from the wheel. The note below the photo read – The fairground had been due to open on 1 May 1986, five days after the disaster, but was never used.

"Do you want to go see?"

I jumped at Dan's words. "Are we allowed to?"

"My Director buddy can take us in there."

'In there' was the correct term for Pripyat. A little more than a mile away from Chernobyl, we drove past the road sign with its chilling radioactive symbol, and on into the ghost town. The silence that engulfed us seemed to be heightened by the thick snow that covered every surface. We passed apartment blocks abandoned in haste, the odd window dangling off its hinges, tree branches growing at an angle from some of the rooms. At the side of the roads sat the wrecks of cars and vans, tyres looted, their windows glassless, while spidery plants threaded their way up through the engine or the cab. There was no movement, not a single sound.

I sat in the front beside the Director, my throat dry with the shock of this place. A garage door suddenly swung open in the breeze, the clank of iron making me jump and spear it with my eyes, half expecting a zombie to reel out. The Director stopped the car for a moment, as if he were operating a ghost train and gleefully waiting for the ghoul to swoop down on me, but the door clanged shut again and he slid back into gear. He continued to drive us around the grid system of flats and office buildings, turning at a corner into the abyss of another street, trundling to its end, turning again into another. The place was completely deserted, not another human, not another beast, although the snow was peppered by a variety of animal prints.

"As if it's post-holocaust," I whispered.

"Right on." Dan's voice from the back seat held a hint of sarcasm.

Before us then loomed the Ferris wheel in the fairground and, as we drove right up to it, I gripped my seat, feeling that it might swoop down onto us. Dodgem cars sat in some random pattern, as if they had actually in fact enjoyed their inauguration on that day in May, as if now still in the dead of night they came alive and whirled around through the trees that had sprouted up between them.

"Can we go now, please?" I asked.

Beside me the Director let out a short laugh. "Few peoples wish to stay long here," he said. His first croaky words to me in English.

As we left the nuclear power plant behind that afternoon, Dan clasped the Director to him in a bear hug. "We'll get this Goddamm place closed down." His eyes were moist as he drew back and pumped the man's hand.

In the Jeep, he confirmed to me that it was thyroid cancer. "He's on a mission to get Chernobyl shut down before he succumbs to his early death," he said.

"Can we do anything to help him?"

Dan gave an imperceptible shake of his head. I drew a deep breath and blew the air out in one heavy sad lungful, resting my hand on his thigh in comfort. We drove on in silence, each of us lost in our own thoughts as we entered the exclusion zone. Our tyres sped over the road, covered with virgin snow; no other vehicle had bothered with the trip up from Kiev that day, and all the people we'd met at the plant now lived in the new town of Slavutich. When we reached the spot where we'd seen our lynx, Dan stopped the car and switched off the engine. We sat in silence waiting and watching, as the sun began to set. Gradually, the sky was washed with a pale blue and then with indigo, and finally the blackness overcame them both. After a glance at me, Dan started the engine and we drove on home. When we reached Kiev, he disposed of our boots.

17

The following weekend, Dan took me to the American Christmas party. This was held jointly by the World Bank, IMF and USAID, in the sumptuous ballroom of the Prince Volodymyr Hotel. He said he had to collect a document on the way there, and I sat beside him in my black evening dress staring out of the Jeep window at the rising moon and wondering what the night ahead held for me. It was early evening, bitter but clear, with a fresh dusting of snow which shimmered on the pavements and lampposts. We drove up towards the Lavra Monastery, climbed to its golden domes and spires, eerily luminous in the dusk, and then Dan drew up beside the World War II Memorial Park. He turned off the engine.

"What are we doing?"

"Come on kiddo, we're going to have us some fun."

Grinning at me, his hair already tumbling out of its combed semi-neatness, he swung himself out the car and tramped around to the boot. He took out a large plastic disc the colour of bubblegum and waved it at me.

"Sledging?" I threw him the most incredulous look I could muster, forehead crinkled into all its furrows. "In a long dress?"

"Nah, got that one covered." He tapped the side of his nose and reached for a plastic bag. "Jogging pants and sweats, come on." Dan was already ripping at his dicky bow, chucking his fur coat into the boot, reaching for snow boots and the warm clothes.

"Dan Mitchell, you are one crazy guy." I laughed, delighted that by association so was I, and I began to get changed myself.

When we were togged up in hats and scarves, I took his face in my hands and kissed him.

"Now there's an idea," he mused.

"You're joking, it must be minus five out here, come on let's sledge." I grasped his hand and attempted to pull off a high-kneed jog to the park entrance, my padded boots sinking to the rim in the snow.

The Memorial Park was headed up by a statue of Mother Russia, who stood in her titanium glory, gleaming nearly 100 metres above us, spookily lit in the darkening park. We scuttled over to our starting position by the trees. And we were not alone. The hill had clearly been swathed in families all afternoon, who had honed out well-ridden runways, though just a smattering of foolhardy souls remained with us in the dusk. I peered down the steep slope, the moon was barely up from behind the trees, but the snow glittered, shooting up the light we needed to take us some fifty metres below. And to me, loved up and swooning, it looked magical.

"All sprinkled with fairy dust," I murmured.

Dan threw me one of his sardonic looks, but I could tell he too was high.

"Get your pixie butt onto here, Tinkerbell," he said, slapping the glow-in-the dark tray down onto the snow.

There was barely room for me, but I made no comment as I slid down between his open legs.

"Yee-ha!" he cried, and pushed us off.

Legs in the air, with Dan's arms fast around me, I whooped and yelled with him as the sledge swept down the sheer gradient. When the slope flattened out and we came to a halt, flopping back into the snow, we shook with silent heaves of laughter.

"Again, again!" I cried.

I hoisted Dan to his feet, staggering backwards with the bulk of him, and we stabbed our toes into the hillside, slowly reaching the top of the slope again. While I waited for him to get his breath, I stood taking in the vast park; the moon was now a little higher and it was a full one, hanging pale blue against the velvet sky, while the Dniepro river stood dense and navy far below us. Closer, through the trees, I could just make out the tanks and wartime aircraft on display, now enveloped in snow.

"All wrapped up for Christmas," I muttered to myself.

"You can see why we had to come right now, can't you? Full moon and all."

I took his gloved hand in mine. Capture a moment, I thought. Here was my life. If ever you're supposed to be able to define the happiest moment of a life, I think that would have been mine, standing on a glittering moonlit hill with the man I thought I'd be with forever. Happiness – I was puffed up with the stuff.

Dan and I made many runs down that slope, and finally we were alone at the top in the dark. We too should have left, but instead we exchanged conspiratorial smiles, sat down and set off for one final go. I knew what Dan was up to even before we hit the mound of snow half way down, because we'd both seen others glide up and over it, flying off their sledges as they hit the other side. And it was me who was planted face down into the snow, with Dan flailing onto his back behind me. Helpless with laughter, I slithered across the ground on my belly and climbed onto him, shaking the snow from my hair into his face.

Finally, we got to our feet, smacked the snow from our clothes and made our way to the park gates. There, at the entrance, we passed a young woman sitting on a bench. Wrapped up in a fur coat and hat, she was reading a novel. Completely absorbed, despite the sub-zero temperature, she showed not the slightest sign of shivering.

I looked at Dan in amazement.

"Aloneness is hard to find," he said.

I guess I knew what he meant, but still, I've never forgotten that girl.

At the party, as we handed our coats in, Chelsea skittered up to us in her velvet gown and air-kissed me on both cheeks.

"Vanessa, you look radiant!"

I observed her with what I hoped was a frosty amusement – I'd been practising more mature looks in the mirror, knowing that tonight the place would be full of Dan's 'generation' as I'd ragged him.

"No I don't, we've just been sledging." I waved my bag of evening clothes at her.

Leaving Dan with the coats, I entered the ladies, where I was surprised to see a group of Ukrainians jostling around the mirrors. Mouths wide as they reapplied their vibrant lipstick, eyelashes spiked as they doused them with yet more mascara. These women spoke in the harsh tones that were still largely incomprehensible to me, even though I'd been in Kiev for several months by then. I ducked into a cubicle to change and found myself sighing morosely. Of course the local staff should be included in the office party, but I realised that I'd hoped for a night off from all that was Ukraine, for some Western immersion. I'd hoped for some respite.

Emerging from my hideout only when I'd heard the gaggle leaving, I sank onto a round vanity stool, the spit of the one my mum used to have in her bedroom, peach velvet with tassels lining the base. I gazed through the mirror, losing myself in my memories of her: standing in her pinny at the sink, clipping her foam curlers at bedtime, the smell of her face cream, her soft smile. And I wished she'd seen me happy.

The door clicked open, bringing me out of my reverie. It was Chelsea. We shot each other false smiles as she slid into a cubicle, and I turned to the mirror pulling a face then at her back. Tongue still out, I dragged fingers through the heap of messy hair and peered into my complexion – which I realised was indeed radiant. No smudges of mascara or smears of lipstick – no make-up at all back then – just a twenty-six year old face, taut and glowing from exhilaration. The youth that is wasted on the young, what would I give for that beauty now?

Back in the foyer I was surprised to bump into Sasha. He was loping from the ballroom, cigarette held expertly, his swarthy smile framed by a purple bow tie. The white linen shirt looked expensive.

"Starsky!" I cried.

"Hutch, Good evening. May I say how beautiful you look tonight."

"So do you!" I actually found myself blushing. "What are you doing here?"

"I am with my girlfriend, Lily, she works for World Bank."

"Oh I see." I laughed. "And does she buy her CDs at the black market?"

Sasha drew on his cigarette and exhaled. "Evident!" He nodded at the ballroom. "Huggy Bear is waiting for you."

"Ah, good one." I pressed a finger to the knot of his tie and moved on.

Inside the ballroom, Dan stood by the door, his own bow tie crooked. He led me to a large round table, where his colleagues made their welcoming jokes, about our tardiness, about Dan's dishevelled state. With dismay, I watched Chelsea join our table, together with several of the Ukrainian women, and held out my glass for a hefty dose of wine.

There's something about overseas aid professionals socialising in-country. Initially the effort is made to find other topics for discussion, films, or books, or family, or home, but the need to get round to their passion – the country they've been posted to – is an excruciating itch. They can suppress it for so long, but eventually they have to scratch, until the blood rises to the surface in livid streaks – sometimes even drawn, thickly and painfully. Each person around that table was a genuine expert in their own field, be it in finance, agriculture, health or the environment, and every last one of them held a point of view – you could see the PhDs tripping over each other across the table. Perhaps it was the arrival of Dan, the respected Deputy Head of USAID, that set them off that night, and they soon launched into an intense rant about the problems of Ukraine.

136

The economy was in tatters, there was no banking system, corruption was rampant, the collectivised farms would never be productive again, the health sector was bankrupt. Oh, give over just for one night, I thought, watching their need to outdo each other – the weighty words, the mid-sentence wiping of spectacles to hold the floor. I felt suddenly sorry for them. They never really seemed happy, any of them.

Fixing my smile, I tuned out and looked around the sumptuous ballroom, but was unable to escape the thuds of zeal bouncing off my head, the currents of misery dragging me down. They were all so righteous. Suddenly, I felt the makings of tears and left the table to seek sanctuary once again in a toilet cubicle, where I wept. Soft, silent tears at the hopelessness that seemed to be Ukraine – which was rum, given that two hours before I had been buoyant with joy.

When I came out of hiding, the dancing had begun. A trio, brought over especially from the States, were romping through a set of big band numbers. I sank into Dan's body; it felt good to be held by him, to be swung by him, and we danced for a long time. And then Chelsea cut in. Just appeared by our side and smiled at Dan.

"You don't mind, do you Vanessa?" Her sidelong glance was feline.

I glared at her. "No, go ahead."

But Dan was clearly annoyed by the interruption and he took her hand with little grace, still holding mine with a lingering, outstretched arm as I backed away to the side of the dance floor. And, as I held his gaze with mine, the love that zipped through my chest seemed to heap itself up behind my breastbone, a physical mass of emotion, sweet and sticky as marzipan. This man. I used to scorn the notion of one love, of one person who fuses with your soul, but that night I was so in love with Dan.

The moments were broken by Sasha, who sidled up and invited me to dance; I guess he must have felt sorry for me. We finished the slow number together, swaying gently to the melodious drifts of saxophone. Afterwards, Chelsea had the gall to swing her arm around Dan's waist and lead him back to our table, while Sasha kissed my cheek and slid his own arm around me, his palm splayed proprietarily at my waist. I grinned up at him, aware that he was mimicking the woman's cheek, and he winked at me.

"We danced that same song together last year, Dan, do you remember?" Chelsea cried, purely for my benefit, as we took our seats again. She leant over to him then, and added in a low voice, "Shame it ain't going to end the same way as last year."

When we left the hotel in the early hours I remember that the night was clear, and so completely still you could hear it. Despite the glistening road, Dan's arm was slung around me as he drove, and I was snug at his side, head lolling back against the seat. The only life we passed was the odd police car parked in a lay-by, though many apartment windows were still lit. I watched them flick by, imagining the vodka-fests behind the curtains as I idly mulled over Chelsea's words. These days I've learnt to sit on things, draft a reactive email but park it for a day's reflection, count to ten in the office before I retort. Above all, not wheedle away at a remark knowing full well that I could get hurt. But all those years ago I wanted instant gratification.

"What did Chelsea mean?" I asked.

"Chelsea?"

"When she said, shame it won't end like last year."

"Oh, that."

As he spoke, a blue light quivered through the Jeep and a siren punched me upright.

"Shit," Dan said.

I looked at him in alarm as he pulled over, wound down the window and reached across me for his papers from the dashboard; the wine on his breath was potent.

"Don't worry, I've got this one covered."

The two uniformed men approached his door, guns clinging to their hips like gremlins ready to pounce.

"Dobryi vecher," Good evening, one of them said.

Dan returned the greeting in Russian, his smile languid.

The militia spent several minutes going over his papers. At one point one of them ducked down and flashed the light at me, and I attempted what must have been a frightened smile. My mouth was dry, my thoughts already crawling round inside the KGB building. Finally the man returned the papers and he put his head to Dan's face.

"Breathe on me," he said in Russian.

Dan took a deep breath and exhaled over the policeman's face, while the man breathed in like one of the Bisto kids.

"Again," he said.

Dan expelled another lungful. Again, the man put his face to the draft of his breath and inhaled. For a few moments, he contemplated the scent of it, nostrils twitching, and then he nodded.

"Harasho," OK, he said. We could drive on.

Dan wound up the window and put the car into gear.

"That was close." My chest was thudding as he pulled away.

"Oh, wouldn't have come to much." He tweaked my knee in reassurance.

Then he let out one of his guffaws and rapped his palms against the steering wheel. "He was sniffing for vodka! That man had no notion of how wine smells, I'd bet he thought I'd been eating candy."

I shook my head in disbelief. "You really think so?"

"For sure." Dan shifted in his seat with the satisfaction of it. "Crazy country."

"Mad country."

We fell into a companionable hush, while I stared muzzily out the window, my hand on his thigh. We passed the Mariensky Park, the Parliament building, its flags lying still, and further down the hill the crescent-shaped Cabinet of Ministers, now distinctly white against the waning moon.

"So what was it Chelsea meant?" I asked him lazily.

"Oh that." He let out a chuckle, still smug at his ruse. "Last year we were intoxicated, like we are tonight I guess, and ... well we ended up in bed with one of the Ukrainian girls from her office."

It was a smack in the face. "You had a three-in-a-bed with Chelsea?"

He nodded, giggled a little. "Might even have been four."

I snatched my hand off him. "Four? Three women and you?"

"Yup." He shifted both hands up the wheel with steely concentration.

"Were you and Chelsea an item then?" It was my jealousy that kicked in first.

"Nah, just the odd one-nighter. You know how it's like."

I did. And I reasoned with myself; after all it had happened months before we two had even met. I myself had had a fling with a guy at the British Embassy just days before meeting Dan. What was left spinning around my head were images of Dan in bed, with three stunning women sprawled across him, pleasuring him – pleasuring each other – maybe it had been a couple of those nubile girls in the ladies. I'd thought those things only happened in films, or in Dutch brothels.

"Why did you do that Dan?" It was all that would come.

He shrugged. "Because I could."

And that was 1994. Ten years before Clinton said it.

139

18

The miscarriage happened on New Year's Day. I had only discovered I was pregnant a few days before Christmas. I'd missed my November period, which wasn't unusual for me, but December brought nothing either, and when I told Dan he whisked me into the American clinic. By then the foetus was ten weeks old. I remember the shock of seeing a baby with arms and legs when they scanned me. Oh they told me it was tiny for the gestation period – a good centimetre smaller than average – but the consultant didn't seem concerned, simply advising rest. And that suited us both over Christmas. We bought a small tree and dressed it, laid gifts for each other beneath, and snuggled down on the sofa to contemplate life with a baby. We hadn't been trying, had even been careful.

"Must have been that time when Carole ..." I said, trailing off.

"Yeah." He pulled me closer. "Three cheers for Carole, I say."

"Would you like another boy?"

"Yeah," he mused, "or a girl."

"Are you OK about this Dan?"

"Vanessa, I'm more than OK with it – it's the most wonderful gift. Earlier than I'd planned, of course."

"Planned?"

"Sure. Well, hoped ... intended ... you know."

"Yeah. But, like you say."

I did wonder about the programme. The baby was due the following summer, probably during a lull, and finding a local nanny to look after it would be easy, I knew that. Bogdan might not be ecstatic, but he rated me highly, I knew that too.

So I was just beginning to allow myself to imagine this good thing in my life, and when it came, it seemed to me that the wrench served me right.

"Nothing should die on New Year's Day," I said, curled up in bed, hands cradling the life inside me, thighs clamped to staunch the blood.

"Ness, we don't know that yet, I'm going to take you in now."

They opened up for him. The consultant was an acquaintance, a single man who seemed ready for some relief to his bank holiday, and he scanned me again. At twelve weeks, my baby then had hands – even the makings of finger stubs – but my baby hung suspended and still, there was no flickering white spot in the grey fuzz of its chest. There was no heartbeat.

At home, Dan let me sleep. When I woke he climbed in beside me and spooned himself around me, encasing me in his thick arms and thighs, shedding silent tears of his own, while I grappled with the shock. Somewhere within me, I knew that I deserved this, that I wasn't a good enough person. I had known that since I was a small child, when my father would snarl at me in close-up, his breath cigarette-thick, his spittle spraying my cheek. We stayed in the apartment for days. Dan wrapped me in blankets and plied me with his John Grisham novels, which at first I resisted and then read at voracious pace. In between times I gazed out of our balcony doors for hours on end.

One time, Dan and I sat together on the bed, fixated on the old woman in the block opposite, who was shaking a rug from her balcony.

"It was the sledging, wasn't it?" I said.

"No, no, no Vanessa, do not go there."

"But we fell off loads of times, and that crash at the end."

"Baby, there was something wrong with it, chromosomes."

"We shouldn't ever have gone to Chernobyl, that could have caused it. And how much did I drink at the Christmas party?"

The woman was leaning precariously over the balcony, lifting the rug, pounding it against the railings, and I remember being concerned for her – apartment balconies were known to collapse in Kiev. I can still picture her today. In fact, she remains my overwhelming memory of those blurred days, when the conflicting thoughts danced like hooped ribbons through my mind. The grief and sadness consumed me for hours, but then they would thin themselves out and be funnelled into a great vat of relief. I was not ready for a baby ... my work in Kiev had only just begun. After a while, the relief would be flattened by guilt, squashed to a pulp – and rightly so. But eventually, the guilt too would spin full circle into sadness and grief once more.

Alongside all of those emotions was a thrill – that I had been proved a woman. Because, at twenty-six, I still felt very much a child. Oh, the empathy, the stuff that drove me into the world of overseas aid was bleeding from the heart, oozing from me like Jell-o, as Dan had once said, but that was instinctive, a primal residue from childhood even. And, in any case, empathy does not a woman make. I knew that there was little intricacy to me, there was no convoluted thought within. Later, of course, there would be far too much.

At first, I said nothing of all this to Dan sitting on the bed beside me. But suddenly he heaved a sigh, its plaintive catch snagging my heart.

"Look at me, Ness." He waited until I could, the tears spilling over again. "This has happened to me before, way back. Sheryl had miscarriages, several of them. On each occasion, the doctors confirmed that it was chromosomal abnormality. She went on to have two healthy babies."

I nodded, rubbing at the tears.

"And we can too, Ness, we can too. And we will, one day."

He clamped me to him and we sobbed together then, the release we both needed, even though I was certain that Dan's release was made of simpler, more genuine stuff than my own. I felt that I must contain my shame. And yet, somehow, it blurted its way out.

"I must be evil. Because I don't know if I feel sad enough."

"What do you mean, Ness?"

"I don't think I'm ready to have a baby. There's a part of me that's actually relieved about the miscarriage. So I feel that I must have caused it. How evil is that?"

"That's baloney. What you're feeling is all quite normal."

"No. It can't be normal to feel any kind of relief about this."

"Listen to me, Ness, there's a whole range of complex emotions going on inside you right now."

"That sounds very American." I smiled weakly.

"Maybe, but I won't have you beating the crap out of yourself, you hear me?"

"I hear you."

"This is a first for you. You've got to let your feelings out, all of them, good and bad. It's probably going to bring stuff up from your childhood too, Ness. You've just got to go with it, let it all come out."

*

When I made it into work some days later, I was hoping that I'd find an empty office, that my staff would have played hooky during my absence, but Irina was solidly at her desk. And she was poring over an invoice from Lancashire for their first quarterly payment.

"Hi Irina," I said, annoyed that she should have opened it.

"Hello." She glanced up at me briefly and then at her watch.

Riled by that, I took the kettle down to the toilet, where I rested my hands on the basin and observed my reflection in the crazed mirror.

"Whinge, whinge, whinge." I mimicked Irina's whiny voice, turning down the corners of my mouth at myself. "I really don't need this today. Or you."

Back in the office, I busied myself with cups. Then, arms folded, I leant against the windowsill and studied the invoice on her desk. It was detailed, I could see that, but my eye was drawn to the bottom line – a quarter of a million pounds – which brought me out in an indignant, angry sweat. I still had not received any progress report from Jeff, which should have backed up the invoice with the detail on their achievements thus far. And he was off in Thailand over the Christmas period, on a whole month's leave.

I wondered about trying some small talk before wheedling the invoice off Irina, but she spoke first. "This invoice, it is outrageous."

Her pronunciation of the word was perfect, onomatopoeic even, and I glanced at the dictionary on her desk. Full marks for selecting that one.

"Can I have it please?" I asked calmly. "I'd like to study it myself."

Irina snapped up the paper between her fingers and thrust it at me. Then, with a melodrama I had never before seen in her, she sank her head into her hands.

"Wrong, all wrong." Flinging her head back she speared me with eyes that glittered. "How you can pay this invoice? How you can pay only fees of stupid experts who come here to my country, to sleep with girls, to watch striptease?"

"Irina that's simply not true …" I stopped, mesmerised by her fury.

"This money would buy medicines and equipments for our hospitals, why you don't do that in my country?"

"This is a technical assistance programme," I said. "We bring new skills and experience to Ukraine, we transfer know-how."

"Know how? In my country we already know how," she cried. "In your country, why do the people not protest about this waste of their money?"

Because they don't know about it, I thought fleetingly, but pushed that one aside. "Bogdan finances the Levshenko programme from his own money, as you well know, Irina. It is not coming from the British taxpayer."

"Still, it is a big waste!"

"It's not a waste. We've only just begun the programme and there will be results soon, we just have to be patient. The micro-credit has begun to flow in Donetsk, the Small Business Centre has already opened, the—"

She jumped in. "No entrepreneurs have yet come to Business Agency. You have provided Viktor with computers and photocopy machine to use for his own business."

"That's rubbish! You should be careful of false accusations like that, Irina, it's dangerous." Her glare smacked me on the cheek, but I managed to keep my voice steady. "And our train the trainer programme for the Task Force will start next month."

"Why have they not begun already?"

"Because they have been developing the training materials for it."

For a few moments, our eyes were locked together and it seemed as if one single thought was bouncing between us like a shuttlecock – duplication. Don't say it, I willed her silently, don't make me face up to the fact that, despite my own outburst to the donors about duplication, I have now condoned the weeks Bobsteve have spent on creating train the trainer course materials that probably already exist somewhere. For a moment, I thought I might have got away with it, but then she kicked her chair back.

"Replication!" she cried. Different word, same meaning. I felt my face sag as she harried me. "You have replicated the training materials which other donors in Kiev have already developed before. Why did you not use their courses?"

She was absolutely right, train the trainer programmes are standard – the essence of overseas aid. You train somebody up, who will then go on and train others – or as the adage goes, you teach somebody to fish instead of fishing for him. And I knew that curricula for this type of training would have been sitting on the shelves of all the donors. Bobsteve had sold it to me by insisting that the materials had to be tailored to the specifics of the situation.

Irina went on, her eyes flickering violently. "Now you will pay this invoice, pay them this huge sum of money which would fund a whole hospital building in Kiev." She stood up, grabbed her coat and briefcase and made for the door. "I go to university," she cried and slammed it behind her.

144

I felt overwhelmed then. For a long time I sat at Irina's desk head in hands, my whole world seemingly having collapsed around me. After a while, I made myself tea, taking short hot sips in a bid to soothe myself, while I watched the feet clipping by on the pavement outside our basement window; I could not allow Irina to be right about this, I had to pull myself round. Finally, invoice in hand and still churned up, I called Carole and launched straight in, my despair turning to anger.

"How can you submit an invoice before you've let me have the first progress report? They should arrive together, you know that."

"Happy New Year to you too," she said huffily.

"Happy New Year," I said. "Was it a good one?"

"St Ann's Square, pissed as farts. How about you?"

"Just quiet. At home." My hand drifted across my belly but I said no more.

"We've got Kevin Reed for you."

"Thanks. That's good news, anyway. And the progress report?"

"Jeff's getting that to you. Thought he would have done so before he left on holiday, that's why I sent the invoice." A lengthy pause played out between us and then, "Can you pay it for me?"

I stared at the total amount on the invoice, gazed into all the noughts, and I felt nauseous. I was impotent and could already see myself sanctioning the cheque.

"Soon as I get the report to go with it, Carole."

I hung up and looked down at Irina's desk, staring through it and then slowly focussing with realisation. The photo of her parents had gone, as had the glass paperweight of the Ukrainian coat of arms, with its blue shield and yellow trident; Irina had cleared her desk before my arrival that day. And she never did come back. Sasha, driver, tea-maker and interpreter, then also became my office manager for the rest of my time in Ukraine. I often wonder if her fury was the catalyst. If it was the seed for my later wilfulness.

The following day, January 6th, was Christmas Eve in Ukraine (Russian Orthodox Christmas being celebrated later than ours) and Yaroslav had invited me to supper. It was a long-standing engagement which I wanted to keep. Dan dropped me off at Yaroslav's apartment in the suburbs of Kiev, saying he'd fetch me at midnight.

"You're a glutton for punishment, Cinders," he said.

In fact, I was feeling in the mood for Yaroslav's moroseness as I took the stairs, which were littered with waste paper and reeking of urine – the habitual indifference of communal living. As with many apartments, at his doorway were two doors, one of reinforced steel and, behind that, one of padded brown, studded with buttons like an upholstered bed-head. I heard Yaroslav swing the inner door, then the outer one opened towards me, and he greeted me with a bow, hand on chest.

"Good evening Vanessa, welcome to my humble abode."

I smiled at his textbook English. Behind him, his mother, small and neat, seemed too diminutive to have been a rocket scientist. She clucked like anyone's mother welcoming a guest on an important evening. His father towered above, his grey hair greased back, or perhaps just greasy, and the brother, a bespectacled boy in his teens, stood by to shake my hand. I handed a plant to the mother, together with a carrier bag containing the toothpaste and shampoo, which Dan was then dubbing my calling card. She thanked me without looking inside.

I followed the family through to the box of a living room. A quick glance around confirmed that Yaroslav and his brother slept there; two day beds were set against opposite walls and the table had been pulled over to one bed that evening for seating. The low ceiling seemed to be crushing me and my eye was drawn to the window, where newspaper had been stuffed into the gaps between the metal frames. Despite this insulation and the thin mustard curtains, the room was chilly. I smiled as Yaroslav's mother pressed me into one of the chairs at the table, and I commented on the embroidered tablecloth, while the four of them stood around looking down on me. The woman launched into animated chatter.

"We have two tablecloths tonight, Vanessa," Yaroslav translated for her, "one for our ancestors, one for our family. And this bread is called a kolach."

I looked at the braided ring of bread, a candle at its centre and smiled up at her. "This all looks very lovely, spasiba Bolshoi." Thank you very much.

"Bolshoe pozhalusta." You're more than welcome, she said before bustling off into the kitchen. The father sat down at the head of the table and his sons shuffled round onto the daybed.

"We are lucky tonight," Yaroslav said with sarcasm. "We have electricity for Christmas Eve celebration."

I looked up at the long fluorescent tube which was blasting the room. It hurt my eyes. It picked out the pock marks on the ill-nourished skin of my hosts, and I wondered if they could decipher the recent grief in my own face. The table candle would have sufficed for me that evening. Yaroslav's

146

mother returned to the room with a jug of stewed fruit juice.

"Uzvar," she said, nudging her son for translation as she poured.

"This is God's drink, Vanessa," he said. "It contains twelve differing fruits. And tonight's meal will also contain twelve dishes, all will be meatless."

"Ah." I took a sip. "Vkusna." Delicious. In fact I had been hoping for wine or even vodka that night.

Over the next hours, Yaroslav's mother proceeded to lay out course after course for us. No pesticides or chemical fertilisers were used in Ukraine back then and the food was exceptional; the mushroom dumplings, the baked fish, the stuffed cabbage. While I had thought myself barely hungry, I savoured every course, ever keen for the next. And I found myself humbled by the plentiful offerings; the family must have been scraping this feast together for weeks. Eventually too, his father did bring out a bottle of wine, and later he served us copious shots of vodka.

While we ate, Yaroslav and his brother translated continuously for the parents, who told me about the history of their country. They held forth about the famine of the 1930s, when six million Ukrainian peasants were starved to death by Stalin. The food shortage was entirely manmade, Yaroslav explained, as the farm workers were forced to grow produce only for Russia, but were left unable to eat anything themselves. It was genocide, his mother insisted, jabbing a finger onto the tablecloth. Her choice of language made me balk, but Yaroslav added that Ukraine was now trying to elicit that very admission from Russia.

"But," he added, "our government could better use their time and their efforts to carry out necessary reforms in our country."

In the forties came the Second World War and invasion by Germany. They told me about the Babi Yar massacre, when tens of thousands of Jews were slaughtered over the course of just two days. Forced to line up at the edge of a pit on the outskirts of Kiev, they were then shot, falling into their grave. I resolved to research that piece of history further and the later photograph I found, of naked women and children queuing for their death, left me bereft.

Then, of course, there was Chernobyl. I allowed them to tell their tale without letting on that I'd actually visited the place, as that might have seemed touristy on my part. I sighed heavily as Yaroslav finished telling me about their history and I locked eyes with each of his parents in turn, wanting to convey my empathy for their country.

It must have been around the sixth course, a fish one of some kind, when

Yaroslav and his father seemed to forget my presence and began a heated exchange. Thawed by the wine, stuffed with food and sapped somewhat by their sad tales, I sat with a muzzy smile, tuning in and out, startled by the odd thud of a fist to bring home a point. Finally, Yaroslav let out the weightiest of sighs, and began cleaning his glasses on his shirt, shaking his head despondently.

"Vanessa, our life here is so complicated. Actually, my father and I agree on our discussions. You see, we must have democracy in our country. As you have heard tonight, we have a sad history but we could have a bright future, very prosperous even, if our Parliamentarians would conduct their jobs properly."

"I've heard that most of them are corrupt," I said.

"Yes, and they have political immunity. They crash their cars and nothing bad happens to them, they take bribes and nothing bad happens to them. We need a statesman to lead us, like Nelson Mandela, or Margaret Thatcher."

I had to smirk at that. "The British miners would not agree with you there, Yaroslav."

"Margaret Thatcher was in charge of privatisation in England, wasn't she?"

"Oh yes. We called it selling off the family silver."

Yaroslav contemplated me for a moment but chose to ignore the comment. "We need the same reforms here in my country, but our politicians rig the privatisation of our enterprises, they take the best bits for themselves or for their friends, who will then reward them later."

"Maybe you have to wait for the next generation to come through," I said, surprised to hear myself echo Dan's view, which just months earlier had seemed so warped to me.

"Perhaps, yes, but I am an impatient man. That is why I became a journalist, but my profession also suffers too much. Your Levshenko programme has taught me how to investigate matters, how to build solid arguments, how to analyse what is happening in my country. But when I report the news on TV all I can say is bla bla bla."

"Must be frustrating for you."

"It is. It is. And you know, many interesting things happen in Ukraine, the people should know about it all. But do they allow it? Not on your nelly, as I think you say in England?" I smiled and nodded for him. "My good friend, Taras, campaigns for democracy, he organises protests, he distributes leaflets. And the police harass him, they go to his apartment at dawn. Last week they have broken his door down."

"That's terrible." I shuddered at the idea of such violence.

"My father is heated in our exchange, because I support my good friend. He is scared for me, you see."

I did feel the hairs on my arms bristle at that, but said, "You're too much in the limelight Yaroslav, you're on telly. Nobody would ever lay a finger on you."

Yaroslav emitted a kind of squeak then, rocking his head to and fro as he weighed up this fact. "I hope so, Vanessa, I hope so."

19

Two weeks later, Jeff returned from his Christmas holiday in Thailand. It was a Saturday, but still I called him into the office with the overdue first progress report.

A quick skim of the document revealed that it focused on the problems hampering progress, rather than on any achievements. Jeff was laying the groundwork to wriggle out of all his commitments. I flicked quickly through the multitude of annexes, most of them padding – lists of people, of equipment, empty GANTT charts. The work plan for the next six months set no milestones, but it listed at least ten new experts, as yet unknown to me, each of them to fly in and out like tourists.

"Do you expect me to sign off your quarter of a million quid invoice on this basis?" I found it hard to control my fury at Jeff.

"We've made substantial progress, Vanessa. Building up the team and everything, it all takes time, you know. The most important thing on an aid programme is for everybody to get along with each other."

I've never forgotten that remark, so astounding was it to me. "The most important thing on an aid programme is to bloody well show results from the three million quid," I cried.

"And we will, very soon, the next six months will be ever so busy, you'll see."

"It will for British Airways! All those people flying in and out."

"We need those people to bring results."

"When are we going to see any tangible results? You haven't even set any milestones!"

"I want to keep things flexible."

"Flexible? You want to get out of producing any outputs, more like. It's obvious that you're lining up a cop-out for Viktor's Small Business

Agency. What is it you've written? The economic climate is not propitious?" I paused for effect. "Big word that, Jeff."

"The programme was unrealistic to expect us to do much on that front."

"It was you who designed the bloody programme!"

Later that evening, I lay on our bed wrapped in a towel and scrutinised the report, while Dan nagged me to dress for our night out to a new Indian restaurant, the first to open in Kiev.

"You need to get your butt into action if we're gonna have some fun tonight," he said, coming out of the shower.

"Isn't it convenient that the list of items under programme expenditure happen to add up to precisely a quarter of a million pounds?"

"You going to sort your hair?" He stood drying himself.

I ignored him. "I mean, they want £180,000 in fees alone, for the days Jeff, Bobsteve, Niamh and Paul Hopkins have spent on the programme thus far." Even Carole had charged twenty days for herself, and slipped in an admin assistant I'd never heard of.

"Ness, let's face it, what are your options here?" He stood naked now, towelling off his hair. "Either you hit nuclear or you pay the invoice. Contract's signed, can't redefine the nitty-gritty now, that's not your role."

"My role is to alert Bogdan if something's going off course from the programme remit, and I'm sure I can find something in here that's not kosher."

"They only started up three months ago, give them a fighting chance."

"Look at the living allowances – nearly forty grand alone. Jeff's apartment costs us £5000 a month and we're paying all the other experts per diems of £200 a day. Wouldn't surprise me if we're paying for that prostitute at the hotel to service Paul Hopkins."

"So, withhold payment, stop the programme, where will that get you?"

"I can at least make them stew a bit. I mean a thousand pounds for photocopying, faxing and postage? That's half the total spend on micro-credit for the women in Donetsk, over the whole duration of the programme. Don't you find that crazy?"

"What I find crazy is you working on a Saturday evening."

Dan snatched the report from me then and skimmed it across the room. I watched it land on a chair and sighed. He was right, I needed to sleep on it before working myself up any further. I contemplated him. His eyes were loaded with love for me. We had not made love since the miscarriage and it was surely time now. Smiling, I undid the towel and rolled onto my back.

"Come on then, if it's fun you want."

He eyed me. "You sure?"

I nodded and gestured at the old lady opposite who was performing her daily rug shake on her balcony. "Is she allowed some too?"

"Why deny her this effigy of Adonis?" Dan primed his muscle, waved to her, then kneeled his way across the bed to me.

When we got down to it, though, our lovemaking was more poignant than droll. And we both shed a tear. Afterwards, we lay on our backs, each lost in our own thoughts.

"Can you ski, Ness?" Dan asked me after a while.

"Er, yes."

"Good, let's go next week."

"Next week? Our train the trainer programme starts Thursday."

"So, we'll go tomorrow."

"Where?"

"Carpathians."

I glanced sideways at him. "Just like that?"

He glanced back. "Figure we could both use a break, don't you?"

*

Our journey to Skole, just below the Carpathian mountains in the far west of Ukraine, was by overnight train, an exotic experience for me. Side by side, Dan and I sat squashed together on the lower bunk of our wooden compartment. Dan had packed caviar and he laid out a rushnik over our laps, gently breaking the thin black bread and loading squares for me, while the train click-clacked its way through the darkness.

"Tysovets is small and it's beautiful," he said, pouring me a plastic beaker of cognac. "Close your eyes and imagine the perfect ski resort – the mountains so white they blind you, the sky a perfect cobalt blue, and pine trees all frosted with snow."

I opened my eyes and smiled at him. "And three whole days alone with you."

There had been a tinge of guilt about the holiday but, as I told myself, it would be the first time I'd taken leave from the programme and it was only half a week, which I could surely squeeze in before our training commenced.

"Ah, now that's the best bit." He nudged his cup to mine and held my smile with a tender one of his own. "I'm gonna spend every minute of them nurturing you. That's, ooh, thousands of minutes just holding you, massaging you. And whatever else it takes to restore you, Vanessa."

I sank down into him and visualised these things too. "It'll make us stronger, won't it, all this?"

"Yep." He kissed my hair. "Unbreakable."

"Unbreakable," I murmured.

"Anyways, now we get to have more time, just us. Later we can do all that zoo kinda stuff. Right now, there's a world out there waiting for us."

"The world's our lobster, as Jeff would say."

"Yeah, well no thoughts from the office for the rest of this week, thank you."

I was nicely sleepy when I settled myself down on the top bunk, smiling over the edge at Dan curled up below me and snoring softly. The train's speed appeared to have been calibrated for a dawn arrival in the mountains and its steady swinging motion lulled me into a deep sleep, feeding my dreams with movement. Mum pushing me on the swing in the park, conkers, an ice-cream van and the embrace of her arms from behind as she slowed me, stopped me, enveloped me.

In the morning, a cab ride from Skole took us up the mountain to Tysovets and we checked into a Soviet hotel, where the prices were also still at communist levels, I was amused to see. Once kitted out, we sipped coffee in the sunshine and surveyed the slope above us. Dan was right, the pine trees seemed as if expertly landscaped across the mountains, the sky was cloudless and the snow untrammelled. Already I could feel myself relaxing, anticipating the day's pleasure as the sun poured down on us.

"There's nobody here." I watched a single skier reach the bottom and turn for the tow lift.

"I had the place cleared for us." Dan grinned. "Let the snow be virginal!"

I threw him a sarcastic grin back. "Are we going to deflower it up there then?"

"Depends. Come on."

He tossed some kopeks onto the table, slung both sets of skis over his shoulder and we crunched our way across to the lift. We slotted ourselves into the skis and I planted my poles, then performed a few wide circles of my arms.

"You said you've done this before, right?"

"Right."

I was unable to meet his eyes. In fact the extent of my experience was

153

on the dry ski slope in Pendle, where Carole and I had been weekend visitors.

Dan turned and grabbed the bar of the next lift. "Meet you at the top."

I watched him leave, my dismay mounting as the next bar and then the next swung past me. Finally, I lunged for one and clung onto it, as it first slackened and then jerked me forwards. My bum seemed to have been left behind like an amateur water skier, but with grim focus I managed to right myself and follow on behind Dan, who himself was casually leaning back from the bar like a professional. Once I'd got the tension sorted, I too began to relax and we trundled on up the slope.

I kept my eyes fixed on Dan, feeling the emotional tug of him, as if I were in his slipstream. His back was smothered in a purple puffa jacket, his long legs encased more narrowly in black, which lent him a wide-shouldered Herculean look. As ever, his stance had that self-possessed air about it, and in those brief minutes of separation, I wanted him badly; the sexual pull of him was strong too that morning.

At the top, I watched Dan let go of the bar and ski on slickly, stopping to turn and see me off the lift. Nifty it was not – a few slapstick steps to steady myself – but I did ski to his side without falling.

"So, I figure this would be a red slope in Europe," he said. "Are you going to be OK with that?"

"Sure!" I set off at full pelt down the expanse of snow, which fortunately was gentle and mogul-free, easier in fact than a dry slope. Dan had soon overtaken me.

"Wow! That was better than sex" I swished to a not unimpressive halt by his side.

"Oh really?" He raised his eyebrows. "Come on, let's go higher."

The next ride up the mountain was on a single chair lift. I studied the way the chairs arrived, the way the skiers stood backs square to them, ready to be scooped up and off. Dan was lifted smoothly into his, and then my own chair came at me from behind, snatching me up into its trivet-like seat. Relieved to have accomplished that much, I then balked at the decrepit state of my chair. There was no bar to protect me from falling and I pressed myself into its rusty back, my ski poles over my lap as some sort of psychological barrier.

At first, the journey hugged the ground just a few metres below, but we soon began to climb, until the deep snow was a good twenty metres beneath me, the treetops at my feet. I held my chin up and looked over at the two ski jumps in the near distance, Dan had told me the Soviet

Olympic team used to train at Tysovets and I busied my mind remembering the ski jumpers on Ski Sunday. The theme tune came to me and I began to hum it to myself.

Then, without warning, the ground dropped away from us. The tops of the trees plunged down, and my stomach too seemed to pitch with them into the void; we were crossing an abyss. Hanging a good hundred metres above the snow, I clamped my eyes shut, willing myself not to jump off, while my bottom seemed to be slowly shuffling itself forward.

I must have screamed, because I was then vaguely aware of Dan's cries. "Sit tight … don't move … almost over." But the thumping beat of my heart – jump, jump, jump – was doing battle with the terror that had frozen me to the seat. The falling sensation swept me, over and over, and I could actually feel myself plummeting. I heard Dan screaming at the operator to stop the lift and fleetingly opened my eyes to see a triangular hut. Then I sensed the chair stop and dangle precariously on its hook, before feeling Dan's arms take me and pull me down to the snow.

"It's OK, it's over," he said, wrapping himself around me.

He led me away from the hut and the few onlookers, who were queuing to take the lift further up from this halfway point. He me down on his jacket in the full sunshine and his own hands shook as he took a flask of cognac from his pocket and handed it to me.

"Have yourself a good long draft."

I took several lugs of the stuff, gulping it back and choking as it hit my throat.

"I'm sorry, Ness. So stupid!" He pulled me closer to him "Why didn't I remember that gorge from last time I came?"

It took an age for me to control the violent shaking of my body. But as the sun blazed against my cheeks and the cognac burnt from within, I began to find some calm again. It must have been a good hour, long enough for the sun to rise to its full height, long enough for us to empty the flask – surprising the capacity of such a tiny object, I remember thinking.

"Let's go back to the room." I threw Dan a loaded sideways glance.

"You sure you're strong enough to ski down?"

"Yep. Let's go."

We slumbered in our room for the whole of that afternoon and awoke in the dark. After showering I lingered at the window, peering into the blackened mountains, which I could only feel, finding no visible shape to them in the moonless night. We ventured down to the hotel restaurant, a large hall akin to some miner's social club, with its fluorescent strip lighting and canteen tables. Dan clapped his hands at the waiter who was sitting behind a newspaper. The man snapped it shut and sidled over to us with a frown.

"Service!" Dan chided, reaching for the menus with a click of his fingers.

"At least he won't nick our plates before we've finished."

"Place needs a good shake up. Been too long in this Godforsaken country, I need to get me some service culture."

"I love this country. And so do you secretly."

"Ah, the people, ah the deep soul of the nation. Just be good to have some easy living alongside all that profundity, don't you think?"

"Doesn't come more beautiful than here though, does it? No pollution, no hurly-burly, wildlife at your tippy-toes."

"You're right, it beats waiting in line in France. Courcheval, that's where I took my boys last winter." He had a glint in his eye. "Have you skied there, Vanessa?"

I screwed up my face. "Truth be known, I've only ever skied on a dry slope before."

"Ah." He studied the menu with mock concentration. "The lady's only ever skied on a toothbrush. Kind of guessed as much."

"Was it that obvious?"

"Nah, you were amazing."

I smiled into the menu. "Did you bring Spencer and Franklin here too?"

"Sure did."

"And we'll bring our kids here too one day, won't we?"

"Maybe." He shrugged. "Plenty of other places on the globe we can go ski."

Back in the room, a bottle of Crimean champagne stood on the sideboard with two mismatched glasses. Dan tossed me my silk dressing gown, a Christmas gift of his, and told me to undress, while he too stripped and donned his towelling robe. Then he led me out of the room. I followed him along the corridor, down the back stairs and out through a fire door into the night, where the icy air slapped my body. I pulled the cream gown tighter around my chest.

"What's this? Another roll in the snow?" I was a little cross.

Dan smiled and led me by the hand over to some wooden steps, which we mounted. At the top stood a hot tub, the steam rising off it in sheets and he nodded at me to get in the water. After a glance around to check we were alone, I dropped my gown, stepped over the edge and sank down into the luxuriant heat, the surface bubbling like a hot spring around my chin. Dan dropped his own robe and climbed in beside me, sighing sybaritically as he sank against the tub.

"The stuff you do for me, Dan. Did you have to bribe someone for this?"

"When in Rome ..."

"Well I guess we could just call it a boost to the local economy."

"Before you go all analytical on me, let's raise a toast to ourselves here, shall we?"

He reached over the side for the bottle and let the cork fly. As he was pouring our glasses, the howl of a wolf pierced the night. Dan's arm jerked with the shock of it, spilling the champagne, and we both froze and scoured the dark mountains, seeing nothing, feeling everything.

"That sounded close," I whispered.

"Wonder how he sounds when the moon's full." Dan clinked his glass to mine. "To us."

"To us."

We sipped the champagne and tipped our heads back to contemplate the night sky. Its perfect blackness was punctured only by stars which were so low down they seemed to be hanging just above us.

"I've never been as close to the sky as this before, I feel as if I could draw those stars down to us." I reached up with a scooped hand.

"I felt I nearly lost you up there, today, Ness," Dan said softly. "Seemed like you were going to jump."

The chill of a shudder rippled across my shoulder – a bizarre sensation against the fierce heat of the water – and I could only nod, no words would take shape.

Dan pressed on. "Some vertigo you've got yourself there. All that, 'cos you saw a kid fall to his death when you were eleven years old?"

I let the pause linger. After a long while, I reached round for my glass and sipped at it. "It was more than that," I said quietly.

"Want to tell me about it?" Dan's face was glowing with the heat of the tub.

"Well ... my dad was there too, you see."

"Aha?"

"And, there was a crowd gathering. People were coming over to watch what would happen. And, after a few minutes there was a whole group of

157

us standing at the bottom of the multi-storey, all of us looking up at the boy." I fell silent for what seemed like an age as I relived the scene, as I tried to push the words out. "And my dad, well … he egged him on, you see." I looked up at Dan, his face a blur through the film of tears. "And, well then he shouted up at him. 'Jump yer coward!' he cried."

Dan nodded and waited.

"Then he looked around him. Grinning. Can you believe that? It was as if he wanted validation from the crowd, like some feckless schoolboy bully. 'Get a move on,' he said, 'we ain't got all day.' Then they were all joining in, all of them goading the poor boy. But it was he who started it."

I closed my eyes and I could see my dad, his hands cupped around his mouth. I could hear the people laughing, see how thrilled he was with the encouragement, his tiny runt of a face bunched up in creases. Then my eyes panned upwards, like a movie camera, up past each of the concrete tiers of the car park – one, two, three, four – right up to the boy in the green plaid shirt, teetering on the very edge at the top.

"And that's when he jumped?"

"Yeah." I squeezed the champagne glass between both hands, my knees hunched up beneath the water. "He just launched himself off. His arms were out, as if he could fly. And he did, kind of. He soared through the air. And then he hit the ground."

The silence that followed was filled benignly by the gurgling water.

Dan drew a deep breath. "You see it as his fault?"

I nodded, squeezing back the tears. "Actually, he went to jail. Not for that of course, but later, for GBH. Mum and I escaped then to my aunt's place in Salford."

"Started over?"

"Yeah."

"Is he still in jail?"

"No idea. Probably – he'll have gone back in anyway."

"Was he ever rough with you?"

"Not really. He did throw my pet hamster on the fire though."

"Jesus!"

Dan scooped at a handful of water and ran it over his face, blinked it away then fumbled for my hand beneath the bubbles and squeezed it. It was some time before he spoke.

"Explains a lot about you," he said softly.

"Think I've always been trying to make up for it."

"It was him, Ness. Not you." Dan waited for me to look at him. "Not you."

"Yeah." I threw him a wan smile and squeezed his hand back. "Come on let's not get all morose, this will be one of our moments, this tub, I want it to be special."

"Sure, baby."

But Dan continued his grave observation of me for several moments. Then he heaved himself up and reached out of the tub again for the bottle. As he filled our glasses, we held each other's look, a depth of understanding between us that no words would have managed. Steadily, slowly, Dan nodded at me and I back at him, a simple gesture of love, which drew us in, one into the other and held us there. Until the wolf's howl once again steeped the mountain and we were shaken from our trance with a jolt.

20

The day after my return, Sasha and I arrived at our programme HQ to observe the first of the Task Force train the trainer sessions. Greatly restored, I felt quite breezy that morning and I put my head around the door of the Business Agency for a fix of Viktor and his can-do attitude. He stood at his usual station, phone fused to ear, but he swung round and beamed at me with a curled finger granny wave.

I blew him a kiss back. "Hi Viktor."

Paul Hopkins sat with his feet up on the meeting table, reading the Kiev Post, an English language newspaper for expats. At first, I thought perhaps he was too engrossed to have noticed me, but then he flicked his eyes up and threw me a sneering glance – one of impunity. You snake, I thought with a shudder, and left the room. I'd revisited his CV to check out which company had seconded him to our programme, almost with the intention of somehow getting him recalled from his stint. But even then it was dawning on me that they might actually have seconded him to get rid of him. As I now know, such action is common in the aid industry, because which firm is going to let its best staff go when it can earn as much with the worst?

Up on the first floor, our model Job Centre had been laid out school desk style. I counted twenty young women, who had been recruited specially by Mrs T from within her own staff to be our Training Task Force. They sat with their backs to us, listening to her hold forth from a lectern, while Yaroslav filmed her. Jeff had secured prime position beside her for his spot on the telly and I nodded at him coolly. At his side sat the Three Graces. Now fully trained, they would be fronting up this model Job Centre, but would first assist Bobsteve to train up the Task Force. With priest-like smiles, the two men hovered over to me in their open-necked shirts. As Sasha pointedly shuffled away to light up, they held out their new training handbook and I winced at the logo on its cover. We had paid them thousands to develop this training course and the handbook should have carried our Levshenko logo, but instead it was Lancashire's logo that was emblazoned across the cover. I wondered how tailored the course materials actually were – tailored for later use by Lancashire on some other aid programme, no doubt. Irina's angry face flashed into my mind, but I pushed it out – Dan had said to give them a fighting chance and I would do that.

"What's Mrs T saying?" I asked Bobsteve, who beckoned to a young girl, someone I vaguely recognised but couldn't place, and asked her to translate for us.

The girl muttered something. "Saying, train, desk ..."

"What?" I frowned at her, but she shrugged and gestured with a jerk of the chin that Mrs T had now finished, then she shuffled to the door and slunk out of the hall.

"Who is she?" I asked.

"Supposed to be our interpreter. It's OK though, we've got another one."

Mrs T strode purposefully towards me and planted kisses on each cheek while I beamed at her; I so loved the gravitas this woman bestowed on me.

"I have given the command to my staff Vanessa," she said. "After learning all necessary skills here, they must then train five hundred staff in the regions of Ukraine. We want to develop the best Job Centres in Europe."

"That's great Valentyna, thank you."

"And look, we have flowers today to improve our image."

With a flourish, she swept a hand towards the carnations in vases which had been dotted about the room and I smiled – as if flowers would lure in the jobless. Leaving wafts of her perfume with me, she clipped back to the front, while I joined Sasha by the window. Bobsteve nodded at Mrs T, then beamed at the women and each man clasped his hands together, rubbing them as if gearing up for a spot of DIY.

"Right, let's get started shall we? First, let's get you all out from behind those desks and into a semicircle. Much more cosy."

A different girl translated for them then. I caught the perplexed, almost fearful, expressions of the women, as they stood about while Bobsteve dragged their desks away and arranged a horseshoe of chairs. Stripped of protection, the young women folded their arms or pulled their cardigans across their chests. The Three Graces, however, were quick to take their seats again, having had a head start to get the measure of this alien team from the West.

"Good. Now, we'll start with an ice-breaker. This will relax us, we'll get to know each other a little better and that will make our task together much easier."

The translation was followed by a palpable silence.

"We'll go round the room," Bobsteve continued. "And what we'd like to know from each of you is – if you were an animal, what kind of animal would you be?"

Pleased with themselves, the men stood back and gazed expectantly around the semicircle. Again there was silence. You've lost them, I thought, with mounting irritation.

"Well, OK, let me go first," Bobsteve said finally, "Let me see, er, I think I would be a ..."

"Twat," I muttered under my breath – which after all was a pregnant goldfish, or so the boys at school used to claim. Beside me, Sasha's shoulders began to shake.

"... I would be a tiger," Bobsteve finished, with a low snarl and clawed hands.

Fascinated by the interpreter's attempt at a snarl, I turned to study the blank expressions. Not one face revealed the slightest trace of inner reflection. Yet I suspected that each and every one of them would be masking a myriad of reaction – consternation, derision, panic, amusement? Still filming, Yaroslav eyed me for some sign of explanation, while Mrs T's smile was fixed and too bright. Bobsteve rambled on.

"Because, well I like to think I'm a rare sort of guy, not endangered, but nonetheless special, you have to respect me, but underneath it all I'm a bit of an old softie."

At that, Sasha and I collapsed into giggles and I doubled over, palms clasped to my cheeks. It was the release I'd needed after my weeks of melancholy and it did feel good. The trainees seemed to perceive our laughter as their cue.

One brave woman raised her hand. "Please? I will be a lion, so I can eat you."

"Ah, I have no natural predators, but lion's a good one. Any others?"

They were unstoppable then, tripping over each other with their choices. They would be bears or wolves, they said, or snow foxes or voles.

I wondered what they must be feeling about these weird teaching methods, when I knew that they were used to copying from a blackboard or transcribing dictation. They would be kangaroos or koalas, they smiled, or frogs or lizards.

"I would be an otter," one trainee said. "I swim all day, eat fish and make people smile."

"I would be an elephant," said another, "and never forget what I will learn here today."

We all laughed at that, and the room visibly relaxed while they shouted out ever more exotic choices. Even Mrs T came up with one – a leopard – and I smiled at her. She must have fought for the extra budget to remove these women from their everyday jobs and allocate them to our Task Force, and I sensed that she'd chosen well.

"You will be our Task Force." Bobsteve glanced then gravely from face to face. "You will help create a Job Centre Network that is sustainable in the long run, when our aid programme finishes and we are long gone. You are all pioneers. In the UK Job Centres have been around for one hundred years, but in your country are a brand new phenomenon."

A hand went up. "We will visit UK, yes?"

"Yes, there will be a visit to the UK to see how Job Centres are run over there. But we have a lot of classroom work to get through here first."

I watched the exchange of thrilled glances between the women as they registered the reality of their study visit to the UK. I later learnt that none of them had ever left Ukraine.

"For the first weeks we will train you all to become trainers yourselves. Then we will begin with the substance of running Job Centres, starting with service culture." Bobsteve paused until all the women had looked up quizzically. "What is service culture, I hear you ask? Well, when I go into a café in Kiev, nobody smiles at me. That is not welcoming and I want to be welcomed. You all have beautiful smiles, ladies, you must learn to use them." Instant smiles flooded the room. "You will learn to receive the unemployed, to build their confidence. Any questions so far?"

A hand went up. "Will we each have computer?"

"There will be some computer training, particularly when we come to the unemployment benefit systems. But the most important role for you will be to scout for job vacancies and match them with the unemployed. Everyone clear?"

There were a few vague nods.

"Also, we will develop a corporate culture right across the Job Centre

Network."

Another hand. "What is corporate culture?"

"So you are all singing off the same hymn sheet."

"We will learn singing?"

Bobsteve laughed with a nervous glance at Mrs T, who speared the men with glittering eyes.

"Not exactly, no. It's a saying, a bit like walking the walk. Anyway, we'll come back to that one."

As the men cleared their throats I wondered how the interpreter was coping with all of this.

"Now, to sum up, let's say this. Job Centres are new here in Ukraine, we two old codgers are new here in Ukraine, and you ladies are all new to training. So, the way we see it is that we will all be guinea pigs together."

Bobsteve glanced at me and I nodded my approval. I thought that was a nice touch, even if the guinea pig idiom caused a flurry of discussion, bringing us full circle to animals and culminating in agreement that rabbits not guinea pigs was the term used in Ukraine.

"Any more questions?"

Another hand. "Please? When will we go to UK?"

"The study visit will take place in the summer. However, there will only be fifteen places available and we will select those of you who perform the best over the course of the training."

In an instant, the excellent ambiance these men had created in that room was destroyed – and it was replaced by one of suspicion. Eyes darted around the group, eyes which had suddenly became hooded and dark, and I had a flash of the old Soviet denouncing of neighbours that Dan had told me about. I fired a glance at Jeff, who gestured to the back of the room and I followed him there.

"I thought all twenty were going on the study visit?"

"Indeed they were, Vanessa, but Mrs T insisted places were allocated to both her and the Minister. Viktor's on it too, of course." He whistled to signify a nifty move by Viktor.

"But how can you expect these women to stick it out if they're left off the UK visit? They'll desert the programme before they've trained anyone else up and all this will have been wasted."

He shrugged. "That's the way the cookie crumbles."

The flippancy of his words incensed me. "Not good enough, Jeff. Your progress report highlights the risk of these women leaving through lack of motivation, and it is within your control to stop that."

"No budget for more."

"You have three million pounds. You'll just have to cut some short-term experts from the programme."

Jeff sucked his teeth. "Can't see Carole budging on the profit from fees."

"Careful Jeff, I haven't sanctioned payment of your invoice yet."

We locked eyes and I bristled, but then Jeff raised his chin. "Pull the plug on it then."

His voice was chilled defiance, challenging me for the first time ever – and I'd thought it had been me playing him. In the silence that hung we glared at each other, and I confess to a shudder or two. My stock was currently strong, but I was a rookie and he an old hand at this; he knew I had only the nuclear option – stop for good, or stop and completely redesign the programme. As yet there were no grounds for either. Our standoff continued as I tried frantically to think of what I could possibly threaten him with. But then the silence was broken by glugging from the water cooler. The girl who had fluffed her translation had re-entered the room and was pouring herself a cup.

"Who is that?" I asked Jeff.

"Our interpreter."

"But she can't speak English."

"She tries hard."

I realised then where I'd seen the girl before – when Dan and I had been in the Mariensky Park.

"That's Balavensky's daughter, isn't it?"

I scowled from her to Jeff, who took my arm and steered me away to the window, lowering his voice. "Don't go upsetting the apple cart, there has to be give and take with an aid programme."

"This is unacceptable!" I heard myself squeaking like some dowager empress. "How much do you pay her?"

"I have a slush fund."

"A slush fund?"

We gawped at each other, both incredulous that he'd let me in on that.

"It's just a small one." He shook his head. "Negligible really."

"Ah," I nodded benignly. "I'm sure you'll find a way of stretching it to cover the UK study visit too, though, won't you?"

While Jeff's face coloured with anger, I swung round to face the trainees. All eyes were fixed on me, alert and gauging, some assessing the chances of any apples falling, others imploring me like puppies in a shop window. All that expectation, all that hope.

That evening, my head swooning with the knowledge that I'd got one on Jeff, which I would somehow use to my advantage, I phoned Bogdan to sanction payment of the first invoice for a quarter of a million pounds. Finally I believed that I'd wrestled some control over the programme.

21

In the early spring I made one of my regular trips to Donetsk, timing it to coincide with Niamh's quarterly visit home to Ireland and thereby supporting Svetlana in her absence. Niamh, my frizzy-haired micro-credit expert, had become a bit of a guru for me, but still I loved having Svetlana to myself and by then truly counted her as a close friend. The timing was perfect. One of Dan's investors was visiting the region that week and I'd persuaded Dan to cajole him over to the coal mine, where he could, I chirruped, assess his potential new workforce. Kevin Reed had now been working on the Job Shop for the miners for several weeks and Svetlana had planned an afternoon rendezvous there for us all. But first, we had the business of the women to deal with, and she'd invited me to lunch at her home in the village.

Sasha drove us out from the airport in a hire car and we parked up at the bus stop by the hedgerows. Though still a chilly March day, it was officially spring and a rich green had once again taken hold of the village. We threaded our way between the houses, the chickens and geese scurrying across our path, bolting from a stop start as if playing dare on a motorway. Small white goats strained at long chains, snuffling the grass on the common land surrounding the houses, and the yap of dogs vying with the shriek of cockerels steeped the air.

Svetlana's elderly neighbour was in her front yard, washing clothes, and I stopped at a distance, lingering to watch her. Bent double over a washboard, her knees were locked straight, with her upper body hanging heavy over the garments in a large plastic tub. She scrubbed what looked to be a shirt up and down the washboard, wrenching it across the ribs with a force I would not have thought possible of someone her age. Eventually she reeled upright, without any apparent discomfort to her back, wrung out the garment and slung it over her garden fence to dry, catching my eye as she did. I realised then that she was probably not so old, though she could have been anything between forty and seventy.

"Zdrasvitsa," Good morning, I called to her and began to move on, embarrassed now at having spied on her.

She greeted me back and stood watching as I opened Svetlana's gate, calling something to Sasha, who shouted his reply.

"She asks if you are the English woman," he told me with a grin. "I said you were big film star from Hollywood."

"Which one would I be?" I asked him, not displeased by the attention.

"Marilyn?" Sasha's gold eye tooth flashed at me.

"A dead one then?" I shoved his arm playfully and he shoved back.

Svetlana was preparing pelmeni for lunch and she ushered us in with her usual cheerfulness and made us coffee. While Sasha took his mug outside to light up, I helped her finish scraping the sautéed herb mixture into the large pasta circles. Together, we folded the dough and fluted it with our thumbs like Cornish pasties.

"Now, to our business," she said, wiping her hands on a towel once we'd stacked them all up on a plate.

I gave her the envelope of karbovanet notes which would be the next instalment for the micro-credit scheme and she secreted it in her bedroom; under the mattress I thought, but said nothing – if £200 were to go missing I would merely replenish it myself. She returned with her ledger, sat down opposite me and ran through the entries for each borrower in turn.

"Lesya has bought a hairdryer." With some gravitas, she traced her finger along the line. "At a cost of five thousand karbovantsiv. And she has made regular repayments to our fund."

"Great news. I've brought her some hair dyes, I had them sent over from the UK. Thought she could give you all a spring makeover."

Svetlana threw me a worried look. "But she must pay you for them, our fund can help her."

"Oh no, it's fine really. I've got fabrics for Olga too, look."

I took out the folds of material I'd bought in the Tsum, Kiev's only department store, on the Boulevard Kreschatyk.

She frowned again. "Olga has borrowed the most money from our fund Vanessa, and she has purchased many bundles of fabric already. In fact Olga has not made payments for several weeks, she owes our fund thousands of karbovantsiv, a total of thirty-four pounds. Look."

Svetlana swivelled her ledger round and jabbed her finger on the amounts – paltry ones to me – which were written in red. I met her eyes and for a moment those grey almonds became a little wolf-like, until it dawned on me what her problem was and I nodded slowly.

"Sorry. Perhaps I could pay her to make some curtains for my apartment with this fabric then? That way it would be more ... official."

Svetlana considered this. "Yes that would be OK, I think. It is important not to give our people something free of cost, because they will not see the value of it."

Dan had advised me the exact same thing. "Even a token payment Ness," he'd said over dinner one evening, "allows them to maintain their dignity, allows them to stay proud."

I'd shrugged and only half agreed with him; the giving of charity was still ingrained in me. In any case, if the miners weren't being paid at the moment, then these women were either having to seek out other non-mining families for their business, or else they were bartering. That or providing stuff for free.

After secreting the ledger once more, Svetlana suggested a walk through the village. "My mother would like to greet you, she is tending her land," she said.

Outside, we found Sasha playing football with some of the small boys in the village, who were dressed in shorts and shirts straight out of a 1960s sewing pattern. He performed an elaborate keepie-uppie for us as Svetlana and I set off through the village. A woman driving a cow to the open pasture stopped to chat to Svetlana. The cow stopped too and swung its head round like a dog looking back for his mistress. We passed the communal well, a neat white structure beneath a small roof which reminded me of a bus shelter. Clearly this formed a hub for the village and many of the local women were gathered there that day, some of whom I recognised and greeted with a warm handshake, their skin paper dry against mine. A little further along, we came to the village hall, where the kindergarten children were playing outside, sharing a single hula hoop. Making a mental note to bring some more appropriate toys to the village, I smiled at Svetlana and caught the sheen in her eyes.

"Would you and Oleg like children?"

"Oh yes, but it is impossible in these times, Vanessa."

I nodded. "You're still so young, anyway."

"Come," she said, "Yelena's bee hives are just inside the woods."

She led me across a field and we entered the woodland on the outskirts of the village, and in to a small clearing where two wooden beehives were humming.

"She has two now?"

"Yes, thanks to you, she has two now."

"Have they produced any honey this year yet?"

"I think they will start soon once the flowers bloom, I know that Yelena has fed them with juice from our sugar beet. She is becoming a real expert."

"I'd like a photo of you." I took out my camera. "For my portfolio."

Svetlana stood behind the two hives, flicked her long hair out to the front and smiled intensely into the lens.

"You will send me one copy?"

"Of course, Oleg will love it," I said winding the camera on.

We made our way back across the field and around the northern perimeter of the village to a series of small land plots, where Svetlana's mother was hoeing with her husband. She wore a headscarf, tucked up in the ubiquitous towel-after-bathing style, which for me in the West smacked of glamour, but in Ukraine of hard labour – the penance of the peasant. The old woman dropped her hoe and clomped over, greeting me with her usual bear hug, the warm smell of earth rising from her. She stood back, my hands in hers, lifting them up and out to survey me, as an aunt might a small child, and spoke as if commenting on how much I'd grown.

"She is waiting for her spring salad vegetables to come up through the earth," Svetlana translated for her. "We hope for a good crop this season."

"I love salad vegetables," I said, in a Russian I'd been practising for this moment. "Vkusna," Delicious, I added, which made her mother cluck and throw her hands up.

"She will prepare the first salad dish this spring especially for you, Vanessa," Svetlana translated again. "To thank you for coming to our village."

"Wonderful," I said, again in Russian. "I have a gift for you."

I took the package from my handbag, a bottle of perfume wrapped in pink foil, and handed it to her. Delightedly, she took the alien package, but did not unwrap it. Instead she laid it down with a small pat at the edge of the land plot, incongruously pink and shiny against the rich black soil. She returned to her labours and we ambled back to Svetlana's home.

Olga, Lesya and Yelena joined us for lunch, all of them flirting with Sasha, who, as the only man present, headed up the table. He sat slightly sideways on to it, legs akimbo, with something of the early James Bond about him, as he maintained a running translation for the young women.

We ate the pelmeni – organic, additive-free and delectable – while the girls stumbled over each other to tell me about their business progress.

Olga had bought a sewing machine, it transpired, and Svetlana made sure to catch my eye pointedly as the woman explained to us what clothing and soft furnishings she had made with it. She did have sufficient orders too it seemed, and I carefully added my own to her list, pulling out the fabric, which was dyed satsuma orange and splattered with crimson poppies. In fact, I'd had it in mind for village dresses rather than my own curtains and I smiled to myself as I pictured Dan's face when these would finally go up at home. Lesya was gearing herself up to take a loan for a hooded hairdryer and had set up a temporary drop-in salon in a corner of the village hall. Yelena planned to branch out into jams, as a canny move to exploit the masses of wild berries and cherries expected in and around the village that summer. As they each told me of their progress, I too found myself swept up by the enterprise of it all and was taken by a sudden idea.

"You know what? Why don't you all come up to Kiev and see what we can achieve there? We could sell your honey, Yelena, and your creations too, Olga." I was as excited as a six-year old, while Sasha translated for me. "And Lesya, someone will want their hair cutting up there."

The woman clapped and whooped, Olga and Lesya even stood and swung each other round in a girlish dance; Kiev was the exotic abroad and as yet unchartered for each of them. I also knew that it would be a chance for them to earn a wad of real cash up there.

As she watched them skipping, Svetlana spoke up. "Our men will be marching to Kiev soon."

Abruptly, the two women sat down and a respectful silence fell. Svetlana went on. "Still they have not been paid, Vanessa, and there will be a march by all miners in Donetsk, with a protest at the Ministry of Coal."

I stared at her. "But Kiev is four hundred miles away."

"Yes." She nodded gravely. "It will take them several days."

"Weeks more like."

"Perhaps, yes."

"Well then it's clear! You'll all have to be in Kiev to welcome them, won't you? We'll drive down and fetch you, won't we Sasha?"

"Evident!" Sasha flashed me one of his looks – it was a six hour drive each way.

After lunch, we set off for the coal mine. I sat in the back, dreamily planning the girls' trip to Kiev, working out how I would make it special for them; surely Dan wouldn't mind them staying in our apartment? Svetlana interrupted my reflections.

"Kevin Reed is very popular with the miners, Vanessa."

"That's good." I smiled at her. "We got it right this time then."

"He's very jolly."

It's true that Kevin was known for his sense of humour. When we'd worked together to cushion the Thatcher mine closures, he was a man at ease with everyone, from post boy to MD, and skilled at winning miners over. Perhaps it was his easy Lancashire ways, or maybe that he was built like a miner and they saw some kindred spirit in him, even if he was a manager at British Coal. I remember him coaching interview techniques, role-playing the boss at some engineering company, or haulage firm, where many of the redundant men would end up. He'd fire his questions at a miner – why do you want this job? Advising that the response should always stretch beyond the pay packet. Equally, I remember him sitting alone with a single phone, calling prospective employers for vacancies, which he would then display at one of the Job Shops. Sometimes the simplest actions are the most effective.

We pulled up to the mine just as Dan was arriving with the manufacturing CEO from Philadelphia. As ever, the house of cards tumbled through my chest to see him. Dan was spending the whole week in Donetsk, nurturing the American's decision to invest in the region, which had now been granted Special Economic Zone status.

"He's a steel baron," Dan had told me as he'd packed his bag in Kiev.

"With a Stetson?" I lay on the bed watching him.

"No but he has a kind of swagger."

Indeed the man was a colossal presence, and clearly a workaholic, as borne out by the lines in his forehead, which had worked themselves into the criss-crossed pattern of a garden trellis, fanning up and out from his eyebrows.

Neither Kevin nor the mine manager had come out to greet us, so Svetlana led us inside the crumbling administration building. We found Kevin behind a door bearing a paper sign marked JOB SHOP, the words emanating felt-tip sunshine rays in patriotic blue and yellow. He was sitting at his desk busy talking with Oleg and he nodded a welcome to us, gesturing to the display of cards up on the wall opposite. Our group moved over to it, Svetlana with a wink at her husband. But I wavered by the door and found myself gawping at Kevin as he put his gentle questions to Oleg, annotating a sheet of paper with the responses of broken English. He'd only been in the job for a few weeks but his face was grey, he'd lost a good stone in weight and had grown a salt and pepper beard. He caught me watching him and smiled, as if it fell to him to comfort me, and I smiled back quickly and made to join the others.

On the wall, Kevin had pinned filing cards with the details of companies in Donetsk, some of them marked with job vacancies, highlighted in fluorescent pink.

"Here's yours, Mr President." Dan took a card from the rack and presented it to the American. "Donetsk Engineering Company Inc. Manufacturers of steel presses. Got all your details on it. Seems to me, you could find yourself some good workers here."

I smiled at Dan, his accent had gone all John Wayne. The man took the card from him and the trellis wire deepened. "I'm impressed, very impressed. So what kinda skills these guys have?"

Instinctively, we all looked over at Oleg, who was now bowed forward at the desk, his back to us, his voice a whisper. He was clearly desperate to escape this gaggle of onlookers and, as if sensing our scrutiny, he scratched the back of his neck.

Svetlana spoke up then, her voice proud and wavering. "These men work very hard, they are skilled to use complex machinery. They are responsible men who follow instructions, they are highly trained to work in a safe manner."

Kevin looked up at us and smiled. "Spot on Sveta, love. Let me introduce Oleg Poliansky to you all."

With an arm round Oleg's shoulder, Kevin gently spurred him to stand and turn to us, and I watched the great miner nearly bow down to the American. "And I'm Kevin Reed, good to meet you, sir. We're just here fine-tuning Oleg's curriculum vitae. I'll ensure that you get a copy before you leave us today, I have them in both English and Russian."

The American took Oleg's hand in a firm grip and shook it vigorously, before Oleg nodded at us and slipped out of the room. Kevin smiled fondly at the closing door and then he pulled up chairs for us around the coal-fired stove. At least he has heat, I thought, glancing at the plaster peeling like butter scoops from the walls, at the corner where a bucket resounded with the steady plop from a leak in the ceiling. I found myself waiting for the next one.

"You can have copies of all the men I've been able to interview so far." Kevin took a file and flicked through some thirty CVs. "It was tough at the outset. Nobody wants to face up to pit closing, but once you've got one man through the door you find that the others slowly follow. Young Oleg there came back to add some details about his hobbies."

Svetlana and I exchanged covert smiles; she'd engineered it so that Oleg would be in with Kevin as we arrived.

"Is this mine closing down?" the American asked. "As I understand it none have to date."

Kevin nodded. "Scheduled for end of year. The World Bank and IMF are piling pressure on with the promise of hefty loans. Any case, coal's no good, quality's pitiful."

"How many men are employed here?"

"Around six hundred at this mine."

Kevin's chunky mobile phone on the desk rang.

"Could you get that for me please, love?" he asked Svetlana. "Can't speak the blinkin' language and my boy's out running an errand."

Svetlana answered the phone and spoke at length, jotting notes on a pad.

"Ah it's that sunflower processing plant I called yesterday," Kevin said, watching her. "I'm glad they've phoned me back. Ask them if I can come and visit them tomorrow will you, love?" Kevin rubbed his hands with satisfaction. "I hear there's money in them there sunflowers and country's full of 'em."

A hush fell on the room. I found myself welling up at the extraordinary effort this man was putting into our aid programme.

"You're a fine man, Mr Reed," were the American's parting words later that afternoon as he left with a tome of Ukrainian miners' CVs under his arm. "I'm gonna need hundreds of good men and I would like for you to act as my personal labour exchange."

Over dinner that evening, at Kevin's pokey hotel in Slagansk, we chatted perfunctorily, the three-way dynamics between us poor. Sasha could see that Kevin and I were holding off on the conversation we needed to have, out of sheer respect for him and his country, and as soon as he'd finished eating he wandered off into the TV room. I ordered more beers, sending one through for him, and wondered how to begin.

"So ..." I looked at Kevin.

"So ..." he echoed, exaggerating the purse of his lips.

"I heard you took a cut to your fee rate to do this job?"

"Yup, and to my living allowance."

He looked around him and I followed his gaze. The long low window was draped in a grubby net curtain with a row of browning spider plants in net baskets lined up on the sill below. Several fat bluebottles lay curled up beside them.

"I try to think of it as a learning experience," he went on. "No point in flying visits, you've got to get these men, got to get them to trust you. Though I'm not right sure what we can offer them. Are you?"

"Well … today went well."

He sighed heavily. "Yeah, if the Yank bites. Anyhow those men won't be quitting the mine until they're pushed, they don't believe it will close. I myself will believe it when I see it."

"What about the World Bank pressure? Ukraine won't receive any major loans if they don't close the mines, will they?"

"Mebbee. Most pressing problem for them at moment, mind, is next wage packet. They've hardly been paid for five months now, you know."

"Don't know how they manage to live."

"Hand to mouth. Subsistence farming. Good job the land's fertile."

I thought of Svetlana's mother ankle deep in soil, the way she'd laboured over her radishes and lettuces. "What's going to happen here, Kevin?"

"Not a magic wand, love, that's for sure. These men are scared, like rabbits in headlights, and they've good call to be. What's happening here is a far cry from pit closures back home. Britain was relatively wealthy, and we had other industries going for us, plus we were linked in to the rest of the world."

"It is bleak," I said quietly, "but we have to do something."

He nodded and sipped his beer.

"The women will keep them buoyant, they're amazing aren't they?"

"They are that. But the men need to work too."

Above me the light bulb faltered momentarily and I looked up into the flickering element, wondering what to say next.

"You're doing a bloody good job, Kev."

"It's a bloody hard job, Ness."

His voice matched the rhythm of my own, his face now grim.

I nodded. "I can see that and, well I want to say a huge thank you. Really."

He nodded back in acknowledgement and took a long draft of his beer.

"Found a cockroach on my toothbrush last night. Great ruddy fat one, and all."

"Oh Christ, no." I put my head in my hands and covered my face.

175

"And you've seen the office. Like Chinese water torture with that leak. Food's crap. No hot water. Bogs stink."

He paused, smiling at the young waitress who arrived to take our plates and waiting until she had wandered away with them.

"And the bog doors are made of glass, did you know that? So yesterday, there I was, taking a dump, as you do. And there was the mine manager smiling at me through the door. He even spoke to me. 'Dobryi Dien' Good morning, he said."

I gasped, but struggled to suppress the smirk that was fighting its way out of me, biting my bottom lip, searching for distraction in the sugar pot on the table. Then I heard Kevin's own snort of laughter and I glanced up at him.

"Said good morning to me, while I was sitting on throne, he did."

I let the smirk go then, let the laughter stream out of me, great sunny heaves of it. Kevin too was shaking, his cheeks bunched up, his eyes streaming with the hilarity of the image.

"You're too good for this world, Kevin."

"You and me both, love, eh?"

22

The miners began their march on Kiev, four hundred miles to the north-west, in early May. It was a journey that was to take them over two weeks. A few days before their anticipated arrival, on a hot afternoon, lush and lime with catches of birdsong, we also set off from Donetsk. Beside me, Sasha drove us through the endless spruce forests. When he and I had begun our journey south from Kiev before dawn that day, they had emerged from the night like spindly beasts, their bony arms reaching out to us.

In the back, if Svetlana, Yelena, Olga and Lesya were squashed they showed not one sign of it, chatting and giggling as they shared sandwiches, reaching forwards with radishes, small early beetroots and hard boiled eggs for us. The back window and boot of the Jeep were stacked with our booty – endless jars of honey, padded out with cushion covers and a cloth roll of new scissors. On top of this heap, a cardboard box held a full honeycomb, its sweet headiness seeking out our nostrils as we sped over the tarmac. Sasha had been on the road for over six hours already, but he made no complaint about tiredness, or his limited rear-view vision.

The girls provided a running commentary on the various crops we passed. This was the Ukrainian steppe, Svetlana explained, known for its chernozem – its fertile black earth – and she pointed out the swathes of spring barley, corn and even watermelons. The fields were universally ploughed, many of them lined with sunflowers. Though squat and awaiting the golden heads which in summer would ratchet around in pursuit of the sun, they did seem to be growing by the minute. No link between soil and supermarket had ever existed in my life and I made a mental note to be more aware of my own country's roadside agriculture when next I returned home, whenever that might be.

We swept past several factories which lay silent and still, the production plant and office buildings stretching out for acres, the trucks semi-abandoned on gravel paths where the weeds spidered themselves around the tyres. Sasha seemed to know what most of them had produced; the military plants which had lost their supply chains, the clothing manufacturers churning out too poor a quality, or foundries which had smelted a cast iron that could now be imported more cheaply.

Nothing was seen of the marching miners, who were being billeted in towns, where rallying meetings were boosting their morale. These gatherings were left unreported by the state television, even though I knew that Yaroslav had produced some footage of the crowds in town squares cheering their support for the miners.

It must have been some hours later when the jolt of our brakes woke me. I opened my eyes to find myself bathed in the evening sun, streaking pink through the windscreen. We were on the outskirts of Kiev, in a queue of cars, at some sort of checkpoint manned by soldiers in combat fatigues.

"What's happening?" I asked Sasha, rubbing at the crick in my neck.

He clicked his tongue. "Now you will see how crazy is my country."

He edged the Jeep forward behind the other cars, which were slowly being let through by soldiers skirting them like feral cats. One of the men gestured to the patch of waste ground to the side of the road and Sasha pulled over to where large metal canisters with nozzled hoses stood waiting for us. Winding down the window, he offered a handful of notes to the soldier and closed it again.

"We are a dirty car," Sasha said, "and we must pay a fine for that."

"What?"

I giggled nervously as four soldiers flanked us and began spraying our tyres, the doors, the bonnet. In the back, the girls were also waking now. Svetlana wound down her own window and began remonstrating with the nearest soldier, who jerked his hose up and sprayed the top of her door, catching her with an arc of water. Sasha swung round to snap at her and she closed the window.

"Such corruption," she cried. "What must you think of our country, Vanessa?"

"I will dine out on this one," I said, regurgitating one of Dan's sound bites.

While Sasha must have been exhausted after our twelve hour round trip, still he gave the girls a mini tour of Kiev on the way to our apartment, pointing out the key government buildings, the splendour of Boulevard Kreschatyk, the ominous KGB headquarters (where he barked at Lesya to put down her camera). I gave him the following morning off, arranging for him to meet us with the goods at noon, and he pulled off, elbow lolling from the open window, the gold eye tooth flashing at some pretty girls ambling alongside the Jeep. Not too exhausted to flirt then, I thought with a wry smile to myself. Dan welcomed us at the apartment door, an apron cinching his waist, a wooden spoon held aloft, and the four girls treated the night on our living room rug like a teenage sleepover party, giggling and whispering into the early hours.

The following day, I led them down into the centre of Kiev, where we spent the morning taking photos. Once again, it was the lilac season, marking the passage of my first whole year in Ukraine, and the sweet scents drifted all around us. Each of the women wore full make-up and the shortest of skirts, which apparently Olga had run up especially for the visit, while Lesya had cut and styled their hair in wedged bobs, the height of Western fashion in the mid-nineties. They bought cheap sunglasses at a kiosk and stood together with pouts and sticky out hips, surprising me with their glamour model poses before the fountains in Independence Square or at the statue of Cossack leader Khmelnytsky astride his brass horse.

At noon, we set up stall on the Boulevard Kreschatyk. Sasha was waiting on the pavement with the boot of the Jeep open. He pulled out some robust cardboard boxes for our table, which we then stacked with the jars of honey and the fresh slab of honeycomb.

"Let's just get a few jars out," I said.

"But I want to sell all of them," Svetlana translated for a frowning Yelena.

"I know, but if we pretend we only have a few they'll be more desirable."

Perhaps it was the four young women in mini skirts with the fresh plump skin of the countryside, or maybe it was the way we allowed passers-by to plunge a finger into the luxuriant honey and taste it – whatever, the first four jars went in minutes. Sasha pulled more out, balancing the large glasses one in each hand.

"We should increase cost." He flashed his eyes at me as he laid them out.

"Yep." I nodded. But Yelena was biting her lip; she'd marked all the jars with sticky labels, which Sasha and I began to peel off. "Don't worry, we can drop the price again if they don't sell," I assured her.

But of course they did sell and we nudged up the cost of each jar, all of the girls eventually getting into the swing of it, until at a certain point the punters stopped buying.

"OK we drop price to what is called optimum price," Sasha said, showing off his knowledge of economics. So we dipped and froze the price, slapping on fresh labels, until all the jars had sold.

"This is market economy?" Yelena asked me, stuffing karbovanet notes into her bag.

"Evident!" Sasha and I replied as one.

That evening Dan treated us all to dinner at a little Mexican place, where the four young women sampled their first Margaritas, and then slept more deeply – a nifty ploy of Dan's. The following lunchtime we repeated the sales operation with Olga's cushion covers. I'd taken her first into the Tsum department store to try and negotiate a deal there for her. A large brick building on the corner of the Boulevard, you'd never have known that Tsum was a shop, with its dirty curtains where a window display should have been, but it had clearly once been magnificent; all marble pillars, and lights set out across the ceiling like an Escher puzzle. My request to meet the manager that morning had met with vacant stares by the shop girls, even though one or two of them had fingered the fabric. Their interest in the vibrant colours, with which Olga had dyed the white cotton, was clear but their snobbery over this provincial peasant girl prevailed and they subbed her with disdain, feigned or otherwise.

Out on the Kreschatyk, our spot was free and we set up stall again. Some elderly women sweeping up lilac petals stopped to watch us, no doubt grateful for some respite from being forced to stoop over their short-handled brooms. At first, business was sluggish and after an hour Olga had sold only three cushion covers. Then Dan pitched up.

"You need to add value," he said, and promptly left us, making for the Tsum.

He returned a little later with bags of cushion pads, which he proceeded to stuff inside the covers, making a show of this domestic task, pushing deep into the corners, clapping the finished item between his hands. I watched in amusement and pulled out my camera. Pose with Cushion, as I called it, is still on the wall of my study today – that winning smile, the self-mocking eyes. Then Dan launched into his market stall routine, quipping with the female passers-by, flirting his way to sale after sale. At one point, the militia showed up, taking their cowboy struts across the pavement towards us. The Donetsk girls became jittery, began patting pockets for their papers, but Dan snapped out his USAID security pass. It was with some wonder that I caught him claiming diplomatic immunity.

"You don't have that, Dan." I shook my head at his dishonesty, as the two policemen smartly left us.

"Nah, but didn't want those petty criminals spoiling my fun here."

By the early afternoon we had sold all of the cushion covers. Olga took a running jump at Dan and swung off his neck. He caught her up and twirled her round, while the lilac sweepers stopped work again to applaud the dance. He suggested a celebratory lunch at McDonalds, where I ordered only chips and enjoyed watching all four girls peel back the bread rolls on their trays and twitch their noses at the slippery mayonnaise gunk inside. They conferred through silent glances and then each of them closed up the burger and scoffed the lot.

After lunch, Dan returned to his office, Svetlana headed off to a suburb of Kiev to visit a friend, and I descended with the others into the shopping subways that criss-crossed beneath the Boulevard Kreschatyk. I stood back as they each bought jeans and high heels for themselves, bargaining hard, with scowls that weren't really scowls but for me were certainly disconcerting enough. I scrutinised their faces in turn, trying to fathom the depths of these women. In the whole of my time in Ukraine, I never really did get there.

We still had Lesya to deal with. She had borrowed the cash for her own jeans and shoes from Yelena (even though I noticed that Olga had made more profit) and towards the end of the afternoon, I took the three of them to the model Job Centre, where I knew a session for the Task Force trainees was underway. As we entered the hall, the women swung around to us en masse. But the first person to catch my eye was Carole. After finally having signed off on her invoice, I had skirted round her. Aware that my power thereafter had diminished, I was hoping to boost it again by aloof behaviour, and although she'd been faxing me tricksy little notes, we hadn't actually met up. I nodded to her, but made for a cupboard at the back of the hall, where, on the sly from Svetlana, I'd stored a stack of hairdressing magazines for Lesya. She gathered them in her arms, a treasure of bright glossies, while the Task Force trainees looked on.

Bobsteve exchanged glances and switched off the projector. "Alright ladies, as we have guests, let's break there for today." They bid us good afternoon and left the hall.

The Task Force women scrambled out from their desks and scurried to the back of the hall. Only once they'd all begun flicking through the magazines, did I raise my head again to Carole. She was standing, back to the windowsill, smoking a cigarette and watching me. I clipped across the parquet.

"Hi." I smiled at her.

"Hi," she said.

"Didn't know you were coming?"

"Flying visit. Just wanted to check progress with the training. These women are amazing, don't you think?"

"I do."

"Hope you're not going to disrupt their training too much though, Ness?" She gestured to the gaggle of trainees and laughed.

"Oh, I view the programme as holistic, you know cross benefits and all that. The Donetsk girls get to earn a little, while the trainees get to glam up their image."

"Of course. Only joshing."

I refused to smile with her. "Maybe you could splash out with some of your per diem and get yours done too?"

Carole glanced across at Lesya, failing to hide her disdain; she probably spent £100 a shot on her hair these days.

"Anyway," I continued, "as you say, Mrs T made such a fabulous selection of women for her Task Force that they'll all be streets ahead in their training."

She nodded. "Bob and Steve are so impressive too, aren't they?"

I realised what she was up to, talking up the programme, and I allowed her what I intended to be an enigmatic smile. "Glad you came up with enough funding to be able to take them all on the study tour to Manchester."

"Jeff managed to make some savings elsewhere." She shrugged. "In fact I'm here also to prepare our next invoice for you, Ness. And progress report too, of course. I know they're both due next month."

I raised my eyebrows. "Please deliver them the right way round this time, will you? And I am expecting a rather more weighty report than previously."

"Of course." She paused, and for a moment my pretentious words hung between us, then she said, "Look, do you fancy meeting for dinner tonight?"

I nodded towards the Donetsk girls, who were now organising a queue by the small toilet at the end of the hall. "Busy," I said.

182

I felt a sudden pang of distress at the frostiness of our exchange, which I was inflicting and, to hide the tear which threatened, I turned and made for the trail of women at the improvised salon. When Lesya finally set to with her scissors, I looked around and saw that Carole had left the hall.

It was a good six hours later that our final client departed, by which time my hands were wrinkled to prunes. Lesya was clearly talented, and despite her cheap offers had made a good profit too, at least half the trainees having opted for a cut. We arrived home to cold beers and an Indian meal cooked from scratch by Dan, with spices brought by a visiting Asian colleague. That was another first for my Divas.

The following day the miners arrived in Kiev. All four women prepared themselves more prudishly than they had done on the previous days, pulling on the mid-calf dresses of their forest parties, but the same hot pink lipstick was passed around. After breakfast we made our way down past the Golden Gate, where the beer bottles left by the drunks of the previous night were being cleared away. Svetlana was hanging back a little, so I too slowed my pace, relieved for the chance to converse in English.

"How are the Task Force women, Ness?" she asked me as we fell into step.

I was confused by her question. "Do you mean what are they like?"

"Yes. For example, are they young? Do they all come from Kiev?"

"I'd say they're all about your age, late twenties, dynamic, very intelligent," I paused. "Just like you really. Why do you ask?"

She folded her cardigan tighter across her chest. "They do not like me. That is the reason I did not go there with you yesterday afternoon."

"But they haven't even met you." I pulled the corners of my mouth down at her.

"They know that I am paid by the programme, while they receive nothing."

"What?"

"They are jealous, I have heard."

As I realised what she meant, a sudden anger swept me and I pulled up short. "But that's ridiculous. These women must be the luckiest women alive in Kiev, we're training them in fabulous new skills, with a guaranteed job at the end of it and they should be bloody well grateful."

"Still. They are jealous. I think it better if I avoid these women."

"Look, we pay you, because you are working on the programme, while the Ministry of Employment pays them, as its contribution to the programme. It's simple."

Simple it was not, as I realise now, and Svetlana did pause, as if she was wondering whether to explain further, but she let it drop. "Yes, perhaps you are right," she finished.

We continued up past the Cabinet of Ministers. I was reeling at the thought of this resentment of Svetlana; not only was it a lack of gratitude, but also a petty mindedness. We walked on in silence, up past the Parliament, its national flags breezy and bright against the clear blue sky, and by the time we'd reached the square in front of the President's office I'd found some calm. I knew not to agitate Svetlana further that morning, but leave her to savour the anticipation of seeing her husband again.

Around the edge of the large square, a series of waist-high barriers had been erected, and we sat down behind them, joining Olga, Lesya and Yelena, who had already bagged a spot on the kerb. The militia were guarding the barriers officiously with the odd soft kick to the metal panels as a warning to keep us at bay, and we eyed them, while we chatted quietly and sipped coffee from a flask. Our mood was sombre as we contemplated the growing crowds of onlookers and what the coming protest might hold.

It was a good two hours later, nearly noon, when the chants of the miners could first be heard. Still some distance away, the sounds rose and dropped, as if on the wind, thrilling and menacing at the same time. The tension among the militia was palpable, as we and the hundreds of other well-wishers got to our feet, and the men began to prowl like caged animals, twitching, jerking their guns, while the noise grew ever louder, sending frissons up my spine and quickening my heart beat. Eventually, the line of miners became visible, a speck at first, then a blur of indigo topped by flecks of flame; the relentless progress of boiler suits and orange helmets. Finally, the shape of real men began to emerge from the mass, the breadth of their shoulders, the bulk of their torsos, then their stoic expressions. The crunch of their boots was exhilarating.

As the first men reached the square, we girls waved them on to us madly. Svetlana's cheeks streamed as she caught sight of Oleg and I fought back my own tears, overwhelmed by pride in seeing her husband near the front of the march. Beside him, Olga's husband Dmitry marched with his chin held high, then came Lesya's and Yelena's, all of them striding it out, though clearly they were dog-weary from the many days of walking. When the front flank of the miners reached the police cordon they stopped, waiting for the remainder to catch up, and their chants grew louder.

'President! President!'

I can still hear them today, the flimsiest of demands. Slowly every last man joggled his way forward, and then they stopped and stood as one, so collected, so still. I strained forwards over my barrier and scanned the vista of men, a mass protest of thousands which stretched back as far as the eye could see. When finally they were all assembled, the marching stopped, with a final, almost military crunch of boots, and I held my breath and waited, my heart thumping, puffed out with admiration.

For a moment, the men ceased their chanting and in the silence my eyes flicked instinctively to the militia. They had no horses, nor did they possess the shields or sinister headgear of the Lancashire riot police during the Thatcher strikes. But what they did carry here were handguns and rifles, which seemed to be so primed for action, jolting about as if with a mind of their own. What if the men charged them? I thought. Would there be a bloodbath? I glanced back at the miners.

And then the strangest thing happened; the miners sank down to their knees. Like a herd of roe deer, they knelt first onto one knee and then down onto the other, and they began to clatter their helmets against the road. Nothing more. The fiery orange steel sprang off the bitumen, clanging as some kind of benign background percussion to their chants.

'President! President!'

The miners turned their faces up to the stony windows of the President's office. Faces which were open and trusting, as if somehow they had been saved, though the reality was far from that. They reminded me of some biblical painting I'd once seen in the National Gallery and, though I have no religion, I found myself speaking silent words – *suffer the little children to come unto me*.

The miners' protests of later years were to be more volatile, more ugly, as eventually the fury would spew out of them; fury about years of sporadically unpaid wages, about disdain for safety, about a precarious future. But that first protest is one of my moments in time, of which there have been few, when humanity or nature overcomes me. The moment when a huge ball of red sun jumped out on me from behind a mountain crag, during a summer's drive through the Alps. The moment when a moon, already full, shot up at the speed of an escalator from the surface of a black ocean. And that unique human moment in the square. Futile and yet life affirming.

When the protest ended, the miners got to their feet and looked around, bemused and disorientated then. With gentle hands on shoulders, the unions began shepherding them to coaches which would take them to hostelries in the suburbs before they would be driven home the following day. Our men, of course, were going to be staying at the apartment. Dan had agreed, had stacked the fridge with Slavutich beers, bottles of champagne, and had stocked up with slabs of pork fat and boar meat sausages. When the nine of us arrived home, he was waiting, Mein Host personified, laying out his offerings together with black breads, plates of salad and potato dumplings.

The men showered and threw open the windows to rid our apartment of the gathering steam, their towels slung over the backs of doors, bookcases or magazine racks. They slumped into the sofas, arms slung around their women who were perched at their sides, and they began to tell their stories of the long march north. Dmitry and Oleg were dominant in the recounting of these tales, while the wives listened with eyes that glistened. Amidst it all, Dmitry launched into a Stakhanovite mining song, moving us all to silent wonder, and Olga's eyes gleamed as if she were falling in love all over again with her husband.

After we'd settled them in, Dan and I left them to it. This was a momentous evening where East and West would find greater depth of existence in separate celebration. Added to which, of course, Dan and I wanted a last night together. He took his suitcase and an overnight bag from our bedroom, offered jovial instructions to sleep wherever the miners and their wives found space, and then he drove me to the refurbished National Hotel. There was no sign of Carole, I was pleased to note as we made our way up to our room, where we ordered caviar and champagne, bathed together in deep bubbles and worked our way through the thick towels.

That night we slept very little, the windows thrown open to the heat of the coming summer, the downy white duvet caught between our legs as we thrashed and clung to each other until, eventually, the dusky light of dawn sought out our bodies and we lay together contemplating the contours we formed. For both of us, thoughts of the past few days seemed easier to handle than those of the days to come, and Dan was first to voice them.

"You've made a lot of folk happy again, Ness."

"Mmm, wonder if they got any sleep last night."

"You can't do this kind of stuff for everyone in this country, you know."

"I aim to get through a fair few."

I felt him smile. He took a deep breath and turned to kiss my temple. "I

186

love you Vanessa Parker, and I always want you by my side, right?"

"Right." I smiled at the ceiling. "Anyway, what happened to all those cushion covers from Tsum? I know that they don't sell the inner pads separately."

"Ah. Those you would find heaped up in the men's room."

"Ah, would I now? That's why I love you too Dan Mitchell and I always want you by my side. Right?"

The following day Dan left for the States on his annual leave.

23

During that early summer of 1995, the programme teemed with experts who flew in and out. Never did they stay for more than two weeks, the adjoining weekend spent adding layers to their personal enrichment with a visit to cultural Lviv, or sultry Odessa on the Black Sea coast. And they showed up in direct proportion to the milder weather, like mini beasts scurrying out to play. We had a statistician for labour market analysis, consultants in vocational guidance and several IT geeks to set up the Job Centre systems.

Carole's second progress report arrived on my desk, together with an invoice for a further four hundred thousand pounds. I let them both linger there, fielding her phone calls with an insistence that Bogdan's imminent visit should have some bearing on my decision to sign off. Not only had I lost some of my power over Lancashire, after having sanctioned the first invoice, but Jeff seemed not in the least perturbed by my having rumbled his slush fund. I watched on frustrated, wondering if I should have taken more steps to intervene and revamp the contract before paying that initial quarter of a million pounds. I knew by then that the grounds to do so were weaker. So it was futile of me to incur Jeff's wrath by sarcastically enquiring if one expert was there to assess time and motion – all time and no motion. Our relations were flamboyantly strained.

"If you can't stand the heat, get out of the kitchen," Jeff sneered.

"Heat? This kitchens' full of Slush Puppies," I snapped. Ha! I was chuffed with that one, though it makes me cringe now.

Dan was away for several weeks, renting a serviced apartment in Chicago to be near his boys. I spoke to both of them on the phone, each of us shy with the other, which was reassurance that Dan had been holding forth about me. Despite his pleas, I hadn't been able to join him, in view of

Bogdan's forthcoming visit to Kiev. But the loss of Dan's presence was staggering. I missed his bulk beside me in bed, his great arms around me. I missed another head on the pillow, the chance to offload and seek advice. Though he called me each day.

During his absence the quarterly coordination meeting of all the aid donors was held. I was by then well known in Kiev aid circles – if not necessarily taken seriously. It opened with the usual exchange of information, each donor spewing forth about their current programmes, spinning the positives, no mention of the glitches. Once the World Bank, the IMF, the EC and the weighty national governments had all briefed us on their latest actions to offload millions of taxpayer dollars in Ukraine, the Scandinavians took the floor. They introduced a new social programme worth $3million, the goal of which would be to set up a model Job Centre in Kiev and train the staff nationwide.

"But, but we are doing that already," I blurted at the Finnish woman.

Beside me the awful Chelsea smirked into her papers; I swear she thrived on my bumblings at these meetings.

"It is always good for the Ukrainians to see different ways of doing things," the Finn came back at me, her stance cool and objective.

"But they'll laugh at us if we set up two model Job Centres in Kiev."

Silence. Looking back, I wonder how many people round that table were thinking that they laughed at us anyway. I glanced at the woman taking the minutes – the sole Ukrainian we deigned to invite to these discussions about aid to their country. She was writing steadily, her face a mask of Slav inscrutability.

I went on. "And we've set up a training Task Force in the Ministry, with twenty staff who will then roll it out to the regional Job Centres. You can't go treading on their toes."

Around me papers shuffled, but still nobody spoke.

"And what about the absorption capacity?" I squeaked on, grasping at some aid jargon for effect. "How can Mrs Tabachuk possibly manage another donor, which will mean yet more Western experts running around her department? We have enough problems getting her to commit time and people to our programme."

That show of weakness was highly naïve. In reality, all the aid donors suffered these same problems, but truth was more mammoth than elephant in that room, and our chairman simply moved on. After the meeting, the Finn approached me, her perfume smarting my nostrils.

"Vanessa, I have a budget to spend by year end. If I do not commit that budget to a project, then I will lose the money. This I cannot allow, because there is public pressure to increase overseas aid programmes and I cannot be seen to be reducing ours. We national governments have to answer to our electorate. Unlike philanthropic donors like Bogdan Levshenko."

You have to give it to the Scandis, I always think nowadays, so straightforward, so technical in their honesty. But her words and condescending delivery incensed me.

"Well spend it on something complementary then," I cried. "You know full well that you'll create chaos with this one. Anyway, if there's one thing I've learnt in my first year here it's that the Ukrainians have to really want a programme. It has to be demand-led. There's no point foisting a project on them."

She eyed me for a moment. "My dear, Mrs Tabachuk has been lobbying us for months to start this project."

The news knocked me sideways. I hadn't actually learnt a thing in that year.

"So Mrs T is playing us off against each other?" I asked Dan later on the phone.

"Sounds like it, Ness," he said gently.

"Have you seen this before?"

I could sense he was resisting the urge to tell me that, yes, he saw it all the time, but instead he said, "Maybe she's lining the Finns up for when yours finishes. You know it takes an age for programmes to get off the ground."

"We still have two years to go, though," I mumbled.

For several moments I heard only the sound and rhythm of our breathing.

"I miss you, Dan."

"Miss you too. Anyways, I've got some news for you when I get back."

"Oh, what's that?"

"Good news. Be back next week."

Just before Dan came home, our long-anticipated expert, Sir Roderick, arrived. And his was a visit that brought things to a head. He was a former Permanent Secretary for Employment, the pinnacle of the department and, now retired, he was ready to extend his largesse as a newly available consultant on the aid market. Carole had claimed he was a coup to the programme, and he was due to spend two days in Kiev, to advise Minister Balavensky on Employment Policy. I too had high hopes of his visit –

finally some gravitas had landed – and it was I who drove out with Sasha to meet and greet at Borispol.

In arrivals, Sir Roderick was instantly recognisable as our man. Of slight build, he wore a fawn cashmere coat with a black velvet collar, despite the hazy summer's day. As he pressed himself into too much of my personal space in greeting, I noticed a worm-like thread of vein at his temple and a scum of white sleep in one eye, which added to the layers of discomfort I'd already tortured myself with. His title had a lot to do with it, of course. He was of the alien upper classes, and back then that made him inherently more intelligent than me, it made him more valid. Although there was to be an erosion of my inferiority during his time there.

On the journey into Kiev, I sat nervously in awe of him and maintained a trail of pre-rehearsed questions. He told me about his granddaughter, about how she would go up to Oxford to read history that year, how they enjoyed visiting ancient English churches together. As we neared the centre, the man showed no interest in the translucence of the Dniepro, or the cloud-like foliage that surrounded us, but then nor had he commented on the spewing chimneys or the anonymous apartment blocks either. I left him at the National Hotel, relieved that he was content to amuse himself that evening, but hoping no prostitutes would show at his door, which would surely alarm such a cultured and superior elder.

The following morning, Jeff had his telephone voice on, fawning and flapping his nicotine aura at the man. The Minister too appeared impressed by Sir Roderick's title, sweeping like a ballroom dancer from office to ante-chamber, his voice more mellow, his eyes somehow lighter, it seemed. I hadn't seen Balavensky for weeks. He still hadn't bothered to visit our programme HQ, and I was wary of how the meeting would pan out.

Mrs Tabachuk appeared at just the prescribed time, sat down beside Balavensky and received from him a mighty introduction, perhaps beyond that befitting the Head of a Job Centre Network, and thus confirming for me that the affair with the PM was ongoing. Sir Roderick sat up a notch as he clocked the silk scarf, the slash of crimson lipstick, and he made a play for her attention. I, however, was still cross with her; she had not returned my phone calls about the Finnish project and now refused eye contact with me.

The Minister began the meeting. "I have many questions for you Sir Roderick," he said through Sasha's translation, settling himself in for the long haul, I could tell. "We hope that you will help us solve all our problems."

Across the table from him, Sir Roderick smiled a little. The vein squirmed in his temple as he clicked open his briefcase, extracted a document and patted it down on the table, clearly expecting the chance to respond at that point. But the Minister continued to bear down on us, in monotone, rehearsing his usual points about his once-great nation. The chernozem, the fertile black soil, by virtue of which Ukraine had been the undisputed breadbasket of the Soviet Union, the production quotas for inter-ballistic missiles which had always been fulfilled. He even added a new bit, a whole diatribe on the life and times of the great Ukrainian novelist Mikhail Bulgakov.

Stick to the point, I urged him silently, as Sir Roderick's foot began to tap. But on he went, regaling us now with the unemployment problems his country faced, the lack of funds for benefits or for job creation, while Sir Roderick's eyes darted across the room for something to relieve the pressure of words hailing down upon him. I guess a man of his position had barely ever had to listen – to really listen – but then he could have made an effort to get the measure of the Minister, to absorb some of the problems. After all, we were paying him a thousand pounds a day.

When the minute hand of the wall clock had clunked its way round for nearly a full hour, Balavensky abruptly came to a halt, knitted his fingers and sat back to await the input. Signs of life hit the room again. Sir Roderick faltered, unsure if it was over, before he himself shifted. Then he began.

"As you are perhaps aware, Minister, for a long period I was responsible for the UK's Department for Employment."

Single-handedly? I thought, as he nodded to Sasha for translation.

"Your nation clearly faces great challenges," he continued, and I waited for more. But nothing came; no attempt to recap on the problems Balavensky had laid out, or to seek common ground with him. Instead, he spun his document round on its axis and pushed it across the table.

"I have prepared an Employment Policy for you, Minister, translated, of course. Perhaps we could run through it?"

That was it, no effort to build a relationship, merely the arrogance of a superior being addressing an inferior one. I flicked my eyes from him to Balavensky and received a momentary glance from the Minister, who then sat back heavily and sighed.

"Thank you. We are most grateful for your assistance," he said.

Sir Roderick urged him with a quick shake of the head. "Shall we discuss it Minister?"

"No there will be no need. Is there anything else?"

Mrs T sat still and silent, her smile as glassy as a child's doll, while opposite her Jeff began his alternate cough/laugh routine, ending on a cough.

"Minister, may I be so bold as to suggest that we take a look at the document," he said, "I am sure it contains some of the finest elements of UK Employment Policy."

"Yes, I am sure it does. However, this is Ukraine and Ukraine has its own problems, Ukraine needs its own Employment Policy. I will leave my office at your disposal to discuss matters further with my colleague."

With striking dignity, Balavensky rose and left the room. For several moments after he'd gone, those of us left around that table sat staring at the discarded policy document. And then Mrs T came to life, as if the doll's string had been pulled in her back, scooping up the document, tapping it into her own papers and beaming at us.

"We do thank you for your assistance, this will be of great use to us." While her eyes held an intense smile, they did seem to be searing Sir Roderick, though he returned the smile with equal fervour.

"Perhaps then we could take a look at my proposals for reorganisation of the Job Centre Network?" he asked hopefully.

"Of course," she said. "Please." The only hint of agitation was her slight adjustment of the scarf, its Hermes logo carefully arranged for observation.

Sir Roderick took out several copies of two organisation charts, which he placed before each of us. I looked down at them. One was the current chart for Mrs T's department, with its trees of job titles – a veritable forest – and the other was his proposed reorganisation – after the loggers had been in.

He began with vigour. "Now, there are far too many people employed in this organisation. It needs to be leaner, much leaner, and I have proposed here a new structure for the network, plus clear roles and responsibilities for your staff."

A hush fell on the room as we each gazed down into his proposed organisation chart. All those people chucked off, you could almost hear them flop with a thud to the floor, where they would surely wither and die. Could this country, these people, bear any more livelihoods lost? I glanced surreptitiously at Mrs T, who was frowning in contemplation at the chart. True, the current Job Centre Network was stuffed with duplicate roles and fuzzy lines of hierarchy, whereas the proposed one was no doubt efficient to a fault, but Sir Roderick was hustling her into the unknown.

Against the silence, I heard the reeds of a blackbird and looked out the window at the mass of foliage outside the Minister's office. Fat cherries hung from a gnarled branch which grazed the sill, and beyond that another sprouted the makings of apples. I remember thinking how incongruous that an orchard should fit within the courtyard of a Government Ministry. The blackbird sat in the apple tree, its eye cocked as if at me, its beak open. Its trills were so poignant. 'Fly home, fly home,' it seemed to be saying. I found myself welling up then and, for the first time ever since my arrival in Kiev, I wondered if perhaps we should.

Mrs T gave us two full hours of her time that afternoon, her reactions consistently bright and searching, as Sir Roderick waded through the jargon, talking of efficiency gains, of natural wastage. At the end of our meeting, however, she left swiftly. Asking Jeff and Sir Roderick to wait for me, I skittered down the corridor after her.

"Valentyna," I cried, seeing her about to disappear around a corner.

She stopped, stood for a moment then swung round slowly, a smile very much in place. "Yes. Vanessa?"

"We're not expecting you to implement these changes quickly. I know it takes time to transform an organisation."

"Thank you."

There was no sarcasm, only apparent gratitude to her voice, but still I blushed at my own callow words; this woman was twenty years my senior. She watched me with a mild expression and I hurried on, blurting rather than phrasing it.

"By the way, I wanted to ask you about the Finns, about their new project with you. I hope there's not going to be any duplication?"

She regarded me for several moments before responding. "Ukraine is a large country Vanessa. And as you see, my organisation is also extremely large." She gestured to the chart in her arms. "But we have not yet decided how we will use the Finnish aid. Which is most welcome. As is yours."

"OK." I smiled, backing away. "I'm very happy to co-ordinate with them, if you like."

"Thank you."

Her voice held that same slow, genuine cadence, she even waited for a moment as if to see if there was more. Then she swung on her toes and left me alone in the corridor, while I stood watching the swish of her skirt, listening to the jangle of her bracelets. Wanting only to take her at face value.

Back in the antechamber, it appeared that Balavensky had asked for a word with me. Only Sasha remained. Jeff had apparently taken Sir Roderick off to some concert which began shortly. The Minister ushered us both back into his office.

"Vanyssa," he began, once we were again settled at his table. "I think you and I, we understand each other."

"Yes," I lied. The failure of the meeting had been partly his fault; if only he hadn't gone on so much, Sir Roderick might have handled him differently.

He stood up and walked to his desk. Thinking back on our past sullen encounters, I surveyed his office. The early evening light had cast an old-fashioned, honeyed glow on his furniture, over by the window his full-sized Ukrainian flag rippled. He pulled out a wad of papers from a drawer, then he shuffled back over and skimmed one of the documents across the table to me.

"From Germany." Then another. "From France." And then another. "From Sweden."

I reached for the papers in turn. Each document, drafted in Russian, was headed 'Employment Policy' and emblazoned with the various logos of these three national aid programmes. Staring into them, I nodded slowly and trawled my mind for an apt response. Finally I raised my eyes to his.

"We understand each other," I said.

Prickles of – well of what exactly? Maturity? – crept up my spine and around my face as we held each other's gaze.

"Vanessa, I need practitioners, I need real experts in their field, who can sit with me and my staff and work through our problems with us."

Balavensky sat with me for a further hour that afternoon, taking me through his needs. Nothing, he said, had been tailored to what he wanted. He was sick of endless fact-finding missions by aid donors and he was sick of the wasteful programmes in which they culminated.

"In you, Vanessa, I see an individual who can truly help Ukraine. You must shape your aid programme for us, so that we can benefit in real ways."

At the end of it all, he let his eyes rest on mine, pressing home his expectation.

"Now Vanyssa I must go to my dacha and tend to my land."

And on that golden summer's evening, the Ukrainian Minister for Employment stood and ushered us out of his office, so that he could go to his country home and dig up his potatoes.

After the meeting, Sasha joined me for a celebratory beer. I buzzed with renewed hope as I gabbled on about how I'd finally got through to Balavensky – and I could tell by his unusual energy that Sasha too was impressed. We parted at the door of the Irish bar and I strolled along the Boulevard Kreschatyk, smiling at the buildings, at the trees, at anyone who passed me.

I was crossing a side road, when I caught sight of Jeff and Sir Roderick standing some way up it. I stepped into the shadow of a building and watched the two men; they were supposed to be at a concert but were hovering outside a restaurant called Lake Baikal. I think I knew what they were up to even then. I watched Sir Roderick, now in shirt sleeves, stepping from one foot to the other as if in anticipation, and I felt suddenly furious. A thousand pounds a day wasted, and there was still one more to go. I found myself setting off up the road towards them, but then I saw a third man approach and shake hands with them – it was Paul Hopkins, and I came to a halt.

"You!" I even said it out loud, but I wasn't about to take all three of them on. So I turned back and set off again for home, seething with all that I would throw at Jeff and Sir Roderick in the morning.

Dan and I had passed Lake Baikal many times, but he'd told me early on that it was a hole, and we'd never eaten there. It struck me then. I came to an abrupt halt and hurtled back along the Kreschatyk, up to the scuffed doorway of the restaurant. The men had disappeared. I went inside, pushing my way through the heavy curtain that draped over a second doorway and entered a gloomy room which was more like a night club than a restaurant. My eyes were stung by the smoke weaving through the darkness, while the bass of the rock music vibrated through me.

The edges of the room were lined with tables bearing tiny pink lamps, and benches upholstered in red plush, all of them occupied, though it was too dim for me to make out if I knew anyone. There was a central dance floor, above which hung a large glitter ball, and waitresses in skimpy white dresses, which glowed purple in the dark, were making their way around. Finally I spotted Jeff, Paul and Sir Roderick sipping glasses of beer at a table a short distance from me. Hanging back against the wall, I observed them and noticed that, quite bizarrely, they were lined up in a row behind the table, their eyes fixed on the empty dance floor. Like men at a football match, I thought, and took another look around the room; all of the men were sitting in similar rows, backs against the wall, while the few women present sat opposite them.

Suddenly the volume was pumped up, making me jump. White lights flashed and the floor beneath the glitter ball began to slide apart, like the famous ballroom on Blackpool Pier. A cage rose from the opening and inside it a girl was wound around a fireman's pole. She was writhing up and down the polished steel – completely naked. I gasped at the sight of her shaved pubes as she raised a thigh, and found myself lurching towards the three men.

"You sleazebags!" I screeched, and they each swung round, gobsmacked, as Jeff himself would have put it. "You come here to help tackle the social misery in this country, and then you patronise a dump like this! Do you think that poor girl wants to have to do this? Do you?"

At that, all our eyes turned onto the girl. Illuminated by the flashing spotlights, she was now upside down on the pole, legs akimbo. For a moment the men did glance down at their beers, but the pull of the scene was too potent and their eyes were dragged back to her body. In the bursts of light, I recognised then many Westerners from the aid world, several of them from the donors' meetings, and I felt instantly soiled. These slavering animals, indulging themselves in this base feast with total impunity, incognito and so far from home. There was a glow about the men's faces – the radiance that comes with desire – and a smugness too. They knew that they would never be caught out in this parallel world, that the wife could never possibly know. Totally sickened, I turned on Sir Roderick, my chest thudding.

"She could be your granddaughter!"

He didn't even seem to hear me, so I screamed instead at Paul Hopkins.

"And you! You disgust me."

He glanced up at me, shrugging as if to shake me off.

"She earns good money – and tips. It's our free time and it's all perfectly legal, so you'd best stop your carrying on."

As if he'd taken courage from this, like the lion in The Wizard of Oz, Jeff then spoke, though his eyes were still on the girl. "Run along, Vanessa."

I glared at the side of his head. "There will be repercussions, you know."

"Ooh I'm shaking," he mocked.

In fact it was me who was shaking. I could feel the fury seething inside, like a coiled viper about to strike. But still, it was out of character for me to reach for Jeff's beer, to flick my wrist across their laps and douse each of them, a little like watering seedlings in a row. It was puerile of course, but I would say effective, judging by the shock on their faces. Then I turned and clipped out of the nightclub.

24

Back at our apartment I poured myself a large glass of Moldovan Cabernet Sauvignon and flopped onto the bed with a pad of A4. Still furious, yet euphoric, and perhaps a little jittery at what might await me, I headed the paper with a large question mark, working out my nerves in the curlicue of its tail. Beneath that I wrote the line Balavensky had praised me with: In you I see an individual who can truly help Ukraine. I was going to take matters in hand and turn this programme around. I was going to stop it and redesign it completely; the nuclear option, as Dan had called it.

I began with the positives, as he always advised. We had some excellent experts on the programme – Niamh, Kevin, even Bobsteve were performing well these days. If I could secure more of their inputs and rid the programme of the short term experts, the tourists who flew in and out, that would be a fine start. I parked the seedy Paul Hopkins to one side, not even allowing him paper space at this stage, though I was aware that he still had 80 days allocated to him, at a cost of £42,000 to the programme – twice my annual salary. And Jeff, well he was useless for everything except continuity but this in itself had a value, I was learning, and I would have to park him too – for now.

Then there were the Ukrainians. I headed that section with Mrs Tabachuk and underlined her name. She had always been my greatest ally in the Ukrainian camp and, while I was still confused by her approach to the Finns, after the clear commitment I believed she had shown that day, I was ready to give her the benefit of the doubt. If I could offer her something more, I was certain that I would secure greater allegiance from her. Then there was Viktor, the Graces, the Task Force and my Divas, plus now the Minister, whose aloof behaviour had finally been clarified for me. I was excited about securing real experts for him, could envisage them bandying ideas around with him to reach the home-grown Employment Policy he truly needed.

I poured another glass of wine, took a hefty slug and lay on my back staring at the cracks in the ceiling, imagining them as pathways to my solution, like a children's puzzle, where the finger traces a maze of lines to the treasure chest spilling with gold coins. Dan always said you had to figure out the specific self-interests of individuals, then move forward with these in mind. I sighed, rolled off the bed and padded to the window. Opposite, the old lady sat watching television, the grey screen flickering. Suddenly, I realised what I should do. Use the media! Mrs T craved power – witness her affair with the PM. She also favoured style over substance, what with her French scarves and her dogged attention to image. I believed that if I could help propel her into the limelight, bestow her with media attention, she would be more passionate about our programme. We could fund Yaroslav to produce a series of human-interest type documentaries on the Levshenko programme, highlight the model Job Centre, follow the roll-out of the Task Force training to the regions, focus on Mrs T as the driving force behind this essential service for the mass unemployed.

Back on the bed, I jotted all this down furiously. In a further flash of inspiration, I realised that I could also offer the empty top floor of our programme HQ to the Finns. With minimum investment, they could use it to add a much needed Vocational Training Centre, for carpentry or bricklaying, say. I would allow them Yaroslav's media coverage alongside ours – which might go down well on Finnish TV too. Ha, I thought, if I could pull this off, it could be the first time ever the donors had achieved genuine co-ordination between two aid programmes. Synergy was the new buzz-word we were all beginning to use in the aid world and I'd pioneer the stuff. The phone rang and I jumped up; Dan always called at this hour.

"Hi kiddo, howz it going?" His voice was languid, I could tell he was at some poolside, drink in hand.

"Hi Dan, it's going great," I began. And then I checked myself. Didn't I want my strategy to be fully developed, watertight, before I regaled my mentor with it? So instead I said, "Well actually, you'll never guess what happened tonight."

"Aha? Let me guess, you set fire to the curtains?"

I smiled to myself, he hated Olga's curtains. Bloodbath in a volcano, he used to call them.

He went on. "Pushkin jump out the window? Please don't tell me you let the tub overflow on the geek downstairs again?"

As he spoke I flopped back onto the bed, grinning at the amusement in his voice. Slipping a hand up my shirt, I ran it down loosely over my breasts, imagining it as Dan's hand, broad and warm and soft.

"No, nothing like that." I paused. "I poured beer over some of our experts."

There was a slight stall and then he said, "Over Jeff?"

"Aha."

"And Paul Hopkins too, I hope?"

"Yep."

"And … surely not over the knighted one?"

"Indeed I did. You should have seen his face."

"I'm impressed," he was laughing now. "Any likely repercussions?"

"Not sure. We were in a strip joint."

"Ah, you were in a strip joint." I could feel him contemplate this, heard him take a sip of his drink. "Well, if they fire you, Ness it's not gonna matter, 'cos I'll take care of you from here in."

I picked up my pad and looked into the hotchpotch of ideas. "I won't get fired," I said, already toying with another one. "It's all going to work out fine."

Instinctively, I knew how to play it with Bogdan. During his trip to Ukraine, I flattered him with an invitation to a party in his honour in Donetsk. If those villagers had climbed into my heart, they would surely move a man whose hankering after his homeland was hard-wired within him.

En route to the village, we stopped by the coal mine, where Kevin quietly showed Bogdan the Job Shop and introduced him to Oleg and Dmitry. I watched them bond instantly; that silent magnetic tug of shared Ukrainian blood. I'd said nothing to Svetlana of my grand designs to tackle Bogdan, but she was intuitive enough to know when a big cheese needed a big welcome. She had orchestrated everyone onto the common land by the village hall, which had been festooned with a welcome banner. Beneath it, the Governor of Donetsk, Vladimir Zukov, stood waiting to greet us and Bogdan was then treated to a sort of Royal Variety Performance, as my Divas, plus a whole raft of other village women, made individual presentations of their enterprise. My boss applauded and nodded, occasionally eyeing me thoughtfully. Finally he threw his head back and laughed heartily, as Tanya led her gaggle of chickens like school children across the grass. She rushed at one with a red ribbon around its

201

neck, ambushed it in a flurry of feathers, and lifted it up for Bogdan, who reached to embrace the fowl with skill and real care, while the cameras flashed about him.

Bogdan was then led on a tour by Vladimir Zukov, both men slapping each others backs as they strolled among the goats and geese towards the communal well. Yaroslav interviewed them against the sunset, a piece I knew would make it to national broadcast, given the Governor's political clout.

Back at the village hall, trestle tables on the grass were laden with the food and wine Svetlana had bought with the budget I'd secured from Jeff's slush fund. The wisps of smoke from the barbecue brought forth the scent of charcoaled pork and chicken, which even I was beginning to savour (indeed I succumbed to my first chicken leg that night) and we set to, as we had in the forest the previous summer. Flanking Bogdan on either side were Oleg and Dmitry with their wives, Svetlana and Olga, and I watched the two men regaling my boss with their endless roars of laughter, their meaty hands smacking the table at his jokes. Opposite him, Vladimir Zukov led a series of flattering toasts to the Levshenko programme.

As twilight set in, the blue coal dust embedded in the flesh of the men's foreheads seemed to glint at me. Still today I can picture the joyous faces of Oleg and Dmitry. It was a joy that perhaps not every man attains in a lifetime, a happiness that may have required a parallel and equal depth of suffering for it to be fully realised. That particular memory of their expressions will probably never leave me. Although it is slotted alongside another memory – a later one – of each man's face.

The following day, I rose at dawn and took a solitary walk through the village, enjoying the sounds of the livestock coming to life. I passed the Governor's cottage, now used only as a summer dacha, and smiled to myself as I wondered how Bogdan had fared in his own billet. He had downed copious amounts of vodka during the toasts.

In the distance, a low mist hovered by the wood, enticing me over, and I made for it. Reaching the trees I stepped in between them, past Yelena's hives and further in, crunching ferns beneath my trainers, swishing past the wet fronds that licked my shins like dogs. When I'd reached a spot where I could see nothing but greenery around me, the trees having swallowed up my entrance, I sat down on the trunk of a fallen oak and sighed. The peace was punctured only by birdsong, the stillness only by the odd rabbit that scampered out and then back into the foliage.

"Perfect," I murmured.

Closing my eyes, I tilted my chin and gave myself up to the morning. Then I heard the crackling of ferns and opened my eyes to see Bogdan picking his way through the woods. He wore a T-shirt slung over shorts and sandals, his face was unshaven, his eyes bloodshot.

"May I?" he asked as he reached me.

"Please do." I grinned at the sight of him and shifted along the log.

"Wonderful party last night, simply wonderful," he said. "I can still hear the music from the accordions in my ears."

"It was amazing, wasn't it?"

"Ah Vanessa …" He reached across and took my hand in his, his breath still fumy with alcohol. "You have no idea how my soul yearns for this country."

"I didn't even know a country like this existed, Bogdan."

"It has worked its way under your skin too, Vanessa, hasn't it?"

"It has."

"You know, I could not have chosen better than you to supervise my programme here."

"Thank you." I felt the heat of my blush.

"You have turned the colour of your hair!" He eyed me. "I am very happy with you, Vanessa, very happy indeed."

I saw my chance. "I've been thinking actually, there's so much more we could be doing here."

"Ah yes, if only we had more money," he said. "Money, always money."

"No, I mean even with the three million pounds we have already."

"I think there is so much activity going on already, don't you?" He chuckled, but he did cock his head a little, so I continued.

"The Job Centre and Small Business Development Agency are fantastic flagships in Kiev, our progress there is brilliant, as you've just seen for yourself. But we could expand things down here. You've seen how committed they are."

"Are you teaching me to suck eggs, my dear?"

"I just mean, well, why stop at this village? At this coal mine?"

"Because we have limited resources."

I took a deep breath. "If we lose some of the short-term experts in Kiev, gain efficiencies up there, we could divert resources down here without any negative impact."

"Perhaps you are thinking of one expert in particular? A rather grand one?"

He twinkled at me then and I realised that Sir Roderick must have complained about me. I felt the blush deepen.

"He was supposed to teach the Minister to fish, not slap him round the face with a cold trout!" I cried.

Bogdan let out a chuckle. "You have a good sense of humour, always a good tool out here. I have heard that you may also be in love?"

I cocked my head at him, ignoring the comment, and knew how to deflect it. "We pay these so-called experts at least six hundred pounds a day. That's not far off a thousand dollars," I paused for effect, "even for the days when they are just travelling."

Sure enough, his jaw twitched at the mention of his money. "Go on."

"We need fewer experts, who can spend longer on the ground, who can invest more time to build the trust that is needed. Because aid will not work without trust."

I held his eyes with mine and waited for him to nod his understanding, before I reiterated it for good measure.

"Doesn't matter how much they know, they can't transfer any of their know-how, any of their experience, unless they have first built a sound relationship with the Ukrainians. And we're kidding ourselves if we think differently."

As the mist swirled at our feet and the day slowly opened itself into so many differing shades of green, I took Bogdan – who was by then quite biddable – through my plans for change. On the flight back up to Kiev that afternoon, I presented him with them in writing, neat and pithy. We should add more villages in the Donetsk region, expand the micro-credit available so that more women could benefit. We should add more mines, open more Job Shops, build on the reputation of the current one. In Kiev, we should add a couple of solid practitioners for the Minister to build an apposite Employment Policy, we should create synergy with the Finns. We should set in motion a media component, to publicise both Levshenko and the fruit it was bearing (he particularly liked that one). All of this would be financed by clearing the programme of those often ineffective, and sometimes arrogant, short-term experts, by a major cut-back of their flying visits, and, hence, of their fees.

By the time we landed at Borispol I knew I'd won Bogdan over. It was within my power to redefine this programme, to make it work, and I was about to do just that.

25

Honduras was just a holiday destination. At least that's how it was first billed for me. Dan told me how he and his boys had scrambled over the Mayan ruins, many of the structures still strangled by dense jungle, the branches wound like pythons around the stone blocks, loath to give them up to excavation. He described sitting atop the Great Plaza where the sacrificial ceremonies were held, and he laughed about the bonding horseplay with Spencer and Franklin, as the local guide had explained how the male members of ancient Maya would pierce their penis, in a bloodletting to pacify the gods.

After his return to Ukraine, we took our own week's holiday together and flew down to Odessa, the so-called Pearl of the Black Sea. On our first morning, we sat with ice-creams at the top of the Potemkin Steps, breathing in air steeped with sea salt, and looked down towards the harbour, a heady hundred metres below us. Made famous by the runaway pram in the film Battleship Potemkin, the gradient was actually quite leisurely and the steps flattened out every so often for a breather, though Dan and I had pretty much jogged up them before breakfast; he was a fit man these days.

It was the height of summer, a balmy breeze stroking my bare shoulders and ruffling my hair as we sat, flanked by chestnut trees, and gazed down at the expanse of cobalt. Dots on the horizon became ships approaching the harbour, bringing the extensive trade that had bestowed Odessa with a certain continued freedom during Soviet times.

"How would you like to live with this kind of heat all year round, Ness?"

That was his opening gambit, I remember, his broad tongue scooping the ice-cream which dripped down the cone.

"Commute to Kiev from Odessa?" I asked, though the lurch of my stomach told me, even then.

"They've offered me promotion. Head of Mission, Latin America."

"Latin America?"

He nodded. "Based in Honduras."

"What do you mean?" I held the puzzled smile in place as I searched his face.

"They want me to move on, Ness."

The strawberry ice-cream turned to bile in my throat. "They want you to go to Honduras?"

He nodded and I watched his eyes narrow as he gazed out to sea, battling with his own emotion.

"To leave Ukraine?"

His head jerked. I turned too and stared out at the blue, so innocuous in the sunshine, the flashes of light bouncing off refracted even wider by the tears that suddenly sprang up. So much light to the morning, and yet the darkness was already closing in on me.

"But you're posted here, you run programmes …"

"I've been here five years now, one more than my due. Swung that one after you arrived."

I fixed my gaze on a tanker moving steadily across the horizon, and struggled to control the miserable tug at my jaw.

"They can't just make you go," I said finally.

His nod was imperceptible.

"But what about us?"

He glanced at me. "I'm kinda hoping you'll come with me."

"When?"

"They want me in September."

"This September?"

He nodded again.

"Next month? Is this some kind of joke?"

"No." The word was a rasp.

"Have I got any say in this?"

"I have no choice in the matter, either."

"There's always a choice! I can't possibly leave Ukraine now, look what I've just done to reshape the programme, this is my life."

I had spoken about little else since his arrival back home in Kiev.

"You could do this stuff there too, Ness. They need people like you."

"This … stuff?"

"I'm just saying—"

"You're just saying you expect me to up sticks and follow you to the other side of the world."

Dan let out a growl of frustration and tossed his cornet to the ground, smacking his hands free of it. "Look, I know I'm not getting this right, but you didn't expect us to stay in Ukraine forever, did you? This is a once in a lifetime for me – for us."

"I didn't expect you to go sneaking behind my back and line yourself up with a cosy little fait accompli."

"It wasn't like that, I—"

"You think I'm some muppet, happy to trail after you at the drop of a hat?"

"No."

"You want me to give everything up and keep house for you in some banana republic?"

"Of course not, there's heaps of work for you out there, too."

"Oh, you've got that all sorted too, have you?" I glared at him, stunned by his bloody-mindedness.

"No. But there's more poverty there than here."

"All those times you've told me I can make a difference here, you were just humouring me, then?"

Dan sank his head into his hands, running fingers through the wad of inky hair, while around us people climbing the steps began to give us a wide berth, but I was unstoppable. I flung down my own cornet.

"I wouldn't even be able to find Honduras on a map!"

"I'm sorry." His voice was muffled. "I didn't mention it earlier, because I didn't think I had a chance. And they won't budge on the timing."

I gazed at the hairs on his forearms, the tears blurring them into dark fuzz, and found that I was beginning to shiver, quite violently. On the step below us, two ice-cream cones lay mouth to mouth, a puddle of chocolate swirling into pink, like a yin yang pattern.

"Well you can go alone," I snapped. "Have a nice life."

I stood and began to stomp blindly away.

I must have walked for some hours through the streets of Mediterranean Odessa, staring through the buildings, refusing my mind the chance to confront the two certainties fighting their way in – that I wouldn't go, that he wouldn't stay. Provided I kept walking, I knew that I could keep that up, so I encircled the Opera House for the umpteenth time, the winged statues at its entrance appearing more ghoulish than cherubic to me, and I stumbled through the Passage Arcade, its lacy plasterwork feeling like cobwebs in my face. Outside, on the main boulevard, the faces beneath the red Coca-Cola umbrellas were laughing, incomprehensibly, and I kept moving on and away from all that, pacing the back streets until finally I found myself in the City Gardens.

By then the sun had no slant left to it, it was brutal on my worn-out eyes. I made for a shady bench, slumped down onto the pocks of bird droppings and sighed, with the resolution of it all. My idyll had come to an end. I was about to be stripped of the protective layer that sustained me.

I sat for a long while, keening silently to myself, stuffing soggy tissues into my pockets, dragging them out again. When I sensed that the realities nudging to get in at me would not be kept at bay for much longer I shook myself to, and sought distraction from my park surroundings. A flea market was underway and I was flanked by two stalls selling porcelain and bric-a-brac. I should have been prepared for it – in the aid world you move on. I'd always avoided broaching the future with Dan, but I'd always been waiting for it too. And I should have realised how long he had been in Ukraine. I'd hoped that we would move on together, in a few years when the Levshenko programme had come to its natural end, that we'd decide where to go next. A rum snort escaped me as I saw an image of us flicking through brochures for our next destination – as if our lives were some sort of city break.

At the stall opposite me, several paintings were propped up. I gazed into them – the fruit bowls, the pots of violets, the vases of sunflowers, and thoughts of the past few weeks of my life came crashing at me, tumbling over each other to be first in. The sparkle of the Donetsk girls selling honey on the Boulevard Kreschatyk, the hopeful trust of the marching miners, the childlike excitement of the Task Force trainees who were about to visit England, the sincerity of Balavensky's plea for me to help him. I felt as if I were living their lives with them, as if they were intrinsic to me and I to them. I found my eyes drawn again into the paintings, seeking out the wilting flowers, which would often be present in Ukrainian still life. Against the strong, fresh blooms, there could be one or two stems that drooped, an odd petal that had fallen and was already crispening, a peppering of pollen on the table top. For me, this was the secret expression of their lives. I knew that I wouldn't be able to leave these people now, they needed the programme and that would fall apart without me driving it, ergo they needed me.

I roused myself, sighed and looked around the park. Across the sandy path, a small fountain was shooting up strings of jets, the droplets at their peak perfectly round as they high-dived back down to the pool. The steady rhythm of the water soothed me; I would get through this. Gradually, I became aware of a presence beyond the jets and my vision adjusted to see Dan watching me from the other side of the fountain. We held each other's eyes, no smiles, no acknowledgement, just the simple gaze of contemplation. He began to stroll around the pond and towards me, each of us still considering the other, each of us perhaps searching for leeway. I took in the rose polo shirt, the crumpled shorts, as he moved towards me, almost in slow motion. I took in the whole man, the physical being that was my love. He was still here now, I thought, so capture him, freeze this frame. Because I knew that I would not get through this at all.

Reaching me, Dan too slumped onto the bench. After a moment he placed his hand on the slats between us, and after a further moment I placed mine over his.

"When Franklin was born I was scared, you know, scared that I wouldn't have enough love left over from Spencer." He spoke softly, his voice seemed thick with spent tears. "But then there he was, all vulnerable in his diaper, clutching my finger with his tiny fist. And, you know what? He climbed up inside me, beside Spence." Dan clamped a palm to his chest. "Right in there. So you see I needn't have been scared at all."

I sat still and silent, fighting back the tears.

"Now you've gotten in there too, Ness." His voice faltered. "Can't live without you."

"Ditto." I squeezed his hand. "So stay."

Dan sighed, shifted along the bench and pulled me to him, kissing my temple.

"What will we live on? Love and fresh air?"

"There must be other jobs."

He threw me a rueful smile, stood and reached for me. "Come on, let's walk."

He led me past the stalls, pumping my hand with his, as if somehow he wanted to imprint the memory of it on his skin. For me, all shape and colour was distorted through the film of tears that refused to be blinked away; an old chamber pot became white slush, a wooden towel rail a sandy plank. I felt like a child, being led through the funfair by a parent trying to make up for the bully that lay in wait in the playground, the lights and music unable to lift the sick pit of anticipation in her tummy.

During the remainder of that week, we went over and over the matter, getting no further than we had on those steps. In our suite at the Londonskaya, with its intricate parquetry and swagged curtains, we made love well into each night. A frantic love, often a desperate love. In the daytime too, Dan was always close by my side, touching me, holding me. I hoped perhaps he might be weakening in his resolve and I do remember being alive again to the pastel-hued buildings, their façades dripping with vines, as we strolled through Odessa. Perhaps it was just that I too needed an imprint of our last days for myself.

"You said we were unbreakable," I was brave enough to utter one morning, as we languished in the claw-footed bath which stood centre stage in the bathroom.

He sat forwards, creating a wave of water, and took my face in his hands. "We are."

"I thought we were going to have a baby together."

"We are."

He held my eyes with his and the emotion swept me then, but I dodged it with an attempt at humour.

"Bit difficult, if you're there and I'm here."

He stood up suddenly, stepped out of the bath splashing pools of water and began to towel himself off, his back square on to me.

"It's a top posting, Ness. And I need the challenge."

"Can't you try the other donors in Kiev first, though?"

"Like I said, I've outstayed my welcome in Kiev."

"Just one more year?" I heard my small voice. "I could be ready to go too then."

He spun around and dried his toes on the side of the bath. "Got my boys to consider here too, you know, they're growing into men now, they need me closer."

He seemed intractable. But then so was I, until perhaps our last evening. As we sat in the hotel's leafy courtyard and drank glass after glass of wine, Dan pulled out the aid card. He told me how he had researched programmes for women farming on scratchy patches of land in the hills, how malaria killed children in the Mosquito jungle region, how they badly needed development professionals, 'like me'. So I turned my imagination to a possible life in this hot new country, where they spoke Spanish and grew avocados the size of melons, and perhaps I wavered a little.

When our flight landed at Borispol on the Sunday evening, however, I

210

was jittery at the prospect of getting back to the programme, my bones already crawling with my plans for the coming week. It was beyond my control. As we taxied to our stand, Dan turned to me.

"I can't go without you, Ness."

"I can't leave these people, Dan."

It was partly brinkmanship, believing there to be real hope in his words, partly my own bloody-mindedness, but mainly it was my gut speaking.

26

Once back in Kiev, our mood shifted. As if the interlude in the sun had been just that, a spell away from reality. If we could have done, we'd probably have swished in and out of rooms avoiding each other, but our apartment was too tiny for that – how whole Ukrainian families must rub along in such confinement. I plunged myself into the programme, clinging to its daily succour. We both worked late, while at home we became overly polite. I was relieved when finally I left on our study visit to the UK, desperate for respite.

When he dropped me at Borispol, Dan switched the engine off. We both sat staring ahead and he let out a morose sigh.

"I'm jaded, Ness, you know that."

"But I've still go two years to go here. Why can't you wait for me?"

"Why can't you come with me?"

"Apart from any sense of professionalism, you mean? Apart from having just re-designed my programme, which will fail without me? Apart from letting Bogdan down? And more to the point, apart from the fact that I just do not want to leave yet. Have you considered any of that, kiddo?"

"Look, it's just the way it is in aid, you can never expect to get two postings in sync, someone's always got to give."

"But why should it be me?"

"Because I have to go now."

"Do you? Do you really, though?"

He turned to me, eyes pleading. "I'm ready to move on, Ness."

"Well I'm not!" I flung the Jeep door open.

Dan followed me round to the boot. "Will you think it through? Please?"

"Only if you will too, I mean about trying other avenues in Kiev."

212

"OK."

His conviction sounded loose, but as we kissed, I wondered how I could even contemplate a life without this man.

*

In the end, we were a group of thirty on the study tour to Manchester, half as many again as planned, so my leverage over Jeff had not been completely wasted. We began at the glass-walled offices of Lancashire. In reception, the group clipped on their badges with high-spirited chatter over the way their names were spelt in the English alphabet, and gathered round the coffee vending machine. While we waited for Carole, I sank into a leather sofa by the window and watched them passing round the capsules, animatedly weighing up the different blends. Viktor, who had once bellowed at Balavensky across a conference hall, appeared now to be thick friends with the Minister, their heads fused together over the labels. In fact, the whole group seemed like a gaggle of friends on holiday together; curious how the hierarchies seemed to have dissipated. Still, Balavensky was first to slot his capsule into the machine, I noticed, while the Three Graces and the Task Force trainees huddled round him, noses up in a show of smelling the coffee.

Svetlana sat down beside me. I'd now witnessed for myself how the Task Force trainees had ostracised her. The young women were universally charming to me, but huffy with her, and I planned to raise this with them at some opportune moment during that week.

"So far, so good?" I asked her.

"Oh yes," she said. "Thank you again Vanessa."

I had insisted that Svetlana join the study tour, adamant that she would double up as translator and thereby avoiding the need for Balavensky's daughter to travel. That girl's presence on the payroll, however, was by then an irrelevance for me – the more programme funds that went into the local economy the better – and I knew that I would never tackle the Minister on this minor corruption.

Upstairs, Carole stood at the front of a meeting room and ran through our itinerary, while the group rummaged through their goodies folders, squirreling the highlighters and logo-ed pens into pockets, as they had done with the toiletries and socks on the plane over. From the back of the room, I observed my friend with a coolness that hid a sheepishness. We were barely speaking now that Bogdan had revised the programme, not only allocating more budget to the study tour, but also shifting sums away from the UK short-term experts to pay for extra micro loans, more local Ukrainian experts and additional office equipment. Profit from fees had shrunk, and with it, I had heard, Carole's standing in the company.

First on our programme was a visit to a Job Centre, which I found myself leading, after Jeff claimed other commitments and slunk off. I herded the group like cats along the busy pavements, waiting patiently as they stopped every so often to press up against the shop windows. Each member had a fifty pound daily allowance and was saving it up for their free day, which we had all clocked on the itinerary. They created quite a stir with their clothes and hairstyles too. Balavensky had forsaken his baggy brown suit for a more dapper cream jacket and shoes to match, an outfit which Yaroslav also sported, while the Task Force girls were dressed up in primary colours and wore bright make-up.

We came across a tramp hunched up on the ground with a dog and a cap. As he slurred for spare change, the group skirted round him.

Viktor sidled up to me. "Perhaps UK needs transfer of know-how from Ukraine in this matter, Vanessa. We have not men who sit on dirty street and beg money in our country."

I knew his comment was tongue-in-cheek, because by then there were many beggars in Kiev, but I grinned and went with it. "So you see, Viktor, it wasn't just Soviet propaganda!"

The Job Centre was full and smelt of fetid socks. Most punters seemed irritated by our jolly presence, their faces incongruous against the smiling job-hunters pictured on the brochures, which the Graces quickly began gathering up.

The manager, a kindly woman in her fifties, welcomed us valiantly. "Job Centres were set up by Winston Churchill, who had them painted green, the colour of hope."

She invited Balavensky to try out the PCs, in a mock search for a job in consumer sales. His impassive face lit up as he typed one-fingered commands and moved through the screens. Then she led us over to the benefits section, where a girl who had agreed to be observed signing on for her dole sat wringing a rolled-up newspaper.

"What jobs have you applied for in the last fortnight?" the adviser asked her.

"Three." She scratched her nose, responding directly into Yaroslav's camera.

"How can you prove that to me please?" The woman continued typing.

She unfurled her newspaper and pointed to the adverts circled in red, while the adviser nodded and pushed a form at her for signature.

Viktor clicked his tongue. "But how do you know that she has really applied for these jobs?"

"I did apply for them." The girl scowled at him. "I called them up, but they'd gone already."

The manager stepped in. "Sadly, we have ten people chasing every vacancy." She led the girl away from our pack, while the next person stepped forward.

Afterwards we paused for photos outside the Job Centre. The hierarchies dissolved further as the group took up their positions in a general muddle, although Svetlana was still out on a limb. When I marshalled the group onto a bus for our next destination, the Task Force girls skipped upstairs, leaving her downstairs with the oldies, so I decided then to act. Such petty rivalry, I thought crossly, as I stomped up the stairs and stood swaying on the top deck, which fortuitously was otherwise empty.

"Ladies," I began, in faltering Russian. "Svetlana is a local expert on the programme and that is why she is paid by us. You are recipients of valuable new skills from the programme and that is why you are paid by the Ministry. Do I make myself clear?"

The women gazed at me. "Da," a few of them muttered.

"Please, let us remain a cohesive group throughout this week."

Odd to me, looking back, that I took this sledgehammer approach. Svetlana was earning four hundred pounds a month, while the women were being paid a quarter of that. I should have empathised, but back then I truly did believe that these women should have been above envy – as if somehow aid recipients should be universally benign, should be better than human. I believe their response to my sermon was to take the bullying underground.

Over the following days, we visited many job creation initiatives, and Yaroslav filmed it all. Throughout the tour, my friend was inconspicuous, but there was one bizarre incident, after dinner one evening, when the copious toasts were underway. I emerged from the ladies to find him screeching at Mrs T and Balavensky. The room fell silent at the sight of me, and I dismissed it as high spirits and booze. Later, of course, that little spat was to fall into place.

On our free day, I decided to go shopping for clothes. I had hoped to avoid the group and had breakfasted in my room at the Holiday Inn, but in the foyer there they all were, poring over maps with the concierge. Even the Minister clutched a shopping sack, one of the flimsy red and blue striped boxes, which always choked up arrivals at Borispol. Only Mrs T was absent. She of course already knew her way around this city and its designer shops.

"Ah Vanessa." Viktor caught my arm as I made for the door. "Will you take us to the shops with good price, please."

Shit, I thought. "Of course," I said, "but make sure you each have a map so you can get back to the hotel by yourselves."

Jeff should have given them all a Paddington Bear name tag, I thought, as I stood on the pavement and watched them spill through the doors to my side. "Marks and Spencer is the UK's favourite shop and very good value." I held up a map and circled the Arndale Centre. "There are lots of other shops here too, and a market with the best prices."

We entered M&S via the food hall. Balavensky was first in through the automatic doors and there he stopped dead, creating a commotion behind him as Viktor and the trainees shunted on into each other, while everyday shoppers tutted and glared at the strange group. Inside, it was like watching children pop out into Santa's grotto with glances up and along the wondrous aisles, except that it didn't bring me warmth and fuzziness, but rather guilt and shame.

The group dispersed into the food aisles. I had once read that a Russian musician visiting the UK in the seventies had vomited his guts up on his first trip to a supermarket, and I was reminded of that as I watched the Graces at the fresh fruit display. Hands clasped to mouths, they reached almost tentatively to stroke the flashes of orange peel and the packs of fat strawberries. Balavensky picked up an Indian ready meal and stood bewitched, turning it in his hands, sliding the sleeve off and back onto the foil dish. I watched Yaroslav filming the trainees, as they swarmed around jars of artichokes, packets of olives and tubs of hummus.

Finally, I turned away and went in search of chocolate for Dan. It was still late summer, but the store was already dressed for Halloween, the shelves stacked with net bags of orange-foiled chocolates. And it struck me suddenly that this country now marked out the passing of time by crass consumerism. Tripping through the seasons – from Valentines, through Easter, to Christmas, and all those occasions for sales and marketing in between. I reached for one of the chocolate bags: the net itself would make a good toy at the kindergarten in my village. In my village?

I dropped the bag back on the shelf and took in the British shoppers, who were charging through the store, heaping gluttony into the wire baskets as if driven to squeeze every last drop of what was their right from their day. We should have study tours for you lot too, I thought. You should know how these Ukrainian people live. Much more profoundly than you, that's for sure. With a sigh which sagged heavily from me, I left the store.

As I wandered aimlessly around Manchester, it struck me that I had lived there for the whole of my adult life, had spent little more than one year away, and yet the city belonged already to my past. Kiev was home now and I was missing the place badly. The thought of having to leave finally caught me out and I realised that I was dangerously close to tackling the soul-searching Dan had asked of me. My stomach churned and my legs fell hollow. That week, he had constantly popped up in my thoughts, like the game Whack-a-Mole, but I'd rapped him back down, only to watch him appear again in some other spot. I found myself in Deansgate and mooched through the door of Kendals in search of further distraction.

"Free makeover, Madam?" A young girl stepped forward.

"Yes." I was flustered by her panache. "Why not?"

I climbed onto a bar stool and gazed at my complexion in the mirror, still pale despite the long hot Ukrainian summer. Perhaps if I began finally to use make-up I could make him stay, I thought, as the girl began to paint me.

"Always use a synthetic brush for cream, but natural bristles for powder, otherwise the bristles will spoil," she said.

I glanced at her pot of brushes, crammed with varying shapes and sizes, and I felt disgust for them. How frivolous, how vacuous, when the women in my village were bent over washboards or straining over the winding handle at the communal well. Still, I sat it out. The girl applied something called a primer to my eyelid, to prepare it for the purple shadow which would accentuate my green eyes, then beige eyeliner to cover up the red rims I'd never even noticed were there. And so it went on, until finally I sat with smoky eyes, bronzed cheeks that glittered, and a sticky crimson lipstick that made my lips creep. OK, *kiddo*, I thought, let's see how easy it is to leave me now. I bought the lot. Then I traipsed to the ladies, locked myself in a cubicle and sobbed. The thoughts came at me, surprising me with the way they clenched and pummelled me. The reality was that Dan was going to leave Kiev. How could I possibly not go with him?

On the final day of the study visit, Bogdan invited the group to tour his engineering works and learn about apprenticeships. Kitted out in hard hats

217

and overalls, we set off through the plant under his personal guidance, joined by Jeff for the first time that week. The group were by then all confident in asking questions and the chatter between them and my boss was animated as he pointed out the manufacturing processes, shouting above the deafening noise of the machinery.

We came across a slight youth huddled over a lathe, and crowded round to observe his work. He was producing threaded machine parts of some kind and we watched a bladed tool slicing up into a cylinder on the end of the lathe, coming at it over and over to produce a perfect thread around its girth. As the youth worked, he shrank from our scrutiny, but Bogdan introduced him as an apprentice learning his trade on the job through a government scheme. Viktor and Balavensky as ever seemed to know nothing of personal space and pushed themselves into the boy's pimpled face, he must have been able to smell their breath.

"How long you work here?" Viktor barked at him above the din.

The boy flushed scarlet. "Ten months."

"How much money you earn?"

The boy glanced at Bogdan who nodded for him to respond.

"Two pounds forty an hour," he said.

"Is lot of money," Viktor exclaimed. "How many hours you work?"

"Thirty-eight hour week," he said, which the group duly noted down.

Bogdan hosted lunch for us in his boardroom. I watched him settling in at his burr walnut table to play Mein Host, but Jeff was on his feet even before the prawn cocktail starter had arrived.

"May I propose a toast to the whole group," he said. "It has been an exemplary study tour and I have no doubt that you have all gleaned many ideas to put into practice on your return home."

Not that you were present for any of it, I thought, looking round for any sign of amusement from the group at Jeff's attempt to impress Bogdan and catching Svetlana's wink. The other faces remained inscrutable as ever, but I suspected that their smiles would be broad on the inside. Clearly annoyed, Bogdan too leapt to his feet.

"I hear Vanessa has made it a fabulous week," he cried, "with excellent experiences for all of you to take home for implementation in Ukraine, and I would like to propose a toast to her."

There were thumps on the table then and the group stood and cheered, tipping their glasses at me, while I indulged in the warm blush of praise on my cheeks.

"To our continued co-operation," I cried and then, bizarrely given the turmoil within me, I added. "Long may it last."

Balavensky was next up. Gradually over the course of the week his eyes had flickered with life, particularly during our visits to the NGOs – back then the charity sector was barely nascent in Ukraine, and played no role alongside the government in job creation. He thanked us for the meeting with senior civil servants from the Department for Employment, who had travelled up from London to spend a day with him. Afterwards, Mrs T was on her feet waxing about her plans for the Finns to expand our HQ with a Vocational Training Centre. Then Viktor told of his visit to a business incubator, where entrepreneurs could rent cheap office space and benefit from free access to PCs, phones and faxes, equipment which Viktor had stroked as he'd toured the place.

One by one, each member of the group stood and toasted the week, how it had been illuminating, exhilarating, and oh so fruitful. We were still sitting in the boardroom at clocking off time, when finally one of the Graces pulled out a form, which set the whole group off rummaging through their bags.

"Vanessa, they need to have their papers stamped," Svetlana explained, "to prove that they have been in the UK on official business."

I glanced at Balavenksy and Mrs T. Surely they would vouch for the group? But they too had forms that needed stamping with proof.

"A round stamp is best," Mrs T muttered.

"A round one …" I echoed and shot Bogdan an enquiring look, certain that he would not possess a stamp of any kind.

But my boss slapped his hand on the table and reached for his phone. "Get me the mailroom," he snapped.

The post boy arrived in the boardroom holding aloft a stamp, to raucous applause, and one by one each of the group placed their forms face up to receive its clunk. The ring of dazzling purple read, Please ensure you use the postcode.

I was packing on that last evening when Carole came to my hotel room. No phone call from reception, she simply rapped on the door and I opened it to see her tight anger, her beauty pinched into frayed lips, the lines at her brow tense. Though I knew the look well, never in my life had I been on the receiving end.

"You'd better come in then." I opened the door wider.

She strode in, quite impressively on her stilettos, slung her shoulder bag onto the bed and made for the window. She folded her arms at me, so I did likewise, but I did edge back to the wall, my shoulders seeking out its comforting solidity.

"Well, thanks a fucking bunch, Ness," she cried. "You totally annihilate me and then you don't even have the fucking decency to face up to me, skulking round Manchester all week."

"How have I annihilated you, Carole?" I began calmly, though my chest was already thumping.

"We stood to make fifty percent of that project at the outset. A profit of one and a half million pounds, do you realise that? And now. Now! That profit's been slashed to a miserable half a million, thanks to Miss Goody Two Shoes."

I felt the sudden surge of my own fury, but remained silent as she screamed on.

"A whole million quid in profit gone. Did you actually set out to destroy me? Did you?"

I stared at Carole, flinching as she took a stride in my direction, but she made for the bed, where she tore at her bag and whipped out a pack of cigarettes.

"Cos that's what you've done. You've destroyed me!" She glared and lit up, her hand shaking over the cigarette.

I let my own anger loose then. "Destroyed you? *Douze points* for melodrama, Carole! That's still half a million quid profit. Still easy money."

"Easy money? I work my tits off on your programme."

"Doing what exactly? Booking a few plane tickets? Writing crap reports? Lording it up at the National Hotel in Kiev?"

She gasped at me. "You try coordinating forty fucking experts on a programme."

"The programme doesn't need forty fucking experts! It needs three or four who can spend more time on the ground, who can slowly build trust. Why can't you get that through your thick head?"

"Who wants to spend more time on the ground in those clapped-out countries? No decent expert is going to sacrifice his career in the UK for that. You get that into your thick head, Ness!"

"What do you know about decent experts? You've only sent us tosh. Sir Roderick? Paul Hopkins? It's a bloody good job I've been on the ball and got Kevin and Niamh involved."

"That's another thing, isn't it? What you really want to do is take charge of the programme yourself. It's us who know the experts out there

220

on the market, not you."

"On the market? That's all it is to you, a market. To them in Ukraine it's a matter of life and death, but to you all this is purely for commercial gain." I was screaming back at her too now. "If I had my way, most of that three million quid would be spent on the ground, on the micro-credit, on the local experts, on equipment." I ticked the stuff on my fingers as I went. "That's what they really need, but you don't give a shit about all of that, do you?"

She shook her head in consternation. "If you had your way you'd fly a plane over Ukraine and drop the three million quid in notes."

"Well maybe that would be more effective!"

That last shriek of mine brought several sharp raps from the neighbouring room. We both glanced at the wall and stopped dead. I found that I had my fists clenched, and realised that we had both edged towards each other in the fight. I took a series of calming breaths and steadily forced my shoulders down, watching Carole do the same, her chest heaving, her eyes steadily losing their blaze. Finally, she sat down on the bed.

"My first ever stint at programme supervisor, after ten years as a secretary, and now I'm a laughing stock at Lancashire. I'm just a bimbo, always was, always will be."

She sank her head in her hands and tears sprang to my eyes as her words hit home.

"No you're not." I sat down beside her on the bed, my arm drifting around her shoulders. "I'm so sorry, Carole. I never saw it that way. I think I only saw the need to get results out there. And I thought that would be important for Lancashire too."

"What do they care about results? They're only in it for the profit."

"They used to care. With the coal programmes here, didn't they?"

"Eastern Europe's different. It's over there, not over here. And it's a gravy train." Carole looked up at me. "Anyway, no results to speak of yet, are there?"

I squeezed her arm. "There will be though, we're poised for a break-through, especially after this week, you'll see. They're champing at the bit to implement some of the stuff they've seen here."

"Oh yeah, as old Viktor likes to say, 'All problems will be solved.'" Her Ukrainian accent was spot on and I laughed.

I stood to scoop out a couple of miniatures from the mini bar and handed her one. We each took a slug of gin and winced.

"I'll fix us a proper one," I said.

When I'd returned from the counter, this time holding glasses topped up with ice and tonic, Carole had shifted up the bed to its head, shoes off, legs stretched out. I shuffled up beside her, chinked glasses and we sipped at our drinks in silence.

"Anyway, if you're lucky you might be seeing the back of me," I said finally.

"What do you mean?"

I sighed, my voice a singsong. "Dan's leaving Kiev, going to Honduras, wants me to go with him."

I watched her absorb this. "You're not going to though, are you?"

I shrugged but said nothing.

"Surely not?" she said.

"I am thinking about it."

"Have you gone stark raving mad? I thought all that was just a fuck fest?"

I felt my eyes prickle again. "No. No, in fact, I do love him."

"But what about the programme? What about Ukraine?"

"Ah, well there's the rub, as they say." I let out a hollow laugh. "I think I might just be in love with that too."

Carole was clearly waiting for more, but I was struggling to compose myself, unable to go on.

"Can't he stay till you've finished it?"

"Says not." I nodded in agreement with the logic of her question.

"Well then he's selfish and bloody-minded isn't he? Thought that when I met him."

"Yes he is stubborn." I grinned at her. "I quite like that about him, though."

"But, what's to say he isn't going to want to move on again, once he gets you to Honduras? What's to say he won't be dragging you off with him on another whim?"

"True."

"Didn't you say that's why his wife left him?"

"Yes, but ..."

My words trailed off with the sting of hers; indeed identical thoughts had crossed my own mind.

"But what?" she asked gently.

"It's different with me. He does love me, we're very close."

"He's a lot older than you, isn't he? Are you sure it's not just father figure stuff with him, Ness? You know, after the shitty Dad you had?"

"Might be. Is it such a big deal if it is?"

"So are you going to go with him?"

"I have no idea. I can't even think straight, Carole, my head's all over the place. I miss him so much while I'm here, I can't wait to get home to Kiev. And yet it's not just him I need to see again, it's the women in Donetsk, the miners, it's the whole programme, you should have seen these people this week, so fired up. The thing is, Carole, Ukraine's worked its way under my skin."

She snorted then. "Tell me about it. It's turned you into a right harpy."

We smiled and sipped our drinks while I wondered whether to go on.

"It's as if I've arrived at precisely where I belong, as if I were born to help the Ukrainian people. I feel so grounded, so real." I searched her face for comprehension, found none, and tried again. "I don't know, it's difficult to describe. Just that, in Kiev I've felt more myself than at any time before in my life and I'm scared that I'll lose all that, leave it behind, that I'll change or something, that I won't be me anymore." I paused. "And then he won't want me anymore, anyway, will he?"

Carole slipped her arm around me. "How could anyone not want you? But if you feel he's going to dump you, then you simply shouldn't go."

That's not what I felt at all. She hadn't grasped it, and I found it hard to grasp myself, but for the first time I realised I was terrified that I would be less myself, that I would lose my very self if I left Ukraine.

"You're still only twenty-seven, Ness, you've never had a problem finding men." She paused. "And if you want kids, do you not think you're better to find someone closer to your own age?"

I glanced at my friend, I'd never told her about the miscarriage, it would have seemed disloyal somehow to Dan, and I decided against telling her then.

"Well I'm hoping he'll stay anyway," I said, shuffling off the bed. "Nothing's settled." I made for the mini bar and took out a bottle of Chardonnay. "Anyway, enough of me, back to you," I said brightly. "Can't we sort it so that you get more credit for the programme? I mean for the successes? Because there are some and there will soon be more, we're poised for a breakthrough, I know it. Why don't we list them, back of an envelope stuff and I promise you that we'll collaborate properly from here on in."

I could hear myself speaking, as if I was going to stay.

27

As we took off from Manchester, a feeling of contentment swept over me. I was going home. I looked down at the red roofs, at the Lancashire landscape and took my mind back over what I'd said to Carole. The interlude in England, the place of my birth, had been just that. Kiev was where I belonged now. I thought too of something my Mum used to say. Be true to yourself, she'd always told me. As a teenager, I was never sure what she meant by that, it sounded too surreal for a working class girl who had always been buffeted by life, rather than taken control of it. But sitting on that plane, I knew precisely what she meant. It was a feeling of equilibrium, of living each day in a way that didn't tug me in the wrong directions, that didn't leave me bewildered in bed at night. A daily output in words and actions that mirrored me perfectly on the inside. Through my life in Ukraine, I had found that equilibrium, and I was fearful that if I were to leave I might never retrieve an even keel again.

And yet, as we reached the Carpathians and flew over the wide tracts of forest, the fields of cereals, the fertile chernozem, I knew that the pull Kiev held for me was intermingled with that of Dan, and I felt powerless to distinguish between the two. Please let him have reconsidered, I said silently, as the plane landed and screeched down the runway.

At Borispol Dan held me. I clung onto him, breathed in the scent of him. We dined at our favourite Italian, the Pantagruel, where he was keen, overly so, to hear every last detail about my week in the UK. I too was eager to linger at the surface, embellishing the many ways in which the study visit had cemented my programme onto a sounder footing. However, beneath my descriptions of the Job Centre, the shopping trip, Bogdan's factory tour, we were gauging each other. His whole face was alert, pupils dilated, assessing me for my decision – and he roared too loudly at my anecdote about the mailroom stamp. Equally, I was scanning his every movement for signs that he had relented and would stay on.

The only lull came as we called for the bill, those moments between the imaginary pen flick to signal it and its arrival at our gingham tablecloth. Caught like this, we smiled broadly at each other. Then Dan whistled a soft tune – Yankee Doodle or something – and glanced around. So I asked him.

"Are you going?"

He pursed his lips at me. "Are you coming?"

I shrugged.

"Ah," he said.

The waiter arrived and received superlatives from Dan beyond his normal gusto, while I sat with my heart thumping. What did that 'Ah' mean? On the brief walk back to our apartment, Dan took my hand, rolling my fingers between his own, but we didn't speak. In bed we stretched against each other, my limbs seeking out his, as if to fuse with them, and his with mine. We moved with our habitual tempo, as if the steady, familiar rhythm would settle our lives back into what had been there before. But in the hazy depths beneath our lovemaking, I think I was conscious that what had been there before was already lost to us.

Afterwards, we lay on our backs, staring up at the wisps of dusk playing off the ceiling. The hubbub of the courtyard, the familiar wafts of heat from the open window, the woody drifts of polish from the parquet, they were all comforting for me, but that homecoming feeling was scuppered by the tension between us. For a long while neither of us spoke, perhaps neither of us dared to. Then, finally, Dan broke the silence.

"Did you know that Buddhists build temples to secure their place in nirvana? The logic behind it being that the more they build, the bigger, the better, then the greater their chances in the next life."

Prickles crept across my cheeks; was he telling me he was leaving?

"My parents divorced when I was eight," he went on. "Mom remarried, and as a consequence I behaved badly. Real bad, in fact. I guess I couldn't handle my dad walking out on me. I used to stick my step dad's golf clubs in paint, cut the sleeves off his shirts, that sort of stuff." He let out a soft snort. "And as a punishment, when Mom wasn't around, he used to lock me in a wall closet with the light off."

My stomach flipped in empathy and I fumbled for Dan's hand across the covers, my mind opening the door on that cupboard to free him.

"I set off building my own temples, scrabbling for some weird atonement, just like you, Ness, making amends for your pet hamster." He turned to me, his face twisted with emotion. "But somewhere along the way, I lost the will, I stopped caring. I don't know, maybe the world just wasn't grateful enough."

I shucked myself up onto an elbow. "But you still do care, Dan. I see only goodness in you, only compassion. The you I love does still believe in it."

"You do that for me, Ness, it's vicarious. You love me and it bolsters me, it makes me more myself than I am. I need you by my side, can't you see that?"

I blinked back tears. "I think I can see it. But I need you to understand something for me too Dan. When we first met, do you remember what you said to me? Stay as you are, you said. Can you remember that?"

"Yep."

He took a breath and expelled it in one short burst, which could have been emotion but sounded like impatience. I went on.

"Well, I'm scared that if I leave this place I will not stay as I am. I'm scared that you need the person you see here in Kiev, doing all this worthwhile stuff. I'm scared that if I give this job up, I'm going to flounder, that I won't be the same person anymore. That I'll be less of myself. And I'm scared that then you won't want me anymore."I heard my voice falter and I let the tears spill.

Dan shucked himself up too then and wiped my tears with his thumb. "How could I ever not want you?"

He kissed me, pressed me back down and slid on top of me once more. The light of day brought a retreat once again, as if the night had been other-worldly, on the other side of darkness. We were distant, cool; in fact, I would say that Dan was irritated with me. He suggested breakfast out at a café, where we sat amidst other people's hubbub while I sipped coffee and took surreptitious glances at his face above the newspaper. Had he even heard me in the night? Had he listened? Did he have any interest in my reasoning? He probably considered that his own soul-baring should have clinched it for me, that his demons were somehow worth more than mine.

After breakfast, we drove out to Sasha's garage to view a fresh consignment of paintings. It was a lengthy journey and Dan switched on the radio, creating a barrier with the breakneck political discussion in Russian, or so it seemed to me. I was becoming more fluent but he knew I still had problems keeping up, and his occasional snorts at some heated point exacerbated the distance between us. *You are selfish and bloody-*

minded, just as Carole said, I thought, working myself up into a rage. *You're a bully, just like my dad was to my mum.*

Sasha was waiting on a wall outside his lock-up and he ground his cigarette into the patch of others at his feet as we parked. Still sullen at being left off the study tour, he shook Dan's hand and nodded to me without the usual flash of gold eye tooth.

"Did you enjoy your week off?" I asked him pointedly, suddenly cross with him too. The corners of his mouth dipped in response.

Inside the garage, stacks of paintings were lined up at one wall and I glanced around to see what other stashes he had. On a plastic sheet across the oil-slicked floor were several rolled up rugs, antique no doubt, and beside them stood a heap of tarnished samovars. Silently, I stood to the side of Dan as he bent to rifle through the paintings, while Sasha, somewhat obsequiously, slid each discarded one away, to allow him full sight of the one behind. I took in the usual vistas of the workers, bodies rigid as if chiselled from stone, heads aloft, a banner unfurling and smoke spewing from yonder chimneys. Dan gave no hint of a reaction until we reached the last one at the back, an enormous painting, as wide as I was tall.

He let out a whistle. "Oh yeah, this one's good."

"This one very rare," Sasha jumped in. "From Eastern Ukraine, from house of old woman after she died."

I stepped back, gazed at the painting and shuddered. Against the backdrop of a typical village with its peasant ribbons, corn sheaves and combines in the distance, it depicted an upper body shot of Stalin, almost life-size. His hand was resting lightly on the downy hair of a young boy. In a flash I was reminded of those TV images of Saddam Hussein's hand cradling the head of a terrified child, one of the BA plane passengers held hostage when Iraq invaded Kuwait.

"Ghoulish," I said.

"Superb," Dan said. "How much, Sasha?"

I saw Sasha silently inventing his price on the basis of the word superb, but the set of Dan's jaw told me who would win out here.

"One thousand dollars," Sasha decided.

Dan laughed. "Three hundred."

"Eight hundred."

"Five hundred, final offer."

They shook hands and I stared at the painting, my heart leaping around my chest as I formed my question.

"Where will we put it?"

"Latin fincas have vast walls." His eyes gleamed at the artwork.

I turned and left the garage, focusing hard to put one wobbly leg before the other, while the blood thumped through my ears. A few minutes later Dan joined me in the Jeep.

"You're going then?"

"Have to, Ness." His voice was gentle. I could tell he regretted his cruelty in front of Sasha.

"So you can't stay for just one more year?" I heard the tremble to my own voice.

"Neither the Bank nor the IMF in Kiev have positions to match Honduras."

"What about the EC?"

"Oh yeah? Like they'd want to employ a Yank." He jammed the jeep into gear and pulled off in a skid start.

"How about you do a stint as an expert on a programme?"

"How about I go stack shelves in a store?"

He was right. I fell silent.

"Why can't you come with me, dammit?" he cried.

"Even Moscow would do," I said, ignoring him. "Have you tried there? Just a year and then we'll go together."

"This job ain't gonna be there in a year, Ness."

"There'll be others."

He smacked the steering wheel. "You just don't get it, do you? There are five of these Regional Director posts in the whole of USAID. Five. How often do you think they come up? Jesus, Vanessa, there's enough poverty in Honduras to last even you a lifetime."

A sudden fury hit me then; he hadn't absorbed a single word of what I'd told him about me in the night, didn't take it the least bit seriously.

"I want to stay in this country, I'm changing things here. My programme is unique."

"Your programme is just like all the others, a charade maintained by both sides that it's fruitful and sustainable, when in fact it's a money-spinning sideshow."

I gasped at this. "You're so cynical! I wonder why you're even in this business. Look at what I've achieved in Donetsk with those women, with the miners. I've even got the ear of the Minister now, you should have seen him in England, he's trusting me to deliver."

"The Minister is playing you big time. How much of a cut do you think he's skimming? Ten big ones? Nah, more I'd say."

"You're just twisted and jealous, 'cos he's let me into the tent which is where you've been trying to get for years."

He shook his head with the smile of an indulgent parent and this incensed me further.

"The reality is that I'm better at this than you ever were!" I screamed.

"Yes you are." He made an exaggerated swerve at a pothole.

"What about those Task Force girls? Am I supposed to just abandon them?"

"Do you think your girls are going to stick around on government salaries when you've trained them up to Western standards? Do you really think any of them will be there once the dollars have dried up at programme end? They'll be snapped up by some foreign investor if not by another aid programme."

"No they won't, because I am going to make personally sure they're not."

"What you gonna do? Pay them yourself? Look, it's just a job! Nobody's indispensable, not even you."

"So how can you leave me for just a job?"

"I've got kids to support, remember? What the hell are we supposed to live on? You earn Jack Shitt."

The sting of that silenced me. I looked down into my hands, knitted together on my lap. When I spoke again it was in a whisper.

"I know why you're leaving. Because you're self-centred and egotistical, Dan Mitchell."

"Oh OK, and you think you're not, right? What drives you is your little ego, you get off on being the benevolent one. You're not saving these people, you are saving yourself, go on admit it, Vanessa Parker."

The tears were spilling now. "I came to this country for a reason. I've... I've found myself here."

"Found yourself." He let out a snort of irritation. "Kids stuff, Vanessa."

He pulled up at the side of the road, jumped out and slammed the door. I watched him shuffle off, stumbling slightly as he went. When he'd turned a corner and was out of view I shifted over to the driver's seat and drove myself home.

Dan stayed away that night. I fretted around the apartment, furious by the way he'd bullied me, but bereft by his absence. As to his whereabouts, well, frenzied thoughts flashed at me – I even considered that he might be with Chelsea, although deep down I knew that to be nonsense.

On the Monday morning, I sat with my coffee and my thoughts, listening to the silence which rang throughout the apartment and bounced off the wooden floors. Odd how you burrow deeper into each other, in and further in, curling around the nooks and turns, reaching such a depth, that you couldn't possibly find your way back. And yet, in one instant, you can be sucked out, bumped and bruised by the flight, and find yourself on the outside of someone again. Find yourself alone again.

I could go with him, I thought. Why didn't I just stop fighting? Had I worked myself up into such a state about the need to stay that I could no longer unravel it? Of course, there was doubt too. I loved Dan completely, but I did question his zeal to move on, even though he claimed us to be unique – unbreakable, as he put it. The way he seemed not to hear me, not to understand me – he wasn't even trying to. And those echoes of my dad's bullying still lingered. I was feeling steamrolled.

Sasha drove me in to work, silent and respectful after being party to such an insight about my future. As we arrived at the programme HQ, a man in overalls was painting the front door green, a rich grassy gloss. Mrs T stood supervising the job personally, providing commentary while Yaroslav filmed her and the brush strokes.

"Green is the colour of hope," she announced to the camera as I slipped past her inside the building.

Indeed, the hope inside our HQ was tangible that morning and I felt myself slipping out of my sulk, eased also by the fact that there were no Lancashire experts in town. In the Job Centre, the Three Graces were unpacking the new PCs which had arrived during their absence. I watched them gliding around the hall with a new-found confidence, a new-found purpose. So touched was I by the scene, that I pretended to busy myself over a PC, uncoiling its cable, plugging it in.

"Damn, it needs configuring or something." I stared into the nonsense on the screen. "Sasha, can you fetch Viktor up please?"

A panting Viktor came through the door a few minutes later, jostling with Jeff, whose presence instantly spiked my hackles. Jeff beat him to our side and rubbed his hands together.

"Have we got a light bulb situation, ladies?" Addressing only the Ukrainian women, he ignored me.

The Graces looked blank, but I decided not to enlighten them on the joke, as Jeff sat himself down and Viktor breathed heavily over his shoulder. The two of them frowned at the screen. Jeff pressed the Enter key while Viktor jabbed at the Escape one, and the PC pinged but the screen remained static. After a few minutes, Jeff sat back with a sigh that was clearly meant to signal defeat despite a superior intelligence.

"Truth be known, I'm actually a Luddite, ladies," he said.

The Graces and Viktor glanced at him, waiting for more.

"Luddite? What is this Luddite?" Viktor asked, stabbing at a few more keys.

"Yes, what actually is a Luddite?" I asked pointedly, with a scornful glance at Jeff.

He scratched his neck. "Well, it's just one of those expressions…"

"No it's not just an expression, in fact Luddites were actually workers who protested against mechanisation in the last century," I said, my tenor far too ugly – I would say a little unhinged even. "Best not to use big words if you don't know their meaning, Jeff."

At this, each of the Ukrainians watched us and waited, while Jeff glared at me.

"You think you're so clever, don't you? If I were you, I'd think seriously about moving on with your cowboy."

"So that you can continue swanning through this three million pound programme with impunity, Jeff? I wonder what other slush funds you might have hidden from me that make your life more comfortable?"

He kicked the chair back on its wheels and stood up, jabbing a finger at me, his foul breath engulfing me.

"You… are a busy body. You have no understanding of the complexities of this country, coming here with your bleeding heart, pussy-footing around at the edges."

"And you've never had to be accountable before, have you? That's the real crux of it. You've made an easy living out of this, all your life, haven't you? You don't give a shit about these people!"

We both turned to look at the Three Graces and Viktor. They were making no attempt to hide their scorn for Jeff, it was etched on all of their faces, and perhaps it was this moment that clinched it. I can't leave you, I thought, I just cannot.

"Looks like we'll have to get the computer fairies in, then," I said lightly, and sat back down at the PC, my hands shaking over the keyboard. I arrived home that evening to find Dan stirring a mushroom risotto at the stove. He glanced briefly over his shoulder at me and then back to the pan.

"Took a hike in the woods," he said. "Hope they're not poisonous."

He looked as if he'd slept in the woods too; unshaven and wearing the same T-shirt as the previous day, though the pungent male drift coming off him did stir a buzz at my crotch.

"Smells good."

"Get a load of this." He offered me a block of parmesan. "Fresh from Rome, guy in the office brought it back for me."

The rich aroma of the cheese lifted me for a brief moment – he'd had it brought back especially for him; this could only mean that he planned to remain in Kiev and eat it. For several surreal moments the parmesan represented the future; this food would anchor him here alongside it.

"Mmm, that is good." I smiled at him.

"Oh and you're on the news, I've taped it for you." His politeness was eerie.

"Thanks." I opened two bottles of beer and slid his across the work surface.

"I leave at the end of next week."

My heart thudded. I managed it through to the living room with my beer, sank into the armchair and flicked on the recording. Refusing my mind any chance to consider Dan's words, I busied it with tiny sips from the bottle and watched the brief shots of me with Balavensky at the Job Centre in Manchester. There I was on the screen. After several replays, I paused the footage and looked into myself. I could feel the intensity, I could feel how vital this was for me, and in that brief moment my resolve was fixed.

Dan brought the dish through and I joined him at the small table by the window overlooking the Opera House. Outside, life continued regardless; commuters sauntered home from work and already jovial queues were forming on the steps for that evening's performance of Tosca. Didn't they know?

"Thanks for this," I muttered, toying with the rice.

"Been thinking," he said. "How about you come out for the holidays. Then after a year you'll join me, right?"

I shook my head. "If you go, then it's over."

He stared at me. "That's absurd."

It was. Totally absurd. "Don't bully me Dan. You have no understanding of what I said to you yesterday. You're going despite everything I've told you about my needing to stay. So don't think you can go off and build yourself a new life, and still dip into me as you wish. I'm not going to sit around torturing myself with thoughts of your three-in-a-beds, waiting for you to pitch up here on a whim."

"What are you talking about?" He was genuinely stunned, I could see

232

that, and yet I persevered.

"I'm staying here to see it through, not just one year, but two more years, until the end of the programme. You're only thinking of your career, so why shouldn't I think of mine? It's what defines me."

"You're being naïve, Ness, look you're young, you—"

"Yes I'm young and I'll meet someone else!"

He eyed me sadly. "Do you think what we have together comes along more than once in a lifetime?"

"I don't know." I dropped my own eyes.

When finally I glanced up, I saw that his were wild. Desolate. I caught the bags beneath them, the thick shadow on his jaw and my stomach flipped. But still I remained silent.

"Christ you mean it, don't you?"

He sank his head into his hands, ran his lovely thick fingers through the unwashed hair and I wanted to reach out and caress them, to pull his head onto my lap and fold myself onto him. But I didn't budge.

"Like you said that night in the mountains, I'm a product of my childhood. Just like you are. I can't help it. It's a need Dan, not a choice."

His head lay in his hands and I said no more. Did I think that by pushing him to the limit, I would somehow force him to stay? Such immaturity belongs now to my distant past and is incomprehensible to me now, all these years later. But then I'm inclined in any case to think not. I'm inclined to believe that I truly meant what I said to him that night.

28

It seemed that my decision was made, but in the few days that remained before Dan left I took myself off down to Donetsk. For validation. Kevin was home on leave, but Niamh and Svetlana invited me to an update meeting of the micro-credit beneficiaries, which I later suspected they had engineered for this purpose. On our drive from the airport, we passed fields of sunflowers, standing to attention before the sun, each dappled gold head on its imperceptible ratchet round as it chased the rays. I saw Dan's smile appear in one, then another, and yet another, before I snapped my eyes away. Push him out, Ness, he's in the past, I told myself, gripping the edges of my seat, this is your future right here.

Inside the village hall, the chairs had been laid out in horseshoe formation, and beside them stood the table with its samovar and plates of cakes, their just-baked sweetness steeping the air. I made a point of crossing the floor to greet my Divas – Olga, Lesya and Yelena, then Marina and Tanya, and found myself engulfed by other arms reaching out to pat or stroke me hello, bringing me comfort. In itself this strengthened my resolve, but also prickled my eyes, as comfort is wont to do with the vulnerable.

There must have been thirty women in the hall, many of them more smartly dressed than before, I noticed, several with groomed hair. Again, I sought out Lesya, patting my own hair in acknowledgement and she hunched her shoulders up at me. Svetlana opened the meeting, inviting each of the women to report back in turn, then enslaving herself to the translation, both of the information they gave us and our follow-on questions. Given that Niamh and I both wished to demonstrate an eager interest in each woman, Svetlana was forced to maintain an intense dialogue for the next two hours, frowning in concentration to grasp our questions and responses. You alone could hold me here, I thought, as I watched my friend in action.

The first to recount her story was a woman with a kindly face who told us how she would rise before dawn to pick flowers – sunflowers latterly – bucket them up, then ride the bus into Donetsk to sell them on the streets. Her friend also made the same hour-long journey each day, buying boiled sweets in the market on the outskirts, then lugging a basket into the centre to set up stall and sell them on at a miniscule profit. It was a matter of just a few karbovanet notes, I thought, as she shuffled over to offer us sticky sweets from a paper bag.

"These woman are incredible," I muttered to Niamh, my words gummed up by a pear drop.

"S'what makes our life worthwhile, honey."

Further round sat another older woman who was still wearing her headscarf inside the hall. Her enterprise was to collect old jars from households and factories – indeed from wherever she found them – wash them and supply them to a pickling plant. "This has been a busy period," Svetlana translated for her. "Our harvested produce must be conserved now for the coming winter."

I know that on that particular day I was open to sentimentality, indeed I was trawling nets of the stuff in to myself, but of all the enterprise I came across in my time in Ukraine, I think that woman humbled me the most. I looked at her hands, raw, red and clawed with age, while she gaily mimed the actions of gathering, cleaning and distributing jars, as if in a game of charades. Still today I can visualise her, trudging for miles between villages, scavenging jars, rinsing them out by hand before negotiating a paltry price with some factory manager.

We continued round the horseshoe until all the women had told their tale, while I sat absorbing one story after another. It struck me that Olga, Lesya and Yelena spoke with a new-found confidence, perhaps as a result of their business trip to Kiev. When all had spoken, we broke for refreshments and I felt duty-bound to make a speech.

"In one short year, this micro-credit scheme has expanded and enriched itself beyond all our expectations. It is because of your success that soon we will begin loans in other mining villages, and I find it truly overwhelming."

In reality though, I was not in the least overwhelmed. I was buoyed up, I was re-energised. The jar lady stepped forward with a curtsey to present me with a bouquet of sunflowers, which I accepted with grace and poise, perceiving no trace of Dan's face in their glorious golden heads. That glow had seeped back inside me. This was where I belonged.

That night, I stayed at the local hotel in Slagansk, where Niamh also lodged during her weeks of input on the programme. The spider plants and bluebottles still graced the windowsill, untouched since I'd last eaten there with Kevin a few months previously.

"When's Kevin back?" I asked Niamh as we studied the menus at dinner.

"Next week. By the way, did you know that he and Yelena are an item?"

I frowned. "But he's married, isn't he?"

She smirked and reached for her tobacco tin. "All men are bastards."

"Guess he must be separated," I muttered, watching her light the roll-up. "She's not though."

"She is now."

I shook my head. "Life here is never simple, is it?" I gestured to the tin. "Can I try one?"

"Sure. Didn't know you smoked?"

"I don't."

She extracted a stub and lit it for me. "Don't draw too deeply first go, hon."

Pinching it to my mouth, I inhaled, the swirl to my brain instant and potent.

"Christ." I gripped the sides of my head.

"You get used to it," she laughed. "Better not to."

My next drag was more tentative and I grinned woozily at Niamh.

"How old are you, Vanessa? Mid twenties?"

"Twenty-seven."

"You'll be OK without him, hon, you've made the right call."

I narrowed my eyes at her. "How did you know about that?"

"Trickle down. Works all ways on an aid programme."

"Do you really think I'll be OK? Because I'm not sure, Niamh. I mean it feels good to be back here, today was just amazing, but still I'm worried that I might be making a bum steer."

"It's you that's amazing, Vanessa, and what you are doing for these women. Look, I'm nearly ten years older than you, and this is the first time ever, ever, that I've felt I'm achieving anything with my life."

"I know what you mean." I paused for a moment. "Are you married, Niamh?"

"Nah. Kick-arse career woman me – all heels, balls and lipstick." She drew back an imaginary pistol, fired and blew on it.

I laughed. "And roll-ups?"

"My trademark. The female must possess some sort of maverick weapon in the banking stroke wanking world." She exhaled and smiled at me. "And then I met these incredible women... and then I found myself on the road to Donetsk."

"I know, it's like a need, isn't it? I can feel it gripping me inside, clenching the marrow in my bones."

"Yep. And how many people ever get to feel that? You tell me, Ness? Across the whole of their lifetime?"

"I wish Dan could see that."

"Like I said, all men are bastards." She went boss-eyed at me.

"No, no. Not Dan. I think he was like me too once." I smiled ruefully. "Maybe we all become jaded eventually."

"I'm not jaded." Niamh took my wrist in a soft grip and shook it. "I'm invigorated, just like you are! Your place is right here, Vanessa. Anyone can see that you're in sync with yourself – the moon, the stars, the planets, they're all perfectly aligned in your universe."

I snorted. "You don't believe in that crap, do you?"

"No." She blew out a wisp of smoke. "But I do believe in fate, honey."

I turned my face up to the smoke trail as it glanced me, and we watched each other in silence, the one contemplating the other. Yes, I was aware that Niamh was playing me, that her continued existence in Donetsk depended on me also staying put, but I was happy to be swayed, because if there was any fate about that evening it was the way she got me. Her words were spot on and they caught me with precision timing.

*

The night before Dan left, he visited Ukrainian friends to bid them farewell. There was nothing left for us to say to each other. We were both exhausted from talking it over and, in truth, I think we were both aching for the end. While dreading it, of course. Poised to spring at the sound of his key in the door, I sat stroking Pushkin in front of the TV, back-brushing his fur from tail to head, which seemed to both bemuse and bewitch him in equal measure. The futile emotional energy of waiting for Dan to return for his final night in Kiev, as if it were a regular return home, as if it would lift me as it always had done. For minutes at a time, I did feel lurches of excitement, thinking, well bring it on, the future cannot start until you have left. But this elation was so obviously manufactured by a misery which was fighting to overcome itself. In reality, I wanted only to hold onto time, to get in front of it and push it back, arms outstretched against its iron mass, all purchase slipping from my feet as it ground on regardless.

Dan came home at 2am. From our bed, I lay and watched him through the adjoining door, shuffling about the living room, his hair dishevelled, a vodka pallor already taking hold of his flesh in the gloom. I watched as he poured another shot of the stuff, placed the bottle on the side table and slumped into our armchair. And for a long time I watched him watching me, in silence.

"It was here before you, and it will still be here after you," he said finally.

I held his look, his eyes were tender. Go with him. Go with him, my dread told me. But I sensed only an imperceptible shake of my head.

"Will you come and lie with me?" I asked.

He stood and still fully clothed he climbed into bed behind me, spooning himself to my back, sliding one arm beneath me, encasing me with the other. We relaxed into one another. I could visualise each part of my body that was in contact with his. I felt his collar bone rigid to my shoulders, his chest flat against my back, his stomach pressed into the small of my spine and his groin resting snugly around my bottom. We fitted each other. That was my last thought, as the dark waves drifted in behind my eyes and sucked me down into slumber. Did I really think I would find that again?

I was woken at first light by the alarm on his wristwatch vibrating against my breast. He showered while I made tea and toast for us, his favourite with honey, and we waited for his driver, his cases at the door. When the doorbell rang, I looked over to him and was unable to control my jaw. The trembling shook its way through my whole body, the tea spilling over the mug as I reached to place it on the table.

At the open door, he held me, my face in his chest, sheathed by the powdery smell of his clean shirt.

"I absolutely love you, you know that don't you?" he said.

I think I did. I said nothing. He breathed in, slowly and deeply, and let the breath out in a long draft.

"If you change your mind, my mailing details are beneath your pillow, and there's an open air ticket to Honduras. My email will remain the same."

"OK." I sank my face deeper into his shirt, clinging to him now and attempted a "Goodbye." Though it came out more like, "Gu-ba."

Down in the street, he slung his cases into the boot and, with a single sweep of the head, he looked up at me. I have never forgotten that final moment between us, the wretchedness in Dan's eyes, though it was a fraction of a moment, because the wash of my tears then blotted it out.

When I'd blinked them down he was already hidden inside the car, which then slowly pulled away.

29

I took a sleeping pill and returned blindly to bed, burrowing face down into the sheet where Dan had lain, scrunching the duvet around me. And I slept. When I stirred some hours later, I let out a whimper at finding myself awake, tossed around in a fever and screwed my eyes shut against the painful sunshine, finally succeeding in forcing more slumber upon me. Subliminally, though, I was aware of life on the surface, of how it was somehow skewed.

Eventually, my body seemed to allow itself to wake. After refusing to concede this for some minutes, I then allowed my eyes gradually to open. It was dusk. I lay still within my silent cocoon and watched the shades of gloom seeping around the walls, across the chair, making the curtain patterns dance in a grey volcanic bloodbath. Dusk had always been special. How many times had Dan and I returned to the apartment at dusk, cold and thrilled, thrown our clothes off and snuck beneath that duvet? The smooth warmth of a palm across a chilled thigh, the singular sensation of goose bumps rippled. How many times had we awoken at dusk, after the doze that followed sex, refreshed and sated, in wonder at finding the other beside us? Always the promise of evening, of a glass of wine, of conversation, always the remains of the day to enjoy. Now there was just a void.

Get up, I told myself silently.

I threw the duvet off, kicking irately at its sticky folds which caught around my legs, padded into the kitchen, took a glass and downed a pint of tap water. The lino was cold beneath my feet. This is your life now, I thought, pressing my soles into its surface. Dan's half-empty vodka glass stood by the sink. I averted my glance and left the kitchen, slunk into the armchair and rested my eyes on the walls before me, now stripped bare of

Dan's paintings.

"Right you," I barked. "No drama needed, just get on with it."

With a slap of the wooden chair arms, I stood and made for our wardrobe. I lugged my portfolio through to the living room, slid a heap of photos out onto the rug and splayed them out. Suddenly hungry, I made myself a sandwich and a mug of tea, careful to avoid sight of that vodka glass. A strange coldness had taken hold of me, deep within my bones, and I wrapped myself in a blanket as I sat down on the rug and began to choose between the photos.

My focus had always been on the curious; an iron manhole cover with its intricate patterns, electrical wires sticking up from a municipal plant tub, a rain gutter that stopped short a little way up a building, spewing water onto the feet of passers-by. Fortunately, the only human content was of Ukrainian origin, a trader in an apron standing before caviar jars in the Bessarabsky Market, a youth hunched at a bus stop discarding pistachio shells, or a militia man with the face of an eagle directing the squall of traffic on foot. There were no images of Dan.

With sticky tack, I arranged a good fifty photos up on the walls, making sure to position them so that they covered the dark edges left by the missing paintings. But when I stood back I saw that, in fact, they had framed the gaps and set the abandoned spaces in even sharper relief – as the voids they were. I sank back onto the rug and gazed into the photographs, one by one, until it became too dark to see past their murky shapes, and I found myself gazing then out of the window into the night.

I must have fallen asleep and I came too with a jolt as the phone rang. Pushkin lay on the rug with me, curled like a doughnut into my stomach. Outside, the night was pitch and, as I knelt my way to the phone, I thought myself at first to be in Manchester, and then that it could be Dan calling.

"Ness?" It was a voice I vaguely knew, but not Dan's.

"Yes," I said, realising with a slump where I was.

"Sasha here."

"Oh. What time is it?"

"Five o'clock. It is Monday morning."

"I'm asleep Sasha." I slunk back down to the floor.

"Yaroslav has disappeared."

"Yaroslav?"

"Last night. His mother thinks they have arrested him."

I sat bolt upright. "Who's 'they' Sasha?"

He paused. "She wants you to help."

241

"Me? How?"

Sasha clicked his tongue, "I will bring her to you now."

"Sasha no, I— you can't do that." The phone fell dead.

I roused myself and switched on a lamp. Despite having spent most of the previous twenty-four hours asleep, I was exhausted and a headache had settled into both of my temples. I showered, lifting my face to the deluge of water and finding some comfort in its physicality, which then became a yearning for Dan's presence. He would have arrived in Tegucigalpa by then, flying in between two precarious mountain peaks to land on a runway, from which the local metal thieves often filched the lights, melting down their casings, he'd told me. I pushed the image away, stepped out and snapped up a towel to dry myself.

I was filling the kettle in my dressing gown when the doorbell rang. Sasha entered, a protective arm around Yaroslav's mother, whose birdlike frame seemed skeletal that day. She shook visibly as I led her over to the sofa and sat her down, while Sasha frowned at the gloom and switched on the main light, casting a sour glare over us and the room. In staccato snatches between her sobs, the woman told me how Yaroslav had left for a democracy meeting the previous afternoon and not returned.

"Are you sure he's not stayed over with a friend?" I asked gently in Russian, passing her a tissue.

She shook her head, an agitated hand at her forehead. "They have taken him."

"But why would they arrest Yaroslav?"

The woman held forth. His friend, Taras, the pro-democracy campaigner, had disappeared and Yaroslav had been noisily preparing to expose his belief that the government was behind the abduction. I gawped at her; I hadn't even been aware of his friend's disappearance.

"It seems that after some glasses of vodka in Manchester, Yaroslav let both Tabachuk and Balavensky know what he planned to do," Sasha added.

I gasped. So that was what that night was about. Still, I shook my head. "No way."

Beside me the mother screeched the names Tabachuk and Balavensky, slapping a palm on my knee to bring them home.

"They can't be involved, they're not like that." I stood and walked to the window, keen to put some distance between us.

Sasha clicked his tongue. "This is Ukraine, Ness."

"Manchester was weeks ago. Why didn't they do it as soon as they got back then?"

"Would look obvious, no?"

"This is crazy."

From behind me came a small voice in English, "Please." And then again, "Gaspazha Parker, please."

Opposite the apartment, the dome of the Opera House was beginning to emerge from the gloom, its cream brickwork gradually luminous against the marble window frames, still dense in shadow. The proposition was ludicrous.

"OK," I said. "Give me ten minutes."

I dressed in the new clothes I'd bought in England and sat at my dressing table to blow-dry my hair. Gazing at myself in the mirror, I wondered what my strategy would be. What would Dan do? I saw his reflection then behind me. It was a few months before. He was holding up his glass of champagne to me with a smile, as we got ready for a night out, and I was tipping my own glass back at him. Then he pulled out a condom. I cocked my head, eyes narrowed in chastisement – we were already late for our dinner party – but with one of those roguish grins, he began to roll the condom over the flute of champagne, fitting it snugly to the rim. I waited, sardonic expression still in place. Gradually, the condom filled with gas, inflating it like a mini balloon, until finally, with a soft phut, it popped off the end of the flute and floated upwards.

Back in the present, I clicked off the hairdryer and attempted a smile, but instead found myself squeezing back the tears. My closed eyelids threw up a vision of Yaroslav in a cell, in the dungeon of that KGB building, and I felt the beads of fear drip down my back. Life in this city had been benign until Dan had left it.

"Let's go and find some breakfast," I said breezily as I strode back through to the living room. "There'll be nobody in the office yet."

Yaroslav's mother was standing at the wall of photos with her back to me, surveying the images. I stopped dead and bit my lip as I caught her tight shoulders. She was studying a photo of her own apartment building, a small tree growing from its roof. Yaroslav had laughed with me when I'd spotted that shot, had made one of his cynical remarks about his country falling apart, but clearly it could also offend. The woman turned to me, her tears for the moment dried, her eyes now dull, with a loss of respect.

So I flung back the door of Mrs T's office a crazed woman – exhausted, emotionally ragged, and now possessed by the need to reassure Yaroslav's mother of my worth. I find it amusing now that I felt I could outwit this woman with my fledgling diplomacy – I was so callow and she so adroit – but I opted for the surprise attack, sat down at her desk and asked her outright.

"Do you know where have they taken Yaraslov?"

There was perhaps a momentary flash behind the eyes before she replied. "Good morning Vanessa, what can I do for you?"

"I think my friend has been arrested, did you know?"

She observed me with that woman of the world look she had and adjusted her silk scarf. Her glossy black hair, I noticed, was perfectly coiffed at 8am.

"Vanessa, I have no idea what you are saying to me, no idea at all. If your friend has been arrested, as you say, then he must be guilty of a crime."

"He's completely innocent! You know him, he's helping you build your profile with his TV documentaries, for goodness sake!"

"You think I know him, do you? And do you think you know him?"

"Of course I do, he's a good man."

Mrs T sighed, sat back and tossed her pen onto the desk. "Vanessa, you oversee an aid programme here in Ukraine, which takes up all of my time and all of my energy. I propose that it should also take up all of your time and all of your energy."

I breathed in, counted to ten, then spoke more softly. "Look, his mother is downstairs, she's in real distress. I know that you are a friend of the Prime Minister, would you please at least ask him to intervene?"

She shook her head. "I do not possess that level of persuasion in our Government."

"Well, you know, maybe a little pillow talk …"

I shocked myself with that – the words seem to be coming from some other being – and I watched her, powerless to retract them, as they filtered through to her understanding. She blanched and for a moment began to range forwards, but checked herself and remained still.

"Do you know how hard it is to be a woman in my country? We need guile, we need ways." Her voice was menacingly soft.

"Yours is not the honourable way though, is it?"

I knew that my behaviour was bordering on feral, and she stood then, but remained sinister in her control, her voice still a whisper. "Leave my office."

"Not until you tell me that you will help. Did one of the Prime Minister's cronies have him arrested?"

"You are a foolish child. You come to my country and think always that your ways are better than our ways, and now you think you can also meddle with our politics?"

"You should be grateful we're here. Your country is on its knees."

"I should be grateful? To you? To you it is all one big game, Vanessa. You burden me with your so-called experts, who are less intelligent than me. You expect me to arrange my day to accommodate them and you expect me to allocate my best staff to their whimsical ideas. You send me trainers who ask my staff what kind of animal they are?"

It was my turn then to gasp. "You asked for this project!"

"Did we? Or did you arrive here and knock on my door?"

"This is ridiculous," I cried.

"Yes, this is ridiculous." She sat down calmly, as if she was floating to her seat in a ball gown, while I heaved myself up and fumbled my way from her office.

Outside, I slumped back against the wood panelling. What do I do Dan? I asked myself silently, but the confusion didn't lift. Hearing footsteps on the stairs, I shuffled to the picture window at the end of the corridor. Shuddering, I stood gazing down onto the Dniepro below and let the memories drift in.

It must have been February, a Sunday morning just before sunrise. The caretaker at Dan's office had taken us there, shuffling ahead of us onto the ice and out to the centre of the river, where he felt the currents were most favourable. Dan had insisted I wear a fur coat and hat, along with our ski suits, galoshes and rubber boots, and we sat together like fairytale bears on the folding stools, a misty fog hanging over us, as his elderly friend began to drill. Just a small hole, with what resembled an over-sized corkscrew. Then he'd scooped the floating ice out, and handed us our miniature rods; they could have been from a children's Hook a Duck game. We shared Vodka to stave off the cold – minus twenty apparently – and watched enchanted as perch after small perch popped up on our jiggling rods. He fished to escape his cramped home-life, he told us. And I'd thought again of the girl reading in the frozen park that night – of how Dan had explained that aloneness was hard to find.

Well not for me it wasn't.

I sighed, turned and made my way up a further floor, to Balavensky's office.

The Minister sat at his desk behind his flip calendar, its date as large as the top line of an eye test chart. It was Monday September 18th 1995.

245

Despite the early autumnal chill, Balavensky's window was thrown open, as ever, to the fruit orchard in his courtyard, the trees now hanging heavily with apples.

He motioned for me to sit. "Vanyssa, it is pleasure to see you."

I looked at him blankly, the ache behind my temples thrumming. Once again, his eyes were dead that morning. It was quite skilful really, as if he could pull a shutter down over himself, slotting a lens to mask any sign of inner life. I looked into those eyes and thought again of our tumultuous relations since my arrival in Kiev; the way he'd provoked me at our first meeting, then dodged my phone calls, shown no interest in our programme other than sidle his daughter onto it. And then how he'd suddenly taken me into his confidence. I thought of his striking dignity in the face of Sir Roderick's belittling that day, and how he'd seemed genuinely moved during our study tour. I recalled the bitter spat with Yaroslav in Manchester, but wondered if he was at all capable of having my friend arrested, of having him interrogated inside that building.

"Were you ever in the KGB?" I asked him suddenly, in Russian.

I'd wanted to throw him. But Balavensky let out an instant laugh and smacked the table. I too broke into a reflexive smile, my own chuckles weirdly high pitched. We chortled like that at each other, his cheeks bunching up like Punch, and I had my first ever sight of his bad teeth, of his coated tongue. When my eyes flicked again to his, I saw that the light had hit them.

"I just wondered if it was a pre-requisite for a Minister?" I continued, "Because Dan used to call you Blofeld, you know." Still smiling, I was gauging him for any giveaway signs.

His head dipped slightly to one side, as if I'd paid him a compliment. "Dan enjoyed the novels of James Bond, I think. He has left Ukraine I hear?"

It was he who had thrown me. In a flash I saw Dan's smile and I had to look away, look down. Only by mentally tracing the figure of eight on his calendar several times over was I able to push Dan out.

I looked up and contemplated the man. "Did you know that Yaroslav was arrested yesterday?"

"Niet." No. His expression remained inscrutable.

"Minister, you once said to me that we understand each other, you and I."

"Da." Yes, he said, spreading his palms, his forehead splitting into furrows of apparent frankness.

"You said that, in me, you saw somebody who could truly help Ukraine. And I think – I hope – I have been receptive to that?"

"Of course, Vanyssa. Let us be clear, with your help I am building a genuine Employment Policy for my country."

"Well, Minister, in you, I see somebody who can truly help me now. Yaroslav is an innocent man, we think that he's been arrested and I need to get him released."

I watched him, waiting for the shutter to drop to deaden the eyes. Perhaps it did hover half way, but then a gentle smile broke over his chunky face and his head dipped.

"OK, Vanyssa, I will make all necessary telephone calls."

"Thank you."

Altogether too simple. But my mind was in turmoil and I knew of nothing else to usefully add; the whole surreal morning had taken on something of the James Bond about it. So I stood and made for his door. Then I stopped and turned.

"One more thing, Minister. May I ask you a simple question?"

"Da." He nodded.

"It was you who invited Bogdan into your Ministry, wasn't it? It was you who requested our aid programme?"

"Kaneshno." Of course.

"I think the head of your Job Centre Network is not so sure."

I waited for some reaction, saw none and turned again for the door. What had I hoped to achieve with that? But he stopped me in my tracks.

"In Ukraine, we have a saying." I looked back over my shoulder and waited. "He that would have eggs must endure the cackling of hens."

"Ah," I said, even more befuddled. "In England we also have a saying. Ask a simple question, get a simple answer."

He laughed again. "Vanyssa, I truly am a simple man. Perhaps one day you will come to my dacha where you may eat my potatoes, and where you may meet the white cat that belongs to my granddaughter."

"Perhaps one day I will accept your invitation, Minister." I threw him a rueful smile and left his office.

With overconfident reassurances and, I believe, some reinstatement of my value, we dropped Yaroslav's mother home. Then I sat beside Sasha, engine off.

"What do you think, Ness?" he asked me. "Was it her, or was it him?"

"She refused to help. He said he would. I have no idea."

Sasha clicked his tongue. "Let's see what Viktor makes of it."

"Viktor?" I actually grinned at him.

"Viktor." The gold eye tooth winked at me as he smiled back.

So we took Viktor out for lunch at the National Hotel, where we were served blinis with salmon caviar, fresh carp and copious shots of vodka. I partook in the shots only and let their conversation wash over me, their mouths moving, lips pursing, as Sasha explained, as Viktor absorbed, as the shots were sunk. I tried to make sense of the morning, of all that Mrs T had said to me. Of what I was still doing in Kiev, when Dan was now in Honduras.

When our lunch ended, Viktor too promised to see if he could help, though in what potential capacity I did not wish to begin to explore. Sasha dropped me home, pulled me to him in the car and hugged me with a kiss to the top of my head.

"I pick you up tomorrow for office, Ness."

Once upstairs, I went straight to the computer and the inbox Dan had set up for me, but there was no message from him. I slunk down onto the sofa and closed my eyes. But the events of the morning hurtled at my closed eyelids, prickling them with image after image, and I knew I would find no peace without a sleeping pill. In the kitchen, Dan's vodka glass still stood on the sink. I reached for it, turned back to the living room and launched it against the wall of photos, where it smashed, transforming one picture into a blur. The street lights, hanging like mint humbugs from a filigree lamp post, became the clawed fingers of a spectre streaking down the celluloid.

"Fucking country!" I screamed at them and made for the bedroom.

30

It must have been a waking dream, because it actually did happen to me. We were in the tiny kitchen, naked beneath our aprons, because Dan said that's how you should truly cook up a dish. It was one of my culinary lessons, as he called them – his pronunciation of the word somewhat dubious. We were chopping ingredients: ginger, coriander, garlic, and stir-frying them in the wok, adding the pak choi, the bean sprouts, all of this stuff brought to Kiev by a visiting colleague. Then Dan tossed in the raw prawns.

"Now we have just two minutes. Otherwise they'll be overdone." He sank to his knees and lifted the apron.

I stirred, smiling at the memory; I'd needed no longer than that. Then the inkling that all was not right crept in, engulfing me and waking me fully. I slumped. He'd been gone for just forty-eight hours.

I phoned Niamh, announced that I would fly down for a couple of days and cabbed it out to Borispol. While Mrs T was questioning my value, the work I was pioneering in the coal regions would bolster me, I knew. At Donetsk airport Svetlana took me in her arms, her breath hot against my cheek. My body felt weak, as if it were succumbing to the flu, and the pressure of her embrace was sore against my flesh. When she drew back, the film across those grey almond eyes triggered a moistness in my own and we both blinked the emotion back. Niamh had told her then.

On the drive to her village, she was animated. Perhaps to compensate for my subdued state, or perhaps because she was now to work full-time on the programme and we had doubled her salary. The battered Lada she drove was also a fresh programme purchase, for travel among the ten additional new villages, each of them to benefit from a micro-credit fund. While it was a cold day, above us the sky was a pure azure, around us the woods were illuminated by the early onset of autumn, and the sunflower headers were forking their way through the fields, decapitating what were now dead, black flowers. With each sunflower head that fell I saw whatever was left of Dan's smile wither and take a lopsided leap.

In the village, my legs felt drained as we picked our way across the long wet grass, and the uneven ground seemed to fall away from me, making me stumble. When we entered Svetlana's kitchen, Niamh and Kevin stood up from the table to hug me.

"Hiya love." Kevin drew me into his mineral smell.

"Hi honey." Niamh's eyes were all concern behind the dark blonde frizz.

"Gosh, what's all this then?" I stood back to press home a meaningful look for them both. "All I've done is added to your workloads. Big time too."

Svetlana's mother came in then, and went for nuclear. Arms outstretched, she hoisted me into her bosom, the lapis fabric of her best dress bunched up around my cheeks, her arms strapped like barrel hoops around my back. So she knew too.

"Poor dear," she cried in Russian, with sharp wet kisses to my cheek. 'Heart' and 'broken' were other words I deciphered as I extracted myself from her, snorting with forced laughter; I knew I would cry if I didn't transform this into farce.

"I'm absolutely fine, all of you. Anybody would think someone has died."

I shifted backwards into my own space, pumping my palms up and down as a moving barrier to keep them at bay. Here, I had always been the boss, the strong one with no emotional issues, the one who flew down to sort out theirs for them.

"Can we discuss the new strategy?" I asked finally, clicking my briefcase open. "I think it's spot-on the way you've linked up the new villages with additional mines."

Kevin and Niamh sat down again hesitantly, while Svetlana guided her mother to the stepped oven in the corner. She donned an apron, greased a frying pan and began to hum. Niamh spread out a map of the region and indicated the compass circle they had drawn around their village, then the green stickers at each of the new locations.

"Svetlana's been to all of them and I've visited six so far," she said. "All full to the brim of your passionate, committed and enterprising woman."

"We have used green stickers, for hope, Vanessa," Svetlana said. "In each village, we have appointed a head woman, and asked her to produce a strategy paper on how they plan to use our micro-credit."

"Perfect. Well done both of you." My voice was assertive. "And the coal mines?"

"Mines fell into place round the villages, Ness," Kevin said, with his comforting smile. "Folks seem to know about our Slagansk Job Shop, so we're pushing at open doors."

There was a whoop from the stove, and I looked up to see Svetlana's mother tossing a pancake. It flew to the ceiling and she caught it neatly in the pan with a gappy smile at me. We all laughed, then applauded, and it struck me that it was lunchtime.

"Can I help set the table?" I asked and closed my briefcase.

The mood livened then. Kevin folded the map and we girls bustled with a dish of tomato salad and a pot of smetana – the herb sour cream which was to go with the pancakes. The mother was not staying to eat with us and as she pulled off her tunic apron, I thanked her and gave her a hug of my own. She drew back and raised a finger to speak.

"If there were no clouds, then we should not enjoy the sun," Svetlana translated for her.

I smiled – all these bloody sayings they had. "In England, we say that every cloud has a silver lining," I replied.

The woman added something and Svetlana spoke again. "My mother says that for you the lining of the cloud will be golden, Vanessa."

As she left the cottage, the woman gave me the most motherly of smiles, soft and so gentle. Be true to yourself, Vanessa, I heard my own mother say. I smiled back at her, feeling the soundness of my decision to stay seeping through my gut and restoring strength to me. Potentially three hundred women across this poor mining region would now benefit from Levshenko small loans. It was I who was at the genesis of that amazing feat, and, by staying, it would be me who would sustain it.

Svetlana took a bottle of champagne from a small fridge in the corner, a new acquisition, I noticed.

"To the expanded Levshenko programme!" she cried, as the cork hit the ceiling and we ducked.

"And to you three special people," I added.

"To you, Ness," Kevin said, "for sticking by us to see this through. It's first programme I've ever known that's brought about real change. And, as well we all know, it would come to a halt without you driving it on."

"To Ness." Niamh and Svetlana spoke as one.

"Thank you." My throat was so tight that the words squeaked out, and I gulped the champagne, feeling the instant glow at my cheeks. "So… you two will practically be living down here now, won't you?"

Niamh nodded, serving herself the tomato salad. "I'm so excited about the work, hon."

"I'm lovin' it too, hon," Kevin mimicked.

I smiled at him, and thought back to his freezing office, to the dripping hole in its ceiling. "And how does our existing Job Shop fare?"

"All CVs completed. Those that wanted them, anyhow. Touching three hundred when all's said and done."

"Fantastic. Any luck with finding new jobs?"

"Yelena's ex-husband's gone to that Yank who owns the engineering works in Donetsk." Kevin paused as if waiting for me to comment. "Oleg and Dmitry have also been for interview there."

"And?"

"Offered them both a job too."

"Wow! You didn't tell me Svetlana?"

Svetlana flushed a mottled pink. "Oleg did not accept the offer."

Kevin smiled at her. "Problem is, Ness, the men don't really believe the pit's ever going to close. I'm hoping in time they might come round, I mean thirty of the others have gone for it. They can be guinea pigs for Oleg and Dmitry, eh Sveta?"

"But it was such an opportunity!" I gazed in dismay at Svetlana.

She shrugged. "They are paying wages again. The interview was very good for Oleg, it has shown him that he can work outside the mine, but…" She flicked her wrist to check her watch. "His bus will be here now, his shift has finished."

"OK," I said, letting Kevin finally catch my eye. He frowned and gestured that we would continue this discussion alone later.

But, after a hasty glance at the window, Svetlana went on. "Myself, I would prefer he leaves the mine. Yes, they pay wages again, but they have stopped all investments. It is not safe to go down, they do not check the methane levels often, but still the men go down."

When she'd finished, we all fell quiet, each of us seemingly lost in her words. But then Oleg swept into the cottage, bringing a waft of carbolic soap with him. Svetlana jumped up, kissed him warmly and busied herself at the stove, while her husband greeted us all with a formal handshake and sat in her chair. He pulled his cigarettes out of a pocket, pushing them back again with a nod of thanks when Niamh slid her tobacco tin across the table. As he rolled up a Rizla, I watched the stress of the morning shift lift from him; his shoulders relaxed and the furrows in his forehead smoothed themselves out a little, revealing the pocks of coal dust for ready scrutiny. He licked the paper and smiled at me, his slate blue eyes intense.

"Svetlana tell you about interview, Ness?"

"Yes." I smiled back.

"Ha, very easy, we talk only about football." He laughed across at Kevin, threw his chin up for acknowledgement.

"You see, it wasn't so difficult, Oleg was it?" Kevin chuckled back.

"He support Manchester United and I support Shakhtar Donetsk, so we talk very nice."

I allowed Oleg the laugh he sought from me. "Which team's best then?"

"Donetsk. Kaneshno." Of course. Oleg dipped his head as if I was an idiot for asking and flicked his ash repeatedly. "He offer me job, but coal mine is better, I think."

As his wife brought over a tray of tea, I nodded my approval of his decision, if only so he wouldn't lose face. Inside, though, I grappled with the stupidity of it; if he'd had the balls, Oleg could have left the mine behind – and earned good money too.

"Later maybe," I said to him.

"Yes, you are right, later maybe."

Oleg nodded emphatically and pulled Svetlana down onto his knee, encasing her with his lamppost arms. At the sight of their embrace, a lurch shot through my stomach, Dan's face flashed into my mind, and I realised that it had been a whole hour since I had thought about him.

After lunch, Oleg went for a nap and we set off for the weekly loan repayments meeting. Svetlana suggested I take a stroll around the village with Kevin. The meeting would be held in speedy Russian and very dull, she said. But her hasty glance at Niamh unsettled me for some reason and I insisted on popping by to at least greet the women. Besides, I had my usual carrier bags of shampoo and medicines.

Inside the hall, the smell of coal burning heartened me. Olga jumped up, keen to gift me yet another scarf she'd made, which I gathered around me, swinging to an imaginary salsa beat. I received only weak smiles and wondered if they too knew about Dan's departure. Then I realised that everyone was just keen to begin the meeting, so I waved my carrier bags around a bit, and sought out Kevin to leave. He was standing behind

Yelena's chair. And he was kissing the top of her head. She, meanwhile, was smoothing her fingers along his hand, her eyes narrowed like a cat coaxing for food.

"Kevin," I said, suddenly disgusted, "let's go."

He hunched his shoulders at me with a lopsided grin.

"You're married, Kevin," I said coolly, as he followed me out down the steps.

"Been separated best part of a year now, truth be known."

"Oh, but you kept your wedding ring on till now?"

"Only to stop anything happening to me! Christ knows this country's predatory. But Yelena's no gold-digger, she's sweet."

Predatory. Was that how it was in Honduras too? I closed my eyes and saw stilettoed women in clingy black micro skirts clipping through the heat of the night. Dan had told me how the balmy warmth dusted your bare shoulders in the late-night bars.

"Was it over with her husband before you two got together?"

"Not that it's any of your business, Ness..." Kevin threw me a pointed look. "But yes. As good as."

As good as. Perhaps Dan had already said the same thing about me to some woman, his hair ruffled by the bar's ceiling fan as he poured his lazy grin on her. It was as good as over before I left.

At the communal well, many of the village women acknowledged me with a smile, their gossip in full flow. It was beginning to rain and we huddled in with them beneath the shelter. found myself watching them chatter and, in my narcissistic state, was convinced that they must know. That they must be talking about me.

"Any case, all's fair in love and war." Beside me, Kevin interrupted my thoughts.

I snapped at him. "Would everybody stop talking at me in riddles? The man I thought I'd marry has left me; in fact he's probably shagging some slapper at this very moment. I've got a friend who's disappeared, most likely thrown in prison. Mrs T, our key Ukrainian partner on the programme, is now telling me she never wanted it in the first place."

As one, the village women fell silent and regarded me with concern. I batted them away with an apologetic smile and shuffled out from the shelter, with Kevin traipsing after me into the rain. We walked on in silence.

"I'm sorry about Dan going, Ness," he said after a while.

"Yeah." I stopped walking and turned around abruptly. "Look I'm freezing, I'm going back to the meeting, even if it's just to sit by that stove."

"OK. We can chat more over dinner." His relief was palpable and we parted company, he to his car and I to the village hall.

When I snuck softly inside the hut again, however, the scene took me aback. Svetlana was standing over Olga, and she was launching into her, her voice bitter, her arms flailing. Olga sat folded in on herself, streaming with tears. Several other women were gathered round in support of Svetlana, and they too were haranguing Olga with their own high-pitched shrieks. Then, gradually, my appearance was noticed and nudges and shushes set in. I looked from Svetlana to Olga to Niamh, and I felt naked with embarrassment.

"What the...?" I muttered, but the silence was steadfast, hostile even.

I turned and hurried from the hall, ran through the village and back to Svetlana's cottage, where I sat silently at her kitchen table, mindful not to wake her sleeping husband. I played the ugly scene out again in my head. It was surreal and skewed – like an out of body experience after all the compassion I'd indulged in around those women. The images of Olga's tears, of Svetlana's anger, of the women's hatred, they all tumbled over one another, and soon they led onto others, of Mrs T's silent fury with me, of Yaroslav beaten and broken in a cell. I let them swirl around me until, ultimately, I was left with just one image – a stark vision of Dan's last glance upwards from the street. How had I possibly let him go? Why had I cut off all contact? So utterly stupid.

I allowed myself no pause for thought as I pulled out his old mobile phone – mine now – and jabbed in the number of his new cell phone, which he'd taped to the front of it. It rang for several seconds.

"Hullo," he said.

"Dan?"

"Ness?"

I fell silent, closed my eyes; just hearing his voice made my head heavy. But then I thought I heard another voice.

"Are you alone?"

"It's 6am."

"You're not alone, are you?"

"Sure I am." He paused. "What can I do for you?"

I shouted then. "What can you do for me? Like we're in some shop, or something?"

He said nothing.

"Are you shagging somebody already?"

"Don't be ridiculous, I've just got here."

"Oh, so next week you might be?"

"Ness, look, let me call you back…"

"You've ruined my life, Dan Mitchell, do you know that? It's all gone wrong and I hate you for that, I hate you—"

The phone clicked, and went dead. From the bedroom I heard Oleg shifting himself out of bed; I had woken him up too.

*

Later that afternoon, when Svetlana drove me with Niamh to our hotel in Slagansk, she had returned to her smooth and jolly self. Still, our tyres slapped against the wet roads, or dropped belligerently into potholes, and we were swung from side to side as if the Lada were negotiating an endless set of speed humps. I eyed her, wondering at this new side to my friend I'd witnessed. But I had neither energy nor inclination to tackle her, or Niamh, and it seemed they too preferred the silence.

In my hotel room, I slept for a while and then took a long bath, the mobile phone balanced on the edge of the sink, in case Dan did call me back. He didn't. And I tormented myself with a few tears at the thought of him with another woman, seeing his craggy smile above her. Then I pulled on my jeans and a sweater, pushed him from my mind, bringing a mental blind down over him, and fixed my professional mask on before heading for the restaurant.

"What has Olga done to deserve that kind of treatment, Niamh?" I began when she arrived at our table.

Niamh was nodding as she took her seat. "I know it looked bad, hon, but Olga hasn't made a single loan repayment for months."

"But it was like a lynch mob, all those twisted faces."

"It's how these credit circles work, Ness. Peer pressure. She knew that from the start."

"Kangaroo court, more like. Her husband wasn't paid for months."

"Same goes for all of them, doesn't it?"

I stared at Niamh as she lit a roll-up. "Still think I could have helped her out. What she owes the fund is peanuts to me."

"Honey, you know that would be wrong. Look, you can't go getting overly sentimental about these women, Olga has to learn the harsh realities of running a micro-business. That's why we're here. Not to mollycoddle them." She rapped her fingernail on the table.

"But if you'd told me, I could at least have paid her for the gifts."

"Maybe that's why I didn't tell you, hon. You'd have paid way over the odds and that would have set the others off into turmoil. It's not our job to play Lady Bountiful out here, we must create a sustainable system for them, one that works after we've gone home and left them to it."

I watched her blankly as she took a series of agitated drags on her cigarette, until, finally, she exhaled with a sigh.

"Look, pay her for the scarf. But don't overdo it, just a few pounds, so she can pay something back to the fund tomorrow."

I smiled at her "Will do. Thanks for giving her a chance."

"But I know nothing about this, OK?"

"OK."

Pleased with my minor victory, I beamed at Kevin arriving at the table in his oversized woolly sweater.

"Evening ladies." He gestured to the waitress for beers.

"In fact, we need to discuss the loans, Ness," Niamh began again, with a glance at Kevin as he sat down. "We're going to have to get a bank involved, especially now we're expanding the scheme."

The smile left me. "A bank? How come?"

"If we're serious about creating a sustainable scheme, which we are, then we'll have to start channelling the loans through a proper financial institution."

"Why can't I keep on bringing the cash down? It's only small amounts."

She cocked her head at me. "The Governor wants us to bring in a local Donetsk bank, a new one."

"A new bank? But what about corruption?"

"Well…you will be on the board, along with me and Kevin, initially at least, until the programme ends. They're offering a sound interest rate, 11%. That's quite good for micro-credit, isn't it, Kev?"

Kevin nodded and sipped his beer. "Makes good business sense, love, formalises things."

I looked from one to the other. "If you really think so. You're the experts."

I picked up my menu and made an effort to study it, but all I saw was fuzz. "I'm sorry, it's just that I've got too many fast balls coming at me this week," I said. "I mean, why didn't Oleg and Dmitry take that job with the American?"

Kevin smiled gently at me. "All in good time. Like I said, love, thirty others have gone for it. Our Job Shop is a real symbol of hope down here, it's a case of chipping away at the men."

I looked again from him to Niamh, like a child pleading with its parents. "It's just that my programme down here is so important to me, I couldn't bear to see it fail."

They both locked eyes on mine.

"We share the same goals as you, Ness," Kevin said. Niamh nodded, closing her eyes in emphasis. "But your aid programme, as you call it, is dealing with changing people's lives." He paused. "And change is scary."

I nodded at him blankly and, feeling suddenly useless and vulnerable, I reached for my beer glass, my grip weak as I tipped it to my mouth.

31

There's something about time. The desperate effort to exploit it, to be for as long as you can, when it's up against you, and then the desperate effort to be nothing at all when it's overtaken you. In those early days I slept as much and as often as I could, stirring each morning with that niggle, then awaking despondent. It didn't take long for me to realise that there had been no other voice that morning, just the long-distance echo, that it had been day two of his arrival there. I waited for his call, but by day ten it still hadn't come. I did pore over the air tickets he'd left under the pillow, my hand did hover above the phone, but the longer Dan made no contact, the stronger I resolved to hold out.

Yaroslav was released after just a few days in custody. With relief, I observed no trace of any bruise as he arrived in my office, although his gait may have been less steady as we walked to the café. When we sat down at our usual table, I wasn't sure what to ask him.

"Were you treated OK?" I spoke like someone from the Court of Human Rights.

"Yes, quite well. Thank you, Ness, on behalf of my mother and myself."

"I'm not sure if it did any good." I waited. "Do you think it did?"

"Perhaps." He was stirring his tea, watching the wake left by the spoon.

"Do you know if it was one of them behind the arrest?"

He shrugged. "It is not so important now, Taras has also been released."

We contemplated each other while he sipped his tea, added more sugar and sipped it again, and I tried to visualise for myself what he had lived through. Finally I nodded, at his wish to brush over it, or perhaps to bury it, and I turned the conversation to more banal matters.

259

There was a brief period of his absence from the evening news, I noticed, but he continued to produce his documentaries on our aid programme as if nothing untoward had happened. As if, for that period of time, he too had been nothing at all. We would meet together with Mrs T to discuss his proposals and he would go on to produce a half-hour television feature – on the Job Centre, the Small Business Agency, or the Training Task Force. I would study the two of them together, but as a political novice in things Ukrainian, I detected nothing of rancour on either side. Rather, there seemed to be a cordiality, some sense of protection from her even, which was unsettling given that I'd secretly assumed her – and not Balavensky – to be behind his detention.

With me too, Mrs T restored herself to a picture of convivial co-operation, even if I would on occasion glance up to catch her observing me with hooded eyes; an unspoken understanding that our business remained unfinished. I think we were both watching, we were both waiting, but in my fragile emotional state I was happy to leave it that way. For the time being.

The first time I laughed again was when Jeff called to say that Paul Hopkins had fallen down a loose manhole in a back street and broken his leg. The absurd image, together with the sudden solution to a problem was too much and my stifled giggles ruptured into snorts.

"Not very charitable of you, Vanessa," Jeff chided.

"No, I hope he's OK?" I managed, before my laughter bubbled over.

"He's off the project, if that's what you mean, he's requested sick leave. Niamh will replace him."

Result! I thought, and spent several minutes musing on the serendipitous boosts that life allows you – timely, and just sufficient to tide you through. Then I called Carole.

"Thanks for bringing Niamh in, when you could have sent another new expert out instead."

She sighed. "You rate Niamh highly, don't you?"

"I do. But I know this means lopping even more profit off your fees."

I sensed her smile. "I'm becoming resigned to that, Ness."

I smiled back at the phone. "Come and stay with me next time you visit?"

"OK, won't be till December now," she said. "No budget left."

We both laughed at that.

"Are you OK?" she asked. "You seem on good form."

"Fine," I said brightly, blinking back a pesky tear.

When I hung up, the sobs came upon me unawares and I was grateful that Sasha was not in the office to see me cry. Finally, I walked home to the apartment, where I sought out Pushkin, who had taken to sitting on the kitchen work surfaces with impunity. Grasping him around the middle, ignoring his yowls and his scrabbling claws, I dragged him into the living room and onto the sofa with me, where I clasped him into submission. Keen that we should suffer this one out together, I huddled with him until it was dark, until it was time for bed and the peace that brought me. It had been over a month since Dan had left.

*

In mid-November, Niamh took over the training at the Business Agency, and I would say that I too turned a corner. Widely advertised in the press by Viktor, these workshops were popular with young entrepreneurs, who paid a token fee to participate. I attended the evening ones myself; no point going home to a lonely apartment and afterwards Niamh and I would dine together. While I was an increasingly frequent visitor to Donetsk, still I thrived on hearing about the explosion of new loans across the region, about the enterprise of the women.

The training session that stays in my mind was one on Marketing. The Agency was full that evening – perhaps word had got around that Yaroslav was to film it – and at least sixty people were crammed in. I sat with Viktor, his silver locks shampooed to sleekness, his pallid cheeks lifted by tinted foundation for TV.

"Marketing," Niamh began. "Who can tell me what marketing is?"

Beside her, Sasha translated and several hands went up – nice packaging, smile at people, print pens with your company name – and I looked to Niamh in anticipation.

"All of those things count, of course," she said kindly, "but marketing, in essence, is to make the bastards want your products!" She turned to the whiteboard and wrote this in capitals, while Sasha translated with all the relish and hand gestures of a symphony conductor.

"Repeat that please, all of you." Niamh turned back to her audience, and a chant went up in Russian.

"Is to MAKE BASTARDS WANT PRODUCTS!" Sasha shouted the translation.

It was a bit like an episode of Please Sir. Afterwards, Viktor produced bottles of vodka, which led to an hour of impromptu networking. Shot glass in hand, I observed the commotion, the scrawling on scraps of paper, the business cards being traded like football swapsies.

"Come and witness this then, Danny boy," I muttered to myself. "If you think your work is more important than me, then fine, because this here is magic."

*

In the week leading up to Christmas, Carole came to stay. I gave her the proud tour of our Business Agency and Job Centre. We flew down to Donetsk for a day trip, where she was plied with cakes, honey, and finally that wash and blow dry – all of which visibly moved her. Back in Kiev, on our return from dinner each evening, we would work our way through my video recordings of Yaroslav's documentaries, the balls of our feet pressed together as we curled up at each end of the sofa, hugging large glasses of wine. Carole understood nothing of the Russian language, but the visuals were vivid.

"This is the best aid programme Lancashire has ever run, Ness," she said to me on her last evening, when we were one bottle in. We were watching footage of animated women in a loan meeting at the village hall.

"I know you've made a huge loss on it, though," I said sheepishly.

"Unprecedented. As the MD would say." She let out a brittle laugh, then cocked her head at me. "But even he knows that you've created a first when it comes to results. He refers to your programme in bid presentations, you know. Must have won us countless other contracts."

"Which bits of the programme?" It was the first time I'd heard this.

"The fostering of relations with the Ukrainians, the focus on the grass roots level, you name it, your Levshenko programme is an exemplary case study."

"Gosh." I bit my lip and eyed her warily. As yet nobody knew anything about my run-in with Mrs T. I changed the subject. "And are you OK? In the company, I mean?"

"Oh, I'm not really cut out for project supervision, am I?"

"Yes you are. It was just me, I've been a bit of a princess at times."

She smiled. "I did prefer working alongside you, Ness. You're dead fierce in opposition. In any case, I've been to some of those bid presentations with the MD and he says I've helped bring in new business, so I'll be shifting to more of that in the New Year."

"Kind of a promotion then…" I said hopefully.

"Yeah." She leant over and pinched my cheek. "So can we be mates again?"

"Hope so."

I shifted round to lean my head against her shoulder, and Carole pulled me to her, the physical contact my first in weeks.

"Sure you don't want to come back with me for Christmas?"

"Nah, I'm happy here. Got the cat to think of, anyway."

"There'll be another guy along soon, you know. Always is with you."

My eyes smarted but I nodded for her benefit. "Maybe."

"I envy you, in a way, being out there all footloose and fancy free. Just think you can have sex with a brand new person."

"Carole!" I sat up and giggled. "I thought your sex life was mind-blowing? Don't you suck each other's fingers and toes?"

"Gawd no." She gave a mock shiver. "Wouldn't go near those fingers these days – picks his nose in front of the telly now."

I shuddered; Dan had never done that, but then maybe if we'd stayed together long enough…

Carole smiled at me as if she'd read my thoughts. "Do you still miss him?"

"Still? He's only been gone for 96 days and 13 hours."

"Ah." She paused. "Have you called him?"

"Nope." Not since day two anyway. "And nor has he me."

I could feel her grinning. "You know you said he was stubborn?"

"As a mule."

"Mm. Call him Ness. Nothing to lose, is there?"

I shook my head. "It's over, Carole, done and dusted."

I guess the following day was when it all came to a head. It was December 24th, Christmas Eve back home, and a morning truly deep and crisp and even, but it was just a normal day in Ukraine, where their Orthodox Christmas was two weeks later. And it was the day that our Task Force graduated from their training.

The ceremony was held at the Ministry of Employment. I stood in a line-up with Jeff, Carole and Bobsteve, beaming at the twenty women as Mrs Tabachuk handed out the certificates and a rose for each of them. While we Brits were wrapped in our coats against the unheated hall, the trainees themselves wore flimsy cocktail dresses. Another step to success, Ness, I thought, as I shook each of their hands. Their bubbling smiles were clear testament to the skills they'd acquired and would now roll out to the regional Job Centres.

After the ceremony, the caviar was piled onto tiny squares of black bread and consumed at the usual avid pace. We Westerners found ourselves in a huddle, as per the norm, while the Ukrainians socialised among themselves, but I broke ranks, cracking open the champagne and pouring it for each of the trainees. I reached Mrs T who was standing with them.

"That went very well, didn't it?" I poured her a glass.

"Very well." She echoed, with one of her genial smiles.

"You see, our training was much more than a survey of the world's wildlife."

She drew a sharp nasal breath. Yes, I'd meant to rile her, but I wasn't ready for our duel, certainly not at Christmas. So I swung round and strolled back to my group. As I reached them, I caught Bobsteve stopping in mid-sentence.

"What's up?" I popped another champagne cork.

They looked at Carole, who glanced from Jeff to me.

"What's wrong?" I asked, bottle in mid-air.

"Not quite sure how to put this, Vanessa," Bobsteve said. "Some of the trainees have resigned from the Ministry."

"What do you mean, resigned?"

"Just that, Ness." Carole stepped in. "They've been poached already. Think a couple have gone to other aid programmes – the World Bank was it, Jeff?"

"I believe so. And three have been recruited by a British chemicals firm which has just set up here."

I gawped at him. "Recruited? But they weren't on the market!"

Jeff seemed to have found an interestingly loose piece of parquet floor to tease with his shoe. I wanted to grab his chin, yank it up.

"So we stand to lose a quarter of our trainees before they've even started the job we've just spent thousands of pounds training them up for?"

All three men were now absorbed by their shuffling feet, while Carole rolled her eyes at me and sighed.

"Right," she said. "Ideas. What can we do to stop them going?"

I glared over at the group of women, who were also studiously avoiding me now. Which ones were they? That they even had the audacity to show up today for their certificates.

"Well, I would have thought that the chance to do good for their country, to help their fellow Ukrainians find new jobs would have been a starter for six," I cried.

Jeff snorted. "No such thing as a free lunch, Vanessa."

"There is such a thing as pride in your job. Not that you'd know much about that, would you?"

"Ness, calm down, will you?" Carole placed a hand on my arm, so I glared at her too.

"But these women should take pride in the roll-out to the regions. They should be doing it for the accomplishment of the task, for their own personal fulfilment. They're being paid by the Ministry after all – a good wage too."

"We'll still have fifteen of them, that'll see us through enough regions by programme end," Carole said.

"But will the others stay?" Bobsteve voiced what we all were thinking. We turned as one to contemplate the group of trainees, animated and enjoying their free lunch.

"We need to pay them, don't we?" It was Carole who finally came out with it.

"An incentive, at least," Bobsteve added. "We could try a performance bonus, a trainee-of-the-week type thing."

"A hundred dollars a week extra?" I said sarcastically. "If they smile the right way."

"If that's what it takes."

Carole drew a sharp breath. "Bye bye profits." Her hand fluttered up towards the window and we stood silently watching the banknotes flying off.

"They've got us by the short and curlies," Jeff said finally. I glowered at him, wondering how long he'd known about this, if he'd even perhaps taken a commission from the British companies involved.

"Right," I cried, "I'm going to have a couple of drinks and then I'm going to tackle Mrs T about this. She should not be letting them go so easily."

I sank several glasses of champagne, while I listened to Bobsteve coming up with various suggestions for cash incentives, and Carole doing the maths on each one. Then I asked Mrs T for a word in private and she gestured to the door – it did feel as if we were going outside for a scrap.

"I've just heard we're losing five of the trainees already?" I began, once we were a few steps down the corridor.

"Yes," she said. I waited for more but she regarded me blankly.

"Personally, I was hoping for a little more commitment from them. And from you too, I think you should hold them to their employment contract."

She raised her eyebrows at me. "Employment contract?"

I blushed; of course there was no such thing in Ukraine back then.

"Well you should do something to stop them from leaving, use your guile, your 'ways' as you call them." I could feel the champagne beginning to speak for me. "But you don't seem to care at all."

"You are mistaken. I care very much about these women."

"You don't care very much about the programme, though, do you? You've already made that very clear to me."

"Vanessa, I am committed to your Levshenko Programme, but not for naïve reasons as you are. You consider yourself clever, but there is a wider picture that you fail to see, the wider politics of international aid."

"Of course I see it. I know full well that we are just one small tool in the grand design of your country's free market economy."

She laughed in my face. "In fact you are a major tool in your own country's foreign policy. Do you understand the high value of Ukraine to the West? Do you understand the strategic importance of my country? We stand at the crossroads between East and West, we are the prize which you and Russia fight over. It is like a tug of war. We possess great resources – minerals and fertile land, and what is more, most of the oil pipelines from Russia to the West cross through my country, did you know that? It is because of all of these things that with your aid you keep us 'sweet' as you would say."

I found myself backing into the wood-panelled wall for its physical comfort, but with each shuffle backwards, the woman was pressing herself forwards at me. She went on.

"And we in my country, we accept your aid for exactly the same reasons. To keep you sweet. Because Ukraine should one day become a member of the European Union, and we should belong also to NATO. So we will carry out necessary reforms here to ensure democracy, to ensure that our borders are secure, that there is stability in the region. But do you really expect that we should welcome you here as missionaries? To show us the right ways? If so then you are misled. Because we are more clever than you. Have you any idea of the intelligence we needed simply to survive under communist regime?"

I found myself shaking my head as she came at me, closing the distance. I was pressed well back against the wall now, could smell the champagne on her breath.

"So, Vanessa. You continue to play your game and I too will continue to play your game with you. We will collaborate together until your programme reaches its end, and then you will leave Ukraine and I will go on with my life here. Perhaps one day when you are older you will also be wiser."

When she'd finished, she seemed to realise how close we were and she stepped back, but we continued to glare at each other, horns still locked. Then I ducked away from the wall and sprinted down the stairs of the Ministry.

Outside on the pavement, I struggled to calm my breathing, to slow the thud in my chest, while my mind was chopped into pieces by her words. It was early afternoon and the parked cars were by then inches deep in snow, which continued to fall relentlessly, layering my black coat white. I stood stamping my feet against the cold and struggled to comprehend the woman's dramatic transformation; I could still see the line of hairs on her upper lip, she'd been that close to me.

I waited some time for Carole to come down, anxious to take her aside and report what had happened, but just as she did so, her minibus drew up, with Kevin, Yelena and Niamh already inside. I watched in a blur, as they beckoned her to hurry, as Carole kissed me and said she'd call me, as she, Jeff and Bobsteve bustled into the bus, de-mob happy, with no inkling of what had transpired between myself and Mrs T. I looked at the last empty seat, even had visions of myself jumping inside and clipping my seatbelt – click-every trip – but I felt strangely rooted to the pavement. With forlorn waves, I watched them leave for the airport.

When they had disappeared from view, I set off for home, head down, slipping several times on the ice beneath the snow. At one point I even slid over onto my back, and I lay looking into the flakes dashing against my face, fighting back tears of pain and anger. I could hear Dan's voice mocking me – your programme is just a charade maintained by all... I got back to my feet and trudged on, conscious of the mink hats around me, which suddenly seemed alien and peculiar, while my own woollen beanie was sodden wet and dripping down my cheeks.

When I reached my building, I took the stairs two at a time, passing a fellow tenant who pressed herself flat against the stairwell to let me past. By then, they probably all regarded me as the madwoman with the cat from upstairs. Inside the apartment, I yanked off my coat and hat, dropped them to the floor and slunk behind the table by the window. I was left with the prospect of Christmas Day alone. I switched on the PC and went to my inbox, desperate to offload what had happened to me that morning on somebody.

The top message hit me square on – Greetings for the Holidays. An email from Dan, posted that day and apparently copied to everyone he knew in Kiev. I clicked it open, read a couple of humorous lines about the heat of Honduras versus the chill of Kiev, and a lurch of elation hit my stomach; perhaps this was his way of making contact with me. I pressed reply and hovered over the keys. Hi Dan, Happy Christmas, I wrote. Then I stopped, unsettled by something, shrank the message and glanced further down my inbox. There was already a reply from Chelsea, which she'd copied to all recipients. Dan, good to get more news, can't wait to hook up with you when I hit Costa Rica. 20 degrees plus, rather than minus, will be a boon I can tell ya.

So he'd been in contact with Chelsea already, but not me. I smacked the side of the PC. And why was she going to Costa Rica? Kicking back the chair, I made for the kitchen, where I popped the cork on the bottle of champagne Carole had left me, and poured it unchilled into a pint glass. I slumped onto the sofa, turned to Pushkin who was spread lazy-leopard on its arm and I stared him out, over and over, until the discomfort took him and he slunk off for the bedroom. I watched him go, sighed and turned on the telly, jabbing the remote from channel to alien channel, until I found some amateur daytime soap to stare through.

Two sticky pints of champagne later, I guess the panic kicked in. The fear that he had truly moved on, whereas before I'd not wholly believed that he would. I snatched up the phone and dialled his mobile, my knee jiggling as the old-fashioned dial wound itself back to base. It rang for too many heart-pumping seconds and then went through to voice mail.

Howdie, this is Dan Mitchell....

I slammed the receiver down and sat gawping at the phone, my chest still thumping. The voice had been rich and familiar as ever, but at the same time it was far-flung and somehow remote. I sat for some time, hearing it again, computing the distance between then and now, mapping all that had happened, realising that this man would have called me long ago if he had cared. Finally, I stood and followed Pushkin into the bedroom. Barely dusk on Christmas Eve, and while my colleagues would have been clinking glasses in the business lounge at Borispol, while my peers in Kiev would have been stamping snow off their boots at the door to the Irish bar, the sleep came far too easily to me.

On Christmas morning, I was woken by the sun streaming in and I turned to stroke Pushkin, who had taken to lying stretched full length on what had been Dan's side.

"Dan's history," I said to him as he opened an eye. "It's just you and me now, Pushkin."

The sky was a baby blue, unblemished by cloud, and I watched a plane fly into view, zipping it up the middle as it travelled away from Kiev. I waited until it had disappeared and swung myself out of the bed, refusing myself any thoughts or feelings. With coffee and toast in hand, I padded barefoot around the apartment. Watching the daily bustle around the Opera House, I attempted to manufacture some pleasure from my morning, but my humming was tuneless, more grunt than melody.

Finally, as I knew I would, I found myself hovering by the bookcase, taking snatched glances at the piles of periodicals which Dan had left behind. Within them were hidden articles about international aid, about Ukraine on the world stage. He would often leave one of them lying around for me, page open at some pessimistic analysis. "Easy reading for the cynics among us," I would tease him, making a show of closing the magazine and slotting it unread back into its shelf.

Now, I crunched my toast and idly picked one out, soiling it deliberately with honeyed fingers, and flicked to the page which Dan had dog-eared. The title jumped out at me: All Aboard the Gravy Train: An Analysis of Aid to the Former Soviet Union. I tossed it to the floor and reached for another: Why Technical Assistance Isn't Working: The Inertia of Ukraine. That one hit the floor too.

"So cynical, all of you," I muttered.

The next one, however, held my eye. Queen or Pawn? : Ukraine's Significance on the International Chessboard. I took it, sat down at the table and opened it. I began to read. I read how Ukraine was the largest new country of the twentieth century, that it was of strategic importance to the West because of its size, its population, its resources and its geographical location. That in Europe it was a key regional actor, exerting an extensive influence on the security, stability and prosperity of the whole continent. I read how some claimed the US wanted to tame Ukraine as a Western beast, to remove it from the clutches of Russia, for America's own geopolitical gain.

When I'd finished reading, I reached for the discarded aid articles on the floor. I read how the Western World had pumped in billions of dollars to the Former Soviet Union in development aid since the fall of communism. How expectations for this aid were excessive – derisible even. How the average three-year aid programme could not possibly bring about change that was lasting or sustainable in any way.

Then I read how, in contrast, minor interventions may still have major impacts at the grass roots level. How they may bring significant benefits for the individuals at stake and potentially also greater regional benefits. The words 'grass roots' brought a sudden lucidity to me and I scored through them with a highlighter. I read each of the other articles, struck again by the significance given to regional actions, to local actions, to smaller actions. I ended up with a neat heap of periodicals on the table and, finally, I threw on jeans and a fleece and left the apartment.

Outside, the day held itself still in the cold sunshine. Each glance around me seemed to capture the city in a snapshot, to illuminate it. I walked past the Golden Gate and down onto the Boulevard Kreschatyk, which lay stately beneath its layers of fresh snow, knowingly even, as if it held its own secrets. I crunched past the Cabinet of Ministers, scanning the darkened windows, and on up towards the Parliament. There, I stood on the hill, pummelled by an icy breeze, as I considered the Ukrainian flag flapping rowdily from its pillars, the strip of constant blue above the solid clarity of yellow. My knowledge of this city, of this country, was now greater, but I knew too that I understood it less than before.

I strode on into the Mariensky Park, where I sat on a bench by the frozen fountain. Whether it was a queen or a pawn, this city was humbling, this nation was complex. How could I have focused only on the human story? How could I have been so blinkered to the wider picture? No, I didn't comprehend it, but I knew that I wanted to remain; that I would continue to work at the grass roots level in my village; that my impulses had been right from that very first meeting with the women, in a lush garden on a hot summer's evening. I knew that my instinct to stay had been sound.

32

International Women's Day on March 8th is widely celebrated in Ukraine. In 1996, it fell on a Friday, creating a bank holiday weekend, and I decided to put on a showcase event in Donetsk on the Thursday before. Together with Niamh, Kevin and Svetlana, I planned to invite Balavensky and Mrs T – both major dignitaries in the eyes of humble villagers – and to ensure coverage by national television in the form of Yaroslav. The Governor of Donetsk, Vladimir Zukov, was fully behind it, and my biggest coup, aided by Carole, was to secure a TV team from Lancashire to cover the day. Viktor was also to join us for the outing, though I kept Jeff at bay in Kiev; he had shown no interest before in visiting the coal region, I told him, and this was my show time. Sasha too remained at home. He had no time for all that palaver, he said, enjoying the use of his new favourite word.

We flew down early that morning and were greeted at the airport by the miners' brass band. I was amazed to see that Oleg and Dmitry were members, their eyes shining at me over their trumpets, while the Governor proceeded along our line, grabbing our hands in both of his and shaking them as if they held high dice. The morning was cold, but the sky a deep blue, with the odd cumulus cloud seeming to trail our drive into the city, as if wishing us well.

When our cavalcade crossed the vast river, I glanced into the rose tubs set out alongside us and a memory of Dan struck me – of our very first day together, when we too drove over that bridge, of his gentle teasing, his sidelong smiles. I had heard nothing more of Dan since the email on Christmas Day. I had made no contact either, and my awakenings each day were by then far less harsh on me; it was always just a matter of time, I told myself as I gazed out at the rose stems. Although pruned back sharply, they were poised, already clawing the air, ready to reach out again, to bloom again. Spring would bring new life to me too, I thought, and smiled contentedly.

Our first visit was to the Governor. Vladmir Zukov had established his own model Job Centre for Donetsk, in a newly decorated hall beside his offices. I watched him beaming for the British camera as it swung around the room, taking in the mint green woodchip wallpaper, and I knew that the slant the UK team would be seeking for their documentary would not be the glorious one he himself imagined. He swept a hand towards the PCs and we all plodded over for dutiful admiration, Svetlana providing a flawless translation for us.

She looked stunning that day. I had never forgotten the vision of her haranguing Olga, but her grey eyes were firmly in almond rather than wolf mode, her cheeks were peachy and her long tresses feathered the side of her face. She had showered in her usual freezing water that morning, no doubt, I thought, as I marvelled at her. I glanced round at the others in our group. Yaroslav was his normal diminished self in the bumptious presence of politicians, observing rather than engaging. Beside him, Balavenksy walked tall for the occasion, the odd dart of his eyes at the British camera proving irresistible, while Viktor seemed to have upped the ante in his choice of foundation tone – he looked positively suntanned. Mrs T held her usual smile – bright or brittle, whichever way you chose to see it. Since our showdown, she had become for me simply a colleague with whom I had to get along, if not actually respect or like, and I was proud of my more professional behaviour since I'd come to terms with this fact. In her words, we would collaborate until programme end and then we would part.

We moved on to a neighbouring room, where two of our faithful Task Force trainers were leading a session for the Job Centre staff. While the roll-out of our training was also underway in other cities, Donetsk had become our prime focus, in view of the Governor's zeal I nodded firmly at both trainers and they returned my knowing look; they were each on a promise of a completion bonus if they saw the roll-out training through. With this carrot we had managed to retain the remaining fifteen Task Force women – at a thousand pounds a head, which Carole had resignedly knocked off from her profits.

After a brief lunch hosted by the Governor, during which the men nonetheless managed to down a whole bottle of vodka between them, we moved onto the Slagansk mine and Kevin's Job Shop. Vladimir Zukov clicked his fingers for the file of all the international investors to Donetsk, and he laid out their glossy brochures for the benefit of the British TV team.

"You film, please," he said to them.

I carefully added a raft of miners' CVs and letters of job offers, fanning them out on the desk.

"You film too, please," I joked with the cameraman.

A shift was ending. Our large group moved as one to greet the bewildered men, who were emerging from their cage in the shaft, blinking into the light. I did have my camera with me that day, and for the first time ever I dared to photograph them, capturing at first an orange helmet with its headlamp and then, in close-up, their blackened faces, etched with humility or acquiescent smiles as the presence of the Governor and a Minister gradually dawned on them. I drew away and began to snap shots of the mine site itself; the wheels of the tower, the criss-cross of its iron girders, the corrugated washing sheds. The smoke billowing from the canteen chimney lent the only hint of warmth to this place, which resonated as some forgotten spot.

A little way off, a patch of snowdrops caught my eye in the sunshine. Tiny white bells, their petals allowing only a modest glimpse of the stamen behind, had fought their way through gritty coal sediment. I bent down over them and captured the perfect shot. Today, that photograph is displayed as a large canvas in my kitchen.

Our bonanza ended early that evening in the village hall, where we were to be the women's guests of honour. The habitual Ukrainian stamina meant that nobody had wanted to freshen up before our dinner, though I caught rich drifts of perspiration coming from the Minister and Viktor, and I myself was feeling stale. The TV team were keen to keep going too, they said, gathering up useful footage for their human interest story; the following day they were to complete their reportage with a visit to the football team Donetsk Shakhtar.

The village hall was kitted out like a trade fair that evening. A line of tables had been set up to display the enterprise in the village, each of them manned by the women. With a champagne aperitif in hand, the Governor led both the Kiev visitors and the cameras around the hall, encouraging his guests to handle the jars of melon jam, the blouses, the boxes of sweets on display, or to study the photos of sunflowers in tin buckets. I beamed at each of my Divas in turn.

273

At the end of the line stood the two Ukrainian bankers from the newly created Slagansk Bank which was handling the micro-credit scheme. Mafia, I said to myself silently each time I had to deal with these unexceptional men, with their thin leather jackets and mousy basin haircuts. When he reached them, however, Vladimir Zukov was in raptures.

"Like saving the icing on the cake for last," I whispered to Svetlana.

"But the icing contains arsenic," she replied and we giggled together. We both relied on Niamh to be the more mature professional in our dealings with these men.

I wandered off from the visiting party and back to the women, taking time to greet them properly and enthuse over their occasion. Olga was sitting alone by the window, still ostracised, even though she was nearly up to date with her loan repayments, I knew. Her ruddy cheeks bunched into a jolly smile which didn't quite make it to her eyes.

"OK?" I asked her.

"OK," she replied.

"Biznez good?"

She rocked her head in a see-saw motion. "OK."

I fingered the net curtains. "You make me more curtains?"

I was ready to pay well over the odds to finally relieve my friend of her debt, but my overt support did not alter her mood, so I tried a change of tack.

"I saw Dmitry in the brass band." I mimed a trumpet.

Olga did laugh then with me, or more likely she laughed for me – cajoled into reluctant cheer to make me feel better. How the strong manipulate the weak.

As we prepared for the grand dinner, Svetlana's mother stepped forward to perform the traditional Ukrainian welcome. The linen rushnik over her outstretched arms held the round loaf of bread with its decorated crust, piled up with salt.

"To our eternal friendship," Vladimir Zukov exclaimed, slipping an arm around Svetlana's waist for his translation.

With a slight bow, Balavenksy was first to break off a piece of the bread, scoop up some salt and eat it. The ceremony continued with Mrs T, Viktor and the UK TV crew, while Yaroslav was last to be served. Odd how these people clamoured for international media attention, but were so blithe about their own – at least when all was well. That was soon to change, of course.

No men from the village had been invited to our dinner. The women shone in their own limelight, passing dishes across the lavishly laden table, stretching to refill wine glasses, while Niamh and I were engrossed in our own celebration of Women's Day.

When the toasts came, each and every one of them was made for the ladies. The Governor and the Minister vied with each other for the most sycophantic toast.

"The shape of a woman…" Zukov began.

"The soul of a woman…" Balavenksy came back at him.

Even Mrs T stood up to toast them. "Women in our country must possess wiles," she said with a quick glance my way.

Then Viktor spoke of their enterprise, of their spirit, of their courage. It was he who received the warmest applause.

Late in the evening, some of the men passed by the hall, on their way to the bus for the night shift at the mine. I stood, a little squiffy after the wine, and threw my arms around Oleg's thick neck, and then Dmitry's, planting kisses on each cheek and bringing broad smiles to both their faces.

"You two are dark horses, aren't you?" I said. "You never told me you played trumpet in the brass band."

Oleg tapped the side of his nose. "We keep some small secret from you, Ness."

Zukov clinked a spoon for his final toast of the night. This, he dedicated to me, spinning it out with superlatives and hyperbole; the delight of our first meeting in his office, the joy of dancing the polka with me in the forest. Without me, they would not be celebrating success, he cried. Without me, the village would not have thrived as it had. And to my amazement, the Governor then bestowed on me the highest of honours, the Key to the City of Donetsk, which came complete with a symbolic key. It looked like something out of a fairy tale. Wrought from steel, it was the size of a fish slice, its head ornate with twists and scrolls, and its teeth cut chunkily with secrets. I grasped it in both hands and through the mist of emotion I took in the beaming faces. The Governor, the Minister and Viktor, Svetlana and my Divas, even Mrs T smiling was applauding me. Oleg and Dmitry were whistling, fingers in mouth, their cheeks still smudged with my newly purchased scarlet lipstick. Capture this moment Ness, I told myself. It is now that you can truly move on.

At the end of the party, the visitors from Kiev were driven off to lodge at the local hotel, while Niamh, Kevin and Yelena left for one in the city.

Niamh was to hook up with her new boyfriend, while Kevin and Yelena were to fly to Odessa for the weekend. Relieved to be free of the pack, I spent the night on Svetlana's couch, the crashing applause and radiant faces drifting through my mind, as I sank into a cocoon of slumber.

I did hear the siren during the night. Only subliminally though. I think I thought it was heralding the end of a shift, like the wail of the factory hooter at noon in the industrial town of my childhood.

In the morning, I woke around ten and pootled through to the kitchen in my jim-jams. The kettle was cold – the stove was cold even – bringing a smile to my face; Svetlana must have also slept late. I remembered her drinking quite fluidly herself. I lit the stove and waited an age for the water to heat, while I idled the time away with a Ukrainian magazine, toying with my new key. There were small pastries left over and I ate a couple for breakfast. Then I stood at the window and looked out over the garden and to the village beyond. Everything was so quiet, so still.

I turned to the bedroom. "Svetlana?"

I tapped on the door. After a moment, I rapped harder. Then I opened it. The blankets had been kicked off the bed, a chair had been knocked over. It was then that I remembered the siren in the dead of night and the chill set in. I hurried out of the cottage and scoured the scene. Across the whole of the village there was nobody to be seen, nobody at all. The goats grunted, the chickens scurried, the dogs scuffled on the nearby pathway, and a cockerel crowed in the distance, but the vista was empty of all human presence. I ran to the neighbour's house, my feet bare against the thin layer of snow that had fallen overnight, and slammed my fist against her door. No answer.

Back in the cottage, I dragged on my clothes, boots and jacket and grabbed my handbag. I made first for the communal well, the hub of the village, but even at a distance I could see it was ghoulishly deserted, so I set off at a sprint across the common land towards the hedgerows. As I ran, a snake slithered across my path, bottle green against the grey grass of late winter, and I let out a scream, almost stumbling upon it. It was this cry that must have brought me to the attention of a man, who called out to me from behind. Swinging round, I saw him rushing out of one of the cottages with blankets heaped in his arms and over his shoulder.

"Hey," he cried out. "You. Help me."

My chest was thumping as I hurried over to him, both with the shock of the snake and with what I now knew to be the gravest of situations. He dumped a load of blankets on me and dashed onto the next cottage, emerging with more.

"What's happened?" I asked, trying to keep up with him.

"Explosion," he snapped.

"At Slagansk?"

"Da. Slagansk," he said. "Come."

We ran together to his car, and set off in a skid start, racing across the bumpy tarmac, crashing through the potholes, hurtling towards the coal mine. We passed ambulances, which came at us with furious sound and speed. The journey to the mine, normally a good fifteen minutes, took us just five.

The car park had spilled out onto the road with both vehicles and people – miners, villagers, officials – but the man thrust his car on through all of them, with the same ferocity as the ambulances, his hand constant on the horn. I sat gazing at the faces which stared back at me as we passed them, and I saw it all – shock, disbelief, denial and grief. A cordon had been set up some way back from the mine shaft and the man pulled up just short of it. I launched into action myself then, jumped out of the car and grabbed the blankets from the back seat, hauling a mass of them over both shoulders and flipping the rest like rushniks across my outstretched arms. A man lifted the tape of the cordon to allow us through.

I made my shaky way to the two ambulances parked up by the mine shaft. Each step seemed to be in slow motion; my boots were leaden like a deep sea diver's dragging me down, my knees were feeble, unable or unwilling to propel me forward. By the doors of one ambulance stood a group of women. As I neared them, I realised that it was Olga with her back to me, heaving uncontrollably, that it was Svetlana, Lesya and Marina who were huddled around her, their arms wrapped up in each other like a Celtic knot. I could not tell where one woman ended and another one began, so entwined were they. And as I felt the weight of the blankets leave me, lifted from me by a medic, I stepped towards the open doors of the ambulance.

The face on the stretcher I had seen less than twelve hours earlier, beaming from ear to ear, my lipstick cheekily imprinted on its flushed cheek. Those cheeks had been again reddened, by patches of burns, although much of the surrounding face remained blackened, either by coal dust or perhaps by deeper burns. The eyes were closed, but the face held the shape of the same man, the same protruding brow, the same large nose. As I gazed upon Dmitry, I found the face strangely beautiful, as if it were sculptured from a piece of anthracite. Then a medic pulled the blanket up and hid it forever.

I turned to the mass of women beside me and reached out for it.

"I am so sorry, Olga." I too began to cry.

I placed my own arms loosely around the huddle, but they didn't fit the shape of it. The knot was tied to perfection, each loop intertwined, each strand of arm laced, and I was superfluous. I dropped my arms to my sides and staggered into the side of the ambulance.

"Out the way!" a medic barked at me.

Heaving myself up, I backed off and strayed to the extreme edge of the cordon, where I found solidity in the corrugated iron wall of a coal washing shed. With my back against it, I watched the mayhem. I watched as another victim was brought to the surface, this man still alive although badly burnt, and was bundled in beside Dmitry. As I stared at the man's black flesh, I was overcome by the smell of it burning and my feet would no longer support me. I slumped to the ground, to the coal dust which had been transformed into a black soup by the melting snow and I hung my head, shivering violently. Before me was the patch of snowdrops. It had been ground to a grey pulp by the awful stomping of boots.

Again, I looked up, forcing myself to confront the scene. More and more men were being brought up now. I saw Viktor rushing past with an empty stretcher, panting as he laid it down. I saw Balavensky kneeling over a man on another stretcher. Beside the mine shaft stood the Governor, his face ashen with despair for his people. Yaroslav stood just outside the edge of the cordon, a camera resting on his shoulder, and I saw that it was shaking as he tried to make sense of the chaos. Meanwhile, inside the cordon, one of the British TV men was in the thick of the melee, his camera protruding into faces, into stretchers, and I watched as Mrs T approached him and put her hand over the lens, then tussled with the man for control of the camera. It seemed the most natural of behaviours, I thought, as he was hustled away by one of the many miners present.

Among them, I searched for Oleg. Blankly at first, and then it dawned on me; Oleg had also been on the night shift. I felt a sob escape me as I hauled myself to my feet and made my way shakily across towards the mine shaft, searching out Svetlana again. I found her standing behind one of the ambulances, her back to me. She was gazing into the maw of the shaft.

"Where's Oleg?" I asked her.

My friend swung round to me, her face was blanched, her eyes red and swollen. Her tears began again, and she turned back to the shaft, wrapping her arms around herself. She too was shaking violently, and it was at that moment that I stopped shaking myself. I removed my jacket and folded it around her, resting my arm on her shoulders in comfort. But then her mother shuffled up to us, and she extracted her daughter from me. Silently, she encased Svetlana in her own arms, with a blank nod at me, while I stood numbly by. We waited like that for what seemed like hours.

It was dark when they brought Oleg out. His face was in repose, his charred body rocking without resistance as the two medics struggled with the stretcher. My belly felt suddenly hollow as they carried it across the yard, laid it down into the coal soup and bent over him. Svetlana too crouched over her husband, while they fumbled for a pulse.

"Zhivoy!" The medic looked up with a muted smile. Alive.

To cheers of relief, they began to bundle Oleg into the ambulance and the emotion of the moment engulfed me, I began to sob. Svetlana collapsed into her mother's arms and the old woman struggled to hold her up, while other arms rushed in to support her. But I stumbled away and out of the cordon. I was not needed here. Had never been needed here.

Blindly, I lurched away from the colliery buildings, without any notion of where I was going, and without caring. I continued through and out of the car park and away from the mine. I stepped aside on the grass as Oleg's ambulance sped past me, its sirens ablaze, its steel gleaming in the full moonlight. I kept walking, walking away along the busy road, perhaps even half-hoping to be hit by a vehicle.

I don't know how long I'd been walking, before I was confronted by headlights. They slowed as they reached me, paralysing me with their full beam, holding me in their glare. I stopped to shield my eyes as the Jeep pulled over and the door opened.

"Sasha?"

"Ness." He got out the car.

"What are you doing here?"

"I have come to take you home."

He wrapped his arms around me and I fell into him.

"Dmitry…" It was all I managed, nothing more would come.

For most of our journey to Kiev, I sat in silence, smudging my tears with grubby fingers, while Sasha drove the whole six hours without stopping. I fell into the occasional guilty doze, my head slumped back, before snapping myself awake again. I simply could not believe that a man whom I had known, had spoken to some hours before, was actually dead. I could not believe that Olga, my friend, was a widow. She was younger than me, she had a small daughter.

On the outskirts of Kiev, we drove through a birch forest, just as Sasha and I had done nearly two years before on that first journey together from Borispol airport. We swept past factory chimneys, spewing their relentless grime into the night air, and we passed the shells of tower blocks, their defunct cranes eerie in the gloom. When we reached the anonymous apartment blocks, I gazed up into the darkened windows. It was precisely at this spot where I had felt the first flash of idealism – the conviction that I could truly help these people. That first burst of utopia. A life's shift away from now.

As we approached the statue of Volodymyr, high up on his hill across the Dniepro, I could hear Dan's wisdom. So lucidly then, as if he were speaking to me from the back seat, and I even glanced in the wing mirror to check he wasn't actually there. *Who says our ways are better than theirs? .... It was here before you and it will be here after you've gone... You can't make it all alright for them, Ness... Walk alongside them, that's the best you can do.* His voice was gentle in my head, but it reached in and further in.

How could I square the profundity of that day's events against my tinkering? My aid programme had done no more than scratch the surface of their existence, and yet it had been at the root of mine, had sustained it. Always, I had believed I was making a difference, that I had become at one with these people, had been drawn by them into the essence of their lives. I looked at my reflection in the window, studied its simplicity, and I felt stupid and suddenly very alone.

We arrived home at 3am, at the darkest hour, the hour when it is said that most suicides happen. The streets were still and silent. When Sasha pulled up outside my apartment, the glance I threw up at the fifth floor to see if there was light, was purely instinctive, purely reflex. Of course, there was none.

"Thanks Sasha," I said. "You probably saved my life tonight."

"No problem. You would do same for me, Hutch. I have seen video."

I smiled wanly at him. "I hope I would, Starsky."

He pulled me across the seat to him and kissed my hair. I sank into the side of his body, it felt so good to be held again, so good to be cared for again. Sasha was waiting for me, I could sense that, and so I lifted my chin up for him. His kiss was welcome, gentle, and sweet from the liquorice he'd chewed to keep awake during the journey. But his tongue didn't meet mine in the same way, in the right way. It was alien. So I stopped the kiss and drew back.

"Sorry, Sasha, I can't."

"No problem, so my balls will continue to ache." His smile was kind.

"Goodnight." I said with a rueful smile and I got out of the Jeep.

The walk towards an empty apartment was a challenge I nearly gave in to that night; it would have been so very easy to have turned back to Sasha. Inside the building, the grief swept me again and I plunged into the lift, jumping up and down on the platform with some kind of death wish. The cage swung precariously, knocking the sides of the shaft, but still the lift reached its destination. At the fifth floor, I yanked back the gate and emerged into the dark, the brass lock on my apartment door gleaming in the moonlight, as I scratched my key into it.

When I opened the door, Pushkin skittered out of the hallway and over to the stairs, where he slid to a standstill with a plaintive meow. I heard breathing then. I swung on the balls of my feet and glared at the stairwell.

"Hey kiddo."

Dan stood from where he was sitting on the top step. I could make out the dishevelled hair, the tanned face even.

"Dan?"

"I saw the news," he said.

"But it's only just happened."

"I was in Geneva. I had to get to you, Ness."

He stepped slowly towards me and took me in his arms, encasing me, folding me in. For a long time we stood silent and still, conscious of the steady reconnection. I could feel myself sliding back inside him and his own energy flooding through me. We fell asleep as the sun began to come up, Dan's naked body fused behind mine. We fitted each other, I thought, as the warm waves behind my eyes swept me down into the heaviest and safest of slumbers.

33

Dan stayed in Kiev for a week. We lay on the bed, face to face, while he listened tirelessly to the outpouring of my grief, while I relived the scenes at the mine.

"Dmitry's face ..." I'd begin, as the memories piled in on top of each other.

"I'm here now Ness." He'd say, and draw me closer.

We took respite in sex, coming back for more through the blurry days and nights. The morning light from the courtyard bore down on my face with habitual warmth, the hushed sounds of afternoon then merging into the clatter of evening meals, and on into the stillness of night, and the occasional brush of Pushkin's fur beside us. We soon found again our familiar rhythm, albeit notched up with an urgency, with the knowledge that this might not have been.

Together, we attended Dmitry's funeral in Donetsk. There I found the grace to hold myself apart, allowing the village the respect to bury one of its own without ingratiating myself. There were other funerals, twenty-four of them in all. But Dan and I left after visiting Oleg in the clinic, his face and hands swathed in bandages, arms suspended robotically.

On Dan's last day, we emerged from the apartment and wandered down onto the Boulevard Kreschatyk, falling into our natural pace. We strolled through the Kiev Passage, up the hill to the Parliament and on into the Mariensky Park, where the fountain lions once again poured forth into the early spring days. We sat down on a bench. Lulled by the water's rhythmic flows, I found Dan's presence by my side intoxicating, hallucinogenic, and I longed to splash barefoot in the frothy water, or skip giddily and pick the crocuses. That he had known to come back for me; that I had at all survived without him.

We sought out our favourite café, locking arms across the table, silently contemplating.

"I've been miserable, Ness."

I looked at him and realised this was the first time Dan had raised his own feelings.

"Why didn't you call me?"

"You were like steel. I picked the phone up, sure I did, but you were so adamant that you wanted no contact."

Leaning forwards, I pressed my forehead into his and breathed his clean soapy scent deep inside me.

"You could have called me," he added.

"I did. Remember?"

"Not like that…not angry."

I threw him a weak smile. Dan closed his eyes and a tear slid out. I watched it fall, and struggled to hold back my own.

At home again, we sat together on the sofa and watched Yaroslav's latest feature on the Job Centre.

Dan nudged me. "Are those men genuinely unemployed?"

I grinned. "No, we rustled up a few guys off the street for the shoot." I nodded at the sheets of job vacancies posted on the wall. "They're fake too. Mind you, since this programme aired we've had whole waves of men in, even found jobs for some of them. Viktor's Agency's thriving too, I'll take you there."

Dan raised his eyebrows. It still felt good to impress him.

"Some bright young things have opened a café next door, so we can go hang out with the Ukrainian youth of tomorrow."

"What's it called? Les Deux Magots?"

"Actually it's called Cossack."

Dan let out one of his guffaws. "You've got to love these people."

I sank back down against him and let the TV footage wash over me. A clever pan of the camera captured a prism of sunshine then came to rest on a vase of carnations and I let out a soft snort. "Mrs T's idea of improving their image."

"Hmm." He nodded slowly.

"So what happens once the cynicism starts to creep in?" I asked him suddenly.

Dan looked at me quizzically. I nodded.

He took a deep breath and blew the air out. "Well. I guess you begin to reassess. You start to see things differently."

"Mm, already I feel as if I'm learning to expect less."

"Yeah, that's part of it. It can be a relief, actually, when you finally let go. I think you become more useful...more valuable."

"You learn to walk alongside them."

He nodded. "Not to feel responsible."

"Would anything have done, Dan?"

"What do you mean?"

"Well, if we'd put up a £3million programme to, I don't know, style the hair of every Ukrainian woman, would that have done too?"

"No way, of course it-would-not-have-done." With each word, he patted his palm against my thigh. "Don't put yourself down, you have touched the lives of a whole bunch of people here, Ness."

"Bullied them, more like."

"Bullshit!" He smiled at me. "You'll come out the other side of this, Ness, it's a part of who you are."

As the credits rolled we fell silent. My name appeared, flowed up and off.

"And I should have seen that," he added. "I'm sorry."

I gazed into the screen, met his eyes in its reflection and smiled. "So what's it like in Honduras?" It was the first time I'd asked him.

"What's it like?" Dan ran a hand over his face. "Let me see. Well, I'm handling the kind of aid that gets on TV back home – hungry kids, big brown eyes, naked kids, scrabbling in wasteland. It's illegal, but they have them working the limestone quarries, which slowly fills their lungs up with dust."

"Permanently?"

"Yeah." He eyed me. "You should come see for yourself."

*

As for me, I remained in Kiev for the final eighteen months of my programme. And there were moments of success. Balavensky got his new Employment Policy, home-grown with the support of Levshenko experts. Jeff left Ukraine, claiming ill health (although he resurfaced in Kazakhstan just days later as an expert on another aid programme). At the next donor co-ordination meeting I received praise for creating synergy with the Finns – albeit just a soft thud of palms on the table top; while I had set a precedent for donor co-ordination, I had also created an undesirable expectation for more. Thirteen of the Task Force trainers stayed to programme end, and we witnessed an exponential impact in the regions, with Job Centres popping up in each of the major cities, their staff being trained to whatever extent was realistic given the circumstances. Once we had paid the £1000 bonus, however, every last trainer dispersed to some other honey pot – taking their new-found Western smiles to another foreign aid programme, either that or to one of the newly arriving multinationals.

On the day I left Kiev, in the autumn of 1997, I found myself in Mrs T's office. It was a perfectly blue day and, as she stood with her back to the window, she was framed against it in that suit, a slightly darker hue than the sky.

"I realise that you have lost your best staff," I said to her, in solemn apology as we shook hands. "I should have known better."

"They completed the job," she replied. Her tone was formal, but it was free of hostility. All of that was spent, I think, and I felt the respect prickle my shoulders.

"They completed my job, not yours," I said. And, finally, she smiled.

We wished each other well, and we went our separate ways, never to meet again. As she said we would.

Svetlana drove me out to Borispol. On the way we pulled up at the same overhead traffic lights where Sasha had stopped on the day of my arrival in Kiev more than three years before. My eyes flicked to the pavement where the old beggar lady had stood, and there, waiting to cross the road, was Irina. She wore a sumptuous grey hat, the size of a small drum, and perhaps she felt my glance, because the ice-blue eyes beneath the fur sought me out and met mine. She stepped out into the road and began to cross, all the while holding my glance, and as she passed in front of the car she gave me that slow blink, that gesture of approval. I nodded at her, with matching grace, I think in thanks. Perhaps she'd learnt about the success of the Donetsk women, or perhaps she'd caught wind of my departure and was pleased to see me go. Whatever, I do know that in today's world we might even have been friends. She disappeared into the crowds, she didn't look back.

At departures, Svetlana and I held each other close. Of course, she and I would meet again many times in the future, but as we parted that day I took out the Key to the City which Vladimir Zukov had given me.

"This is for the women of Donetsk." I pressed it into her hands, folding them around it. "For their inspiration, and for their wonder."

*

I've always considered myself lucky that Dan came back for me. I could have ended up a bitter and lonely woman – already Pushkin was taking on significance for me. On that last evening in Kiev, we lay together beneath the duvet at dusk.

"I thought you'd moved on," I said, gazing up at the ceiling shadows.

He let out a soft snort. "I never moved anywhere, Ness, I've been here with you all that time."

"I thought perhaps you'd gone back to Chelsea."

Dan shucked himself up onto an elbow. "Chelsea? It was Chelsea who called me in Geneva about the explosion, it was she who told me you were in Donetsk that day."

I contemplated him blankly, grappling with this. "But she came to visit you, right?"

"No. She took a vacation in Costa Rica, yes she invited me along, no I didn't go." He shook his head. "Ness, I thought about you constantly. When I woke, I'd see you padding about in those ridiculous pyjamas with the dog motifs."

I smirked. "They're rabbits."

"Whatever." He waved the comment off. "I hunted down your shampoo, so I could breathe you in when I took a shower. It's only you. It's only been you, for a very long time now."

For a while, we watched each other quietly. Then I lifted my face up to his messy hair, mussed it and smiled at him.

"Much as I tried for it not to be," he added, smiling back.

"So what's it like living there?"

"Hot. Dusty. Most Hondurans secrete guns in their homes for protection."

"You're not exactly selling it to me."

His smile broadened. "Do I have to?"

34

Now, I lie in my hammock in the shade of the old stone patio and look out over the flowering trees, with their clusters of startling blue or spears of pale orange, and on into the shimmering heat of the distant hills, while I capture some of these memories for my daughters.

I am still an aid professional and I continue to focus on women. As Vladimir Zukov proclaimed in his toast on that fateful night in the village hall, it is the women who hold beauty in this world. As Balavensky added, it is the women who hold the deepest souls. And as Viktor too declared, it is the women whose spirit, whose courage will always lead them to enterprise. In a bid to hold their family together, the women in Honduras will take on arduous labour, hoeing the scratchiest patch of land to throw up something, anything, of nourishment. In business meetings, I stand alongside them, and wonder at their toughness in negotiation, the hidden sinews within them tensing, later then relaxing to become conduits for the love which flows into their children.

It was a good lesson to learn in my twenties, that we never really know other people, other cultures. And yet we will always meddle. International Development has become a fashionable degree course and occasionally, on my trips home to England, I am invited as a visiting lecturer to one or other of the universities that offer it. Imagine, I say to the students, imagine the wealthy Chinese arriving in England with aid to solve our homeless problem. Unbidden. What do they know of the deep-seated flaws at the root of our families, of our education system, of our very culture, of all that has lead to such homelessness? Audacity aside, how could they possibly hope to act with any success?

These days, I keep people at bay with my cheerfulness, and I can tell they don't know how to take me. So much so, that some of the old timers in the donor circles have accused me of naivety. At such moments, I smile quietly to myself; no I am not naïve, I have come full circle, that's all. I do see something of myself as was in the rookies who arrive in their planeloads, fresh from their graduation ceremonies. These kids are canny enough to sense that it's not a naivety in me, that it's not the same stuff they themselves are made of, but they can't quite place what it is. As I see it, I have no wish to exist in cynicism and so once more I have decided to accept at face value. For me there is no other way to pursue my work, or my life; I am as selfish as I am selfless.

While my harsh start in life was the platform which launched me, in sharp contrast I have protected my children – we both have – from its knocks. But I'm aware that their honing will not be as sharp as my own, that it could leave them without any grit, and in some ways I regret that they will not endure the scuffs that set me on my course. Because a part of me believes that there has to be some damage to a life for it to notice. My daughters were born in a country where so many of the population live on less than a dollar a day, but both are still young and oblivious to the poverty which surrounds them. I believe it will soon be time to make them notice. As Dan once said to me – it was here before you, and it will be here after you. It is here before they are conscious of it, and yes, it will still be here when they have left this world, but at some point in their lives, I hope that they will act on it in some small way. I guess I hope that my memories thus recorded may trigger in them a genetic need to do so. For it is a worthwhile use of a life.

But what of Ukraine? When an agreement was signed some years back, with the ultimate goal of EU accession, it seemed that the West was winning the tug of war with Russia. And for a while, Ukraine chugged nicely along towards that safe haven of EU membership. And then, abruptly, and with little forewarning, this year, all that changed. Now it seems inevitable to me that a sliver, maybe more, of the East will be sliced away, back to Russian rule.

Before he left government, Balavensky did see his Employment Policy become law, whether by rubber stamp or by democratic vote is not clear to me. In any case, there are no funds for unemployment benefits, certainly none for active re-employment measures, so the law is a sideshow. I believe the Minister retired to his dacha, the one I never did visit, perhaps with millions stashed under the potato sacks. Whatever, he seems to have got out before the witch hunts. Mrs T was less fortuitous on that front. Her PM lover is long gone and she herself was hauled up on corruption charges some years back – they say she siphoned off from the telecoms privatisations. She got off, of course; the feckless among her peers would not have welcomed the attention. Interestingly, Yaroslav confirmed that it was she and not Balavensky who had intervened for him, that in fact it was the Minister who was behind his arrest. Think Blofeld with cat, as Dan had once advised.

The Business Development Agency folded a year or so after my departure, but Viktor is now a businessman, at the helm of a successful car hire company in Kiev. Sasha married his World Bank girlfriend and now lives in the States, where he does 'import-export'. I visit them in their Georgetown home whenever I'm on business in Washington, and I know that the trappings of their wealthy existence are not simply the product of her salary, so his nebulous affairs are paying off.

I admit that I never really knew any of them. Not even Yaroslav, who to my astonishment showed up on the telly as a presenter of the Eurovision Song Contest a few years ago. His face even held a smile, albeit a sheepish one more suited to a children's TV presenter bewildered by his embarrassing start in the business. You have to work with what you have, he wrote in reply to my letter afterwards, you have to get inside the system and change it from within. I wonder if he is involved in reporting the current troubles.

Two years after programme end, Bogdan, who still invests his personal wealth in Ukraine, had an ex-post evaluation carried out to assess the long-term impact of his three million pounds. This found that there were no Project Survivors – an amusing but genuine term for any tangible successes which remain once an aid programme has ended. That we expect a programme to bring about a lasting and yet so radical change in three short years is unfathomable for me – although I did genuinely expect this back then. As an expectation, it is still rife in the aid world.

In any case, of course there were survivors. All those people who came into contact with our programme took with them skills and experience into the local economy, into their future, even if the institutions we created disintegrated after we'd gone. Perhaps we even bolstered others we did not know about, perhaps we anchored them, preventing them from sliding backwards, simply with our presence in their lives. As Dan said, we Westerners walked alongside them.

And then there is the component of our aid programme which was so minor in financial terms that it eluded the evaluation team, who didn't even bother to visit a single village during their research and analysis.

Then there are the women.

We were due to visit the village in the summer, but that seems unlikely now. Svetlana had invited us to spend some time with her and Oleg, and with my godson, who is now twelve years old. In her regular letters, she keeps me posted on Oleg's job as an engineer in Donetsk, although they remain in the village – they could never leave the village, she says. "Even if you have to take Russian passports?" I asked her over the phone. "Kaneshno." Of course, she replied.

And I can see her point. There are thousands of women throughout that coal mining region who are now involved in kitchen or home industries of some kind, and how could they up sticks and leave? She herself has made a career out of aid and she moves from one programme to the next as a local manager, commanding a lucrative and steady salary. Olga, still cutting and sewing at her kitchen table, has remarried and has another child, while Lesya has opened a salon in the town of Slagansk, and Marina now caters for corporate events – mainly those Svetlana drums up for her through the aid circus. Niamh left to do good works in India, but Kevin, now married to Yelena, became such a valuable asset that he too works steadily through the never-ending cycle of aid programmes. The EU has him, currently, I hear. Though I imagine all aid programmes are on hold now.

The mines have still not closed, even though the IMF and World Bank maintain their coercion by means of loans on a dizzying scale. And there have been other explosions, because levels of the silent and odourless methane gas remain high, and are often poorly monitored. I close my eyes as I remember that terrible day, taking my mind back to relive the hours, out of respect for Dmitry, and for the others. Twenty-five men died at Slagansk. Elsewhere the numbers have been much higher. And still the men go down. Across the coal regions of Ukraine, hundreds of thousands of miners are still going down today. In my village, and in villages across the region, still the women draw icy water from the communal well each morning, still they scrub their men's shirts over a washboard, their spines creaking as they right themselves. Still the villagers dance and sing in the forest. And still they spend hours at table, in a spirit of unity, in a spirit of simply being.

Our finca does have vast walls. I have, however, consigned my husband's socialist realism paintings to his study, hanging instead jolly scenes of Honduran life, of dancers in skirts of naïve hues, wishing to capture the lightness of being that permeates my home. The kitchen wall holds the canvas of snowdrops – and you can take them whichever way you wish. Our visitors are often entranced by the beauty of such delicate flora from a cold climate, and so am I at times. But I also know their fate.

Dan is still with USAID, and he travels often, taking in the whole of Latin America. As he told me, it is indeed a top posting. In fact the building that houses the USAID headquarters is so large that it is rumoured to accommodate also the CIA. And while Dan is once again inspired by his work, in a way that I imagine he was when he first set out, it is not for me to dwell on that here. After I joined him, we allowed ourselves several years together before the girls, and the way we have settled into each other has mellowed him. He is less cynical and I less idealistic, though we are careful to sustain those qualities in each other, and that in turn sustains us.

My husband gallops out of the patio doors, grinning broadly with our youngest on his back; she is giggling so sweetly as only five-year olds can. He flops her down onto the hammock beside me, and she lies with huge but silent heaves of laughter. She laughs like me, Dan says, and watching her I am taken back to a snow-covered hillside and a moonlit night high above the velvet Dniepro river. To a moment I captured when we were flung off a sledge, our own laughter so intense that it too was silent.

Our eldest steps out from the living room into the heat of the afternoon and struggles up beside her sister, while Dan too makes his usual comical show of climbing in. As we begin to sway, the hammock sags, but it can easily take all of our weight, for this is a common family pastime. Dan and I swing ourselves higher, out and upwards, sending giddy thrills through our daughters, who squeal and grip at our shirts. The bougainvillea above our heads has reached its zenith and, nudged by the flying hammock, it sets smatterings of petals free, which waft down onto us, smothering us with their papery lilac. The joy to be taken in the spirit of unity, in the spirit of simply being.

There is mention of ice cream and the girls clamber off, abandoning us for the kitchen. I watch them go and then smile to myself as I recall the thrills this hammock has witnessed, from above and from below its hoops of netting, while Dan kisses me, his palm straying to the nape of my neck. It still brings a flurry. Soon it will lead us through into the cool stone-walled bedroom and down onto the duvet, where the breeze off the hills through our open windows will drift over us, and where we will find our rhythm – one which is familiar, but still with a trace of wonder.

Acknowledgements

I would like to extend my warmest thanks to Stephanie Zia and all at Blackbird. Special thanks also to those who scrutinised drafts of *The Road to Donetsk*, particularly my early readers: Ruth Hunter, Cath Hurley, Barbara McKinlay, Susie Howells, Harry Melton, Elizabeth Franey, Karen Mchugh. Thanks too to my kindred souls at Writers at Work who gave assiduous feedback from the start, and without flinching, especially Judith Evans and Wilma Ferguson. To everyone who contributed with snippets of research, notably Tony and Vica Howson, Kathleen Goldhammer-Copeland, Fionna Gibb, Inigo Arencibia. Thanks too to Nic Ladha for his continued support. Also to Lyudmyla Pogoryelova, of the Taras Shevchenko Museum in Toronto, and Lorna Clark, daughter of the late John Weir, for permission to use his translation of lines from the poem, *A Reflection*. To Pan Macmillan for permission to use lines from *The Making of Modern Britain*, by Andrew Marr, published 10th February 2009. Also to Lynn Curtis for her brutal comments on the first draft, and to Susan Lee Kerr for her illuminating notes on the penultimate one. Thanks to Maddie, for being sunny and funny. And, most of all, thanks to Nick, for always being there.

About The Author

Diane Chandler worked first as a political lobbyist in Brussels, and then at the European Commission for several years, where she managed overseas aid programmes in Ukraine just after the fall of communism. Ukraine soon worked its way into her heart, and she travelled there extensively. Back in London, when Diane married and her daughter was born, she was able to pursue her passion for writing in those few hours she could snatch. Ukraine became the subject for this, her first novel which won The People's Book Prize for Fiction 2016. Her second novel, *Moondance*, is informed by her personal experience of the emotional and physical impact of IVF. She is currently working on her third novel..

Keep up to date with all Diane Chandler news and new titles, join the
Diane Chandler Mailing List
http://eepurl.com/9QUyn
(All email details securely managed at Mailchimp.com and never
shared with third parties.)

Bibliography

Collision and Collusion, The Strange Case of Western Aid to Eastern Europe 1989 – 1998, Janine R. Wedel, 1998. St Martin's Press.
The Bottom Billion, Paul Collier, 2007. Oxford University Press.
The White Man's Burden, William Easterly, 2007. Oxford University Press.
Borderland, a Journey through the History of Ukraine, Anna Reid, 1997. Weidenfeld and Nicolson.
The Selfish Altruist, Tony Vaux, 2001. Earthscan Publications Ltd

Book Club Questions

1. Did you like Vanessa? Did you find her a good person who only wanted to help, or an interfering busy-body?

2. Do you think Vanessa deserved the welcome she received from the Ukrainian characters in her first few weeks in Ukraine?

3.How did you feel about Dan?

4. What did you make of their relationship?

5. What did you make of the chemistry between Vanessa and her driver Sasha?

6. What aspects of overseas aid, as portrayed in the novel, struck you most?

7. What was your impression of Mrs Tabachuk (MrsT) and how did it change throughout the novel?

8. How did you feel about Minister Balavensky? Was he not to be trusted, or simply trying to survive in a complex country?

9. What did you make of the Ukrainian women portrayed in the novel? The Three Graces? The Donetsk Divas? The Task Force?

10. What does Yaroslav, the Ukrainian journalist, bring to the novel?
11. What was your view of the British experts working on the programme? Which ones were competent, in your view, and which not?

12. Do you think Vanessa should have gone with Dan when he left?

13. What did you make of the climax to the novel?

14. Did you expect Dan to return? How did you feel when he did?

15. How did the novel make you feel about Ukraine?

More Original Fiction From Blackbird

MOONDANCE (2016) by Diane Chandler

Bittersweet, at times funny, and always emotionally raw, this
is by far the most moving and honest novel you'll ever read
about IVF and its impact on a marriage.

The Dream Theatre (2011) by Sarah Ball

That Special Someone (2014) by Tanya Bullock

The Modigliani Girl (2015) by Jacqui Lofthouse

Valentina (2016) by S. E. Lynes

Nightingale Editions
Dark Water (2016) by Sara Bailey

Blackbird Digital Books

Discovering outstanding authors

#authorpower
http://blackbird-books.com
@Blackbird_Bks

DIANE CHANDLER

Moondance

How can you long for someone
who doesn't exist?